For Jacob —
I hope you will
enjoy meeting my
Annaliese. Put on your
seat belt.

Warmest regards,
Lindy Carter

Annaliese From Off

A Novel

Lindy Keane Carter

ISBN: 0692244344
ISBN 13: 9780692244340

Acknowledgements

This novel was inspired by the tales that I heard throughout my childhood from my mother's best friend, Betty Scott, of Athens, Georgia. Betty was a raconteur without equal. Her stories of southern politicians, wayward husbands found out, and bourbon-drinking church ladies were absolutely true (with names) and delivered with a delicious punchline perfectly timed, but when she talked about her educated, Catholic grandmother's arrival in the north Georgia mountains around 1900 as her husband set up a lumber business, I was just as enthralled. Those stories, loosely adapted, provided the platform for this novel. All of the characters in this novel are fictional, except for Gifford Pinchot, the first Chief of the United States Forest Service.

There are so many people who have encouraged me during the creation of this book. A special thank you to my Charleston, S.C. writer friends who gave feedback in those early writers' groups and then ongoing encouragement and counsel for many years: Marjory and Peter Wentworth, Mary Alice Kruesi, Patti Callahan Henry, Kate Adams, Denny Stiles, Linda Ferguson, Billy Want, and Frances Pearce.

I am grateful for the unwavering love and support of dear friend Karla Taylor, who taught me how to write tight copy and get the rhythm right and gave me a beautiful brass book stand many years ago for this very book. Lifelong friends Nancy Bryant Hardeman, Libby Weaver Hollett, and Dellita Kobold – thank you for your encouragement and blind faith.

I wouldn't have known why mules are better than horses in the lumber business and many other such practical matters without my interviews with James Edward (Bitty) Aycock and Boyd Maynard Aycock, both of Lincolnton, Georgia, whom I hereby acknowledge.

For excellent editing and insight, I send thanks to Kathleen L. Asay, a writer and editor in northern California, and for terrific advice about publishing and marketing this book, a shout out to Susan Sloate.

And to my most enthusiastic and longstanding cheerleaders, my children Katie, Will, and Mary Lee, I give thanks for your enduring love and support. Especially the tech support.

For Karla, Marjory, Mary Alice
and Elizabeth Tate Scott, whose stories of north Georgia
inspired this one

I

He would have bought her any house in Louisville that she wanted. She could not have known that this bay-windowed Victorian on Pendennis Club Avenue would be a mistake, that at dawn the sounds of the detested docks coming to life on the Ohio River a mile away could travel all the way to their bedroom.

On their first morning there, she awoke to those sounds carried by the wind to the open window and regretted her choice even as unpacked crates encircled their bed. Finally, she shut the window and curled back into his sturdy arms to wait for the childhood memories to fade—slippery-eyed men rolling barrels onto the decks of her father's rotting boat, wharf rats scurrying for fish heads beneath its bow. But as the weeks went by she softened, for the house needed her. She filled its porches with ferns and urns, hung golden silk panels at the windows. On sunny mornings, she pulled the drapes aside to invite the light to puddle on the gleaming heartpine floors that she had reclaimed from grime and abuse. On rainy ones, she lingered in the soothing enclosure of its long halls, swaddled and secure. By the time their son was born, if the bustle of the Ohio at dawn still woke her, the sound had lost its power over her. It was enough for Annaliese to roll over to look at John, still heavy with sleep, and see the rest of her life unfolding in the embrace of this home with this man, the right man. John was a balm for her rootless soul, too.

She felt that he was as solid as the Kentucky soil beneath them, and though he had been hurling himself at the world for most of his 33 years, he had landed on most marks. People all over the state said John Stregal was a better lawyer blindfolded than any of the Old Guard with a crystal ball. Annaliese had chosen a lawyer—and her suitors were many—for a reason. Before she was even out of her teens, she could see that lawyers stayed put. They had to, to forge alliances and get traction in the community, traction such as being invited to join the Pendennis Club, which John recently had. For Annaliese, this had opened doors to new parlors, though she wasn't interested in building status as much as making friends who, down the road, would be able to say they had known her children all of their lives and she the same about theirs.

But around the time their second child was born, the sunny Emeline now four years old, people had started whispering less complimentary things about John. She thought it was just jealousy talking, but she had seen things, too.

On a frigid November morning in 1900, she lay in bed alone thinking about what, exactly, she had seen lately and what she had perhaps denied. He had been leaving for his office before dawn for months. She knew his mother's complicated estate had to be settled, but she saw a shift in him, a new hunger beyond even his usual ambition that rendered him dissatisfied, agitated. Dinner to dusk, he spoke of the headlines screaming of enterprise and opportunity as the twentieth century opened. There were fortunes to be made in these years following the Spanish-American War, he said. Immigrants were pouring into America to sew clothes, pack meat, hammer out furniture. Railroads were expanding, bank accounts growing. The country was afire, he said, and he didn't intend to let opportunity simply wash over him on its sweep across the nation. At dinner, she nodded at him, but she was laying out next spring's flowerbeds on the west side of the back yard. Later, when she had paid enough attention to realize that investments were in the air, she did ask what he was planning, and received a meandering answer involving natural resources. She decided to trust the limits of their finances to keep his plans within Kentucky's borders. When she curled into him these days, it had to be at the end of the day. She would pull her blonde braid off her neck to invite his lips there, mostly to stop the rant.

Annaliese got up and went to Samuel's room to wake him for school. She shook him gently, whispered the usual urgings, and tugged until he finally sat up. The boy was in his second year at the cathedral school, all bony six-year-old elbows and knees, but baby fat still pudged on his forehead. Sometimes, she kissed him there just to confirm with her lips that it was still there—the soft, spongy flesh of infancy on top of hard bone—and sometimes just because he would still let her. Samuel rubbed his eyes and whined while her hand made circles on his back. Finally, his feet hit the floor and she was off to the room next door to check on Emeline. The child lay sprawled across the foot of the bed, thumb in mouth, her face covered with a wild tangle of blonde hair. Annaliese pulled the quilt over her and went back to the hall where she leaned over the railing to listen for the cook in the kitchen, the maid with her sweeper. She ran her hand along the polished oak of the railing, smooth except for the nicks and knots well known to her fingers.

By four o'clock, the day was winding down in familiar rhythm. Annaliese was in her room writing at her desk when she heard John's voice downstairs. She straightened at the sound of it—too early in the day, too loud. Then another man's voice. She ran down the stairs and found them at the open front door, slapping each other on the back. John and his law partner saluted her with their cigars and fell into each other laughing, weak-kneed and sloppy.

"Mrs. Stregal." Jeremiah Lowery took off his hat.

"Mr. Lowery." She smelled liquor on him, not that she needed confirmation.

"Looks like you might need to learn to shoot a shotgun." Lowery pointed his cigar at her.

"Excuse me?" She spun around to her husband.

John threw back his head and laughed.

The servants seeped out of doorways to stare.

"John?" Annaliese gripped the newel post and tried calm questions, but John turned toward the street where several men were spilling out of the family carriage. They staggered over her threshold as he waved them in. They pulled off their hats, pounded his shoulders, his back.

"Bully, John," one of them said.

"Just like John damn Rockefeller," another said.

Cigar ash flew.

John shouted, "Go on, go on, past Mrs. Stregal there. Library's on the right."

Though she knew all five of them, they went quiet as they passed her, eyes down or forward, sucking their trail of smoke down the hall.

The cook was at Annaliese's back. "What's he gone and done now?" she asked.

Annaliese hurried to John as he closed the front door. "You're drunk at this hour? And bringing this home? What on earth is going on?"

"We're celebrating, of course."

"Celebrating what?"

"The deal." He started down the hall.

"What deal?"

"I've told you." He stopped at the library's pocket doors.

"You most certainly have not."

"Then you've had your head in the sand, Anna. As usual."

"What's this about a shotgun?" She grabbed his sleeve.

"Oh, Jeremiah was just kidding." He pulled the doors closed behind him.

She put her ear to the crack. "Timber. It's gold on a stump," someone said.

A knock on the front door sent one of the maids running to open it. A young man held out an envelope to her, which went straight to Annaliese. Her eyes scanned the yellow paper that read, "John Stregal, Esq., 1420 Pendennis Club Avenue, Louisville, Kentucky." Annaliese straightened and stared down the hall. Why a telegram? By now most people had telephones. Through the paper she made out his brother's name. She held the envelope up to the sidelight window and squinted, but couldn't see more and the glue on the flap wouldn't give.

"I'll get the kettle," the cook said.

Minutes later, Annaliese had pried the envelope open.

Have signed the contract, too. Stregal Brothers Lumber Company a reality now. Hope to God you're right about this. – Ben

"Well?" the cook said. "What's it say?"

The maids crept toward them like forest creatures emerging from a fire.

A roar of cheers rose in the library.

Annaliese stared past the servants at the noise. So they bought a lumber company. Odd for two lawyers to do that, but maybe an investment? But no, it was more than that and Mr. Lowery wasn't kidding about the gun.

The library doors rattled apart. She shoved the telegram into her skirt pocket. John bounced against a table before he spotted the cook and waved the empty decanter at her. She took it and disappeared through a doorway.

Annaliese tried to keep her voice low. "John, what is—"

"The deal, Anna. I've told you. Ben and I just bought 17,000 acres of timber land with Mother's bequest."

She pulled him away from the servants. "All that money on trees?"

"Hell, no, not all of it on trees." He looped an arm around her corseted waist. He was a head taller than her five foot six, with the thick chest and solid shoulders of a laborer, though he had never picked up anything heavier than his children, and certainly no tools. His cool, gray eyes shone with the look she knew meant he wouldn't hear a word she said. "We saved some to build the mill, start the payroll." He planted a sloppy kiss on her neck.

"Build the mill?"

"A mill generally goes with a lumber company."

She grabbed his wrist. "What's this got to do with me?" She caught movement at the upstairs landing—the nanny holding Emeline—and Annaliese couldn't breathe. *With us.*

"Oh, don't worry, darling." He looked down the hall for the cook. "The black bears are shy and there aren't many Indians left there." He pulled her into his chest.

"Bears! Where?"

"Georgia. North Georgia. Some of the last virgin timber on the east coast. White pine, poplar, chestnut, and white oak four feet around. Gold on a stump, Anna, and we can't delay in getting to it. Country's afire with people building homes and furniture, wagons and ships, whiskey barrels, railroad ties. While thousands of acres of timber still stand and before the stupid feds move to protect them, we've got to go down there and get it. I'm telling you, 1901 is going to be the best year of our lives."

"We?" Her heart banged against her chest. "You and Ben, you mean."

"Yes, me and Ben. And *you*. And the children, of course."

"You can't be serious."

John looked down the hall again. "Where's my bourbon?"

"But what about your clients? You'll lose them after you've worked so hard—"

"Jeremiah will take them. That's what partners are for. Look, this will take only about two years. Ben and I want our families to be there to see—"

"Ben's family? Lucenia's coming? Oh, no. No, no."

John lowered his voice. "Here I've come home to celebrate and you're—"

"John, you know what our home here means to me."

"Not your childhood again."

"If you'd been the one growing up on a boat on that river—"

"Jesus, Mary and Joseph. I told you we'll be back in a couple of years."

"Leave my mother and sister? Our friends? And why? Why on earth?"

"Annaliese, aren't you proud of me? They are." He pointed at the library.

"Where will we live? You can't be serious. What about school for Sam? He's just started second grade. Where will he go to school?"

"I'll take care of that."

"What about your friends at the Pendennis Club?" She grabbed his arms. "My friends."

"You'll have Lucenia."

"Oh, no."

John pulled out of her grasp. "Enough. Ben's already referring his clients elsewhere in Cincinnati. He and I will leave in a few weeks to clear some land, start the mill, build our houses. You and the children will come in April."

"For how long?" Her nose started running. She put her hand in her pocket for a handkerchief, found the telegram.

"I told you, Anna. Just two years, for Christ's sake. We'll have cut most of the timber by then. Then we'll return to Louisville with a fortune."

The cook emerged from the back of the house with the decanter. She stole a sideways look at Annaliese as she handed it to John.

He staggered back to the library. "And we'll be set for life. You'll see."

∽

II

Annaliese followed her mother around the breakfast room, teapot in hand, ready for cups. For once, Eleanor Lewis was moving slowly. She took her time at the drawer gathering the spoons as though each required an inspection, at the cabinet withdrawing cups and saucers with arthritic caution.

"Mother, please," Dorothy said at the table.

"All right, all right," Eleanor said, sitting down. "Your sister isn't complaining." She laid out the cups.

Dorothy tapped her spoon on the table. "He's gone mad."

"Oh, for heaven's sake," Eleanor said.

Dorothy pulled out a chair for Annaliese and reached to take the pot. "Well, he has. Asking her to leave behind Louisville, family, friends."

"What's wrong with that?" Eleanor smoothed a napkin onto her lap. "Sounds like a wonderful adventure."

The sisters exchanged a look. If their mother had had her way, the three of them would still be living on the river, churning north and south and back again on the Delta Star with its mildewed mattresses and unsavory passengers. Eleanor was a hummingbird of a spirit, unable to settle for long and resentful of convention. Even as children, Dorothy and Annaliese had understood that in raising them on a riverboat while clinging to the last threads of her marriage to its captain, Eleanor was trying to seed in them resistance to society's constraints on women. But as they approached their teens, they yearned for the conventional, which they could see when visiting relatives or roaming the docks. Eleanor's trust fund ensured that they had had silk sheets on those mattresses and tutors as long as they would last, but Eleanor was the only one who valued those. The girls wrote to her brother, Edward, who found them in Indiana and yanked all three of them off the Delta Star and into his magnificent Louisville house to be folded in with his seven children for a life of mayhem and music, three squares a day, and a real school with gloriously normal people. As for Eleanor, she found herself mistress of little but the kitchen, and her sister-in-law's kitchen at that.

"Some of us like this town, Mother," Dorothy said.

"It's just for two years." Eleanor pulled a shawl off the back of her chair and wrapped it around her slender shoulders. She wore a white blouse, ironed and crisp from waist to collar, and the expected black skirt but no corset—all that was left of her civil disobedience.

Annaliese looked at her tea.

"Just the meals alone." Dorothy waved her spoon. "She'll have to learn how to cook on a wood stove. What's gotten into him lately, Anna?"

"Oh, Dottie," Eleanor said. "You know he'll find her a cook."

"I don't know that. He's so unpredictable lately. He's not the man she married."

Eleanor shot a look at Annaliese, still focused on her tea.

"The children, Mother. Sweet Samuel and what about Emmie? Just four years old." Dorothy put her hand on her sister's. "Tell him you won't put the children through this. Tell him you've had time to think about it and y'all just can't go."

Annaliese's gaze shifted outside to the rolling avenue of grass bordered by gardens, quiet and brown under the November sky. Patches of snow laced the edges. Her son knew each knoll and tree, knew where the wild violets popped up after the thaw. Every April, they searched for the robins' eggshells, watched the painted buntings forage in the grasses. The daylilies under the spreading oak she had put in herself, not that she could see them now, but she knew where they slept. Their yellows and oranges would reach for the sky come spring. She had cut back their foliage a few months ago, leaving just enough at the crown to sustain them until their roots would begin to rustle.

"Of course, she'll go." Eleanor caressed the blonde tendrils that had fallen from her daughter's hasty bun.

"But why is he doing this?" Dorothy asked. "Why isn't all that he's built here enough? The man simply doesn't make sense any more."

Annaliese watched the bare tree branches bending to one another in the wind. Two nights of quarreling and still she didn't have a good answer from him on that. Ambition and fortune, yes, she got that. Well, what else could she expect from this man? She should have seen it coming, or at least listened better at dinner. Wasn't it his intensity that had drawn her to him in the first place? In their courting days, John had listened to her as no other man ever had, elbows tucked as he leaned in, eyes drilling into hers, and nodding as if the things she said were the most fascinating remarks he had ever heard. Later, he could even repeat them. He bought the best theater seats, sent the biggest bouquets, and though she recognized this as mere strategy, she admired him all the more for knowing there should be a strategy, other suitors having proven that they failed to understand that.

In her marrow, she was proud of John for what he was, fire and storm, and for all that he intended to be. She trusted him, hard as that was lately. But why did it have to be Appalachia?

Just two years, he had said. Aren't you proud of me? he had asked.

"North Georgia is beautiful country. I've read about it," Eleanor said. "The Appalachian mountains—the waterfalls, and those wildflowers, what precious miracles. They say people stand in awe in those ancient forests of towering oaks, feel the place throbbing with life from soil to sky, and leave full of peace. Cathedrals of the earth, they call them."

"Mother, will you stop?" Dorothy pleaded. "There will be moonshiners, isolation, wild animals, no electricity. And she'll have to live with that Lucenia."

"She can handle her," Eleanor said.

Dorothy grabbed Annaliese's arm. "Leave the children with me and Phillip."

"They need their father," Annaliese said. Her look across the table said the rest—that Dorothy knew what that meant.

As their teen-age years rolled by with fewer and fewer letters from their father, the girls' yearning for his lap and the smell of his pipe did not ebb, nor did their fear that the river or its crowd would eventually claim his life. But it was a rusty can that did him in, as they learned when the man who bought the boat found their mother's name inside a moldy book and took the time to write about his septic end. The sisters had appreciated Uncle Edward—steady and generous—but they could not claim his attentions before his own got theirs, and they were many. Annaliese meant for her children to have every bit of a father's love.

Dorothy went back to her teacup.

Annaliese ran her finger around her saucer. A lot could happen in two years, especially with John.

Dorothy leaned forward to make another point, but Eleanor clamped down on her wrist. The room was silent, save the hum of the new icebox. A maid came in with fresh laundry and stopped at the sight of the three huddled figures. Annaliese looked up. "Y'all know anyone who can teach me how to cook on a wood stove?"

III

Six Stregals sat in their private train car, three to a seat—scrubbed, packed, and ready to get there. Most of them stared at the landscape that was getting more rugged by the minute but Emeline, still grouchy from being awakened to get ready, was trying to burrow into her mother's chest.

The conductor came to their doorway to stand too long and say yet again that this was the wettest April he'd seen in all his years on the Atlanta, Knoxville and Northern. And that they were about fifteen minutes out from Pinch, Georgia.

"Population 'bout four hunnert," he said. "You ladies sure you want to get off there? Someone's meetin' you?" He made no effort to hide his once-over of Annaliese, whose curves were evident even under a high-collared white shirtwaist and black skirt. She tried to keep her face dignified while he took his sweet time.

Lucenia Stregal said yes with such force that the man reared back, as good as slapped. He touched his hand to his hat and left.

"Pinch," Lucenia said. "Pretty much describes our lot, doesn't it?" She balanced a hatbox on her knees, clutched navy blue gloves in one hand. Glass buttons ran down the skirt and jacket of her blue traveling suit. Shiny black leather boots peeked out from her skirt. The feathers on an enormous hat bounced along with her considerable bosom.

Annaliese smiled to herself at such excess on this train to the middle of nowhere, but accessories were all the woman had to work with.

Dorothy had once observed in an uncharitable moment that Lucenia's best hope for beauty came in jars. She was a large woman, five foot nine, with a head too small and hair too skimpy for such bulk. *Perhaps that explained the enormous hats,* Annaliese thought. And then there was the paint. Even today, she had on a little rouge at the cheeks and something dark outlining her eyes, which definitely crossed the boundary of morality. The only thing Annaliese envied was her complexion, flawless and uniformly alabaster, while Annaliese's bore the whitish scars of childhood small pox.

Annaliese caught Lucenia eyeing her hands, which she had ruined handling stove wood. She tucked them under her skirt. It had been a long two days and two nights on this train.

Lucenia's sons sat pinned beside her. James, age five, had been given the window. Nine-year-old Darrison strained to see past his mother's bosom and her hat.

A soggy valley stretched toward the east before it rose into walls of forest and rock. At their crests, jagged granite tiers rose still higher into the froth of damp clouds. The flank of a mountain sliced in front of them, and they saw the details of those distant ridges: hillside coves, mossy boulders, waterfalls. From the cleft of a hollow a hawk rose, pumping enormous wings in startled retreat. The train rounded a bend and brought a canyon into view. Along its rim, boulders formed a mangled, toothy border, except where gaping holes revealed red, moist earth. Rust-colored rivulets raced one another down the canyon wall. Hundreds of feet below, a swollen river swept them away.

"Dear Lord." Annaliese closed her eyes and reared back from the window. She wrapped her arms around Emeline, who objected with a grunt. "How did they ever get railroad track laid through here?"

Samuel shot his mother an anxious look. John had charged him with her care.

"Took them until 1890 to figure it out," Lucenia said. "Hard to get in."

"Hard to get out," Annaliese said.

Samuel stared at his mother. "Mama, it'll be all right." He stroked her arm until she opened her eyes again. She smoothed his straw-colored hair and leaned over to kiss it. He had left his school bravely. Now, a one-room school, if that, awaited him. "Yes, honey. You're right."

James wiggled forward. "Tarzan lived in a jungle and he liked it, Aunt Anna."

Lucenia pondered the thickets. "As long as Montgomery Ward's rural delivery can get through."

Another bend in the track, another tangle of evergreens slid by, and the landscape flattened into a narrow valley. Two horses, wet and slick as the mud they stood in, pressed their heads against the doors of an ash-colored barn.

A string of simple, neat cabins popped up. Annaliese was heartened to see their yards alive with flowers she knew: larkspur, yellow jessamine, lilies, and heartseases. More fields and split rail fences came and went. The clouds seemed to thin out. On a far-off slope, a shaft of sunlight splashed across the glistening granite. One by one, the signs of commerce appeared: a livery stable, a blacksmith shop, Callaway's Feed and Seed. More homes closer together followed. Here was the beginning of Pinch, where John and Ben Stregal were waiting for their families in a bare bones depot.

The porter opened the door. "Looks like the rain's stopped just in time for your arrival." He smiled down at his passengers hopefully, as though he expected a tip for this news. But all eyes went straight back to the window. He shrugged. "Y'all need any help?"

Lucenia rolled her eyes. "Take care to see that this goes with our trunks, please." She handed the hatbox to him. He leaned in to take it, but before she let go she looked him in the eye. "Great care."

"Yes, ma'am," he said with a little tug. Finally she released it to him. "Yes, ma'am." He backed out, bobbing.

Annaliese put Emeline on the seat and pulled her boot up to tie the laces. The boys were out of their seats, elbowing each other to follow the porter. She said, "Boys, why don't you go to the lavatory one more time."

They were outside the door now.

"We have a long wagon ride yet," Lucenia called after them.

"Yes, ma'am," came a reply.

Annaliese dug around in her valise and found Emeline's pink silk hat, crumpled and coated with biscuit crumbs. She brushed it off, set it on Emeline's head, tied its ribbons beneath her chin, fluffed the limp bow, watched it wilt, and tried to fluff it again in vain. Emeline popped her thumb in her mouth and dropped her head into her mother's lap. Annaliese looked out the window. John was on the horizon. Five months since she had seen him. He would be all excitement and energy. She felt like Emeline's bow.

The train slowed to a crawl. The families gathered at the open door that separated their private car from the next—a passenger car that had been added in Knoxville during the night. A few of the passengers looked up from their newspapers. When they saw that the well-dressed women and their handsome children were about to get off at Pinch, their eyes widened. Lucenia stared them down until they went back to their newspapers. Annaliese focused on straightening Samuel's jacket and smoothing his hair.

The question she had avoided putting to Lucenia for five months and now these last two days on the train was boiling up again. She'd held onto it for too long, she now realized. When the scheme had first been sprung on them, they should've talked, should've pieced together what they knew, conspired to negotiate one year not two perhaps—anything!—but the distance between them had always been too vast, their differences too sharp, and Annaliese couldn't bring herself to reach out. But now she blurted out, "Why did you agree to come here, Lucenia? You of all people."

Lucenia pulled on gloves. "Why, because you did, darling."

"Pinch, Geooooorgia," shouted a man who came steaming through the passenger car. Here was a new face, a stub of a man with a barrel chest crammed into the black uniform.

Lucenia leveled her chin at him. "No need for you to bellow like a sea lion, sir. We are as ready as we can be."

"Yes, ma'am," the conductor said. He touched his hat to her and then to Annaliese. "Y'all got someone meetin' you here? Rough country, ma'am."

"Papa's at the station," Samuel said.

Annaliese worked up a smile. "That's right, sweetheart." Why couldn't she picture John's face? His letters said he had lost weight, stopped shaving. But it was his old face that wouldn't form in her brain.

"Our husbands, thank you," Lucenia said as she thrust a hand out to brace herself against the braking.

"All right then." The conductor craned his neck for a look out the door.

Samuel and Darrison were already leaping down the steps. One, three and out.

John and Ben emerged from under the station's dripping roof. Their boys plowed into them. Ben, thirty pounds heavier than John's one-seventy-five, was unable to pick his sons up, but his ham of a hand pounded affectionately on their heads. John hoisted Samuel up to his chest, where the boy draped himself like wallpaper. John struggled to walk toward his wife and daughter coming off the train.

"Annaliese! Emmie!" John held out a hand. "Finally."

Annaliese stepped carefully onto the slick platform. "John. Thank God." His face was clean-shaven, pale at his jaw where the beard must've been, sunburned above.

"Down for a minute, son." John lowered Samuel to the boards. He pulled Annaliese into a hug. "Wait till you see it," he said too loudly.

She took him in, heat, energy, and stink. He smelled of wood smoke and saddle leather. His heart was pounding and so was hers. Back on the train, she thought that she would be pressing him at this moment for some acknowledgement of her efforts. She was going to tell him she had learned to shoot that rifle and so much more. But now, she realized that she was getting all that she needed with this long, public embrace that neither would have dared back home and the very real admiration coming off him.

Emeline pulled on her father's coat. John picked her up. "Look at you, Emmie," he said. "Four inches taller."

Behind the Stregals, fingers in the passenger car were pointing. Mouths moved in speculation about such a family in Pinch. John took off his bowler hat and yelled, "Stregal Brothers Lumber Company. You'll hear about it." More faces came to the window.

Meanwhile, Ben had his hand at Lucenia's back and his lips at her ear delivering something that made her smile. Darrison and James stood by watching with goofy grins.

"Ben, their trunks," John called. He directed his family toward the station. "This might take a while, so y'all can wait for us in there." Already, the porter from their private car was unloading trunks and bags.

"I'm hungry," Samuel said.

"Well, you can get something to eat at the boarding house. Just go through the station doors and you'll see it on the right. I'll meet you there."

Annaliese nodded. "Very well. At the boarding house."

Inside the station, Lucenia and Annaliese and their children peered out a grimy window at Pinch.

Two rows of weathered buildings lined the main thoroughfare that was more bog than boulevard. Scrawny men and women loaded wagons and horses with sacks, boxes, baskets. Three hogs wallowed in the muck around the trough at Chastain's General Store. A clump of motherless, puny puppies huddled under the porch of Meddling's Boarding House. Somewhere, a rooster was crowing. Copper-colored slime coated nearly everything three feet off the ground or lower.

"Downright antediluvian," Lucenia whispered.

Annaliese heard only her own pounding pulse, felt it in her throbbing eyes. Fighting tears, she tugged her daughter's hand. Emeline stood glued to the floor, but Samuel had already pushed open the door.

"Come on, Mama," Samuel said. "It's not raining any more."

"Yeah," Darrison said. "Let's go."

The women gathered up their skirts. Lucenia eyed the mud, then her leather boots. "Montgomery Ward will send new ones," she said.

Into the red muck the women and four giddy children went. They waded toward the boarding house porch. Samuel peeled from his mother's side to get to the puppies, and she called to him to stop. A horse trotted by, flung mud in her face. She dropped Emeline's hand to wipe her eyes. By the time she could see again, he had scooped up a puppy.

"No!" she yelled as the train whistle blasted through the air. She plowed toward him, her anger rising with each sucking step so that by the time Annaliese got to him, she shook the boy too hard. "Put that filthy thing down," she cried.

The pup fell from Samuel's hands. His eyes were frantic, sorry. At the sight of her twisted face, he burst into tears.

Lucenia—skirts hiked high with one hand, gloves in the other—was trying to get to Emeline. The child wobbled on one foot for a second but down into Georgia's clay she went—stockings, rose-colored silk faille coat with black crocheted buttons, and matching hat. The two women reached her at the same moment, struggled to pull her up, and finally yanked her out. Emeline's wails drowned out her brother's. Both children clamped their arms around their mother's legs.

Annaliese was immobilized, trapped, as she had known all along she would be. She closed her eyes and surrendered to the sobs that had pressed for five months. The children clutched even tighter. Annaliese could not perceive the horses passing too close, did not hear the second whistle blast of the departing train, never saw John as he slogged toward her. She felt only the warmth of her precious children and the knowledge that here they were going to be her trial in this place as well as her comfort. Something within her, something small and fragile, was flickering. Anything could extinguish it now—a puff of wind, the air trail off a bird's wing, but it was all that was left of the fortitude she had mustered for the trip.

ᘒᔓ

IV

"How much farther?" she said as she pulled her shawl up around herself and Emeline. The sun had just dipped below the tree-tops and her bones felt every rut in the road. She looked at John beside her on the swaying wagon seat. He seemed to know what he was doing as he steered the horses away from the worst of them. His hands were scarred and rough—the mark, she guessed, of other things he had learned.

John pointed to a knob of granite beside the road. "There's our landmark. Sawmill's just around the bend."

A few minutes later, John and Ben halted the mud-caked horses at the edge of the Stregal mill grounds. In the back of Ben's wagon the three boys wobbled to their feet to stare. Emeline stopped twisting in her mother's lap and looked up, too. The quiet was as heavy as a fog.

Six wood buildings clustered in a red clay bowl that had been gouged out of the forest. Largest among them was a barn-like structure capped with a second-story string of windows and vents. One end of it opened through three doors—cavernous portals for the ramps that fed down into the millpond. A dozen glistening tree trunks, stripped of bark, floated gently in the water. The other end of the building opened onto a railroad track. Several men were loading the remains of the day's labor into a railcar. Everywhere in the train yard, on every slab of open space, sat stacks and stacks of finished boards.

A pair of yellow hounds erupted from under the sawmill, but went to wagging their hind ends after a better look at the horses. The workers straightened up from their loading, peered at the wagons, and waved.

Stregal hands rose in response, some more energetically than others. "There you go, Mrs. Stregal," John said. "And yonder's the office."

Yonder? Annaliese thought.

Three smaller buildings stood to the left of the sawmill—a two-story office displaying a "Stregal Brothers Lumber Company" sign, a windowless building, and another simple structure with only a door and two windows. This door wobbled open and shut as men entered and left, some carrying bulging bags to their wagons. Still others were walking straight into the woods that circled the bowl. In a corral at the edge of the compound, a few scruffy mules stood at a trough, heads down.

Annaliese and Lucenia leaned forward in their seats to see, as though ready to pull the wagons the rest of the way themselves. While John pointed out the buildings where Stregal Brothers' lumber was cut and dressed, the office where their fortune would be invoiced and tallied, and the vast drying yard where their future literally stood in towering stacks, the women strained to find what really mattered. Finally, on a distant hill about 500 yards away, they did: two white clapboard houses. They seemed to sprout from the side of the mountain like pearl mushrooms. They were close together. Very close. Eavesdropping close.

"Oh, no," Annaliese said.

John gave her a puzzled look. "What?"

"How could you do that?"

"What?"

"Nothing." Annaliese realized that there were too many things in life to think to tell John not to do.

"What are we waiting for? Let's go," Lucenia called out. "You boys . . ." she swung a commanding arm in their direction, "sit down." The boys dropped like stones. John urged his horses up the red dirt road and Ben's followed.

After the raw earth of the lumberyard they moved into a broad, green meadow. Annaliese squinted at the houses but daylight was dying quickly. The horse's slow plodding added to her agony.

"Which one is ours?" she asked.

John raised an arm. "On the right."

It was square, two stories, two chimneys, but that was all she could make out. Annaliese closed her eyes. She smelled the damp, sweet meadow grass that spread before them. A gentle wind carrying evergreen and honeysuckle whispered across her face.

Emeline squirmed in Annaliese's lap. "What's that smell, Mama?" she asked.

John said, "Fresh air, Emmie. Ain't it great? You won't smell that on the streets of Louisville."

Samuel and James scrambled over the trunks in Ben's wagon to get a better look at the rushing stream beside the road. In answer to an ancient beckoning that water makes to boys, they began hurling things from their pockets at the water.

Finally, the exhausted horses brought them close enough. Annaliese saw that porches on both stories wrapped across the front and down the left side. The front door separated a pair of bay windows. Chimneys rose on the left flank and the right. Modest but comfortable, he had said in his letters.

"Indoor water?" she asked. He had promised that.

John put an arm around her. "In the kitchen."

Annaliese's hands worked her lower back again. "No hot bath tonight then."

John shrugged. "That would take electricity, Anna. It isn't what you're used to, no question. But it's comfortable. It'll offer a body ease." He saw her shoulders wilt. "Well, the beds are set up." John slapped the reins on the horse's flank.

Annaliese looked at the other home. It had twin porches on the two levels, too, but these ran across the front only and it was barely 15 yards from hers. Why would the men build the two houses so close together when they had all this open space?

Two people came out of the front door. A woman and man walked to the edge of the porch to wave.

"The cook?" Annaliese asked.

"Yes. Name's Martha."

"I thought she was a colored woman."

"Aren't many coloreds up here in these mountains. Never have been. Land's too poor for large scale farming."

"And the man?"

"Joe. Runs the commissary. Good man."

Finally, both families arrived in front of their homes, igniting a flock of chickens into a frenzy. Martha and Joe started down the stairs, with Martha splitting off to help Ben's family. A platoon of geese swept around from the back, which brought the boys out of the wagon. The geese thrust black tongues out of wicked beaks while the chickens flapped to get out of their way. James climbed back in the wagon.

"Geese, John?" Annaliese asked.

"Good watchdogs."

Emeline sat like granite in her mother's lap, thumb poised just outside her mouth. The boys decided the chickens were the easier prey, so off they all tore toward the back yard—chickens, boys, geese.

The commissary man raised a lanky arm. "Hey, Mrs. Stregal. I'm Joe Rosetta. Sure am pleased to finally meet you, ma'am."

She judged him to be in his twenties, swarthy and as lean as a strip of beef jerky. She mustered a smile and nodded.

"I know you must be plumb wore out after two hours in that wagon. I'll get the bags so Mr. John can help y'all get into this house. Martha's got a good, hot supper waitin'."

John helped her and Emeline out of the wagon, and they climbed the porch stairs. "Well?" he said, gesturing at the house. "What do you think?"

Annaliese had to smile. The house glowed with fresh white paint and there was a pair of new rockers, and two more tiny ones, on the front porch. Light streamed from the front door's glass window, suggesting warm relief inside.

The entry hall was a stunning display of golden woods. Every surface glistened in the flickering light of the kerosene wall sconces. An oak staircase rose to the second floor. On the walls, paneled wainscoting ran as far as she could see. Above her head, an oak cornice embroidered the ceiling. Even the parquet floor was an artisan's masterpiece with oak and walnut strips hammered into a delicate latticework pattern.

"You thought it was going to be plain, didn't you?" John said.

She didn't trust herself to speak. It was suffocating, just too much, like three pieces of chocolate cake. Looking to her left, she saw that the parlor was bursting with even more fanciful creations: spandrels, carvings, more paneling.

No hot water, but this. "Well," Annaliese said slowly, "it's quite a surprise."

"Pretty amazing, eh? And in just five months." John came behind her to rub her shoulders.

"It would appear that you are in the wood business, Mr. Stregal," she said.

His hands ran up and down her arms. Every fiber in her muscles, every joint and bone ached, but she let him turn her around. He wiggled her by the shoulders, took her face in his rough hands and lifted her chin up. In an instant his lips were on hers, pressing hard, desperately delivering what he could not at the train station. Annaliese kissed him back despite the child between them. His mouth was rougher than she remembered, his smell so gamey and strange. Emeline's fingers clawed at their elbows. They let their kiss go, but pressed together one more time before Annaliese took Emeline's hand.

John waved toward the stairs. "Why don't you go upstairs while Joe and I get the trunks in? Beds and washbasins in all three bedrooms. Lie down? Wait till you see the wooden Venetian blinds. Stregal wood, of course."

As he slipped out the front door, Emeline raised her arms again to her mother, who yanked at the coat's filthy sleeves until it slid off. Two of the black buttons were gone. Red mud encrusted it from shoulder to hem. After the coat came off, still Emeline reached for her mother.

Annaliese took the child's hand to pull her up the stairs, but she buckled into a tantrum on her father's parquet floor. Annaliese abandoned her, dragging one leaden foot after the other up the stairs. She saw a door, a knob, a room, the bed. She fell upon it, muddy skirt and boots and all. Within seconds, Emeline had brought her fit upstairs, into the room, to the bed, into her mother's face. Mustering her last wisp of energy, Annaliese dragged the child up onto the bed. Her dress and underpants were soaked with urine. Annaliese ripped them off, threw them into a corner. As she pulled a quilt over the two of them and Emeline wiggled under to press her sticky, reeking body into her mother's warmth, Annaliese barely heard the sounds downstairs—John and Joe lumbering about, shouting to Samuel and James to help unload the wagon, to open and shut doors for them, to come here, do this, no, not that, get out of the way, to just go. The trunks bumped and banged up the stairs for a while.

An hour later, when John came to wake her, Annaliese begged him to let her and the children eat in their kitchen.

"Oh, come on," John said. "We have to celebrate." She washed her face and cleaned Emeline as best she could in the basin and hurried everyone next door.

Lucenia and Ben's dining room glowed in the light of sconces and candles. The surfaces glistened with equal excess—the grains of golden oak, black walnut, chestnut. Lucenia was smoothing her hand across the linen tablecloth with a smile.

As the cook brought out the meal, Annaliese's hands fluttered about her head in pointless tucking of disobedient strands. There had been no time for hair.

The aroma of Martha's fried ham, gravy, potatoes, string beans, and biscuits brought everyone to life. Napkins were tucked swiftly under little chins. Forks and knives got busy. No grace was said, Annaliese noticed, but it wasn't her place to say anything in someone else's home. She peered into Samuel's glass of milk for a moment, brought a candle over for a better look, and pushed it back to him with a nod. Martha moved between kitchen and table to refill platters and bowls as they emptied.

Ben smiled down on his sons who were shoveling food onto their plates. "Sure is good to have you here," he said.

Darrison got enough biscuit down to be able to say, "Yes, sir." He stared at his father for a minute. It was unusual for Ben Stregal to talk at the table. Eating was his priority, generally, as his girth testified. Though he stood only an inch or two above John's five foot ten, he threw twice the shadow. His round face was as pale and damp as a cucumber slice. In its center sat a beacon of a nose, a bulbous, crimson thing that made it hard for people to know where to look when they spoke to him. He blinked his eyes, orbs that were too big for the sockets, which didn't help people's comfort either. But eventually, somewhere around the time dessert was being spooned onto plates, he would begin to talk and that was a problem. Family and dining guests had come to dread dessert at Ben's table. A Stregal cousin had once confided to Annaliese, "He doesn't seem to be aware of the function of any punctuation, most especially the period." John, on the other hand, measured his words out like precious spices.

Darrison's gaze went to the steaming food just inches below his father's mouth and then back up again. The table fell quiet as the other adults caught this, held their forks above their plates and made amused exchanges. The only sound was the scratch of Martha's boots on the floor as she moved behind their chairs.

Ben put his hands up. "Oh, all right, y'all. Can't I be glad to talk to my family? Pass the biscuits, would you, son?"

Darrison passed the platter to his father and settled back into his meal.

John laughed. "Martha's a good cook, isn't she, Darrison?"

Annaliese looked up from sawing the toughest ham she had ever met to scrutinize the cook. Martha's straw-colored hair was parted and twisted and curled into an unfortunate goulash of several popular hairstyles. *Such a lot of effort for kitchen work*, Annaliese thought. Had the cook directed her blue eyes at either of the women, Annaliese might have thought the hairdo was in honor of their arrival. Instead, Martha's gaze bounced over the children's heads and straight to Ben. She tilted her head girlishly and put her hand on a round, fleshy hip. Her pouty lips curled into a smile, revealing a wide gap between her top front teeth. Ben never looked up from his potatoes and gravy.

Annaliese shot a look at Lucenia. She was fussing over a gravy stain on her sleeve.

"Yes," Annaliese said loudly. "Very nice meal."

Martha dropped back into the shadows to dish up something at the sideboard.

"So, what do you think about these mountains, Emmie?" John said.

Emeline dropped her head into her mother's lap and stuck her thumb in her mouth.

John turned to his son. "Well, how about you?"

Samuel was chewing the ham leather. After he got it down he said, "Must be lots of Indians out there."

"Well, not what you think," John said. "They're—"

"So we're going to build a fort tomorrow," Samuel said.

"Now y'all just hold on," John said. "You're going to come see the lumber mill first thing tomorrow." He pounded Samuel on the back. "You want to see it, don't you, son?"

Samuel put an elbow on the table and glanced at his mother.

"And in the afternoon you're going to help us unload a railroad car. Your beds and toys from home."

James bounced in his chair. "Railroad car? Oh, boy!"

"And your mother's piano." John pushed back from the table, dabbed his napkin to his mouth. At the sound of his chair scraping the floor, Martha rushed over to pick up his plate. Annaliese got a better look at her, this time noting the flimsy dress that hugged her unfettered breasts. No corset! Even here, a servant would know to wear a corset or at least a slip. This was no oversight. Martha turned away and resumed her circuit, like a schoolmarm circling during a test, except for the swaying hips.

Still, Lucenia seemed oblivious. She tucked a piece of biscuit into her mouth. "A piano here?" she said. "How wonderful. Annaliese, you must play for us every night before supper."

Annaliese, suddenly resistant to ever playing the piano again, said, "Oh, no, I was just planning to teach the children a little." She stroked

Emeline's head in her lap. The child's thumb hung halfway out of her mouth, releasing a trickle of drool onto her mother's napkin. Her eyes had been closed for a long time.

Annaliese motioned to the cook. "Martha?"

Martha bent toward her. "Ma'am?"

She smelled of cheap toilet water and cheaper face powder. Her eyelashes were so fair, she appeared to have fallen into a flour barrel. "Emeline's fallen asleep. Please put her on the chaise in the next room. I brought a blanket over and left it there."

A cold look sliced through Martha's eyes. She tried to blink it away, white eyelashes bouncing, but she reached for the child. When Martha returned, Ben waved her over to take his plate. He touched his napkin to his lips and looked right past her swaying hips to the apple pie on the sideboard. Martha took his plate, stole a look at Annaliese, and moved on.

"So," Ben said. "Piano lessons, eh? Excellent. Aunt Sophronia Jane was a piano teacher. Remember, John?"

At this, the mention of a long-dead relative, James and Darrison slumped in their chairs.

"Smelled like that salve she used," Ben said. "Cloverine, was it? Remember? Mother was appalled with everything about her, but I was fascinated. Not with her swearing, of course, but with her knowledge, especially when she explained music history to me." He leaned into his audience, though no one was making eye contact. "Here's a question for you. Do you know why Gregorian chant is called plainsong?"

John put his head in his hands.

Martha stopped moving. She had arrived at the end of the table opposite Ben, behind John, where she smiled at Ben like the newly converted in the first pew.

"Well?" Ben's bulging eyes bounced from face to face.

They all knew he was eager for someone to give the wrong answer. No one said a word. His lids went up and down imperiously.

Martha threw her shoulders back. Her breasts shot out over John's head, and Annaliese thought for a startling minute that she was going to try to answer the question.

John waved his brother on.

"Gregorian chant is called plainsong because it's monophonic music, you see," Ben said.

Darrison put his napkin on the table. "May I be excused, please?"

"The chants are classified on a system of melodic formulas and scale relationships known as the eight church modes. They fall into three main classes of—"

John finally looked up. "Ben. Not on their first night."

Martha's shoulders fell a little. Her eyes melted at the corners as she watched Ben lean back in his chair.

Annaliese stared a hole in Lucenia.

"We were talking about furniture," John said. "You have some shipments coming, too, don't you, Lucenia?"

Lucenia picked up her dinner plate and waved it in the air. Annaliese's eyes strained at their sockets as she tried to watch both women at the opposite ends of the table.

"Just . . . our . . . bed . . ." Lucenia replied slowly, with extra energy on the last word.

Martha jumped like a scalded pup. She hurried over to take the plate, but Annaliese saw her deliver a look that stabbed the back of Lucenia's head before she disappeared into the kitchen.

Darrison spoke up. "But Mother, what about my bed?"

"That's right, Darrison. It is coming," Lucenia replied. "What was I thinking?"

Annaliese hid a smile under the napkin she brought to her lips.

"Well, let's have that pie now," Ben said. He twisted around in his seat to look over at the apple pie.

"Mother," Darrison said. "May I be—"

Emeline's shriek from the drawing room jolted them from their seats.

Annaliese put her napkin on the table. "It's all right. She's just scared waking up in a strange room. But we should go."

Outside, Annaliese held the oil lamp for John as he carried Emeline down the steps into the darkest night Annaliese had ever seen. Samuel grabbed his mother's skirt and walked beside her. A new slip of a moon hung just above a distant brooding ridge and gave only enough light to outline its spine against the gray. A gust of wind rolled down from the mountain to bite their cheeks as they made their way home. She wished for the cozy glow of one electric light in one of her windows. Outside the weak ring of lantern light, there was nothing but the deep, black water of night. Thousands of invisible trees swayed in it, rubbing against one another to make the soft wash of sound that arrived with the chill. An owl's cry floated down, too, then another's answer, and the images of other creatures stirring as they began their night business made Annaliese pick up her pace.

The children wanted to sleep with them, of course. John piled quilts and pillows high on the floor beside the bed, pointed to the pile, even laid down there himself and began telling a story they loved. But Samuel and Emeline climbed into the bed beside Annaliese, one on each side, closed their eyes and went limp. John stood up to glare at them. Annaliese shook her head. He went back to the floor to wait them out. On the bedside table, the lamp gave off a glow that she hoped would last all night. Two windows were cracked open a few inches. Outside, a chorus of animal cries rose and fell, an antiphon of yips and replies.

"Mama, what's that?" Samuel whispered.

"I don't know," she said. "Hush now if you want to stay here."

"Maybe they're small. They sound small. Like cats. Not wolves, I don't think. Do you? Mama? They're small, right?"

"Shhh, Sam. It's time to go to sleep." Annaliese pulled her arm out from under Emeline, who had actually gone to sleep, and swept the boy's hair off his forehead.

John muttered on the floor.

"We didn't say prayers," Samuel said.

Oh, I've said mine, she thought. "You're right, Sam. Let's say them. Say lots of prayers, Sam. Tonight and every night we're here."

When he was finished, he clamped his hands over his ears and rolled over on his pillow. She listened for a long while for John's snoring. When it came, she finally relaxed, unburdened for one night at least of the reunion expectations of a long absent husband.

_____

V

In the morning, the room was freezing. Annaliese rolled over Samuel, stepped over John, and closed the window. Finally, in dawn's light, she could see this place not of her choosing. Within a hundred yards behind the house, a slope took a steep rise and became a wall of evergreens and trees she didn't know, but she recognized the purple redbuds. John's forest was stunning in its simple, quiet beauty, sobering in its vastness. There was not one human sign or sound. *It could be the year 1401 as easily as 1901,* she thought. Annaliese shivered and rubbed her arms against the loneliness sweeping over her. Louisville's streets were so far away, and with them Mr. Frazier's cozy bakery and his caraway seed bread, her mother and Aunt Gertrude's arguments over the seasoning of whatever was on the stove. Celeste Parker's baby would be born soon, then baptized in the cathedral, and afterward everyone would gather to celebrate in her little house on the cobblestone street Annaliese loved for the clip clop of the horses' hooves as they pranced by. Louisville would dance on without her. Here, there were no sacraments or celebrations or libraries with honeyed light. Only John's forest and creatures, two-legged and otherwise, full of dark potential.

On a distant ridge, something moved—a ribbon of smoke rising from an ashen roof. She pictured a shotgun beside the front door, listless people inside, like the ones described in the *Harper's* article as pale as boiled cod. She wondered if there were children out there and whether they would soon be at her door.

Annaliese wandered the second floor. For a new house, it had a lot of smells. A musky, piney scent came off the floors. There were two more bedrooms in the back of the house. Wooden blinds hung on every window, just as John had said. The morning light insinuated between the slats onto another golden floor. The bedrooms were still empty, but rugs and mirrors, tapestries, water basins, draperies, clocks, chests, and lamps were on their way. Company would be coming, Dorothy had promised.

Downstairs, she found the room she would call the drawing room, which led into the dining room, which led to the kitchen. The kitchen, pantry, and a closet spanned the width of the house. She opened the closet door and found a tub shoved against the wall, no tubing or faucets in sight, but a tub at least near the hot water source and a door with a key. As for the kitchen itself, John had installed the latest white glazed ceramic wall tiles and smooth pine cabinets. There was an icebox that actually held ice (*and where were they going to get that?* she thought) and a spotless new wood stove with a blue enameled coffee pot atop. A crisply folded yellow towel lay on the table next to it. Back home, she had spent hours with an elderly woman learning how to feed in wood of just the right size at just the right rate, how to put your hand in to test the temperature, which varied depending on what you were cooking. In the winter, this stove was going to keep the room cozy. In the summer, it would drive her mad.

She had to hire a cook. She did not want that Martha in her house.

Above her, quick, light footsteps skittered across the bedroom floor. Annaliese hurried outside to the privy. As she went down the steps, she heard, "Mama! Outside. A pig. Where are you? Mama?"

After a breakfast of canned peaches, canned potatoes and last night's ham served again in Lucenia's home, the children started down the hill with their fathers to see the mill. Their mothers, pens and papers in hand, pulled up rockers on Lucenia's front porch. Underneath the porch, an enormous sow banged about.

"Number one," Lucenia said, putting pen to paper. "Fence this pig down at the mill."

Annaliese waved her hand. "Peeuuw. Pigs. Wolves. He never wrote about that."

"Wolves?" Lucenia looked up.

"Well, perhaps they were foxes." Annaliese pushed her rocker into motion. "Didn't you hear them last night? Did they sound like foxes to you?"

"Number two, we get the men moving on bathroom plumbing."

Annaliese nodded and rocked. That privy was cold.

"All right, number three. We subscribe to *Woman's Home Companion* . . ."

Annaliese kept nodding.

" . . . and the *Journal of Public Vocation*. Now that's expensive. But you'll split the cost with me."

The rocking chair slowed. "What is it?"

"My dear." Lucenia leaned back in her chair. "It's about the movement. Women's work in the cities among the poor, the hungry. Our right to vote."

"Oh, that." Annaliese flipped her hand. "That activist stuff."

A puzzled look crossed Lucenia's face. Her lips parted briefly, but she turned back to her list. "You'll pay half, yes?"

Annaliese shrugged.

"And we'll order the Harvard Classics series for the children. We can read to them about the Greek philosophers, the great poets."

Annaliese watched the children ricochet around their fathers on their way down the hill. "How about baseballs and bats?"

"My dear, they'll make them into weapons. James and Darrison will, anyway."

"Well, what about horseshoes?"

"More dangerous than baseball bats."

"Slingshots, then." She allowed herself a grin.

Lucenia sat back in her rocking chair and tapped her pen on her knee. "All right, horseshoes," she agreed. "In your yard, not mine."

"Fine."

They watched the tiny figures of their children and husbands disappear on the grounds of the mill, quiet on Sundays. They could see the buildings and millpond laid out before them at the breast of the meadow. Beyond that, waves of mountains rose to the sky. The mill was closer to them than they had expected. Tomorrow and every day of the next two years, they would hear the saws, the freight cars screeching on the track, the steam whistle at the beginning and end of every shift. Sawdust would drift uphill to land on every clock and book and pillow.

Behind them, the clinks of flatware being tossed into drawers and pots being banged met their ears.

"Four," Lucenia said, tilting her head in the kitchen's direction. "Teach her to know her place."

"Where did they find her?"

"Ben said she's from one of the sorriest farms in the county. Came up to him in town one day, said she heard they were looking for a cook. So he hired her."

Hired those breasts and hips, thought Annaliese, though it was hard to imagine that Ben would notice anything other than food.

The clinking and banging stopped.

"She seems to be very interested in plainsong," Annaliese said.

Lucenia came out of her chair. "Come with me."

They found her at the kitchen sink. Last night's hairdo was wilting in the rising steam. She brushed a few errant strands aside with a wet hand as she turned to them.

"Martha," Lucenia said, "we have some questions. Where shall we put our dirty laundry?"

"In Joe Rosetta's wagon, I reckon."

"Pardon?" Lucenia asked. She straightened into her Stonewall Jackson posture.

"He might could carry it into town for you. Pearlie Wiginton does folks' laundry there. I can't handle any more laundry than what I'm doin' right now, which is Mr. Ben's and Mr. John's."

Annaliese froze. Of all the things she had fretted over before the move, uppity servants wasn't among them.

"Oh, really? Well, we'll see about that," Lucenia said. She moved deeper into the kitchen to stand beside Martha at the sink. "Mrs. Stregal and I need to plan the meals. What's ready in the garden?"

"Garden's just coming in." Martha's lips curled in amusement. "It bein' April." She wiped her hands down her apron, then back up to plant them on her hips.

Lucenia squared her shoulders further. "Then we'll be ordering food to stock the pantries. Mrs. Stregal and I will let you know what we've planned." She turned to leave and bumped into Annaliese, slack-jawed at the theater of watching someone poke Lucenia in the eye.

"No need for that," Martha said. "I done planned and ordered food for nigh two weeks. Train'll carry it up from Atlanta in a couple days."

"Well, how thorough. When did you do that?"

"Yesterday." Martha crossed her arms across her chest.

Annaliese waited for Lucenia put Martha in her red dirt place, but she said nothing. The only sound in the kitchen was the swish of her skirt as she left. Annaliese did not trust her own face so she turned it quickly away from Martha and hurried after Lucenia. As they entered the front hall, Lucenia hissed, "We have to act fast." Then she stalked up the stairs.

"We?" said Annaliese as she watched her go.

❧

VI

Annaliese was in a bedroom unpacking a box when she heard the children. She went to the window.

"Aunt Anna," James shouted outside. "Come see. Pigs and chickens and those loud big birds all over the yard!" He held Emeline's hand. Near their feet, two hens and their chicks worked over the weeds. Emeline broke free to lunge at a chick.

"Where's Uncle John?" Annaliese leaned out the window. "Where's Sam?"

"Down there." James pointed to the sawmill. John, Samuel, and Darrison were coming up the hill.

"Stay right there." She ran down the stairs and shot out the door. James had picked up a stick and was heading toward the sow. "James, stop." She turned to grab Emeline and saw that she was barefoot.

"No, no, Emmie. Where are your shoes? I told you that you can't take them off here."

Emeline beamed as she held up the prize that peeped and strained between her chubby fingers. "Baby!" she squealed.

Annaliese picked her up. James ran back to his aunt, stick swinging wildly in his hands toward all of his body's soft spots. "Mr. Rosetta says pigs like to eat some kind of acorn, chinka something, that's on the ground in the forest and that makes 'em taste good so you got to let 'em run around free." He grinned up at her.

"You were in the commissary?"

James froze. "Uh . . ."

"By . . . your . . . selves?" Each syllable was louder than the last.

The boy's face went pale and he took a step backward.

Annaliese sat down to pull Emeline into her lap. She brushed dirt off the child's feet. "Where are your shoes?"

"Down by the creek, Mama." Emeline pulled the chick closer to her chest.

"You can't go barefoot in Georgia. I told you."

Emeline's face fell. "Why?"

"You could get very sick, Emmie. Something called hookworm. It's in the ground." She yanked her daughter's foot up for a close look, smothering the child, the chick, and its frenzied peeps under her arms.

"What's that?"

James watched his aunt with a frown. "Something on your feet?"

"Well, through your feet . . ." began Annaliese, but she stopped at the sight of Emeline's wide eyes.

James lit up. "It's worms, Emmie. They hook on your feet."

"What!" Emeline banged into her mother's chin. The chick fell and took off.

"Ow!" Annaliese grabbed her chin. "No, James, stop—"

"Then you squish them when you walk on them and they turn into lots more worms."

Emeline grabbed one of her feet and ran horrified eyes over it.

"No, James, that's not it. Stop—"

But the boy was waving his stubby arms and his bright eyes were locked on Emeline's twisted face, feeding off it, Annaliese realized. She reached out to cover his mouth. Too late.

"And then they chew your feet off."

Emeline tried to climb deeper into her mother's chest. Her screams sent the pigs running.

"No, Emmie, they don't. James, look what you've done. Shame on you." An elbow slammed into her breast. "Ow."

Finally, the boy fell silent. He dropped his stick.

"Go get y'all's shoes."

James passed his uncle on his way to the creek.

"Hey," John said as he arrived huffing. "They took off on me. We were throwing rocks in the stream when Emmie and James . . ." His brow softened as he took in Annaliese's expression. "What's wrong?"

"You can't let them do that, John. And they can't take their shoes off."

"Why not?"

"Hookworm. I told you."

He bent down and picked up Emeline's foot for a look, then the other. "Hmmm." He winked at his daughter.

"You think I'm crazy?" Annaliese said. "I've read about this. These worms, they're in the dirt. They get in your feet and work their way up into . . ."

John flipped up a palm to stop her. Emeline was listening intently.

"Anyway, she's only four years old. Who knows where she might've wandered off to."

"Had my eye on her." He reached down to stroke Emeline's hair.

"I had a baby chick," Emeline said, working her way out of her mother's lap.

Annaliese pulled her back down. "Wait on your shoes."

John put his hat on. "They all saw my mill. Your turn this afternoon."

Annaliese looked up at him. "I've got to set up the house."

"Suit yourself." John turned downhill, stuck his fingers in his mouth and punched out an ear-piercing whistle. Darrison and Samuel looked up and picked up their pace coming toward him. "Be sure to set up the children's beds. So they'll sleep in their rooms tonight." His grey eyes said the rest.

Down at the mill, the steam whistle signaled the mid-day break.

Dinner was again in Lucenia's dining room. Martha brought out a platter of fried trout and bowls of vegetables without a word and left. Lucenia smiled at Annaliese when they heard the back door slam.

John looked up from pouring bourbon into a tin cup. "The Johnson company contract arrived a few days ago? Why didn't you tell me?"

Ben sawed away at his chicken. "Well, I was mullin' over whether we could meet their production deadlines."

"Why didn't you just ask J. C. about that?"

Ben did not look up. He never prevailed in their tussles. As a boy, he had once overheard his father tell someone that Ben had just missed being a genius. The ten-year-old Ben pictured himself in heaven, sliding off the genius ledge while little John watched from above. As John grew up, no one in the family was surprised when he emerged as the dominant force, so when John and Ben set up the lumber business and divided the day-to-day duties, John told Ben what he would do and Ben merely nodded, as John had counted on. Ben was overseeing the mill operation and commissary and John was handling the land management, finances, and general operations.

Ben held a forkful of food at his lips. "J. C. and I have been distracted with another steam whistle gone missing."

John put his fork down. "Damn. Not again."

Lucenia stopped pestering James about his elbow on the table to look at John. "Such language," she said.

"Fifth one." Ben brought the food closer to his mouth.

"You find out who's been stealing them?"

Darrison and Samuel stopped shoving trout into their mouths. Annaliese looked up from cutting Emeline's beans.

Lucenia said, "Someone's stealing the mill's steam whistles?"

"Why?" Darrison said.

Ben lowered his fork. "Their wives put them to simmering on top of the stove kettle, and when the men go into the woods to tend to their stills, the women watch for federal agents on the property. If the woman sees one, she'll crank up the heat, blast the whistle in warning."

Lucenia squinted at Ben. "Your workers are moonshiners?"

Ben sighed.

"Did you or J. C. nail down the thief?" John asked.

"Oh, yes, yes." Ben finally looked at John. "It's been Lum McArthur all along. Three of the five, anyway."

John nodded. "Knew it. So you've told him that making mash can now be his sole source of income, right?"

"What's mash?" James said at his father's elbow.

"And just how close do these moonshiners live, Ben?" Lucenia asked.

All eyes were on Ben. Beads of sweat glistened on his forehead. He rubbed his chins.

"You told him to go to the office, get his time, and go, right?" John said. His grip on the table had killed appetites.

"Well, no."

John sat back in his chair. Underneath his sunburned cheeks, jaw muscles worked.

"I can't fire anyone, John," Ben said quietly. "You know that. Man needs the money. You know that, too. Lum's a good worker otherwise. Besides, I figure he can't possibly need any more whistles." Ben smiled and looked at his wife to share the joke, but she was just staring at him, one hand smoothing the tablecloth over and over. He waved at James to pass the potatoes.

John picked up the Jack Daniels and poured again into his cup. "Got to come down hard on this kind of shi . . ." John's eyes slid from Ben to the faces of the four children watching. "This kind of bull. This afternoon, I'm going to tell him to go."

"What's mash, Uncle John?" James asked, louder this time.

"This moonshiner fellow obviously lives close by," Lucenia said.

"And where there's a still there's a shotgun," Annaliese said. "You just know he's got a gun."

Darrison was putting it all together. "He'll get mad if Uncle John fires him."

John leaned forward, lowered his voice as though he could exclude the women and children lining the table, and said, "Let's talk about this later." He shot a look at Annaliese that told her the same thing.

Everyone shifted back in their chairs. Lucenia's hand swept over to Ben's and she squeezed it gently.

"But Papa . . ." Darrison said.

"Let's talk about what we'll do tomorrow," Lucenia said. "My, my. Where shall we start?"

"We're going to build a fort, right?" Samuel said, nodding at Darrison.

That afternoon, after Emeline had finally fallen asleep in her arms, Annaliese slipped away to her front porch and sat down in a rocker. For the moment, the sawmill was quiet. The serene valley stretched out before her in all of its freshest spring greens. Her eyes lingered on the odd color of the earth around the mill. They called it red clay, but to Annaliese's eyes it was practically orange, the color of yams. Already she knew it was slick and sticky when wet. How would their garden do in this muck?

"Pssst!" Lucenia hissed from next door.

Annaliese winced. She had forgotten to see if that porch was empty before she came out. She dropped her head back against the rocker and closed her eyes.

Chickens scattered as Lucenia swept across the yard, fleshy arms pumping as she came. The steps creaked under her weight. She plopped down next to Annaliese.

"We need more information about her," she said, "so we can plan." She leaned over to brush dirt off her boots.

"We?"

"I figure that Joe Rosetta knows her. You must go and dig something useful out of him."

Annaliese stiffened. "Me? Mr. Rosetta? Oh, no. You go."

Lucenia slapped the last of the dirt off her hands and folded them in her lap. "You'll get more out of him than I would."

"I'm no good at that sort of thing." She didn't have a dog in this fight. Martha's sights were on Ben.

"But he's a man and you're a woman." Lucenia nudged her arm. "A beautiful woman. Just look at your hair today, the way those golden strands of hair caress your lovely neck."

Annaliese smiled and fingered the strands for a moment until she realized what Lucenia was doing. "I have to stay here to watch the children."

"Emeline's asleep, isn't she? It won't take long."

"Oh, Lucenia . . ."

"Perhaps there is already some mail waiting for us there at the commissary."

Mail from home.

Annaliese began rocking. "Well, what would I say?"

She found him stacking cans of lard on high shelves in the back. From the doorway, she watched his simian arms swinging the cans in an upward arc. He was the brownest white man she had ever seen.

"Afternoon, Mrs. Stregal." As Joe came to the front, he raked long, thin fingers through his black hair. It coiled back into a glossy mass of curls.

"Good afternoon to you, Mr. Rosetta." She sent him a proper smile. "I understand two of the children were down here this morning."

He was already nodding. "Yes, ma'am. James and Emeline. I gave 'em some rock candy and waited for someone to come lookin' for 'em. We visited fer a spell. I told 'em to stay away from that mill and the pond."

"Yes, that's right. But they shouldn't be down here on their own. It will take them a while to get used to the rules, but until they do, will you send for me if you see them down here alone again?"

"Yes, ma'am." His gaze on the boss's wife was warm but guarded.

"Thank you." She walked along an aisle and peered into a flour barrel. He watched her look at the flour he knew she didn't need, and then spit in the corner. She walked deeper into the store across floorboards sticky with sawyers' chewing tobacco. Her boots stuck and snapped in the amber veneer. A tower of metal buckets leaned against the wall. At her elbow, a shelf full of boxes of soap flakes, saddle soap, salves, and elixirs ran along the wall. From behind a stack of horse blankets she called, "Martha says we should send our laundry to town with you. When are you going in?"

"Later today. Who should I carry it to?"

"Pearlie Wiginton."

A whoop of laughter sliced the dusty air. "Oh, no, ma'am. You don't want her."

"Why not?" Annaliese took a few steps back toward him.

"Pearlie's bad to lay the clean clothes on her bed."

She was back at the front counter. "So?"

"And then her bed bugs crawl right on in. Big ole' brown things. They'll bite youuuu . . . Oooh, Lord. Worry you to death."

She clamped her elbows to her sides. "How do you know this?"

"Aw, everbody knows 'bout Pearlie," he laughed. "Some folks just tolerate them bugs." He shook his head. "That Martha. She sure enough knows."

"But why would Martha want that to happen to us, Mr. Rosetta?" She attempted the tone of a customer asking the price of water dippers.

"She's biggity."

"Pardon?"

"Got to have her way. Proud. You know. Biggity."

"And why's that?" Annaliese ran a finger through the mantle of sawdust on the unplaned counter and examined it as if she cared.

"Well, I lay it to a couple of things." Joe wiped an oily rag across the counter in circles after her finger trail. "First, she's white. She figures she don't have to act like colored help. Then, too, she thinks she's a good cook. Maybe she is, maybe she ain't, but it's true enough that it's hard to find cooks up here. And then there's y'all arrivin' yesterday. She . . ." Joe's circles on the counter stopped and he looked up at her.

Annaliese panicked. *She what?* She did not trust herself to speak so she just nodded. Still he was silent. She began another trail calmly. "She what, Mr. Rosetta?"

Joe's stiff arm did not move. "Well, I just think she didn't believe y'all would really come here."

"But now that we're here, why would she jeopardize her job? She's got decent wages, good food, a clean bed. A sweet situation it seems to me."

Joe tucked the rag under the counter. "Maybe she figures it might could be sweeter." He picked up a broom and began sweeping.

"Afternoon, ma'am," he said to the floor. "Sorry there ain't no mail for you yet."

Lucenia stood on her front porch tapping her foot. Three baskets of the women's and children's laundry sat beside her.

Annaliese came huffing up the road, then into the yard, elbows out to hoist skirts above the goose and pig mess. "Where . . ." Annaliese's chest heaved as she tried to catch her breath in the thin air " . . . is she?"

"Inside." Lucenia waved her up the steps. "What'd he say?"

"She's biggity."

Lucenia rolled her eyes. "Indeed."

Annaliese put her hand to her chest and fought to breathe. She inched closer to Lucenia than she would've preferred and whispered, "We're sure to get bedbugs in our laundry if we use the Wiginton woman." Annaliese looked at the laundry and began scratching her arms.

Lucenia took a step backward. "Bedbugs? What else did he say?"

"Sounds like she's up to what you think." Annaliese was careful to say "you", not "we."

Lucenia stared into the distance. In the house, the older boys were arguing. It didn't sound serious, so neither mother moved. James walked out the front door eating an apple and sat down on a step.

"Annaliese," Lucenia said, "go get John's laundry."

"But Martha will do it."

"Not this time. Pearlie's going to do it."

Annaliese clutched at her skirt. "Lucenia, didn't you hear me? Bedbugs in John's shirts? His undershorts? You know how he is. If those brown bugs are in his clothes, there will be an ugly scene."

"Precisely."

Samuel's argument with Darrison was growing louder and Martha had joined in. It did not sound like she was mediating.

"Oh, Lucenia, I don't know. They'll eat him alive."

"Darling, do you think John is worrying about your precious skin right now?"

Annaliese scratched at her arms again. "Does it have to be John's laundry? Why not Ben's?"

Lucenia took a step closer to Annaliese and lowered her voice. "Remember the steam whistle?"

Annaliese nodded.

"You think Ben could dismiss her?" Lucenia shook her head.

Annaliese looked down at the porch. "Well, I just don't know."

Darrison and Samuel burst out of the front door with Martha on their heels, raised broom in her hands. "And stay out! Y'all can't take food out of my kitchen 'less I give it out."

Darrison shot down the steps to the yard. Samuel ran over to his mother. Martha flipped around and stormed back into the house.

"I'll get John's things," Annaliese said.

That night, he lay on their bed and watched her undress, as she knew he would. Standing at her bureau, Annaliese removed her blouse and shook it out. A cloud of red dust settled on the bureau. She longed for a bath, but the wood stove's fire had long ago died out while she soothed the children to sleep. Instead, she lifted the porcelain pitcher and poured cold water into the basin. Her hands met at her belly to begin unhooking her corset. As it fell away, she exhaled in relief. She dipped a cloth into the water, ran it around her neck and across her chest to the edge of her chemise. Down a naked arm went the cloth, then back up again on the underside to the soft hair under the curve. In the mirror, she watched John with weary eyes. He was still fully clothed, right down to his muddy boots crisscrossed on top of a fresh quilt.

He rose up on his elbows. "So, what do you think?"

"That I'd like some hot water."

The bouncing foot stopped. "That's not what I meant."

"The house is fine, John. Nice and comfortable, like you said."

He did not relax, did not move at all save his eyebrows, which he raised to question her again.

She unfolded the damp cloth, streaked with the dust that had been on her neck all day, and rinsed it in the basin. "Yes, it's all very impressive. It's amazing what you and Ben have accomplished here in just a few months." *Your turn.*

He swung his feet to the floor to tug his boots off. "We're shipping two million board feet a day, Anna. Four million more drying in the yard. White oak, red oak, American beech, black walnut. By June, it'll be twice that. We can't fill the orders fast enough."

She squeezed the cloth in her hands, watched the copper-colored water stream between her fingers, a wretched taint that reminded her of blood. *Say thank you for doing this for me. Say you missed me. Or at least tell me why we're here.*

In the dim light of the lamp, she groped around the top of the bureau for soap but found only John's shaving supplies lined up in their familiar uniform way, one inch between. A stack of his immaculate handkerchiefs, folded to precisely the same size, stood at the corner.

John walked over to stand beside her at the basin. Hooking his thumbs in his suspenders, he yanked them down and began unbuttoning his shirt. She ached to take off her chemise, but she was not in a generous mood.

He took off his shirt. "Forty men on the payroll, in the mill, out in the hills and on the skid roads. Trees this big around acre after acre." He made a circle with his arms. "I am going to make you so proud of me, Annaliese."

"I already was."

"Just wait."

She sighed. *All right, let's get on with it. It's a safe day of the month so there went my last excuse.*

His cool gray eyes softened at the edges. He cupped her face with his hands and forced her to look at his gratitude there long enough to make her soften in his arms.

"Thank you for coming," he said.

She broke into tears.

He kissed her gently, then urgently as she kissed him back. Her hand swept up to pull the pins from her hair. His fingers flew to her chemise, where they fumbled, too big for the tiny buttons but eventually succeeded, one by one. Even after their eightyears together, she would not allow herself the arousal of watching him work the buttons, so ingrained were the nuns' warnings about erotic pleasure and her childhood fear of the mysterious moaning behind the captain's cabin doors.

She reached for the lamp to kill its flame.

"But I want to look at you," John said. His hand halted hers. "Your body. I've missed you . . ."

She turned it off and he didn't say a word. They eased out of the rest of their clothes and into bed. Instantly, every part of him was on her—legs, chest, hands, lips. His mouth was sunburned and cracked, his arms rock hard. When his mouth found her breast, she cried out.

"Beard too rough?"

"Maybe a little," she said.

Her legs gave way to his heated parting. His penis was hard against her, *hard as one of his oaks*, she thought as it sank inside. Her hands were limp on his damp back.

"Not too heavy on ya?"

"Fine."

The rocking began. Like an animal unleashed, John left her then. His soft moans rose into cries of near anguish. He buried his face in her neck and she twisted to try to get her ear away from his mouth in time, but it was too late. He was bellowing into her ear, then the pillow, and when she thought her insides couldn't burn any worse he finally made his last thrust. Shivers rumbled through him, slower and slower until his quaking body went limp.

She gripped his back and stared into the dark.

A few days later, after dawn's watery light had begun to spread across the sky, he bolted out of his front door wearing nothing but shaving soap, an undershirt, and undershorts. Spewing suds and curses, he goose-stepped his way down the steps to the yard. He ripped off the shorts, tore away his undershirt and hurled them to the ground. Arms flailing, he stomped the clothes, sent the hogs running. Annaliese came to the bedroom window and opened the blinds cautiously, like the traitor she was. She felt guilty for telling him that Martha had recommended the new laundress, disloyal for putting his clothes but not hers in their bureau and keeping the secret the whole long night when she didn't sleep for listening for bed bug scufflings. But she felt a little wicked pleasure, too, with the feel of justice in her hands.

Next door, the bedroom curtains moved apart for a moment, then closed.

That afternoon, Joe brought the wagon around to Ben and Lucenia's home. He spit into the dirt and pretended that he didn't see Annaliese watching through her parlor blinds. Moments later, Martha emerged, yellow hair deflated, head down. She carried two bags. Ben and Lucenia came out onto their porch. Neither man moved to help her throw the bags into the wagon. She climbed upon the seat beside Joe. The wagon lurched forward and Annaliese watched it circle around to head down the hill. Long after it had disappeared, she could not bring herself to leave the blinds. Cooks are hard to find up here, Joe had said.

℮〜ᓚ

VII

By eleven the next morning, Annaliese was already a day's worth of mad.

The women stood on the slope of ground behind their homes, their energy and civility toward each other spent, staring at Joe Rosetta and the log fire he had built. A black washpot sat atop.

Joe opened a box of Red Devil Lye and poured it into the steaming water. A hiss went up as the water churned into a milky brew. "Once the water gets to boilin', throw the clothes in," he said. "Get you a stick and push 'em 'round. After a spell, you fish 'em out and rinse 'em in the other pot, wring 'em and hang 'em on the line out yonder." He pointed toward the clothesline he had strung between two slender oaks.

The women looked at the clothesline as if they had never seen it before. Anything but look at each other. Their morning in Annaliese's kitchen had not gone well.

While they had tried to put together breakfast, Annaliese discovered the limits of Lucenia's cooking skills. She refused to crack eggs and get her fingers messy, so Annaliese had to make the griddlecake batter. Because Lucenia couldn't tell when the griddle was too hot, she burned the first four. Cooking bacon was beyond her—it wouldn't cook fast enough to suit her. Eventually, Annaliese had narrowed Lucenia's responsibilities to one: getting the wood stove's oven to the right temperature to bake the biscuits. Annaliese showed her how to test it with her hand just inside the door. Lucenia stuck it in too far and burned it.

Jerking back from the oven, she barked that there was no reason that the wife of Ben Stregal, lumber baron, should have to deal with a wood stove, that John should have had her an electric stove by now, and never mind that there was no electricity for seven counties, and she stalked out. Annaliese threw the blackened griddlecakes at her on her way out.

Now they were supposed to do the laundry, the infested laundry. Annaliese slapped at the flies that circled her damp neck.

Joe brushed off his hands. "Anything else I can do?"

Lucenia walked over to the three laundry baskets and peered in. "Now these things, these bedbugs, Mr. Rosetta. They're big enough to see? Not tiny, like fleas?"

"Yes, ma'am. And no, ma'am. Big ole' brown things." He swiped the back of his hand across his mouth. Smile lines crinkled his eyes.

Annaliese eyed Pearlie's work, too. It *looked* all right. Shirts were still folded, pinafores and stockings looked immaculate. But the women had to be sure. With a shudder, Annaliese scratched at her arms. "Mr. Rosetta, could you dump the clothes in?"

Lucenia picked up a basket. "I'll handle this. You go on back to the store, Mr. Rosetta. If we need more firewood, we'll call the children to bring it."

Joe threw his axe over his shoulder and headed downhill. Watching him go, Annaliese guessed that he had figured out what had landed Martha in his wagon the day before. That she had been blamed for the bedbugs. That John Stregal had not hesitated to rid his household of such a dimwit. That the wives had counted on it.

Annaliese looked up again at the cloudless sky that offered no break from the sun that was cooking her from the top of her bonnet down. A bead of sweat rolled between her breasts.

Joe called over his shoulder, "Don't lay clothes on them bushes neither, or you'll pick up chiggers."

Annaliese threw up her hands.

"Well, the water's boiling," Lucenia said. "Come on. Pick up a basket."

"I'll get the stick." Annaliese turned to go on a long search.

Lucenia reached down for the stick Joe had brought them. "Here."

As the clothes tumbled into the steaming water, the women's eyes swept over the surface. Nothing came back up. Annaliese gave a half-hearted poke. The women brought their faces closer. Something plaid went by, then back down. Underneath the iron pot, the fire spit and popped, sending the boil into a furious froth that spilled over the rim.

Annaliese stirred again. "We should've asked him if they would float."

"Of course, they float."

An apron went by. As Annaliese went after it with the stick, Lucenia leaned in further to peer in.

Two brown bugs popped up.

"Gracious!" Annaliese said. Considering that John had recently shared his shorts with them, they were huge. Lady buggish, but flatter, like a beetle. Reddish-brown. *The same color as this confounded red dirt,* she thought. "Look what I brought into my house just to get rid of Martha."

Lucenia's head snapped around. "It's not as if they're all over your house. They were just in John's clothes." Her mouth curved into a wicked smile. "In fact, just in his underwear, from what I saw." Lucenia began daintily stomping her feet, tearing at the air with fluttering hands and ripping imaginary undershorts.

Annaliese fished out an apron and hurled it at her sister-in-law. "Look at all this work you've made for us."

"I made?" Lucenia yanked off her work gloves and threw them on the ground. She gestured at the furniture parts in the yard behind them. "It wasn't my idea to take your bureau apart."

Annaliese hadn't meant to go so far, but she thought she saw a brown leg in a drawer joint, so she had hammered the drawer front off. Nothing there, but she could not stop. Now the drawers were in pieces all across the yard. She leveled the stick at her sister-in-law. "Of course, I blame you. You just had to go and get rid of Martha. Martha was your problem, not mine. Now we have no cook."

Lucenia pulled off her bonnet and fanned herself. "She was most definitely *our* problem. She didn't want us here. Not you, not me, not the children. Remember? She was probably spitting in our food in the kitchen. But now *we* are rid of her." Lucenia threw up her hands. "You should be thanking me." Finally, she stomped away. Near the steps at the back of her house, Darrison and James sat in the dirt playing marbles. They saw her coming—a storm of dust and chicken feathers, angry skirt, and big boots—and they scrambled away on hands and knees. Just as she thundered through their game, Annaliese shook the stick at her and screamed, "You come right back here and finish this."

Lucenia jerked the back door open and went inside.

"Mother?" James said as the feathers settled.

Annaliese stabbed the stick back into the brew and furiously stirred for something belonging to Lucenia. Out came one of her camisoles—paydirt—so Annaliese sent it flying. Next was one of Emeline's pinafores. Annaliese took it, dripping and reeking of lye that made her eyes water, to the rinse pot, then the clothesline, where she poked it apart enough to drape on the line.

She had been at it for four shirts and two pairs of pants when she saw John climbing the hill to her. At dawn, he had left the house to saddle up and cruise hills with Hoyt, the timber foreman. He was wearing the black felt hat and overalls that still astonished her. As he came steaming toward her, she saw a big grin spreading across his shaded face. She took her gloves off and leaned on her stick to watch him with sour eyes.

"Anna, we found a stand of enormous white oaks," he called. His chest heaved as he stopped on the other side of the washpot. "Some are eight feet across at the base."

She threw her gloves down. "John, I've had the most horrid morning. I . . ."

"Ah, yes, the laundry." His eyes scarcely skimmed the washpot between them before he began walking around it, hands held out to her. "Doing a great job, great job, Anna." He pulled her into a shallow hug and pounded her on the back. "Listen, these oaks, you gotta see them. Beauties. Hard to get to, the hills are so steep, but we'll get a mule team up there somehow."

She looked him up and down, her Louisville attorney in blue overalls and a flannel shirt with sweat rings. Again he smelled so strange. Today it was sweat and pine resin. As he plucked off his wide-brimmed hat, his dirty hair sprang in several directions—the disheveled look she recognized from their morning bed. He swatted at his hair as if to arrange it, but he was beaming at her. *He loves this,* she thought.

"I'm a wood hick," he laughed.

"And I'm a hack."

"What do you mean?" John dropped his hat and reached under the bonnet's brim to pull her hands down from her face. "You're not a . . . whoa! What's happened to your hands?"

"See what I mean? They're ruined." Annaliese pulled one hand away but left the other for scrutiny. "I have been washing clothes in lye. Before that washing dishes, scraping for bed bugs, peeling potatoes, chopping stove wood. That's why they feel like bark, John Stregal."

"Why didn't you get Lucenia to help you?"

Her head fell back. "That woman."

John fixed his gray eyes on her.

Annaliese pulled away from him and jabbed a finger at Lucenia's house. "She left me here. We had an argument . . ."

"An argument? Look, you two can't . . ."

"Don't you tell me what I can't do." She glared at him. "I'm doing the best I can with what you've done to me."

Shock flooded his face as visibly as if she had slapped him. He opened his mouth to speak, thought better of it, shifted from left foot to right, then back again while she wailed into her apron. Finally, he pulled her hands up around his neck and brushed his whiskered face against her cheek. She arched her back. Pulling her apron up again to wipe her nose, she said, "I need help. Hired help."

John was already nodding like a man in the dark who had finally groped his way to the light switch. "I'll take you into Pinch next week and we'll see about finding a laundry girl."

She leaned farther backward. "And a cook."

He nodded and tugged her closer.

"And someone to watch the children. And a man to manage the garden, tend our animals, and fetch things from town."

He finally let go. "Don't get your hopes up, Anna. Help's hard to find here and you'll be wanting a cook who can read. They're few and even if you find one, people from these hills, they're, well, different. They're Scots-Irish. Bull-headed, I mean to tell you."

Annaliese pictured Martha, hands on her hips by the kitchen sink, squared off with Lucenia.

"But we'll see what we can dig up." He picked his hat off the ground and brushed it off.

"When?"

"Depends." He ran his hands around the hat's edges as he stepped backward to eye her with fleeting warmth. "Maybe Saturday."

Saturday was fifteen meals away. "But . . ."

John squared his hat back on. "I've got timber to get to."

Down in the valley, the sawmill whistle announced a shift change.

"Got to go." He stole a quick look at the fire. "Make sure Joe puts that out when you're done."

"Wait."

But he didn't.

Annaliese pulled her bonnet off as she came through her kitchen door. One foot in, she stopped hard at the sight: Lucenia at her kitchen table, knife in hand, slicing into an apple. At her elbow, Emeline stood on tiptoes, mouthing the table's metal edge and watching the fruit fall away from the blade.

Lucenia met Annaliese's raised eyebrows with a shrug. "She woke up wet. Sam called me over to help."

Annaliese looked Emeline over. She wore a clean, crisp dress and boots tied up with precise, identical bows. Her hair had been brushed and plaited into a smooth braid.

Emeline eyed the fruit that was almost hers. "Want some, Mama?"

Lucenia put the slices on a blue enameled plate. "Let's wash your hands, Emmie." She pulled a chair to the soapstone sink and the child climbed up to put her hands under the pump's mouth. Lucenia pushed the handle up and down until water poured onto the child's fingers.

Annaliese watched from the doorway, heart in her throat as her baby's hands were taken into Lucenia's and soaped. Leaning over the child, mouth just above Emeline's petal of an ear, Lucenia uncurled each tiny finger with soft coaxing. Emeline giggled as her aunt blew bubbles into the air from the suds she had wiggled between the child's splayed fingers. Then, hands pressed together, they made circles against each other's palms.

Annaliese walked over to the sink. She pushed the pump handle once more. As Lucenia reached for a towel, Annaliese stood closer to her than she could have imagined an hour ago and thanked her.

Lucenia nodded as she finished drying the little fingers, but she barely looked up into Annaliese's eyes. The afternoon sun poured in the window highlighting Lucenia's flawless complexion. Annaliese stared at this woman who was so unlike any other she had ever known. Pinpoint freckles sprouted across her nose and under her eyes. For the first time, Annaliese saw that her eyes were blue. They were blue and they were somewhere else as she fussed over the child. Suddenly she looked up at Annaliese and said, "A girl child. What a blessing." A smile flashed for a second before she looked away again.

Emeline jumped down and went for the plate. She sat down in the pantry doorway on a stepstool. The kitchen was brilliantly white now in the April sun. The rays splashed across each white ceramic tile that lined the immaculate walls. Emeline sent soft smacking noises into the golden air.

Lucenia slumped against the sink as she gazed at Emeline. "No child should ever go hungry," she said softly.

Annaliese blinked hard and stared at the floor. Were they were talking about little girls in the slums of Cincinnati or certain little girls in Lucenia's past? She turned her face fully to Lucenia and saw in one unguarded moment such a look of sadness that Annaliese instinctively reached for Lucenia's arm.

"Oh, don't mind me." Lucenia walked over to the pantry and stared, hands on hips, at its shelves. "Well, what shall we do about dinner since I didn't have time to wring a chicken's neck this morning?"

Annaliese joined her at the pantry door to eye the cans, sacks, and barrels that Martha had left neatly stacked. "Maybe we'll have a new cook soon."

"Oh?"

"John's promised to take me to town Saturday to see about finding a cook and laundress."

"What about me?"

"You, too."

"We'll need to find two cooks."

"Well, we'll see."

Lucenia took off her apron and stepped inside the pantry. "Ever think about reorganizing these shelves?" She reached for a can of tomatoes.

On the afternoon before the trip to town, Annaliese tiptoed to her front porch doorway and pushed the screen door open enough to peer next door. No one there. She went outside, pen and paper in hand.

April 14, 1901

Dear Mother,

Since I last wrote to you, our furniture has arrived and with only slight damage. It seems so irregular to see some of my things in this new place and now I wish I had not shipped my piano at all, for the sawdust and pine pollen blanket it so thoroughly that the keys are sticking. All of the china and stemware survived, so you must come as you promised so I can use it.

I cannot get accustomed to the hogs loose around the house nor believe John thought I would tolerate it. Fortunately, they run from the children and that provides some degree of entertainment, though I worry that one day the tables will turn. John says ranging hogs taste better. Small reward, if you ask me.

Samuel and Emeline are warming to this place, though they are still afraid of the night sounds (as am I). Every night, we hear a chorus of far-away yipping in the mountains. John says it is foxes. Last night we heard a terrifying scream just as the children were saying their prayers. A screech owl. And then there are the tree frogs with their croaks and burps that are so big for such little bodies. I long for those afternoon naps I took for granted.

Mother, my hands are so horridly raw. Please send several jars of Beulah's Salve in your next parcel. I think I will be ordering many things by post. I suppose if there is any luck for me in this fiasco it is this new free rural delivery service. Lucenia tells me that Congress has mandated that companies must deliver to rural addresses—and just in time for her. I believe she is planning on single handedly keeping Montgomery Ward in business. Once a week, our mail comes up from town on the company freight cars. She and I are going into Pinch tomorrow (with John, of course) to hire the staff.

The cook did not work out.

Please pray for me. I do. Just last night I suddenly recalled the prayer Sister Regina taught me in the ninth grade, the one about through the valley gloomy and dark I cross without fear, with God as my guide the right way is clear. I suppose it took my sitting in a valley gloomy and dark to conjure it up after all of these years. You and Dorothy are more dear than ever, and I promise you I will come home soon for a visit once I get things a little more settled here.

Love,

Annaliese

The streets of Pinch were teeming with people on their Saturday errands and as John threaded his way around horses and shoppers, Annaliese and Lucenia gave the place a thorough look. Their memory of their last time here—a week ago, just—was like a vapor, more a feeling than an image. Now they had the luxury of time as the wagon crept along and they craned their necks to look at the wares in storefront windows, sidestreets gray with shadows, and the people. The farmers were easy to spot right off, in their dirty overalls and felt hats. Their thin, bonneted wives walked behind them. More robust were the clerks and shopkeepers in gray serge pants and a few women in straw hats crisscrossing the road as they lugged shopping baskets. Annaliese and Lucenia wondered where the women lived, where they gathered with other women, what they read, if they could read, where their children were. John muttered about not being able to find a place to tie up, but he finally spotted a post and pulled the team toward it.

As John watered the horses, the women walked toward Meddling's Boarding House, which had a stream of men going in and out.

"That seems to be a good place to begin," Lucenia said.

Annaliese reached for the door. "I'll do the talking."

They opened the door into a wide main hall that ran the full depth of the house. Green and white wallpaper of pheasants and ladies lounging alongside picnic baskets ran along the walls ceiling to floor. At the end of the hall a stout woman at a desk did not look up from her reading. As Annaliese and Lucenia approached her, they heard the clink of forks and knives on plates and the low hum of conversation. The dining room on the left was packed with men. The aroma of fried chicken and biscuits filled the air. On their right, more men jammed the parlor benches as they waited for tables to clear. It was a cheerful, well-cared-for place, right down to several shiny brass spittoons on the floor.

A sign on the desk read: "Meddling's Boarding House. Thessalonia Meddling, proprietor." Then, in smaller print, "No drinking. No Cherokees. No Republicans."

Indians, thought Annaliese. *I knew it.*

Finally the woman looked up. She laid her magazine aside and tried to sweep her blonde, wispy hair into her nub of a bun. Her face, as pale and dull as eggshells, was wary, but she offered a professional smile.

"Good afternoon," Annaliese said. Here was a woman with at least some familiarity with wallpaper. "My, what a pleasant establishment this is."

The smile held. "Thank you. This here's my place. I'm Thessalonia Meddling."

Annaliese nodded and rested her fingertips on the desk. "I am Mrs. Annaliese Stregal and this is Mrs. Lucenia Stregal."

Thessalonia nodded. "Yea, I know. You're those women from off." She looked them up and down. "Kentucky ain't it?"

Lucenia blinked. Her eyelids sported a faint shade of blue. "A pleasure to meet you, too."

"Y'all lookin' fer some dinner?" Thessalonia laced ten plump fingers together and placed them atop her belly. "Might be a while."

"No, thank you," Annaliese said. "We're wondering if you could suggest a laundress."

"Someone to come out yonder to the mill?"

Lucenia came closer. "What about Pearlie Wiginton? We've heard she does laundry."

Annaliese smiled. *A test.*

"Lord, no. She ain't got a lick of sense." Thessalonia wagged her head side to side. "Naw, you want anybody but her. Maybe Nellie Evans or one of her daughters. They help me with the laundry here time to time."

"Where can we find her?" Lucenia asked.

"Back over yonder. Other side the depot." Her eyes fell on Lucenia's eye shadow and she leaned in. "Would you look at that."

"What about someone who would cook for us?" Annaliese said.

"Naw," Thessalonia straightened. "Cain't think of nobody who'd be willin' to live plum out there like Martha done."

Annaliese ran a finger around her collar. *No secrets in this town.* "How about a man who might come to tend our garden and livestock, drive the wagon into town, that sort of thing?"

"Maybe ask old man Simmons—he runs a grist mill over to Chattawattee River—about his boy, Herschel. That boy is itchin' to leave town."

"Why?" Lucenia said.

"Oh, he's alright. He just can't work side by side with his daddy is all. Old man Simmons is bad to drink. Been falling from grace for, oh, 'bout 40 years now."

Lucenia put both hands on the counter. "So this young man, Herschel, he abhors spirits?"

Thessalonia stepped back, fanned her hands in front of her. "I don't know nothin' about whores and spirits, Mrs. Stregal. What's haints got to do with this anyway? I'm talking about drinkin'. Ruckus juice. You know, whiskey. Herschel's sure enough had a lifetime of his daddy's mean side because of it. But Herschel's a fine young man. No drinkin'.

We just welcomed him into the Freewill Baptist Church. Baptized him into the glory and righteousness of our Heavenly Father near to two months ago in the Etowah River."

Lucenia slapped the counter. "Not a drinker? We'll take him."

"What? Wait," Annaliese said.

Thessalonia finally came out from behind the table, smiling at the common ground she sensed, eyes fixed on Lucenia. "Well, now, speakin' of baptizin', y'all got a church home here yet? Why don't y'all come to the mornin' service tomorrow? Or are y'all Methodists?"

Lucenia's chin shot back up. "We appreciate the information. We'll go find this Herschel." She turned to Annaliese. "Ready?"

"Well . . ." Annaliese looked into Thessalonia's eager face and offered a shrug. "Thank you."

Thessalonia held her plump hands up. "What'd I say? Y'all ain't Hardshell Baptists are ye? That's it, ain't it?"

Annaliese caught up with Lucenia as they passed the dining room. A knot of men stopped talking and tipped their hats.

"Reckon you're not, then," called Thessalonia. As they pushed through the door, she said to herself, "Not with that paint."

They found John on the whittlers' bench outside the dry goods store. After trips to the Evans' home, the post office and the mercantile, all of which turned up no recommendations for cooks but did produce several confirmations of the moral rectitude of Hershel Simmons, they rode out of town in search of their leading candidate for hired help.

The Simmons place was not hard to find—the only lean-to cabin next to the river with a mill beside it. As John halted the horses, he and the women heard the thwack of an axe behind the cabin. John helped them out of the wagon. Calling as they came, hoping to come upon the son and not the father, they were relieved to see a young, smiling, red-headed man come from around back. John shot out his hand, which the man shook heartily. He said he'd heard about the Stregals, the cash money they paid. Annaliese looked him over. His pink face was still a work in progress—malleable and soft-whiskered and sprinkled with enough acne to distract you from the features. Barely out of his teens, she guessed. He listened to John, nodding, feet planted apart, arms crossed, weighing his proposal. She liked that—the thoughtfulness. His arms were work-hardened. He was sober. She looked over at Lucenia who raised her hands as if to say what question was there that he was their man.

Herschel threw his axe toward the river. "Let's go."

"You mean right now?" John said.

"Now is good," Annaliese said. *He can peel tonight's potatoes.*

"I just need a few minutes to get some . . . uh, things," he said looking over John's shoulder at the cabin.

John spun around for the women's approval. They nodded. "All right, then," John said. "We'll meet you at the wagon."

On the wagon seat they waited, wary, silent, half expecting the older Simmons to come barreling out the cabin's front door, cursing at them. The sun sat just above the cabin's roofline; the air was cooling fast. Annaliese pulled her shawl tighter. Minutes later, the door opened and Herschel emerged holding the hand of a wispy-headed female about half his size. In the darkened doorway, she looked to be older than he, judging from her hunched shoulders and skeletal body that seemed more bones than flesh. His mother? But as they came forward, the female offered a hearty wave that belied old age.

Annaliese and Lucenia raised their hands against the sun's glare for a better look. She was indeed just a girl. Her thin cotton dress hung on a body still budding. Her face shone at them with pure innocence. She was about 16. Maybe.

"This here's Ruth," Herschel said. "We got hitched last week."

"Hey," Ruth said. She held a cloth-wrapped bundle and a tattered Bible to her concave chest. Her brown hair, parted in the middle, was tied back with a strip of burlap bag, braided below the tie.

John shifted the reins from one hand to the other, then stared at the floorboard, mashing his lips together to fight a smile. His face held no answer for her this time; this call was hers. Annaliese looked over at Lucenia who was scanning the girl from her Bible to her hand clenched tightly in Herschel's to her tiny, copper-stained bare feet.

Annaliese said, "Well, can she cook?"

"Oh, yes ma'am," Herschel said. "She can fix up squirrel and dumplings just as good as you want."

"Sure enough?" Lucenia laughed

"Let's go," Annaliese said.

❧

VIII

Samuel clutched his father's hand as he gaped at the whirring band-saw towering over them. Ten feet tall, it was a loop of jagged steel spinning on upper and lower flywheels. Streams of water splashed across the flywheels, then bounced onto the saw's steel teeth slashing the air.

"Headsaw," John shouted to Samuel. "First saw the log comes to after the bark's been chipped off."

The boy offered only a stiff nod, as if talking might disrupt his careful watch on those hideous, lurching teeth. John tapped his shoulder. He pointed to the massive log creeping toward the saw.

"Head rig," John screamed.

Coming toward them—heading *into* the bandsaw—was a man standing on a moving platform that carried the shuddering log. His boot tips nearly touched it. His hands gripped a pair of open levers, but his eyes were on the approaching saw. A shout from the head sawyer pierced the noise, the man on the rig jerked the levers closed, and their steel claws bit into the log. Samuel's hands flew to his ears. Flashing steel teeth tore into the oak, sending sawdust and water and wood bits flying. The man on the carriage held on, hands quivering on the levers, mere inches from the saw as it tore. As soon as the log cleared the saw and the plank fell away, two sawyers rushed forward to pick it up. Samuel looked anxiously at the rig rider—still gripping his levers, sweat running into his eyes—and waited for him to jump off. But his grip only tightened, for the rig suddenly bolted back to its starting position. Man and oak started their trip back toward the saw again for the next slice.

John bent down to search his son's face. Samuel's hands were still clamped to his ears, but he was nodding. John waved one of the mill-workers over and handed the man a small square, brown box. They spent a few minutes going over it, turning it over, yelling to each other above the noise and pointing at its buttons. Finally, John backed away toward Samuel and the rig and with his strong hands planted firmly on his son's shoulders he nodded to the man. Samuel straightened up, tried to smile and keep his eyes on the man. The man lifted the camera to his eyes and pushed a button.

Annaliese was having a fit as she watched from the millpond door-way, but a quiet fit lest John send her home. She knew she was getting in the way of the two men working within inches of her to wrestle soaked logs off the spiked chains and onto conveyer carriers. Their soured sweat made her eyes water. One of them was missing two fingers. The other man had an oozing gash on his arm. After the photo was taken and John steered Samuel toward a door, she finally stepped outside.

A hard glare rose from the millpond's rippling surface. Four men stood on logs that bumped into one another like dazed cattle. With long pikes they herded them along to the intake ramp, gently poking and pushing, their bare feet gripping the slick wood. She imagined the fate of a man who might slip off his log. Should he survive being crushed on the way down, he would slip beneath the surface, only to claw at the sky of logs above him, trying to find a sliver of air. *Why on earth would a man take such a job?* she wondered.

Out of the corner of her eye she saw John and Samuel moving between the mill and the smaller building beside it.

John was saying, " . . . and so most of our lumber needs to be smoothed out at the planing mill for finer things like furniture."

Samuel stretched his legs to match his father's long, confident strides. He spit on the ground. "Papa, can I have a job? I could be the water boy," he said.

"Well, maybe when you're a little older."

Annaliese arrived beside her son. "Time to come home. Ruth's made an apple betty." She stretched out her hand to him.

Samuel left his hand at his side, looked at John.

"Anna, we're on our way to the planing mill," John said. "Then the dry kiln where we dry the green lumber so it won't shrink and warp later. Come on. I'll show you, too." He picked up his pace.

Annaliese followed. "Is it *hot?*"

"Better be," John said. He pulled off his hat, dragged the crook of his arm across his brow, turned his sweaty face toward her. "The boy's got to see what his father does, Anna."

"It's just that . . ."

"I won't let anything happen to him." In John's eyes a darkness flashed so quickly that she stepped back. He dropped his voice. "A father's got to do this for his son." His eyes softened at the corners. "You know what I'm saying."

She did, just as she knew that now with this family ghost in the air, there would be no winning this battle. She cupped her son's chin in her hand. "Y'all will be up to the house for dinner after a while, then? By 12:30?"

"We'll be along soon," John said. He flipped the hat back on his head.

She headed for the commissary, slowly weaving her way among the mill yard's buildings. One of the dogs crawled out from the shade of one. She quickened her step, but the yellow mutt was soon at her heels, licking her hands. As she tried to wave it away, the dog jumped up and planted two paws on Annaliese's waist, knocking her to the ground. Sprawled in the dirt, she screamed for help. Joe Rosetta burst through the commissary's screen door, fly swatter in hand.

"Hey, now, you git!" Joe shouted.

The dog backed off, hind end still wagging. Its rheumy eyes pleaded, but Joe swung at it again. Finally, the mutt slunk back to its hole.

Joe reached down to help Annaliese to her feet. "Mrs. Stregal, are you all right?"

"Ugh!" She screwed up her face as she got her feet under her. "Can't you do something about that dog, Mr. Rosetta?"

"Why, it's just a mill dog, Mrs. Stregal. Keeps the rats and snakes away."

"Pee-ew." With the backs of her hands she tried to wipe her face.

"I reckon nobody never tried to pet it before."

"I didn't try to pet it." She ran her hands down her skirt. "Lord, that dog stinks."

"Yes, ma'am." He untied his apron, handed it to her. "But she scared off a bear once. Right feisty dog."

"A bear." She wiped her hands on the apron. "There was a bear here."

"Yes, ma'am. Backside of the mill 'bout a month ago. Someone left some food scraps out. Just a little ole black bear." He shrugged.

Annaliese brushed her hair out of her eyes and handed the apron back. "I was just coming over to see if there was any mail."

"Sure enough. Railcar brought it up from Pinch this mornin'." He held up an index finger to her and ran into the commissary, returning quickly with two bundles. "I wrapped a little string around 'em. One for you and one for . . ."

Annaliese snatched her bundle. "Finally." Her fingers flew through it. A catalog, two letters from John's law firm, a book she had ordered for Samuel. "You're sure there was nothing else for me, Mr. Rosetta?"

"Sorry, ma'am. That's all there was in the sack." Joe spat a stream of tobacco into the dirt and kicked some dirt its way. "You waitin' on somethin'?"

"Just letters." Annaliese picked up the broken string, which she looped around the letters pointlessly. *Just news from the civilized world,* she thought. *My mother's scent on her cream-colored paper, her flowing scrawl, her loving words that caress me as soothingly as silk on bare skin. Reports from Dorothy about weddings and parties.*

"I'll keep an eye out, ma'am."

She tucked the packages under her arm and turned toward home. Halfway up the hill, a cream-colored envelope fell out of the catalog. She flipped the envelope over, saw her mother's handwriting, lifted it to her nose and inhaled. Slipping her fingernail under the flap, she tore into it and picked up her walk again. Eyes off the road now, she stomped her feet to scare off snakes and read the letter.

April 12, 1901

My dear Annaliese:

I have not received any news from you so it appears that deliveries may take two weeks or more. I long for news of your train ride, your reunion with John, your new home, how the children are faring. Knowing you, you have put many letters to me in the post, so I'm sure I'll have all my news very soon. Annaliese's Georgia adventure!

I little dreamed how your absence would leave such a void, but my heart is filled with pride at your courage.

Dorothy and your cousins have their health, including Michael who has recovered from his bad throat. He sends his best wishes and warns that he'll be at the station with his banjo when you come home no matter what you say. Jane sends her love and says she'll write soon. Clarke and your uncle have recently commissioned a new ship for the company.

I have enclosed the newspaper's account of Margaret Sommers's debutante party. Though this holds no interest for me, I trust you will find the details about her dress, which apparently was a bit much, and her decorations, even more so, quite entertaining. Her escort was Franklyn Fitzgerald. Dorothy says Margaret has no eye for style nor ear for her mother's desperate suggestions. Hers was the most eagerly awaited debutante party in Louisville this year, but not for the reasons Margaret thought.

Forgive this short epistle, but the hour grows late and I need my ointment rubbed into my shoulders and knees or there will be no peace tonight.

Is there anything you need for me to send?

Love to my baby girl,
Mother

Annaliese had to sit down to savor every morsel of the Sommers clipping. Just when she'd gotten to her second reading of the description of the frothy pink gown, she heard something on the path. The yellow dog dropped to the ground and began a slow crawl to her side, pink tongue lapping at the air. Annaliese laughed at the ridiculous hound but leveled a stern finger at her. The dog stopped and stretched out near her feet.

"Oh, all right," she said. "Maybe you can run the geese off for good."

Annaliese peered into Lucenia's hefty bundle. A catalog from Sears Roebuck and Company, a *Woman's Home Companion*, a letter to Lucenia from a Madame Yale, an almanac. No letters from friends or family, though Annaliese knew she had a sister in Cincinnati.

As she neared home, she winced at Herschel's hammering behind the house for that cabin for Ruth meant roots going in. Entrenchment. This life was supposed to be temporary, yet now another building was going up. Already there were the homes, the barn, the spring house. She wanted to look out her kitchen window and see nothing but mountains, as though the house in which she stood and everything behind it didn't exist, all the easier to abandon when her time was up. Oh, Ruth. It was all her fault. Had Herschel been a bachelor, he could have bunked in the room beside the dry kiln. But here was this child bride in the bargain. She was no cook. She seemed eager to learn—Annaliese had to give her that—but because her skills began at squirrel and ended with dumplings, Annaliese had a lot of ground to cover. The girl did not know how to use a wood stove, how to gauge its temperature, how to measure, and, of course, how to read. It would be months before Ruth would cook by herself. Annaliese chafed at the time the girl required, so she was brittle and impatient with her, finding fault even with the girl's laugh, which discharged like a Gatling gun. She smelled bad, kept taking the boots Annaliese had given her off, and was so nosy. Her little squirrel eyes drank in everything about the families—the books, the mirrors, the piano, but especially Ben. She watched his every move, hung on every bloated word. Just when suspicion dawned on Annaliese, Ruth called him "Old Lizard Lids" in front of Lucenia, who stopped her second reorganization of the pantry, looked at the floor for a while, then shrugged her shoulders and smiled. Annaliese went into the dining room and shook with silent laughter. Still, that girl was a burr in her shoe.

Annaliese arrived home with the dog bouncing at her heels. The geese swarmed up from under the porch, raised their snakeheads at her, saw the dog with hackles up, and raced away.

She opened the front door and dropped the mail on a hall table. A cloud of sawdust and pollen flew up. As she passed the doorway to the drawing room, she paused for a moment to admire her arrangements in this one room that she had been able to finish. In the farthest corner, to the left of the window, the piano was flanked by two parlor chairs with hand-carved backs and yellow satin seat cushions. Draped across the piano lid was a green silk shawl, its fringe spilling over the sides. On the opposite side of the room a pair of brown velvet settees faced each other beside the fireplace. The oak mantel bloomed with a candelabra, gilded boxes, and figurines. As her eyes moved to the naked window and she again pondered what to do about drapes, sounds coming from the dining room made her move on.

She found Emeline, Darrison, and James setting the table under Ruth's spirited direction. Ruth, barely taller than Darrison, seemed to be one of the scurrying children, but she held the platter of pork roast and vegetables with confidence and successfully lowered it to the table without so much as a carrot rolling off.

Well, it smells all right, thought Annaliese as she watched the platter being lowered.

"Hey, Mrs. Stregal," Ruth bellowed. "Grub's on."

"Ruth, you must learn to say dinner is served."

Emeline ran up to her mother. "Mama, look." She reached into her pinafore pocket.

"Dinner is served y'all," Ruth laughed. She rubbed her palms down her apron. "I worked in the garden a little more today, Miss Annaliese."

Since the day she had arrived, Ruth had worried over the little plot of struggling sprouts behind the house, hoeing and cow-manureing it to death. It was clear that she felt that Martha had doomed the whole enterprise.

"Now about them taters," Ruth said, hands on her hips. "You know whether she planted them on the dark of the moon?"

"What?" Annaliese said. One hand was on Emeline pulling at her skirt.

"Bet she did. Them beans, too, they'll be all gone to vine." She shook her round little head. "Jest you watch."

"Ruth, what are you talking about?"

"The signs. Any good plantin' calendar tells you which zodiac signs rule over each day. Looks like Martha didn't hold to it or," Ruth's blue eyes settled on Annaliese's, " . . . maybe she did that on purpose."

Emeline's fingers dug into her mother's hand.

"Ouch!" Annaliese cried.

Ruth's eyes grew wide. "Like she knew ahead that you and Miss Lucenia was gonna run her off."

"We did no such thing," Annaliese said too quickly.

"Mama, look," cried Emeline again and finally her mother squatted to look at what had come out of the pocket. "Rufe showed me where the chickens nest." The pudgy fingers clutched a brown egg. "In the trees."

"You got you some rebel hens out there," Ruth laughed. "They don't want to be in no chicken house." She squinted at Annaliese. "How'd you get your hair to do like that?" She pointed a wafer of a finger at Annaliese's soft topknot. "Reckon you could show me?"

"Dinner's getting cold."

"Come on, y'all." Ruth put her hand on Emeline's back to nudge her toward the kitchen. "Time to wash up." She leaned down to whisper to Annaliese. "You, too, Miss Annaliese. You been rollin' in somethin'? You smell like one of them mill dogs."

John and Samuel came in the front door. They threw their hats on a chair and headed for the kitchen. A few minutes later, Ben came through, handkerchief to his glistening forehead, followed by Lucenia holding a jar of buttermilk from the spring house. Chairs scraped across the floor until everyone was seated. Ruth stood near the kitchen door and bowed her head. When Annaliese finished saying grace, Ruth launched into hers, imploring divine benevolence on countless kin on earth and six feet under. At the end, Ruth shouted "Amen!" and began pouring milk.

"Saw the sawmill this morning," Samuel said.

"No fair," Darrison said. He shot a dark look at his mother beside him.

She reached for his wrist and forced it to the table while she hissed into his ear. Ben and Annaliese looked away.

"Now Lucenia," John said. He held out the platter of pork to her.

"He's not to be down there," she said.

"But there's nothin' to do up here," muttered Darrison into his plate.

Ruth clicked her tongue as she poured. "Y'all got to get out of this house." She stood beside John's chair. Annaliese saw that she was barefoot. Again.

Ruth's face lit up. "Let me show y'all the mountains. How 'bout that?"

"Wait, wait . . ." John said.

"Yea!" shouted the boys.

"You mean the mountain behind our house?" Annaliese said.

"Shoot, that's just a hill."

Samuel bounced in his chair. "We could hitch up the wagon and go up into the mountains. See the logging roads."

"Oh, no," Annaliese said.

"Pass the pork roast on down, would you," Ben said, waving his fork hopefully.

"We sure enough could take out the wagon," Ruth said. "Herschel knows them hills. He could go with us."

John held both hands out above the table. "No. This is not a good . . ."

"I can show y'all the wildflowers, how to find arrowheads in the branches." Her eyes grew merrier with each young face they landed upon.

"Ruth, you have work to do," Annaliese said.

"There are arrowheads in the *trees*?" Lucenia said.

"Like the eggs?" Emeline said between shoving beans in her mouth.

"Miss Lucenia, you tickle me," Ruth laughed. Her cackle bounced off the walls. "A branch is a creek. You know, *water*."

"We play in the water?" Emeline said.

"Wait . . ." Annaliese said.

"Stop this!" John bellowed. He slammed his palms on the table. The table fell silent. "Y'all can't go tromping around these mountains like a bunch of Central Park picnickers. It's dangerous. There are snakes, cliffs out there."

"Moonshiners," Ben said.

"Right. You might stumble onto one of their stills. And one of the prime locations for a still is beside a creek."

"But . . ." Ruth said from behind Lucenia's chair.

Girl, thought Annaliese.

"Ruth, don't you understand? If they think you'll turn them in, they'll burn us out," Ben said.

"Turn them in?" Darrison said. "To whom?"

"The sheriff, son," Ben said.

"Not that he'd do nothin'," Ruth said, hands on hips. "The election ain't for another three years." She let loose another piercing cackle.

"Yes, *thank you, Ruth*," Annaliese said. "Perhaps there's something in the kitchen you should tend to?"

"No, ma'am. There ain't nothin'."

"They would set the woods on fire?" Lucenia said. She reached for Ben's arm.

"Might," Ben said.

Silence fell on the table again. The children slumped in their seats.

Annaliese put her elbows on the table and looked the young faces over. "Well, what if we start with our little mountain, hill, whatever you want to call it, behind our house . . ."

"Aw, Mama," Samuel whined. "We've already been all over that."

Darrison and James went rigid. Their mother narrowed her eyes at them. Darrison spooned baked apples onto his plate and passed the bowl to her.

Ruth said, "'Course, if we was to visit the south side of a mountain, we wouldn't see no stills."

John leaned back and looked up at Ruth. "Hoyt, my timber fore-man, did mention that yesterday on our ride. Said they're usually on the north flank."

"Wait," Lucenia said.

Ruth moved closer to him. "Sure enough. And if we was to look along the trail sides for signs of supplies we'd know for sure whether they was nearby or not."

"Signs?" John said. He turned in his seat to focus on the girl

"Yep. Like a brick in the road. That's a sure a sign a furnace done been built nearby. Spilled meal and sugar—they's signs. Broken glass from jars, burlap sacks."

"Really?" John said. "Got to tell Hoyt about that."

"So we can go?" Samuel asked.

"I didn't say that." John pushed his plate away.

James got out of his chair to stand beside his father. "Papa, please?" He put his hand on his father's broad arm.

Ben looked down the table at John.

Ruth caught it all. "How about Skipjack Mountain, Mr. Stregal, just th'other side of the hills beyond yore mill? You been all over that mountain cruisin', ain't ye? And it's south facing. We won't go far. We'd be in spittin' distance."

John shifted in his chair. "Y'all would have to promise me you'd make lots of noise as you go. Don't surprise anyone or any thing."

"John, you can't be serious," Annaliese said.

"Yes, sir," Samuel said.

John reached out to ruffle his son's hair. "You may go up to Skipjack only, and you have to stay on the logging trails I specify. Herschel must go, too."

"Yay!" the boys shouted.

"And play in da water?" Emeline said. "Take off my shoes?"

Lucenia leaned in front of Darrison and sent a whisper down the table to Annaliese. "Well, out of the frying pan . . ."

John picked up his fork again. "Herschel has to bring a shotgun and y'all take that dog that seems to have found a home under our front porch. And Ruth . . ." He pointed a finger at her.

"Sir?" She stopped wiggling.

"You keep them away from anything poisonous, like berries or mushrooms, and that confounded devil vine that itches you death."

"It ain't out yet, Mr. Stregal."

"Dog?" Lucenia asked.

∽

IX

By the next morning, it was all arranged. John had mapped out a ten-mile route over Skipjack Mountain, sent Herschel to inspect the wagon and horses, watched him clean and load a shotgun, and grilled him about landmarks and streams. Herschel, a man who could pick his way down a mountain on a moonless night, did not smile.

After breakfast, Herschel brought the horses up from the sawmill stables. The women and children burst out of their houses into the brilliant day. As Herschel hitched the bay mare to the wagon, Darrison stroked her velvet nose. The younger boys climbed in the wagon to stake their spots and the dog—christened Slick—leapt in behind them. Annaliese gave Emeline a boost in. Geese swept in to pick at Ruth and her picnic basket.

Annaliese yelled, "I don't like those things, but it's the hogs I absolutely cannot stand. Herschel needs to build them a pen."

Ruth pulled a shriveled ear of corn from her apron pocket, waved it over the writhing heads, and threw it toward the hills. The flock raced away. "Naw, it's a good thing to have hogs around the house. They eat snakes."

"Heavens." Annaliese hurried into her seat.

"Sure enough. I've seen 'em put their hoof on a snake's head, strip the body clean. Yes, ma'am, hogs are good to have around a house."

Annaliese twisted her straw hat on. "You actually watched that?"

"With pleasure. I'm tellin' you, I hate snakes. All three kinds of snakes. A live snake, a dead snake, and a stick that looks like a snake."

Annaliese smiled. "What about dogs?" She looked over at Slick pacing between the boys, slathering them with germs.

"No, ma'am. I don't hate dogs. I like 'em well enough to . . ."

"No, no. I mean do dogs eat snakes?"

"Some dogs git after 'em. I seen a dog bite into a snake, flang it around to break its . . ."

"All right, all right." Annaliese held up her hand. "Let's go." She waved at Darrison and Herschel. "Y'all ready?"

Herschel gave the harness a tug and patted the flank of one of the horses.

Lucenia hurried out her front door tucking a canvas bag under arm. She wore an immaculate white shirtwaist and a straw hat. "Oh, I wish that Brownie I ordered had arrived by now."

Annaliese sighed. "Plenty of time for photographs, Lucenia. A year and 11 months to go."

"I heard that," said John from the porch. He grinned at them from under his hat.

Lucenia and Annaliese looked at each other. Something conspiratorial passed between them, joined them in common understanding for a shocking second, then they looked away. Lucenia climbed up to the wagon seat. Ruth scrambled into the back and slapped a rag at the whirling Slick until she fell into a curl. Finally, Herschel shook the reins at the horses.

"Herschel," John called. "Did you check that latch across the wagon gate like I told you?" He started down the steps toward the wagon.

"Yes, sir. It ain't goin' nowhere."

Ruth gave it a good kick to show it was holding firm.

"Now remember," John shouted to them as they pulled away. "Be back by two. I'll be looking for y'all."

Herschel guided the horses downhill past the sawmill and took an eastward turn away from the route to Pinch. Soon, the bottomland narrowed slightly, bringing the walls of rock closer. Massive tilted shelves of limestone and granite hung from these cliffs, reminding Annaliese of drawings she had seen of Indian warriors out west lined up along ridge tops. She drew in a shaky breath and looked over at Herschel. His face was calm. The horses' ears were floppy and relaxed. The gun was under the seat.

At the base of a slope, a jagged trail of raw, red earth appeared and Herschel guided the horses toward it. "Skid road," he said to the women and they understood that they were looking at one of the trails that the loggers had hacked out of the woods for hauling timber out. Except for the road, there was little sign that Stregal Brothers had been here. No debris, no broken limbs or trampled saplings on the sidelines. John had seen to that.

The forest closed in on them, thick with new life. Massive black trees rose from the moist earth, their trunks laced with the delicate, white gills of fungi as big as plates. Awakening buds sprouted from every branch. The beginnings of a lush canopy fluttered on the limbs overhead. Mountain laurel and wild hydrangea carpeted the forest floor. Though it had not rained recently, the smell of damp leaves and softened moss hung in the air.

Soon, the horses were climbing steeper hills, sending Ruth and the children into a pile against the gate latch. When the grade flattened, Herschel pulled the horses over into a clearing paved with granite outcroppings.

"Ain't no snakes here," he said. "We can keep a right good eye on everbody, too." He turned to Ruth. "You seen any signs on the road?"

"No."

"There's a branch over yonder. I'll look around just to be sure."

The women were content to watch him from their seats, but the children bailed out, shrieking with delight, startling the horses enough to make them shift sideways. Darrison went over to one, stroked its head.

"Darrison," Lucenia said. "I told you."

The boy shot his mother a black look, but he stepped away from the horse. Herschel was waving everyone out of the wagon anyway, so

Darrison headed for the stream. Ruth helped Emeline out, and they ran after them.

Lucenia and Annaliese only half-eyed the forest, for they did not really want to see anything or anyone that would send their weary backsides back into the wagon. On a grassy spot away from the stream where the children played, they snapped quilts open above the damp ground. Lucenia smoothed her skirt and leaned back on her elbows. Annaliese removed her straw hat and lay down, eyes closed. Barring gunshots or bloody murder, she would not open them no matter what Lucenia came up with this time.

There was no escaping the woman's monologues, not even on Annaliese's own front porch, just as she had feared. At fifteen yards apart, the porches were close enough to oblige Annaliese to speak if Lucenia was on her porch when she came out. The response would come back, Annaliese would return the barest of nods and make a show of reading her book or writing her letter, but Lucenia would stand at the railing and lob a question. Annaliese would put her book down and answer, and so another lecture would begin. Annaliese knew what Lucenia thought about feminist agitation for the right to vote, Tula Water for the complexion, Alice Roosevelt, temperance, and social justice for the starving immigrants packed into America's tenements. Lucenia never asked what Annaliese cared about.

"You're not going to try to nap, are you?"

Annaliese draped her arm across her eyes.

"This doesn't look so dangerous, do you think?" Lucenia said.

"Herschel's stomping around out there in the woods, isn't he?"

"Yes."

"We're fine."

"I just hope we're on whatever side of a mountain Ruth said we should be on."

"Uh huh." From the stream, the sounds of happy discoveries drifted over. Annaliese got up on her elbows to look. The three boys were hauling and stacking rocks into a dam, getting filthy and wet. Ruth had a squealing Emeline in her lap *taking off her boots*. Annaliese lay back down.

Lucenia heaved a big sigh. "Oh, Darrison. He's such a trial." She twisted a stem around her finger.

"Why, Lucenia, he's just being a nine-year-old boy."

Lucenia snorted and released the stem. It sprang away.

"You're not used to boys, are you?" Annaliese said. She smiled at the memory of her aunt running her four sons out of the kitchen or the house even, those slightly scary but mesmerizing moments when the boys were feeding off of one another's energy and whipping themselves into a laughing, punching, swearing cyclone. Out the door they would go, Michael and Clark first, the youngest two who always got the worst of it from Ted and Patrick. Her aunt had always said boys are like dogs—you just had to run them and feed them, so she sent them to the baseball field or the school track. Girls, she would say, are like cats. Wary. Plotting. Always something going on behind the eyes. How her aunt had survived raising five girls (seven counting Annaliese and Dorothy) Annaliese would never know.

"You don't have brothers, do you? Just the one sister," Annaliese said.

Lucenia pressed her lips together. "Rose. She lives in Cincinnati, where we grew up." She wound another green stem around her finger. "He just won't do right." Lucenia shook her head as she twisted the stem until it broke.

Annaliese got back up on her elbows. "He minds you pretty well. What else do you want from him?"

"I wish he were more like his father. It's so simple to get Ben to come around."

From what Annaliese had observed, a circus monkey could lead Ben around. Darrison was smarter than both of his parents put together. "Darrison isn't just a smaller version of Ben, Lucenia. You might be able to bend him for the moment . . . " She took the remains of the stem from Lucenia's hand and wrapped it around her own finger." . . . but he won't stay." She released the stem and it sprang away. "He's his own person." She contemplated the potential misery of raising miniature John Stregals and thanked God this was so.

Lucenia stared at the ground where the stem landed. A soft cleft formed between her eyes. Her head dropped to her shoulder, an unguarded posture that surprised Annaliese.

Annaliese said, "Think of something he's interested in, something you can talk to him about. How about horses? Perhaps you two could ride..."

"Oh, no!" Lucenia's back straightened. "I'm afraid of horses!"

"But why? I grew up riding horses and..."

Back at the stream, Ruth was scolding Slick, soaping up the hapless hound until she slipped out of grasp and headed straight for the women. Before they could get to their feet, the wet dog plowing into Annaliese, trying to get behind her, claws grinding into the quilt. Immediately, Ruth was on her, slapping again at the dog with the dishrag and yelling "Git!"

Annaliese held her hands up. "Ruth, stop."

"Tryin' to give that dog a bath, hit smelt so rotten." Ruth wiped the dog's back.

Lucenia crawled away on her hands and feet.

"Lord Amighty!" It was Herschel running in from the forest. "Stop your hollerin', Ruth. You'll scare the horses."

Ruth took a few more jabs at the dog.

"Everything look all right out there, Herschel?" Lucenia said as she stood up.

"Yes, ma'am." Herschel nodded and raked his hand through his red hair. "Nothing to worry 'bout."

When the children rushed up to show their finds, the quilt was turned over and the picnic basket came out. Darrison presented what he hoped was an arrowhead with a questioning look up at Herschel, who nodded. James pulled a frog out of his pocket and held it in his mud-stained hands for Emeline's cool but steady inspection. Ruth nudged her to show her prize, a handful of silvery mica chunks.

The last of the chicken bones and apple cores were being tucked back into the basket when Ruth stood up and screeched, "Who wants to look fer bird nests?" She raced off, elbows flared as though about to take to the sky herself. Slick sprang from her exile and was soon on Ruth's heels. The boys shot up from the quilt like popcorn. Emeline was the last one on her feet scrambling to catch up with Ruth.

"Wait! Put your shoes on," shouted Annaliese to her back. "Sam!"

"I got her," Samuel said, hoisting his sister onto his back.

"Reckon I'm goin' lookin' fer bird nests," Herschel said. He dragged his hand across his mouth and went to the wagon for the gun. "Got to be gettin' on back home soon, though."

"Wait for me," Annaliese said as she got to her feet.

"No, no." Lucenia patted the quilt. "I have something I want to share with you." She flared her eyebrows at her. "Something ever so appealing."

Annaliese looked over at the fleeing children. The sound of Ruth's Gatling gun laugh echoed in the forest. She sat down.

Lucenia pulled the California Perfume Company catalogue out of her bag. "Have you heard of Madame Yale?"

"Of course. The newspapers adore her."

"And well they should. Don't you just love her quote 'Women may be divided into two classes: Those who have good hair and those who don't'?"

"Well, hair is one thing. Paint is another."

"When she came to Cincinnati, I just had to go and hear her lecture, 'The Religion of Beauty, the Sin of Ugliness'."

Annaliese looked in the direction of the children again.

"Now, dear." Lucenia opened the catalog. "See this? Why won't you let me order a little rouge for you? Some blue for the eyes? What about your fantasies? What about romance? How will you ever know just how desirable you can be?"

Annaliese had all the desire she could handle. She shook her head.

Lucenia flipped the pages and pointed to an ad. "Have you ever tried this? Hunter's Invisible Face Powder?"

Annaliese's ears burned. Since her teens, she had hated the clusters of smallpox scars on her cheeks and one on her chin, but she would never consider covering them with a cosmetic. In Louisville, she had seen the Portugese rouge dishes and Chinese boxes of color for the cheeks and eyebrows. But ladies just did not buy such products. Ladies understood that there was a distinction between masking the skin and improving it. To *protect* her pock-marked skin, her aunt had taught her to make a powder of starch and rice powder. But commercial cosmetics that *masked* were immoral, as everyone knew.

"Lucenia, I was brought up to believe that appearance is a function of one's character. Regular attention to one's breathing, sleeping, and excretion are the habits that ensure natural beauty."

"My dear, clean bowels do not the dewy bloom of youth make."

"If you believe that the purest beauty resides in the soul, then it is not the outside upon which one must work."

"Yes, I've watched men in a drawing room crowd around the maiden with the most inner beauty."

Annaliese leaned back on her elbows. "Paint masks God's handiwork."

A sly smile bloomed on Lucenia's face, pushing the apples of her flawless cheeks toward her eyes. "Perhaps it honors his handiwork."

Annaliese let her head drop back. "What's the point, anyway, out here in the middle of nothing?"

"Well, it's all about domestic leveraging, of course."

Annaliese pulled her head back up and cut her eyes over at her.

"You know, using the power inherent in our . . ." Lucenia lowered her face closer to Annaliese's "pleasurable bodies."

Annaliese's cheeks grew hot.

Lucenia was nodding. "The only power a woman has over a man is the ability to say yes or no. Now don't look at me that way. Power is power even if it's just in our narrow little sphere of marriage and family." She smoothed her hand over the ripples of the quilt. "It's a beginning for us. Who knows what it might lead to? Especially if we band together."

Annaliese sat up. "This sounds like feminist agitating."

"So? What's wrong with that? Don't we want to have some say in our society?" Lucenia gave her a long, hard look. "And closer to home, you might get somewhere with John. Well, that's why you're here isn't it? To convince him to go back as soon as possible."

"That's none of your business."

Lucenia held up her hands. "All I'm saying is give it a try. Men are easy to lead around given sufficient . . . reward."

Annaliese's face was on fire. "We shouldn't be talking about this." She found her straw hat and began fanning.

"Oh, settle down." She pushed the catalog toward Annaliese. "Now about your complexion . . ."

"Oh! You are as arrogant as you are . . ." Annaliese's brain afire couldn't form words. Finally, she blurted out, "Bulky!" Her hand flew to her mouth, but she wasn't taking it back.

Lucenia got to her feet. "Let me tell you something." She pointed a finger at Annaliese.

"You've said quite enough already."

Lucenia whispered, "You've always had everything handed to you. Men especially. You don't know anything about working for what you want, do you? You don't know anything about clawing and yearning . . ."

"Oh, yes I do." Annaliese stood up and stalked into the forest.

Ruth's cackles helped her find them. Emeline took her mother's hand. The boys moved through the trees hitting the trunks with sticks. Ruth pointed to the top of a chestnut tree and they all puddled around its base to see a brown thrasher gliding toward a nest. The party moved on in hopes of finding something a little closer to the ground.

Herschel led them to a stone ledge from which they could see mountains rolling away for miles. The hill closest to them rose diagonally to the sky, its spine so narrow that only a single line of trees ran along it. Each majestic cedar stood out against the brilliant blue, solitary and erect.

Samuel said, "Look at those trees, Mama. Don't they look like soldiers marching single file up the hill?"

Annaliese nodded. She smoothed his hair, as downy as dandelion fluff, to calm down.

"Are those our trees, Herschel?" Darrison asked.

"Yup. That's lumber company land. Seventeen thousand acres takes y'all clear across this area here on Skipjack to over yonder at Tomassee Flats" – he pointed to a distant valley – "to Noyowee

Bald" – a grassy, treeless meadow on top of a mountain – "and beyond." As though introducing the neighbors, he went on to point out other valleys and hills, all bearing lyrical names. He spoke of the rivers Oostanula and Etowah beyond, coursing through those hills out of view.

If Georgia history had once just been background reading on a long train ride to Pinch, it now lived and breathed before Annaliese. She knew these to be Cherokee names. She knew that General Tecumseh Sherman's troops had marched up and down those hills—40 miles away—on their way to burn Atlanta. Peace and war. Blood and birth. So many struggles were etched on those tablets.

"Will Papa cut my soldiers down, Herschel?" Samuel asked.

Herschel took his time to answer. He reached for Ruth's hand. "Don't reckon so, Sam. He cain't hardly get to them trees."

No one asked about the thousands of others that he could.

Ruth looked at the sun sinking in the cloudless sky and said, "Better be gettin' on home."

Lucenia had packed and loaded everything. She sat on the wagon seat leafing through her catalog and never looked up except to check on her sons.

On the way back, Ruth sat on the front seat beside Lucenia. Annaliese jostled along in the back with Slick and the children. Looking up at the sun, she guessed at the time and doubted they would meet John's two o'clock deadline. The boys bounced against each other, watched the forest roll by with heavy-lidded eyes. Emeline curled up in her mother's lap. Ruth began singing. Her voice rose in a clear, sweet sound that made even Lucenia turn and stare.

On Jordan's stormy banks I stand, and cast a wishful eye
To Canaan's fair and happy land, where my possessions lie

We will rest in the fair and happy land, by and by, just across on the
evergreen shore
Sing the song of Moses and the Lamb, by and by, to Canaan's fair and
happy land

Where my possessions lie

We will rest in the fair and happy land, by and by, just across on the evergreen shore
Sing the song of Moses and the Lamb, by and by, and dwell with Jesus ever more.

She whispered, "That there was in honor of Herschel's recent baptism, praise be to Jesus."

"Amen," Herschel said.

Next came "Just As I Am Without One Plea" and by the time the wagon approached the lumber mill, she was wrapping up with "Lord, I'm Coming Home."

They were thirty minutes late by the watch Herschel pulled out of his pocket. Annaliese let a breath out slowly. John would be angry, tapping his foot at them in the doorway of the company office. As they neared the office, they looked for him. The mill dogs barked and wagged as usual, but no one came to the door. Herschel slapped the reins on the horses' flanks. If he hurried, he could be somewhere else when Mr. Stregal showed up at the house.

Finally, the wagon pulled up in front of the two homes. Annaliese poured Emeline into Samuel's lap, leapt out, and ran up her steps and into her home. A few minutes later, she rushed back out with a Venetian blind under an armpit and a hammer in her hand.

Herschel and Ruth and the children stopped unloading and turned to watch.

"She's got a mouthful of nails?" Ruth asked.

Annaliese put the hammer in her pocket and dragged a chair toward the railing that faced Lucenia's house. With one hand she held the blind in place and with the other she pulled a nail out of her mouth and hammered.

"Mama!" Samuel said.

"Hush," Ruth said. "Don't nobody say nothin'."

Herschel climbed out and went to help her. Lucenia ignored it all. Her sons slipped out the back of the wagon and ran off.

Soon, the blind was up. Annaliese stepped down and pulled the cord to the side. The wooden shades clattered down and that was the end of Lucenia's view of Annaliese's porch.

Herschel hurried down Annaliese's steps just as Lucenia was climbing them. He drove the wagon, Ruth and Samuel and Emeline still in back, to the back of their home.

Annaliese dropped into her rocker and gripped the hammer in her lap.

"Oh, all right," Lucenia said. She rubbed her arms.

Annaliese stared ahead.

"I apologize for what, in your opinion, might have been offensive remarks."

Annaliese tapped the hammerhead in the palm of her hand. "In my opinion?"

"My goodness! Do you always make it so difficult for people to apologize to you?"

"Only for the relentlessly offensive."

"How dare you. Here I am trying to . . ." Lucenia said, but the sound of boots on gravel made her stop.

John and Ben walked toward them, rigid as pallbearers. Their hands swung mechanically at their sides. John still wore his cruising hat and overalls. Ben was shaking his head. Annaliese came out of her rocker to join Lucenia at the steps.

The men looked up, stared at their wives for too long, sending them down the steps to grab their hands, unable to breathe.

John took off his hat. His jaw was working hard under his stubble. "Hoyt and I went out cruising the north side of Sharp Mountain today."

She realized his face was white.

"We ran across a still."

‿◦

X

As John told it, he and Hoyt were walking along a stream looking for a clear, flat place where they could pen a mule team. John led the way, eyes mostly on the ground for snakes. Out of the corner of his eye, he thought he saw something shiny, out of place, and he put his arm out to stop Hoyt. About 30 yards ahead in a rhododendron thicket, they saw a copper still, a furnace and four barrels of mash.

"Aw, shit," Hoyt hissed.

"Stregal." The call came from the other side of the stream.

John's pulse pounded in his ears.

Slowly, he and Hoyt turned only their heads toward the voice and saw the cold eye of a rifle. Beyond it, a black felt hat. Instantly, they turned away so as not to seem to be looking for the face.

Hoyt held his hands up. "We don't mean you no trouble. Don't know who you are. Don't care."

"You there, Stregal. Ain't you a lawman?" The voice was as tight as a deer tendon.

"No," John said, feeling the venom of the gaze. "I was a lawyer, it's different. Besides, now I'm a lumberman. Don't care what y'all are doing up here."

"A body's got to make a little cash money."

"That's right," Hoyt said, still looking away.

Silence.

John, standing on his own land, slowly raised his hands, too.

The voice came again. "Shit. I jest got this thing set up."

"We won't be back," John said.

"I know where yore house is."

"There won't be any trouble from us, ya hear?"

Silence.

"So, do we have an understanding?" John asked.

The only response was a rustle of leaves. After a few seconds, the men dared to look across the stream, where they saw nothing but the thicket he had been in. Then, the ragged voice floated in from beyond. "These woods is mighty dry. Makes good kindlin'."

Twigs snapped under his feet as he slipped away, each crack an eerie threat floating through the pines. They walked back to their horses, and their eyes were everywhere but on the ground.

The next day, John and Ben spread the word at the mill that the company was not interested in reporting stills, that burned-out acreage would put people out of work, maybe even close down the company. John sent men to clear the underbrush on the hill behind the homes. Annaliese watched them from her back porch while she tried to mend socks. Behind her, the floorboards creaked.

"Just a precaution," John said.

"I'm scared," she said as she put her work down.

"He won't do anything." He stared out at the workers.

"How do you know?"

He shot her a look so withering that it took her a moment to find her voice again.

"Maybe the children and I should go home," she said.

John shook his head. "No. Nothing will happen. We put the word out." He picked up the shotgun he had left in the doorway.

The sight of him holding a gun startled her. "You know how to shoot that?"

"Nothing will happen," he said. "You'll see." He turned on his heels and left.

Five days passed quietly but miserably for the women and children forbidden to leave the grounds. Lucenia and Annaliese arrived at a working civility, but the Venetian blind remained lowered.

On a brilliant, warm morning, Annaliese brought her box of stationery to her porch and sat down. As usual, she first had to stop and think of all the things she would not tell her mother and then see what was left.

May 5, 1901
Dear Mother,
We have survived our first picnic. Lucenia and the children and I went with Herschel and his wife to a place with a breathtaking view of the valley. The mountains and valleys have such beautiful names. Herschel says the river closest to our home is the Oostanula. Then there's the Etowah near town. His wife, Ruth, is showing some promise as a cook if she'll just mind my instructions. But she is wonderful with all four of the children, so there's a surprise benefit.

At supper, John has been telling the children what the various woods are used for, so I have learned that our property has some of the most important timber in North America. White oak, for instance. John says this wood is used for flooring and furniture, whisky and wine barrels. Red oak is so strong they use it for heavy construction timbers. The American chestnut's wood is reddish golden and prized for furniture, fences and caskets. But here is a surprise for you. The lovely dogwoods that flower across Louisville every spring, well, you would never know that this wood is so hard that it is used for shuttles and spools in the textile industry and golf club heads! John doesn't harvest dogwoods, of course. He just threw that in to surprise us. The sycamore is solid and tough to split, so it ends up as meat cutting blocks and handles.

Thank you for your continuing stream of letters. Please tell Dorothy and Aunt Gertrude to write more often. In my next letter, I hope to have some news about schooling for the boys.
All my love,
Annaliese

Next door, a floorboard creaked as someone sent a rocker moving. Annaliese peeked around her blind and, seeing Lucenia writing, wondered if she was describing their plight or writing around it as she did.

If she thought Lucenia hadn't seen her, she realized that wasn't so the next day when she heard hammering coming from Lucenia's front porch. As she looked through her parlor window, she saw Herschel installing a Venetian blind in the opening that faced hers.

Eventually John loosened his grip, for May was unfolding with one day hotter than the one before. At last the children were allowed to go to the streams and cool woods, as long as an adult and Slick were along. Slowly, all of the adults relaxed, too. The days grew longer and lazier, the wildflowers brought their cheerful spectacle to every hill and hollow, and life inched back to normal.

On the first Saturday in May, John and Annaliese set out for Pinch to pick up the new sawmill foreman arriving on the train from Knoxville. As their wagon left the company grounds, Annaliese took a last look back at the homes perched on the hill, two pearl mushrooms set against that vast forest, so vulnerable to any vengeance that might sweep down.

John patted her knee. "I've asked Herschel to stay close to the house until we're back."

They rocked along on the springboard seat. All around them, she heard the distant thwacks of axes and the thud of trees crashing to the earth as the forest was being reeled in tree by tree. The fortune was rolling in, too, she had been told, but one would never know it with John's sullen mood today. She looked over at him, jaw grinding, hooded eyes staring ahead. He hadn't slept well the night before. An hour later, she had gotten not even ten words out of him and gave up.

The bustle in Pinch was a welcome brew of color and sound to her starved senses. John straightened up from his slouch and reached over to pat her hand. She ran her finger up against his beard. Just for her, he shaved every day, but this morning he'd skipped it for the luxury of a professional shave and haircut.

"First stop, the barber, Mrs. Stregal. Think you can stand going in there?"

She looked at him, startled. The barber was known to be as profane as he was ugly, and even if she could have stood him and his clientele and the shop's foul miasma, why would John ask her to? It wasn't like him to forget that the place was no place for a lady. But she simply said, "I've got my own list, you know. The teacher, remember?"

John guided the horses to a hitching post in front of the bank. "All right. Meet here so we can be at the depot on time."

"And what time does the foreman arrive?"

"The 12:15 train from Knoxville." He helped her out of the wagon. "See you then."

"Watch out!" He pointed to a pile of cow manure in her path.

Skirts in hand, she swerved around it.

In the dry goods store she handed the clerk her letters. He squinted at her over thick glasses and greeted her by name, though they had never met. She scooped up one of his baskets and headed for the rear of the store, past pine shelves sagging with buckets of nails and bolts and farm tools. She lingered at the back wall to pick out the things the family had requested. Linament for Ben, kerosene and soap flakes for Ruth. Finding a dusty box of buttons, she poked through it like a child with a little candy money and a lot of time. Further down the aisle, she picked up spools of thread just to roll their jewel tones in her hand and match them to the buttons no one had asked for. She tossed them in her basket and returned to the front.

The clerk had his hand on a stack of newspapers. "I jest realized that these papers are yours, Mrs. Stregal."

"Oh, good. I was waiting for those." She pushed her purchases toward him. "And I'll take a copy of the most recent Pinch newspaper, too."

"Oh, no, ma'am, we ain't got no newspaper." He swept the buttons into a bag and rang up the items. "That'll be eighty two cents. There's been talk of startin' one, but between the Methodist women's circle and court week, we don't need no newspaper."

She paid him. "Court week? Court is held only one week a year here?"

"No ma'am." The clerk chuckled. "There's another week in October."

"I see." Annaliese smiled.

"Criminal cases one week, civil cases the other. Got one coming up soon."

"So lawyers from Atlanta will be here?"

"Every once in a while. But mostly it's lawyers from nearby counties who come in to defend or complain, one. And we got one lives right here."

"There's an attorney in Pinch?"

"Why sure. Colonel Chastain."

"A war veteran?" She pictured a withered old man with tobacco stains on a white beard.

"Why no, ma'am. That's just what we call 'em, the lawyers. Colonel this or Colonel that."

"Sounds like the trials are well attended."

Finally the man came around the counter. He was a skinny character, thin as a dollar bill, with eyes that lit up even through the thick glasses. "Sure enough. People will be spillin' out the winders, standin' shoulder to shoulder in the back. 'Course the cases done stacked up for a year so you can imagine the wagers goin' around." He shook his head. "Some of them Atlanta lawyers, they wear clothes that are all wore out."

She gave him a perplexed look.

"You know. For the jury," he said.

"Yes, I know how cagey those city lawyers are," she laughed. "Well, thank you."

He opened the door for her. "Watch yore step, ma'am."

On the street, she looked left and saw at the top of a hill the two-story marble courthouse. As she passed it, she noticed a group of men hanging around the side. Amidst all the Saturday hustle and hurry, the three stood out in their idleness. Their hair, so black it was blue, fell to the collars of their work shirts in stringy ropes. One turned to look up at her and she saw a pair of dark eyes set in a tanned, leathery face that watched her pass with enough curiosity to make her think he knew she was new in town.

The schoolhouse was a one-story clapboard building perched on stone pilings. Newly painted white with a door and four windows trimmed in black, it was in better shape than she had expected. Violets and mounds of pink phlox sprouted inside stone circles beside the steps. Annaliese walked up the steps, which sent a hog running out from under the stoop.

She brought her hand up to knock but paused. Lucenia had argued for boarding school for Darrison and even for Samuel, saying she had found a school in Maryland that would board boys that young. Annaliese wouldn't even speak of sending a six-year-old away. Ben argued for a family tutor. That possibility—another woman in the domestic mix—had made both women clam up. Then John, quietly watching the dinner table exchange, had proposed that Annaliese tutor the boys. She was doing such a good job teaching Ruth to read, wasn't she? Suddenly, Annaliese found herself arguing for the school in town, even while she squelched doubts about the quality of the curriculum, the teacher and students, not to mention the daily trip. Lucenia got in the last word for boarding school, though she said she would wait for Annaliese's report on the schoolmarm. All of it seemed to Annaliese an odd conversation to be having in May, but the county's school term was July and August, followed by a short break so children could help with the harvesting, then school started back up again in September.

She knocked on the door.

Inside, chair legs scraped against a wooden floor. A voice sang out, "I'm comin'."

Please let her be all right.

The fortyish woman had the bearing of a military commander, if not the physique. All bulk and bulge, she filled the doorway. Pink flesh spilled over the high collar of her shirtwaist. Small fissures clustered around her mouth like ice crystals at a puddle's edge. Something about her pasty skin, her wispy blonde hair brought Martha to Annaliese's mind, though this woman clearly had better control of her hairpins. Or was it just the similitude in this Scots-Irish crowd? No, she wasn't imagining it—this woman looked at her the way Martha had.

"Why, if it ain't Mrs. Stregal." The woman looked her up and down. "Well, one of 'em anyways. Whar's the big one?"

She was not all right.

"I'm Mrs. Annaliese Stregal." She extended her hand. "Pleased to meet you."

The teacher shook it. "Corinthia Meddling. Headmistress."

"Meddling? I know that name."

"My sister, Thessalonia."

That was who she reminded her of. "Oh, yes," said Annaliese with a smile. "She runs the boarding house."

"She owns the boarding house."

"I see." Annaliese kept the smile up but shifted on her feet. Corinthia continued to look her over, mouth twitching.

Finally Annaliese said, "May I come in?"

"Yes, of course." Corinthia stepped back. "You must be here to register your boy."

Daylight streamed in through a pair of windows on the left side of the room, but a chill still clung to its dark corners. Small tables and benches were pushed to the side in a heap. A broom rested against them. Corinthia walked ahead to the plain pine desk at the front. Behind it, a sign hung on the wall: "No talebearers allowed." In a corner stood an iron stove, six feet wide, with a pipe funneled to the outside.

As Corinthia sat down behind her desk, she waved Annaliese to a cowhide-bottomed chair beside it. Annaliese removed her straw hat and put it on her lap.

"You'll have to excuse the mess." Corinthia gestured at a pail of water under a window and a heap of rags. "I'm jest now gettin' things rearranged from last school term."

Annaliese cleared her throat. "You've been a teacher for some time?"

Corinthia tapped a finger on the desk. "Twenty years September last."

"That long." Annaliese detected a trace of bitterness in the way she said twenty.

"Folks in this town respect me near as much as the mayor."

"I'm confident of that." Annaliese shifted in her seat. Cowhide hairs shot into her backside.

"No, wait. Near as much as a good cyclone preacher." Corinthia tilted her head at Annaliese as if to gauge whether Annaliese fully appreciated that kind of status.

"Yes, I've heard how well-regarded you are."

"You know, it took me twenty years of switchin' little legs to win that respect."

Annaliese felt her cheeks get hot. She looked down at her hat. The woman was very much not all right.

"Since your family come to town, seems like all everybody talks about is your fine house. That and the other one's clothes and paint on her face. Them expensive hams and all goin' up yonder ever week on the railcar."

So that was it. Annaliese thought about fanning her scarred hands out under the woman's nose to show her the mark of her fancy life. "It's true we're new in town," she said, "but I've already heard what an accomplished teacher you are."

"Sure enough? Who said that?" Corinthia's eyes went to slits.

"Well, just everyone, of course. At the mercantile, at the barber's . . ."

"You tellin' me you were in the barber shop?"

Annaliese looked at her hat again and tried to think of what to say so she could leave. She dared not move again in the chair from hell.

"You know, the census takers have been up in them hills near you, finding families what moved from somewhere else to work at yore sawmill, I reckon. A load of young 'uns sprinkled about. Don't know how the county expects me to teach all of them, it jest bein' me here."

Annaliese had suspected children near her, but had no way of knowing for sure. Suddenly, she saw a glimmer of hope. "How many children? Did they say?"

"About 15."

Annaliese wiggled forward despite the cowhide. "What if a new school was built on our side of the county? That would ease your load, wouldn't it?"

Corinthia leaned back in her chair. "County school commissioner would have to have a say on that." She shook her head. "Shoot, I know what he'll say. He'll say we might could build a school or hire a teacher, one. Ain't got the money to do both."

Annaliese stretched her hand out on the desk toward Corinthia. "If the Stregal Lumber Company built a new school, do you think that the commissioner could provide a teacher's salary?"

"Might." Corinthia stared at Annaliese.

"Wouldn't it be wonderful if we named the school after you?" She ran her hand through the air to lay out the sign. "The Corinthia Meddling Academy."

Corinthia's fissured mouth began to twitch. "Where are you sayin' you'd build it?"

"Well, we would find some place near us that would be central to all, easy to travel to. We could clear out a road."

"What about books, furniture?"

"Not a problem." Annaliese flipped a hand in the air. "So you'll talk to the commissioner?"

Corinthia slapped the desk. "Better'n that. I'll talk to his mama."

"You can send word to me next week. Someone comes in to Pinch for supplies and the mail on Thursdays." She placed a finger on one of the spelling books. "May I borrow one of these? I'll have it back to you long before school starts."

Corinthia handed it to her.

Outside, Annaliese released her shawl to bask for a moment in the sun's warmth and her success. Corinthia would get the approval, she being a woman given the same respect a good cyclone preacher got, and so would Annaliese from John.

She screwed her straw hat back on and hurried to the barbershop, where she opened the door only enough to wave at John and look away from the barber's leer. The place reeked of pomade and yesterday's coffee and the barber was wiping the last of the shaving cream from John's face. He rolled out, pulling his watch from his pocket with one hand and sweeping his hat onto his head with the other.

The train roared in as they entered the waiting room. The smell of the smoke and metal, the sound of the wheels scraping on the rails reminded Annaliese of her own arrival. From the depot building, she looked out onto the platform and watched John shake hands with a man wearing a homemade collarless shirt and blue-serge pants so rumpled that she guessed he had slept in them last night. They stood for a while talking, then came her way. He was much taller than John, a few inches over six feet, and heftier. His long, square face began with limp hair clinging to his forehead and ended in a black muff of a beard.

John led him into the waiting room and held his hand out toward Annaliese. "Mr. Lowman, I would like to introduce you to my wife."

"How do, ma'am. I'm Slivey Lowman." He lifted his hat and she saw that his eyes were dull and milky and something else: proud. Too proud. She wondered how much John knew about this new employee.

"Mr. Lowman," she said curtly. "You have an unusual first name."

"Yes, ma'am. It was supposed to be Silvey. But my mama, she couldn't spell." He shrugged as though this was a well-worn explanation and smiled, revealing two crooked rows of amber teeth.

❧

XI

About a mile out, they heard the mill's three o'clock whistle. By the time they pulled up to the company offices where Lowman would get off, the last of the workers were trickling out of the mill. John halted the horses and climbed down from the wagon.

"We'll be just a minute. Need to introduce him to Ben, show him a few things," John said.

"Fine," she said. Her thoughts drifted to supper, and she began fretting about the fate of the chicken and vegetables she had left in Ruth's care that morning. She looked up at the homes on the hillside. Distant as they were, she could usually make out a child or even a goose. But there was no one, nothing moving there, all of it too still. In the middle of the afternoon, Lucenia would have made sure the children were outside. Annaliese stood up.

"John," she called softly. She put her hand to her forehead as she peered. Even if the children were occupied with something out back, there would be an animal or Herschel around front.

"John!" This call startled the horses.

He opened the office door.

"Something's wrong at the house." She jabbed the reins at him. "We need to get home."

He walked to the wagon eyeing the homes where there was nothing to see, but asked no questions as he climbed in and took the reins. He urged the horses uphill. Before the wagon stopped in front of her home, she jumped out. She was heading for the steps to the front door when she heard Slick's frantic barking in the back and veered that way. John was already ahead of her, running around the corner of the house, when a gunshot pierced the air followed by children's screams. Just as they reached the back yard, John slammed to a stop and held his arm out to halt Annaliese.

A mountain lion paced back and forth in front of the chicken house that stood about 60 yards behind the home. Slick crouched against the door, yellow hackles up, biting at the air. The snarling cat answered with angry yowls. Beyond the two animals, Herschel stood trying to aim his rifle, but he was also sweeping an arm through the air, as though waving someone away.

Ruth was creeping toward the chicken house straight into Herschel's line of fire. Annaliese screamed at her to stop, igniting a chorus of wails from the back porch as Lucenia and the children saw Annaliese. John ran up the back steps, pushing children aside, and disappeared into the house.

Slick was wild with barking. The cat closed in.

Annaliese realized that the terrorized cry on everyone's lips was her daughter's name. Her eyes raked the back porch where the children writhed against Lucenia's skirt. One, two, three boys. Where was Emeline? Everyone was pointing at the chicken house. In its single window, a small bonnet appeared, then a tiny hand. Annaliese fell to her knees. John came out cursing and leapt down the steps with rifle in hand, nearly stumbling over her. He ran into the yard and circled around behind the cat.

The mountain lion paced left and right, moving ever closer to Slick still backed up to the door. Herschel fired a shot in the air and everyone waited for the cat to run. Instead, it sprang at Slick. Ruth ran to the window and began clawing at the wire mesh. Annaliese raced to join her. Another gunshot blast came from Herschel, this one aimed at the animals locked in a whirling knot of amber fur. Slick broke free, but before she had completed her turn to face the enormous cat, it was on top of her.

John raised his rifle, tried to steady it, scurried sideways, raised it again.

Ruth finally worked the wire mesh out and she and Annaliese reached into the window, but it was too high for either woman to get a grip on the child. Lucenia pushed them aside and plunged her long arms in and yanked Emeline out.

John stood 20 yards from the animals, quivering elbows out, gun to eye while Herschel cursed at his jammed rifle. The mountain lion had clamped its teeth around Slick's neck and was whipping her limp body side to side.

"Shoot!" Annaliese screamed as she ran up to John.

Back and forth his arms went as the whipping continued, the arms that were shaking too much.

She grabbed the rifle, lined up the cat in her sights, and pulled off a shot that sent the cat flipping. Slick got up on her feet to challenge again, squeezed out a couple of thin barks, but collapsed. The cat struggled onto its forelegs, hindquarters up, back legs trying to push forward. Its cries grew in fury with each push. Annaliese ran closer, aimed again and took her final shot. The mountain air finally went quiet.

Meanwhile, inside the kitchen, it was bedlam. Emeline was shrieking at Lucenia's dabbing at the scrapes on her arms. Samuel ran for bandages. Ruth sat shaking in a corner with both Darrison and James trying to climb into her lap. Ben ran in and stopped in the doorway, clutching his heaving chest, eyes bulging beyond even their own usual bizarre limits.

"What . . . what. . ." he gasped. He lumbered to his wife's side.

John jerked the back door open. His wild eyes found Emeline and he fell upon her, pulling her head into his chest. When he looked up, all eyes were on him.

He shook his head. "Slick's gone. She was. . . that cat . . . badly injured. Just didn't make it."

"Papa, no!" cried Samuel, back in the kitchen with a roll of gauze.

John raised his hands. "That cat was probably rabid or it wouldn't have been so close. Nothing else could've been done. Dead now."

"John," Ben gasped. "You shot a mountain lion?"

John waved him away.

"Where's Annaliese?"

"Right here." Annaliese came in, breathing hard. She pulled her daughter out of John's hands and dropped to the floor a few feet away.

At dusk, the families gathered around the fresh grave. Samuel and Emeline held candles, making up rambling prayers. Darrison and James, not knowing any prayers, echoed the ending syllables. A few yards away, Ruth and Herschel stood watching. These particular prayers were unfamiliar to them—some holy ghost was being mentioned—and a religious service for a dog was certainly odd. To them, dogs were like raccoons and other wild but harmless creatures. Still, Slick had saved Emeline, so Ruth flipped open her Bible and went straight to a passage that mentioned something akin to dogs—lambs—and sent up her prayer, too.

A whippoorwill's melancholy song rose from the darkening forest as if to add its own farewell. Its familiar, sweet voice soothed the adults, reassured them with its calm report from the woods. Soon, they were guiding their children to bed, certain that sleep for any of them was still hours away.

But by nine o'clock, Emeline and Samuel were somehow asleep. Annaliese covered them for the fifth time and entered her bedroom across the hall. John lay on their bed fully clothed, staring at the ceiling.

She removed her blouse, stained with Emeline's blood. Again there was no fire downstairs in stove nor fireplace and no hot water, so she dipped a cloth into the basin and wiped grime off her neck and face. She watched him in the mirror. "You said you learned how to shoot a rifle."

"I did." His face betrayed him in his effort to nonchalantly deflect what he knew was coming.

"How about being sure, John? Being sure that you could aim true and shoot true because we are living in, in case you haven't noticed, the wilderness? Did it never occur to you that you might have to shoot a mountain lion to save your daughter's life?"

He rose up on his elbows. "Hold your tongue, Annaliese Stregal."

"I can't count on you." She put the blouse back on and stomped over to the bed. "What's next, John? Bears? Fire that will sweep down the mountain out there and kill us all in our sleep? Dear Lord, John, why did you bring us here?"

He jumped off the bed to loom over her. Annaliese stared into the hardened, distorted face of a stranger, but she felt that she was a stranger herself, she was so defiant. He raised a finger to her nose.

"I have to do this," he said. "I can't tell you why right now, but I have to. And you must support me."

John picked up his boots and left. She heard the sound of glass clinking downstairs and knew he was in the liquor cabinet. Barely breathing, she waited long enough for John to be beyond hearing her come down and walk through the downstairs rooms. On the back porch, she found what she was looking for. Only when she was back in her room did she exhale. She pushed the rifle under the bed and lay down, wishing she did not have to extinguish the lamp before going to sleep, so she did not. It ran out of oil before she had absorbed the knowledge raw but sure that the only person she could count on to protect her family here was herself.

∽

XII

Annaliese looked out her kitchen window as she finished drying the last of the breakfast dishes. All four children played near the house, literally under her gaze and happy to have it. Beyond them, Herschel was digging postholes along a perimeter that would be a fence around the chicken house. Farthest away was John, aiming his rifle at cans on a tree stump. From what she could see, he was hitting about every other one, which was better than last week's every fourth one.

Samuel stood up from his game of marbles to shade his eyes and peer at his father. She knew the boy wanted to climb that hill and take the gun in his hands, too, line up the sights, hold 'er steady and squeeze the trigger, see the can cartwheel away. In his own childish words, whispered to her instead of his prayers last night, he had said so. He had begged her to let him learn to shoot.

She was thinking about letting him.

On the other side of the yard, the garden was finally delivering its promise. It was truly Ruth's garden now with her calamus root and weedless, tidy rows of bright green onion tops and potato vine. Pole beans were beginning their climb up the corn stalks, as she had intended. In about eight weeks, Annaliese knew, the kitchens would be steaming with simmering vegetables headed for green Mason jars. Her mouth watered at the thought of fresh vegetables.

Today, however, she and Ruth were going to bake bread if Annaliese could get her nose out of the cookbook.

Lucenia walked in tying an apron around her waist. "Room for one more student?" she asked.

"Sure," Annaliese said. So the lesson began with two students, only one of whom could read the recipe under her floured fingers.

"I can't make no sense of these letters, Miss Anna. S-U-G-A-R," Ruth said. She scrunched her thin eyebrows.

"Yes, that's a tough one. It's sugar." Annaliese placed her finger on a different word. "Try this one. It's easier."

"S-A-L-T. Ssss - aaaah - ul - t. Salt. Salt! It's salt sure enough, ain't it?"

Annaliese answered the girl's merry eyes with a smile.

She poured warm water from the kettle into an earthenware bowl and dipped a finger in. With a nod to Ruth about the temperature, she crumbled a yeast cake into it and stepped back to allow her students to add the other ingredients. Ruth was first with her cup of flour.

Annaliese held out a long wooden spoon to her. "Add the flour just a little at a time, Ruth, and mix the dough thoroughly after each addition."

When Ruth had mixed the dough to the right texture, Lucenia turned it onto a floured board. With the considerable strength of her meaty arms, she pushed the heel of her hand into the dough, pulled it back over on itself, gave it a quarter turn, and pushed and pulled again.

"I used to watch my mother do this," she said.

Annaliese's eyes flew open at this mention of her childhood.

"Then how come you ain't got no idea how to do it?" Ruth asked.

Lucenia froze, arms stiff as rods, and stared at the dough for a few seconds before responding. "I remember standing at her tin top work table with my lips resting on its edge, you know, the way Emeline does on this table. It tasted cold and bitter. She'd sprinkle flour on the table and jam her hands into the sticky mound. Couple of times, I asked to try. But she always shooed me away."

"Why?" Ruth asked.

"I suppose we would've just slowed her down."

"We?"

"My little sister, Rose, and I."

Behind them, Annaliese listened carefully.

"That the one yore always sendin' letters to?"

Lucenia raised an eyebrow. Her body rocked back and forth with the rhythm of her kneading. "Yes. Anyway, Mother had boarders to tend to."

"Boarders?" Ruth leaned against the table. "So you ate pretty good, didn't you, with them in your house?"

Lucenia did not answer. The dough began to stick to the board. She threw a few pinches of flour onto it and kept going.

The drone of a fly bumping along the ceiling was the only sound in the room. Ruth looked at Annaliese who looked back just as puzzled. Lucenia's silence had elevated a simple question to something else.

Finally, Lucenia said, "Sometimes."

Ruth turned to Annaliese. "What about you, Miss Annaliese? Who are your people?"

"Well, my mother and sister are in Louisville, as you know."

"They lived on a riverboat," Lucenia said.

"Sure enough?"

"Well, only until I was eleven," Annaliese said quickly.

"Your Daddy's done passed on?"

"Yes. We got word of that."

"What? Why didn't . . . ?"

"So anyway, I spent the rest of my childhood with seven cousins. We had wonderful meals—Aunt Gertrude's and the cooks'. But when dinner was served, you had to move fast if you wanted seconds. Meals were a race, especially if Ted and Michael and Patrick were at the table. To this day, we all eat too fast. Ruth, add some more flour here. The dough's getting sticky again."

Ruth held the flour sifter above the dough. She cranked its handle, sending a shower of flour down onto Lucenia's hands. "Ain't this gadget somethin'."

Lucenia stepped back, waving away the dust. Annaliese moved in to poke the dough. "Lucenia, you're just about there. See how it bounces back?"

Lucenia nodded.

"Ruth, feel this. You need to know how it feels when it's ready to rest," Annaliese said.

"Nine of y'all?" Ruth said, grabbing fistfuls of the dough and squeezing it until it oozed into tubes between her fingers.

"Lord, no, not that hard," Annaliese said.

Lucenia reached for the pieces. "Never mind. I'll finish this."

"Gently, Lucenia," Annaliese laughed. "Yes, Ruth, nine." She smiled, remembering her aunt's kitchen, crammed with five aproned girls on Sundays when the cooks were off. The oldest three—Dorothy, Kathryn, and Charlotte—did the measuring, chopping, skinning, and slicing. The youngest two, Annaliese and Irene, danced along the edges of the action in supposed cleanup—happy to be crowded out of any actual work. Only when impending marriage forced the issue did Annaliese return to her aunt's kitchen with a more receptive attitude.

Annaliese gave the dough one more push and nodded back at Lucenia. "And then I met John Stregal."

"Your first true love," Lucenia added in a girlish tone.

Annaliese stared at the worktable for a moment. She reached for the sifter and sprinkled flour on the dough again.

Lucenia and Ruth searched her face, but it was as blank as a new tombstone.

Annaliese handed a jar of oil and a new bowl to Ruth. "Rub some of this around this bowl."

"Yes, ma'am." The girl hooked one arm around it. "I can rub this oil in just as good as you want." She poured a thick ribbon of oil into the bowl.

"Well, a light coating is all . . ."

Ruth's bony elbow pumped wildly in the air as her hand swept around. "Well, what was you lookin' to do with yore life back in Kentucky? After you married and all."

Lucenia gently removed the bowl from Ruth's grip and inspected the coverage.

"Raise our children. Plant my gardens and enjoy our friends."

"Help those less fortunate?" Lucenia said into the bowl.

Annaliese took it from her. "I simply wanted to live in a place long enough to be part of the landscape, to know the smell of its dirt when the rain came, to attend a wedding of a young woman whose first steps I had seen. Something wrong with that?" She dropped the dough in, turned it to bring the oiled side up and covered the bowl with a blue cloth. "Ruth, open the stove door. See if the fire's dying down."

The girl opened the door and peered in. "Yes, ma'am. Should I test it with my hand, like we been doin'?"

"No. We're going to use the warming drawer below."

Ruth closed the oven door.

"Now open the drawer and put the bowl in."

After she closed the drawer, Ruth went to the sink to wash her hands. "Reckon me and Herschel could get some of that pipe water there to come into our place?"

"Oh, I don't know about that, Ruth," Lucenia said as she rinsed her hands. "Ben says it was a huge job putting in the pipe between the spring and these houses. They dug out a channel, bored out some logs, lined them up, sealed them into one long artery and brought it all the way down here. He said they hated having to split it into two pipes then for the two houses, it was so much work." As she dried her hands, she looked out the window at the distant hills. Suddenly, she slapped the towel against the sink. "So that's why they built these two cotton-pickin' houses so close together."

All three of them were at the window now, focused on the mountains, the source of this cool, clear water that the Stregal women took for granted in their homes. Perhaps some of the other confounding decisions made by John and Ben would make sense one day. Even Ruth fell quiet in the warm and milky morning light. They savored this rare peace, this moment when no one wanted anything, bellies were full, there was enough clean laundry. Eventually, their eyes settled on Darrison and James, sprawled on those full bellies shooting marbles through a circle of red clay.

Lucenia shook her head. "Look at those two." She pointed one of her thick fingers. "Just covered in that red dirt. There is no soap on earth that can get it out of clothing."

"Lucenia, there's no point in worrying about that," Annaliese said.

Ruth moved away from them to push a damp rag across the work-table. "My mama always said you are your dirt."

The women turned to look at her.

Ruth worked the leftover flour off the table into her cupped hand. "It was her way of tellin' me I wasn't goin' no further than the edges of that field she used to plow ever' spring. It weren't no use for me to go to school, she said. Better to learn how to plant by the signs, dress a hog, sew. It was kinda like she was sayin', 'That dirt between your toes, girl, it'll sprout your roots.' I know she thought she was doin' right by me. She loved this red dirt, said we owed it somethin' back." Ruth pushed her hair back with the inside of her elbow. "Now I love this old red clay, too, slippery as lard when it's wet and harder'n flint when it's dry. Nothin' smells better than a fresh turned field of it. But I'm tellin' y'all . . ." She shook her head. "I ain't that dirt."

Annaliese and Lucenia stood as still as bookends, staring at this sparrow of a girl who had just told them more about her family and fortitude than she had in all the weeks they had known her.

"I ain't." Two more shakes of the wispy head.

They could only stand quietly to regard her with surprise. Where in the girl's world of doing without had such hope spring from? They knew she had grown up in an isolated hollow, far removed even from Pinch. What exposure could she have had to other people's lives, other than fellow worshipers at church revivals? Perhaps it was the Bible stories glorifying postponed reward that made her confident of a better future. But Ruth sounded like she was interested in the here and now. It was a hunger the Stregal women understood. Beyond these hills, such spirit was building a new America. Weren't thousands of uneducated immigrants arriving on American shores every day bent on forging a new destiny? Wasn't John's enormous gamble born of the same hunger? But they could also see some truth in the mother's credo. Place as destiny. Sit in your dirt long enough, it worms into your pores, limits your vision, defines your horizon.

Lucenia and Annaliese looked out the window again at their children. Emeline, barefoot again, was jumping off a boulder into a cloud of red dust. The boys were breathing it in above their marbles into their pale, innocent, receptive little bodies.

Annaliese said softly, "They are sucking in their very futures."

"Well, anyhow," Ruth said. She took the flour scoop into the pantry and dropped it into the flour barrel. "Is that all for now?"

"Yes, Ruth," said Annaliese. "We'll check on the dough in about an hour. Why don't you start on that rice pudding we talked about?"

"Yes, ma'am."

Annaliese brushed her hand lightly over Lucenia's. "I need to speak with you," she whispered. As the women moved toward the dining room door, Annaliese said over her shoulder, "And put some shoes on."

Lucenia followed Annaliese through the dining room and into the drawing room where they settled into two chairs by the window. Annaliese flicked at the draperies for a moment, stirring up a cloud of pollen and dust. Her fingers fluttered to her neck to grope for fallen strands of hair. Finding none, they moved upward in unnecessary tucking.

Lucenia leaned back on a bent arm, waiting.

Annaliese smoothed her skirt. "You know that I would not ask you to breach a marital confidence."

Lucenia sat up.

"That is not my intention in asking you this question."

Lucenia did not move.

"Has Ben ever said to you that this lumber company absolutely must succeed?"

Lucenia burst into laughter and went back to her slump. "Noooo. But isn't that . . . understood?"

Annaliese looked at her lap. "I meant has he seemed desperate to you, ever made you wonder if he wasn't telling you everything?"

Lucenia slowly shook her head. "What's going on?"

Annaliese pressed her hands together as she leaned toward Lucenia. "John speaks of succeeding as though his life depends on it. I was wondering if we could, you could help me, find out if there's something going on."

"I think you're imagining things. He's got, well, we've all got, a lot riding on this."

"No." Annaliese shook her head. "It's more than that."

"Well, even so, Ben may not know anything considering how John keeps him in the dark," Lucenia said.

Annaliese stiffened but said nothing.

"You know," Lucenia cut her eyes over at her, "if you want to know what a man is up to, you get him around a group of men. His peers. They forget you're there, start boasting. You learn a lot."

"Peers? Where are we going to get peers?" Annaliese straightened. "Wait a minute!"

"What?"

"Court week."

"It's next week, isn't it?"

"Suppose we could get some of the visiting lawyers to come out here?"

"Well, we could try. By Friday, they may be quite weary of Thessalonia and her fried chicken."

"We could invite them to dinner."

"Wear our finest. I brought the most divine red dinner gown."

"Gowns? Oh, for heaven's sake, Lucenia."

"No, no, don't you see? We are wives of lumber barons. We shall be elegant and charming and we shall massage the dinner conversation until we find out what you want to know."

Annaliese jumped up from her chair. "This will be good for the children, too, Lucenia. They will see and hear people of our . . ."

"It's all right. Say it, dear. Our standing." Lucenia was nodding vigorously. "An exceptional idea."

A wail erupted from the kitchen, then a crash and the sharp sound of broken glass scattering across a floor. Now Lucenia sprang from her chair as well. Annaliese was already crossing the dining room.

The next day, Ben and John left the mill in the care of the efficient Slivey Lowman and traveled to Pinch, having agreed to invite a few of the lawyers to dinner after watching the trials. They said it was unthinkable for their ladies to attend court, an event where unsavory topics might fall upon delicate ears and Ruth piped up to say that, of course, that's what filled up the court house seats, balconies, and windows. Lucenia and Annaliese would have protested a little, starved as they were for theatre, but there were guest preparations to get to. They would dig the best of the court stories out of them later.

As night fell, John and Ben returned home and delivered the news that Mr. Henry Chastain, of Pinch, and Mr. Arthur Garland, of White County, had most graciously accepted the families' kind invitation and would arrive Saturday afternoon.

☙

XIII

Preparations began the next day. Floors were oiled, rugs were beaten, and guest beds smoothed. Supper would be in Annaliese's dining room, Sunday breakfast in Lucenia's. Annaliese unpacked a set of English china, the best she had dared bring, and found a bottle of holy water, still full somehow, which she handed Ruth to sprinkle around the house to bless it. The girl stared at Annaliese and the bottle, but did as she was told, dousing herself with some in case there was something to it. Next, Annaliese gave her detailed instructions on how to wash the china properly lest she be tempted to stack and slosh. It came through without a nick and was set out in the dining room. Dinner would be mock turtle soup, leg of lamb, mint jelly, aspic, parsley potatoes, and ambrosia.

On Saturday morning, Annaliese stood in the doorway of her parlor looking it over once again. She winced at the still-naked window.

"It's good to see you so excited and happy." John slipped his hand around her waist. "Mmm." He buried his nose in her neck. "You smell good."

Annaliese smiled as she accepted his kiss on her cheek. "It's going to be an enjoyable evening for all, I hope." She put her hand on his face. Today his color was better. In his eyes, she saw an energy she had not seen for several weeks and he had been sleeping better. "You seem to be rather spirited yourself."

"Of course, I am," he laughed. "Why wouldn't I be?"

At the back of the house, the door slammed into the broom closet. The children were arguing again. Annaliese and John walked down the hall and found the boys following Emeline, clutching something to her chest. They were reaching around her shoulders and arms.

"Y'all just hold on now," Ruth screeched at the boys. "She's gone squeeze 'em to death if y'all don't let her be."

"Mine," Emeline squealed as she scurried toward a laundry basket in the kitchen. "Rufe, make 'em stop."

"What's going on?" John asked. He and Annaliese peered over Emeline's shoulders as she emptied her load out of her pinafore and onto the fresh towels in the basket.

Baby rabbits. Five furry, brown baby rabbits squirming to hide under one another.

"Oh, no," Annaliese said. "Not in the house."

"Ain't they jest the cutest things?" Ruth said.

"Mama, we found them near the spring house." Emeline started to jump up but returned to her crouch over the basket as the boys tried to close in. "Stop." She stiff-armed James.

"Ouch! I just want to look, Emmie," James said.

"Now, y'all just settle down," Annaliese said. "Ruth, what's going on?"

"Emmie and I was gettin' some butter out of the spring house when I seen somethin' movin' in the bushes, somethin' flangin' somethin' around."

"It was a fox, Mama," Emeline said.

"Sure enough it was, Miss Annaliese, with a rabbit in its mouth. It ran off with it, 'course, and I wouldn't 'a paid it no heed but somethin' told me to go look in them bushes and look what we found."

Annaliese gave her a look.

Ruth threw up her hands. "Well, I couldn't jest leave 'em there. They's just gotten to be cute." She leaned over and whispered, "New borned rabbits is the ugliest, nakedest things, ooooh I'm tellin' you." Then back up for all to hear, "Why these critters surely woulda died from cold or animals, one."

John whispered in his wife's ear, "Got to admit, they're cute."

"So we can keep 'em?" James said. His wide little face pleaded for the right answer.

"But they need to be fed, kept warm . . ." Annaliese said. "Wait. What am I saying? I don't want these things in the house. Especially not tonight."

"We'll put them in that there warming drawer of yours." Ruth pointed at the wood stove.

"What!" Samuel shouted. "You'll cook 'em in there."

"Naw," Ruth said. "I heard that Ida Bell Cobb bought her one of these ovens from a traveling drummer—you know, bought it on a time plan with her egg money so Mr. Cobb wouldn't catch on that big cash money was goin' out the door?—and she put her baby chickens in that there drawer when the weather turned cold."

Annaliese put her hands on her hips. "But it's May, Ruth."

"Let's try it," shouted Samuel, closest to the basket. Before Emeline could stop him, he reached in and picked one baby up and presented it to his mother. She stroked the tiny creature with one finger. Its ears were so soft the fur barely registered to her touch. It lay in a soft curl, its downy brown abdomen moving gently up and down.

"You're a goner," John whispered.

"Oh, come on, Emmie," James said.

Like the proprietress of royal jewels, Emeline scooped one up, looked at James reproachfully, and placed it in his hands. Next, Darrison got one, and then Emmie picked up the last two and headed for the stove.

Ruth opened the drawer, slid out the holding tray and spread out a towel onto which all five babies were lowered. They wiggled back into one another, like puzzle pieces come alive. The tray was pushed back inside. "See?" Ruth tucked in the towel. "Jest got to keep a fire goin' is all."

"Just not a roaring one," Darrison said.

"Wait a minute," Annaliese said, remembering the leg of lamb. "What will we do with them when we need a big fire going in there?"

Ruth fluttered her hands at Annaliese. "We'll put 'em beside the stove, wrapped up real good. Or in Miss Lucenia's oven."

"Drawer," Samuel said.

" 'Course."

"All right, all right," Annaliese sighed. "But, Ruth, you're responsible."

"Now we can call our mountain Bunny Mountain," Emeline said.

"Aw, heck no," Samuel said.

"What do you mean, Emmie?" John said. "It's already got a name, I'm sure. Didn't you ask Herschel?"

"But we want to name it. It's our mountain, isn't it?" James said.

"Bunny Mountain," Emeline said.

"What? No, not Bunny Mountain. It's . . ." James said.

"Nope." John held out his weathered hands over the children's heads. "Bunny Mountain it is."

"Bunny Mountain. That's right cute," Ruth said.

Annaliese bent down and put a finger inside the drawer to stroke the nearest baby. It buried its nose under another's foot. She decided not to bring up the subject of how to feed them.

That afternoon, they fed the children early. By 5:00, Samuel and Emeline were bathed, dressed, and warned to stay inside. James and Darrison soon arrived at their aunt's front door, equally clean and rigid from threats. After sending them all upstairs, their mothers bustled into the front parlor and settled into chairs at the window. Lucenia had shown some restraint with her choice of a blue plaid dress with small puffs at the sleeve tops and a white collar and cuffs. Annaliese had chosen a rose-colored dress of dotted Swiss.

The aroma of fresh baked bread wafted through the house, the rabbits having been sent to Lucenia's kitchen. Annaliese had timed the baking to end just as the guests would arrive. "To awaken the senses and set the stage for the pleasurable evening to come," she had explained to Lucenia as she pushed the pans into the oven.

"So, too, with perfume," she had replied.

Lucenia sat closest to the window. The late-day sun poured over her confident face and Annaliese smiled at the artificial rosiness that glowed on her cheeks and lips. The eyebrows were distinctly defined in brown arches, the lids lined lightly in kohl. What would the men think? She made a note to watch their faces as they were introduced to her. With a righteous smirk, she patted her face, enhanced only by Tetlow's Gossamer Powder.

John and Ben came down the central hall, combed and suited. They passed their wives, glasses in hand, and went out the door to stand on the porch.

Soon, they heard the sawmill dogs barking. Two horses with riders emerged from the woods. The women came out on the porch to watch and try to be patient with the horses' crawl. Annaliese saw one of the riders wave.

"That's Henry Chastain," John said.

He was the first off his horse. Chastain's body came down in one fluid movement. His feet landed hard and sure, and he turned to face his hosts. He was younger than she expected—probably in his early thirties, she guessed, with energy coming off him despite the journey. As he came up her steps and shook John's hand, then Ben's, she had a moment to take in his amiable brown eyes, his confident smile. When he removed his hat to her, a mass of glossy black hair tumbled onto his forehead. He swept it back then reached forward to gently press the hand she offered while John made introductions. Annaliese could not find her voice when his hand took hers. She just nodded. John looked sharply at her but moved quickly to introduce Mr. Garland, a man of middle age, white-haired and piggy-eyed.

Herschel arrived to take the horses. She watched Mr. Chastain lay his hat on top of the bag going to Lucenia's home. As the two guests lingered at the front door politely listening to John's descriptions of the craftsmen's work on the walls and floors, Annaliese realized that Lucenia had been watching her rather than the other way around. A sly smile came to her painted lips.

Everyone settled into the parlor while Lucenia went upstairs for the children. Annaliese chose the most remote chair she could find and tried to pull herself together.

Henry said, "I am certain that I speak for Mr. Garland as well when I say that we are delighted to finally meet you ladies." He was sitting on the settee on the other side of the piano from her. "Mrs. Stregal?" He had to lean forward to see Annaliese.

"Why, thank you, Mr. Chastain. We are pleased to make your acquaintance, too. I was surprised to learn that a town as small as Pinch could support an attorney," Annaliese said, suddenly realizing how condescending that sounded.

"It's the county seat, Anna," John said. He stood at the corner table holding a decanter. "You've seen the courthouse."

Annaliese smiled weakly. "Yes, of course."

"Ben and I met Henry on our first trip here, right after we bought the land." John handed Henry a glass of whiskey. "You remember."

She did not.

"Henry is local counsel for the Atlanta, Knoxville and Northern Railroad," Arthur said.

"Delightful," Annaliese said.

John shot her a puzzled look.

"I mean . . ." Annaliese smoothed her skirt. "I must check on something in the kitchen. Will you please excuse me?" She stood up, the men rose, and she swept out of the room.

As she opened the kitchen door, she saw Ruth standing over the stove, stirring the soup and muttering, "I hope to God it's fit to eat." Annaliese closed the door. She dabbed her handkerchief over what was left of Tetlow's Gossamer.

Back in the parlor, the four Stregal children, stiff as the lead soldiers they had just stuffed in their pockets, performed their hospitality duties beneath Lucenia's dragon eye. Herschel arrived to take them next door, giving Ben the opportunity to explain the family crest, which Arthur had made the mistake of noting on the engraved glasses.

"Yes, the Stregal crest originated in England, some two hundred or so years ago. The first Stregal came to America—Philadelphia actually—in time for the American Revolution. Bad timing, I should say," Ben chuckled. His eyes, watery under normal conditions, ran over now with the effects of pollen. He pulled a handkerchief out of his pocket and dabbed at the red rims.

"Is this a plow I see?" Arthur asked as he held his glass close to his eyes.

Annaliese returned to her chair beside the piano. She smoothed out her skirt again and smiled across the room at Lucenia.

"My father had that added to the crest," Ben said. "He was an executive with B. F. Avery and Son Company in Louisville. Largest producer of plows."

"In the world," Lucenia said.

"I imagine that he's proud of your venture here," Henry said as he leaned against the settee, draping one long arm along its spine.

"I'm afraid not," John said, shaking his head. "He died when he was 35. Ben and I were just boys."

Henry's chin dropped. "I'm sorry."

"Well, he certainly has some handsome grandchildren," Arthur said brightly.

"Oh, thank you," John laughed. "But they have their mothers to thank for that." He raised his glass to Lucenia and even higher to his wife barely visible beside the piano.

"Indeed they do," Henry said, raising his glass at Annaliese.

Her cheeks were on fire. She could not understand it, this pulsing that was rendering her senseless. Certainly Mr. Chastain was conducting himself impeccably. He was doing nothing improper. She was doing this entirely to herself, driving herself mad. That was it. She was losing her mind in Georgia after all.

Ruth appeared at the doorway that connected to the dining room, wiping her hands on her apron. Annaliese snapped her head around. "What?"

"Lord a-mercy." Ruth took a step back. "What's wrong?"

"Nothing. Not a thing. What are you doing in here?" Annaliese eyes fell upon Ruth's feet. They were shoeless. She looked back across the parlor, where conversation had ceased.

Everyone was looking at Ruth's knobby, mud-stained feet.

Ruth twisted her apron. "I came in to ask you somethin' about the soup."

Annaliese rose from her chair to stand in front of Ruth. "John? Perhaps our guests would like to get settled in their rooms? Recover a bit from their journey?"

John looked down at his whiskey glass, half-full. "In a while."

"Well, excuse me for a moment again." Annaliese grabbed for Ruth's waist but the girl lurched ahead of her toward the kitchen.

Supper was served at seven. As Annaliese led everyone to her dining room, she was grateful for the meager light thrown by the sconces and table candles. The less anyone could see her face, which she did not trust at the moment, the better.

Lucenia swept in, swathed in red silk. Her skirt was a swirl of vertical crimson panels embroidered with yellow flowers and trimmed in black stripes. An overlay of black lace covered her torso and flared in ruffles at her shoulders. A gold-rimmed cameo peeked out from the black froth at her neck.

Annaliese stifled a smile. Had she been a child pretending again to be an actress, among her cousins, in the middle of the night in their bedroom, she could not have worn such a get up. For her part, her gown was simple: a yellow satin messaline with tulip-shaped skirt that clung to her slender hips and flared at the hem. It was an old frock, the last item she had thrown in a trunk simply because there had been room, not because she actually thought she would ever wear it. But if male eyes fell on Lucenia tonight, Annaliese was glad, for then she could focus. This dinner had a goal, it was best to remember.

She stole a glance at Henry as he rounded the corner of the table. Head bent and bobbing in response to Ben's chatter, he was moving away from her seat at the end of the table.

As John pulled her chair out for her, she smiled at the other guests settling in. Ben sat at her right. On her left, Arthur Garland exuded happy expectation. For the first time, she really looked at him. His mass of white hair, slicked back from his widow's peak, had misled her about his age, for she could see now that his freckled skin was unlined, still firm. They exchanged pleasantries, then turned their attention to the other end of the table. Lucenia was lowering herself into the chair Henry held for her.

Ruth waddled in from the shadows struggling to carry a soup tureen. Unnoticed by all except Annaliese, she put it on the sideboard and scurried away, as if to demonstrate obedience, or perhaps, Annaliese thought, she was anxious to get the soup—a subject of earlier rebuke—out of her possession.

"So, Mrs. Stregal," Henry was saying to Lucenia as he sat down. "I trust that you are finding things not too uncivilized here for your taste."

Lucenia looked away from the mirror on the opposite wall in which she had been admiring herself. "Oh, not uncivilized at all. We are doing fine adjusting to certain boundaries of comfort, but have had our adventures, let me tell you."

"Oh?" Henry sat back in his chair.

"Yes." Lucenia delivered a shiver worthy of the stage. "A little mountain lion incident."

"Really? What happened?"

"It was the most terrifying thing."

Annaliese felt the muscles in her shoulders seize and she looked down the table at John. He held his hands out over his plate. "It was all over in seconds, Henry," John said. "The big cat was after some of the chickens, the dog chased it off, and it was shot dead at the edge of the woods." John smiled and shrugged. "That's all."

Henry, unfolding his napkin stiffly, nodded as though he sensed there was more but he should let it go. Arthur shot a quick look at Annaliese and Ben, saw nothing but smiles, and smoothed his napkin across his knees, too. John raised a toast to his guests, a simple grace was said, and the meal began. With the first taste of soup, Annaliese began to relax. Ruth had actually left it alone.

"So, John, how do you find the local men to be? As workers, I mean?" Henry said.

"Well, there seems to be a common trait known as 'stiff neck'," John chuckled.

"One could say that their spirit of enterprise is wanting," Ben said, prompting even heartier acknowledgment. He dabbed his napkin at a droplet of soup on his belly.

"For the most part, except for Blue Mondays, they're all right," John said with a shrug.

"I hope they're not asking you to let their children work in the mill," Arthur said.

"You know, the textile mills in Whitfield County work them as young as six," Henry said.

"Surely not," Lucenia said. All faced turned to her. "That is . . ." she sputtered, "anyone would agree that's wrong." She paused. "Well, it's just immoral. Isn't it, John?"

John gave her an icy look. Annaliese's shoulders seized again. "Of course it is," he said calmly.

Lucenia's brow furrowed. "Our workers haven't asked you for that, have they?"

John turned in his seat to open the sideboard door. "Never come up," he muttered into the sideboard as he poked around.

Henry and Arthur concentrated on their soup spoons.

Annaliese extended her hand on the table toward Arthur to stir up the conversation she had in mind. "Mr. Garland," she began, "we hear that a Cincinnati man, Henry Bagley, has started a lumber company in your county. Have you met him?"

"Not directly, ma'am. But I know of the operation, a mighty big one. I've heard they turn out 70,000 board feet a day."

"Is that right?" John said. He had turned back around in his seat, bottle of bourbon in hand.

"Now I know you to be a responsible lumber man, John. A careful harvester of our forests," Arthur said. "So I'll be frank with you about Bagley. Those wood hicks of his go out logging and they strip even the steepest ridges, I tell you. If it's vertical, they will cut it down. Even the saplings. Cut them smack off. Leave a mess behind."

Annaliese watched John pour the liquor in his crystal glass, which she had set out for water.

"No, we don't cut anything smaller than eight inches at the base," John said.

"And we clean up. Burn the detritus," Ben said.

"Slows us down, though. Drink?" John said to Henry. He held up the bottle.

Arthur and Henry sent their glasses his way.

Lucenia settled back in her chair and dipped into the soup again.

"Gentlemen," Annaliese said, trying another tack to get the men talking as she wished. "What's this I hear about a lawyers' lying contest every night of court week?"

Arthur laughed. "Why we get together after dinner at Meddling's, gamble a little, tell a few tales is all."

"Snake stories, surprise verdicts, character assassination, that sort of thing," Henry said. He delivered the last of his sentence down to her end of the table, a gentleman's gesture to include all in the conversation. Annaliese returned an amused smile, a genuine one at the prospect of championship fibbing from lawyers, but Ben seized this topic as an invitation for his own storytelling. Pushing his empty soup bowl away, he launched into a ramble about the dangers of cross-examination.

As soon as soup bowls were emptied, Annaliese rose from her chair. "Lucenia, will you help me bring in the main course? Gentlemen, please forgive our informal ways of serving here, but under these rural circumstances . . ."

Lucenia dabbed a napkin to her mouth and pushed her chair back. All four men sprang up. "I assure you that we ladies will be sorely disappointed if you tell any captivating stories about the court week business while we're gone," Lucenia said.

"Or the lumber business," Annaliese said quickly.

In the kitchen, Lucenia said, "This won't take long with that bourbon flowing."

Pushing her into the pantry, Annaliese hissed, "It will if you keep getting them off track! What was that bit about child labor? Let the men talk."

Lucenia's shoulders drooped. "Yes, yes, I will. But six-year-olds in factories, Anna." She twisted her hands as they stood beside the flour barrel and the hanging hams.

Ruth was at the sink, washing pots quietly. A pair of Annaliese's boots peeked from under her hem. "Should I go get the soup bowls?" she asked.

"Yes," Annaliese said, still looking at Lucenia.

Ruth wiped her hands on her apron and went through the door.

"All right." Lucenia straightened. "Next course."

The women returned to the dining room with a platter of roasted lamb, the vegetables, and a tray of water glasses, which Annaliese added to each place setting. As she bent over Henry's shoulder, she caught his scent, noticed the sheen on the thick furrows of his hair.

He was finishing a story. Ben and John were leaning forward on their elbows, smiling.

"So," Henry said, "when the jury came back the foreman stood up and said . . ." Henry straightened his back, held out an imaginary sheet of paper, affected the air of the farmer foreman enjoying the courtroom spotlight, and said in a hard twang, " 'We, the jury . . ." Henry held his stiff posture but his mouth twitched at the corners " . . . find the hog guilty and the cow not guilty.' "

The room exploded with laughter. As Annaliese took her seat again, she saw that Henry's hold on the men was clear. His brown eyes drew his audience in and, once in his embrace, people obviously found his rich voice, his masterful timing intoxicating. A new atmosphere hung in the room as the next course began.

"Tell them the one from yesterday, Henry. The headlight verdict," Arthur said just before he put a slice of lamb in his mouth. "Oh, ladies. This is delicious." He nodded his white head at Annaliese, then down the table to Lucenia.

Henry put down his forkful and smiled. "I was defending the railroad company in a case where an animal—this time a calf—had been killed by a train. As my first witness I put up Lamartine Cobb, the passenger train's engineer. For twenty years at least."

Ben said, "So that's why the locals say, 'Yonder comes The Lamartine'."

Henry nodded. "He testified that the calf had jumped down from a hill into the train's path so quickly that he couldn't stop the engine in time. Next I called the fireman, the railroad employee who maintained the oil-burning headlight. He testified to the same circumstances. I asked him the time of day of the accident. He stated that it was 7:30 at night, so the role of the headlight was quite clear. I asked, 'And your headlight was burning as usual?' I should have left well enough alone.

"The man said, 'Naw, sir. That old lamp was smokin' so bad you couldn't hardly see fifty yards in front of you. I got off at ever' station and wiped it off, but we couldn't go a quarter mile before it was all smoked up again.' "

Henry dropped his head to his chest in mock despair. John and Ben hooted with laughter and pounded the table. Annaliese grabbed her wobbling glass.

"Being sure that I had just lost the case, I didn't even make a closing argument to the jury. Next thing I know, the jury's back saying that they ruled in our favor. The judge, the distinguished Jackson Wiginton up from Royce Ridge district, was dumbfounded. He barked at the jury foreman, 'But the railroad was negligent!' The foreman said, 'We know that, Judge. But when that young fireman there told about that lamp, it was the first time we'd ever heard a railroad witness tell the truth in court, so we decided to reward him.' "

John pounded the table so hard his glass of bourbon fell over. Ben wiped away tears from his eyes, proclaiming Henry the only raconteur he had ever met whose skills surpassed his own.

For the rest of the meal, despite the women's steering attempts, Henry and Arthur drove the conversation all over the hills of the county with tales of hog stealing and ballot tampering. By the time Annaliese passed the dessert platter of dried cluster raisins and pecans, she realized that Lucenia had given up. Mr. Chastain was filling her in on the Meddling sisters, that "long, sad string of old maids." John lounged in his chair, soggy with bourbon. The candles were sputtering their last in shimmering pools of wax.

Annaliese turned to Arthur. "Mr. Garland, when I was at the courthouse, I saw a group of men standing around outside near the steps. They were dark-skinned and small. Looked different from everyone here, and yet they seemed like they knew the place. Might they have been Indians?"

"Probably, ma'am, what's left of 'em," Arthur said. "Army rounded up twelve thousand of them to walk them to Oklahoma but some of them escaped, hid in the hills till the Army was gone."

"Walk them to Oklahoma?" Annaliese asked softly.

Lucenia shot a look of shock at her.

"They keep to themselves a lot," Arthur said. "The blacksmith at the livery stable, he's a Cherokee."

"Where was their land?"

"Right here."

"This very land?" Annaliese's voice rose.

"Anna, the Cherokee nation was vast." It was John, coming to life down at the other end of the table. "It included eastern Alabama, middle Tennessee."

"Everyone knows that," Lucenia said.

"And it was 30 years ago," John said.

"I see," said Annaliese.

"Well, John," Henry said, putting his napkin on the table, "I hate to bring this entertaining evening to an end, but it's been a long day."

"I understand, Colonel." John slapped him on the back. "You tell the best damn stories. I haven't laughed this hard in a long time."

"Nor I," Ben said.

"Ladies, we do thank you for your gracious hospitality," Henry said.

"One more story before you go?" John asked.

"Very well. On my way out the door."

The party moved into the darkened hallway, where coats were picked up. John opened the front door into pitch black and everyone filed past him. Henry accepted from Ben a lantern he had just lit while Lucenia took the second one from her husband. On a distant tree, an owl hooted and the wind kicked up, but in their circle of light they were cozy and happily expectant, like children at a campfire.

"Henry, tell them the one about Bill Fudge," Arthur said.

"Ah, yes," Henry said. "Well, a number of years ago there was a representative in the Georgia legislature from one of our smaller counties here in north Georgia. Bill Fudge, the 'watchdog of the treasury' they called him because he fought most annual budget increases."

John, his hand wrapped around Annaliese's waist, was already chuckling. Ben had his handkerchief ready.

"One day, a bill was being put forward to increase the appropriation for the lunatic asylum, and he was actually for it. On the capital floor, he argued that we owed the unfortunates, flesh of our flesh and blood of our blood, the duty of care and attention, and that from his little Forsyth County, there were twenty people being cared for in the asylum."

John's hand came off his wife's waist.

Henry, looking at Lucenia and Ben above the glow of his lantern, continued. "A representative from a larger county asked, 'Mr. Fudge, why is it that your small county has twenty there and my county, twice as large, has only half that many?' And Fudge replied, 'Why, when a man from my county goes crazy we send him to the lunatic asylum, while if one in your county goes crazy y'all send him to the legislature.' "

Arthur and Lucenia crumpled with laughter, but Ben was blinking in instant sobriety, as was John. Annaliese caught the somber look they exchanged and then it was over. They brought their heads up to present polite smiles to Henry's joke, shook their heads in compliment, but Ben draped Lucenia's shawl over her shoulders as her cue to begin down the steps. Henry followed, not as smooth in his movements now, issuing thanks and compliments again. Finally, John came along behind him to gather Samuel and Emeline from the house. Watching him go, Annaliese hugged herself against the chill and the certainty that she had just seen something she wasn't meant to.

XIV

"Well, Emeline, today's the day," Ruth said. Her fingers worked Emeline's hair into a tight plait as they stood on the back porch.

The child was bent over a basket crammed with the five rabbits that had outgrown it weeks ago. Her head jerked back and forth with the pulling, but she managed to shake it. "Not yet, Rufe," she said as she reached in to stroke a long, silky ear.

"Now, we agreed on this yesterday and you know it. Them rabbits is all growed up. Time to let 'em go and be with God's other creatures. Then we'll take our little trip." Ruth tied off the first plait and set upon the other half of Emeline's hair.

Emeline's lower lip curled down into a pink crescent so exaggerated that Ruth had to laugh. Emeline huffed and went into a deeper hunch over the basket.

Darrison came rushing up the porch steps with news that Herschel was bringing the wagon. The girl glared at him. "I don't want to go."

James and Samuel arrived with the same news and received the same reception. They looked over at Ruth, weaving the end of the second plait now, and then down at the top of Emeline's head.

Samuel knelt beside his sister. "Emmie, Mama says we're lettin' them go home."

Emeline nodded slowly. "I know."

Annaliese's voice came through the kitchen window. "Did I hear my name?"

"Let's go, Aunt Anna," Darrison said. "Herschel's going to be here soon."

Annaliese came out the back door wiping her hands down her apron. "All right, I know." She kissed the top of Emeline's head. "But first things first. Ready Emmie?"

Emeline slid her tiny hands under a rabbit and held it, feet flailing, up to her mother. Annaliese tucked the frantic little feet into one hand and caressed the soft head with the other. "Just think how glad they'll be to see their cousins," Annaliese said. She cupped the rabbit's rear end in her hand and turned its face toward Emeline. "Just look at those happy eyes."

Emeline gave the second one to Samuel, muttering its secret name under her breath as she handed it over; her mother had forbidden her to name them. Then one went to James, one to Darrison. Finally, Emeline clutched the last one to her chest, stood up, and led the solemn procession toward Bunny Mountain. As they climbed the hill, they heard a porch door slam. Lucenia came running to join them.

In the shade surrounding the springhouse, the children bent down and relaxed their fingers until the rabbits hopped forward. The children gave little pushes, but the rabbits crept around for a moment. Then ears went up, heads flipped left and right, and the rabbits bounced off. Annaliese was the last to let hers go. As her children pried her fingers loose, she bent down and let the animal bound away.

Emeline backed into her mother's skirt. Her face clouded over. The lip came out again.

"Now don't you worry, baby," Ruth said. "There'll be more rabbits for us to find and raise in the warming drawer I reckon."

"Yay," Emeline yelled. She took Ruth's hand and they headed downhill to Herschel.

Behind them, Annaliese shot a look at Lucenia, whose face reflected her own feeling that Ruth was more child than woman still.

In seconds, all the children were in the wagon. Annaliese and Lucenia—settling into their seats—told them to sit down, threatened to leave them if they couldn't mind, which sent the boys back down, but only to their haunches. Herschel grinned as he turned the horses toward the mill.

Annaliese had promised Corinthia that the new school and furnishings would be in place by July 11. It was up to Corinthia to provide books and the teacher. Teacher candidates, rather, for she had warmed to Annaliese enough that she had agreed to let the Stregal women have a say in the hiring. Three recent graduates of the Normal School in Athens had made their way to Pinch and among them a Miss Johnson from Tennessee was the best in their estimation. They liked her mild, jovial way and her firm command of the King's English. Her description of her lesson plans was impressive, and she had the spunk and height it would take to intimidate the roughest mountain boys. Even Lucenia was impressed enough to put aside talk of boarding school. Corinthia gave the final approval, made the offer, and Miss Johnson would be moving into the living quarters behind the school as soon as it was finished, which was just days away.

The journey to the school was short—thirty minutes on the new road leading to the hill called Jackson's Thumb. Not a bad daily trip for the Stregal boys and Herschel. As for the other students who were scattered throughout the hills and still being hunted down by Corinthia for registration, they were used to walking long distances.

The sky sagged like sodden, gray gauze on the brink of dropping its load. No breeze stirred the trees. The birds were still and seemed on edge, as if waiting for others to sing first. Before the women and children left home, Ruth had stood on the porch, scowled at the sky and said, "I don't like it. Somethin's dead up the branch and it ain't got nothin' to do with the weather." Herschel shushed her in front of Annaliese, said nothing was going to happen, and hadn't yesterday's sky been just as dark and not a drop had fallen?

Annaliese knew there was no putting the children off any longer. So they loaded the wagon with four giddy youngsters and moved ahead.

Beneath the wagon's wheels, the cracked red clay made for rough going. Herschel looked at the fissured road and then up at the roiling sky. One cup of water could make a gallon of slick on a Georgia dirt road, but there was no thunder so far, and he knew that if a summer shower was going to roll in, it would most likely be in the afternoon, which was hours away.

The familiar road to Pinch soon offered up the new, raw road to the school on the right. Herschel guided the horses toward it, but their memories were stronger than his reins. They pulled to the left, toward Pinch, where food and water waited. Herschel pulled the right rein harder. His made his voice deeper.

"Now get on, Buttercup," he boomed. "It's me back here today. Not Ruth."

Buttercup finally bore to the right and the other horse had no choice.

All around them, the forest was so thick that three men could not have walked abreast. Annaliese leaned forward and peered down the road. She almost had the road's features memorized by now and she knew that after the next few bends the forest would open to reveal the valley to their right. She had heard the Stregal logging teams were working up there, but at the moment, she could not see beyond ten feet on either side.

"How much farther?" Darrison asked.

"A ways," Annaliese said.

"You are beginning to sound like them," muttered Lucenia at her side.

Twenty bone-jarring minutes later, they broke through the forest onto a rocky slope where the view opened onto Black Face Mountain. Herschel pulled the horses to a stop. A river swept through the narrow valley, cupping a few gray cabins in its bends. To the east, steep ridges furry with oak and pine climbed to the sky. But at the foot of the ridges, where the land sloped more hospitably, mules and loggers had moved in. What they had left behind looked like a face after a bad shave, all fresh stumps and red streaks. But the young trees had been spared, and workers had taken the time to drag debris and limbs into piles for burning, so there was some sense of order about the scene. Annaliese's gaze continued downhill. The muddy, vertical tracks of log slides led down to the river. To the west, the hillsides of Black Face mountain were untouched.

"My, they really are moving fast," she murmured.

"Good," Lucenia said.

"Mother, let's go," James shouted from the back of the wagon.

Herschel shook the reins at Buttercup. The wagon turned back toward the road.

A few minutes later, they came to a place where a brook cut a shallow but broad swath across their path. The sparkling water bounced over glistening pebbles and mossy logs. Buttercup flattened her ears and stopped.

"Aw, Buttercup," Herschel sighed, "we ain't havin' this."

He jumped off the wagon and grabbed the horse's reins to lead her into the water. Suddenly the wagon shifted as someone in the back jumped out, too. Darrison appeared at the other horse's head to grab its reins. Lucenia gasped and lurched forward toward her son.

Annaliese put her hand on Lucenia's wrist. "Let's just see," she said.

Darrison pulled, Herschel pulled harder, and Buttercup finally moved forward. The wagon rumbled over the cobbled brook. On the other side, after sharing a few words with Buttercup, Herschel came around the other horse to slap Darrison on the back. The boy beamed at everyone but his mother on his way back to the wagon

Finally, they arrived at the schoolhouse, where the wagons of several workers dotted the grounds. Horses turned their heads toward the arriving wagon's clatter. Two men carried desks up the stairs to the simple, one-room schoolhouse, behind which was the home for the teacher. The gray clapboard buildings blended seamlessly into the gray day. Annaliese had specifically ordered that the buildings be as plain as possible and unpainted, like most buildings in the county. Everyone would know that the Stregals had built them. For the sake of the Stregal children, the simpler the better.

A sign hung above the schoolhouse door: "The Corinthia Meddling Academy."

As usual, the three boys bounded out of the wagon without a hand offered to Emeline, so Annaliese came around to lift her out. Darrison and Samuel were already climbing the steps, trying to edge under the desks the men were easing through the door.

"You two, stop right there," Lucenia screeched.

The men smiled, for they were mill workers who knew the Stregal children. One of them said, "New teacher's here, Mrs. Stregal."

"What a nice surprise," Annaliese said. Then, to Lucenia as she joined her at the foot of the steps, "Looks like Miss Johnson is eager to get started."

"We'll tell her y'all are here," one of the men said. He and his partner pushed their load on through. For a few seconds, the doorway was vacant. Darrison elbowed past Samuel to the next step. Lucenia yanked him back. Then, they heard a female responding to the men.

The new teacher arrived at the door.

"Well, if it ain't the Mrs. Stregals," she said. A familiar gap-toothed smile spread across the pasty face. Her hair, still wispy as corn silk, floated around her head at its own will.

Martha.

Annaliese's brain shut down. The only thing that came to mind to say was, "Oh, no" and "You're a teacher?" So she said nothing.

"You're a teacher?" Samuel said.

Annaliese pulled him down the steps.

"And why wouldn't I be?" shot back Martha. She arched her back and tried to smooth her wild hair.

"What happened to Miss Johnson?" Annaliese blurted.

"Took sick." Martha crossed her arms and gazed down at them. "Or got married, one. Cain't rightly remember what Corinthia said."

"Corinthia." Immediately, Annaliese regretted her tone.

"My sister," Martha said saucily.

"Your sister. Ah, yes," Lucenia said. "It's all so anthropological, isn't it?"

The boys were inching back up the steps to see around Martha's skirts. Emeline suddenly darted in front of them. They tried to grab her and a wrestling match commenced.

"Emmie, boys, y'all come back here," Annaliese said.

"Why?" Darrison howled.

"We're not going in."

"What!" Samuel cried.

"Come here!" Annaliese said as she pointed to a spot in front of her.

The children inched back close enough to suit but filled the air with questions.

"We shouldn't bother the teacher right now," Lucenia said.

"Aw, it's just Martha," Samuel said.

"And you must call her Miss Meddling now."

"That's right," Martha said with a little bounce.

Darrison, watching the women struggling with their faces, turned toward Martha. "Boy, you sure are a lot better cook than Ruth."

"Sure enough?" Martha said with glee.

"Time to go." Annaliese sank her fingernails into Samuel's shoulder. The boy crumpled under her grasp. "Sam, say good-bye to Miss Meddling." She curled a finger at Emeline, who quietly came toward her mother's skirts.

"But . . . when are we coming back?" Samuel said.

"First day of school."

"But we just got here," Darrison said.

"We are leaving now," Annaliese said through clenched teeth. She took Emeline's hand and turned back toward the wagon.

Lucenia beckoned to her two sons, who stayed well beyond her reach.

"Bye now," Martha called out. "I sure do want to thank y'all for this here opportunity. Twenty-seven dollars a month."

Herschel squinted at the group returning to his wagon. He had not seen nor heard the exchange in the doorway, but it was clear enough that they were leaving. The women hurried the boys into the wagon. Annaliese pulled Emeline into her lap and squeezed her until she yelped. Herschel looped the wagon back into the path it had just made. Thunder rumbled in the distance.

"Corinthia's sister? Thessalonia's sister, too, then," Annaliese said.

"Then why didn't they name her 'Phillipia'?" Lucenia said.

"Different mamas," Herschel said.

"Miss Meddling," Lucenia muttered. "We have to call her Miss Meddling."

"That's the least of our problems," Annaliese said under her breath.

"Boarding school," Lucenia said

"No!" said the back of the wagon.

Herschel looked at the darkening sky and snapped the reins.

From the back of the wagon, the questions came flying, but the women only sent back vague answers. Eventually, the boys returned to throwing rocks and spitting on the wagon wheels. Emeline fell still in her mother's rocking arms.

They were still hunched in thought when Herschel stopped the wagon in front of Annaliese's home.

Ruth came out of the house wiping her hands on her apron. For the tenth time that day, she eyed the churning sky. She hurried down the steps to take Emeline from her mother's arms.

"Praise God y'all are home. Nothin' dead up the branch after all," Ruth whispered.

"Oh, yes there was," Annaliese said. She went to her porch, lowered her blind, and plopped down in a rocking chair. But a minute later, Lucenia, arms crossed, was standing in front of her.

"Don't say a word," Annaliese said. Her rocking stopped.

Lucenia walked up onto the porch. "You couldn't have known Corinthia wasn't to be trusted, dear, but had I been there when you and she came up with this plan . . ."

Annaliese held up a flattened palm. "And don't say boarding school again either."

Lucenia put her hands on her wide hips. "Wasn't going to."

Annaliese picked up her rocking again. Why hadn't Corinthia told her about the switch after all the care she had taken in selecting Miss Johnson? One couldn't just drop one teacher in for another, like changing socks. Her pitch to Corinthia had worked too well. Once the idea of her Meddling Academy took hold and the way was cleared, nothing was going to stop her from seeing that sign go up. And if Miss Johnson had suddenly made other plans—took sick indeed—well, what was wrong, in her hillbilly view, with hiring someone who was available and needed the work, never mind troubling oneself about credentials?

Worse, with Corinthia not to be trusted, she was back to one ally in the county, the one who stood beside her now tapping her foot, the one who had a stake in this, too. Annaliese softened a little.

"I don't mean to be so harsh, Lucenia. I'm just worried about what we'll do now."

Lucenia sat down.

"She'll be looking for us to do something spiteful," Annaliese said.

Lucenia raised her arms. "Let us endeavor not to disappoint her."

"But the boys will pay."

"But we'll get rid of her."

Annaliese had heard that before regarding Martha. She shook her head. "Perhaps John and Ben . . ."

Lucenia hit the arm of her chair. "John and Ben nothing. We are going to figure this out ourselves."

"All right, then. Let me think." She pointed a finger at Lucenia, then moved it in a slow arc to her porch.

Lucenia's eyes followed. "Very well, then." She stalked back to her house.

Annaliese said to her back, "We have to tell the boys something."

Lucenia went to her rocker and lowered her blind.

A few days before the school's opening, they made the trip again, this time loaded and cocked.

They saw Martha come to the doorway at the sound of the wagon. She raised her hand to shield her eyes against the morning sun and stared at the man on the seat between them, as she was meant to.

He stopped the wagon at the foot of her steps. A cloud of grit rolled in behind it, and everyone spent a while coughing and flailing at the summer dust. Finally, Annaliese and Lucenia got out of the wagon, each carrying a basket. The man lumbered out on the other side and tied up the horses.

"Good morning, Martha," Annaliese said.

"Lovely morning, isn't it?" Lucenia said.

Martha shrugged. "Hit's a hot one." She cut a quick look over at the man, still fiddling with the harnesses, then back to the women's baskets, full of something covered with blue kitchen dishcloths.

"We brought you a welcome present," Lucenia said. She lifted a dishcloth corner and held the basket out.

Martha came down the steps, took it and peeled back the cloth. Her eyes bounced from object to object before she pulled out a jar. "Dew of Youth Cream," she said. A smile bloomed on her hard face. Sitting down on a step, she put the basket on her knees and began pulling jars out.

So she can read, thought Annaliese. She shot a quick look over at the twitching Lucenia from whom she had pried these goodies.

Lucenia wagged a finger at the basket. "There's Parisian Hand Balm, the most fabulous face powder, some hairpins, Beulah's Wrinkle Magic, which is so hard to find . . ."

"Well, ain't that nice," Martha said. She pulled out the box of hairpins.

"The catalog's in there, too." Lucenia looked over at Annaliese.

"As for my gift," Annaliese said. "Something cuddly." She put her basket beside Martha.

Again Martha peeled back the blue cloth but this time could not hide her surprise. She lifted out a small rabbit, still dishrag limp from sleep, blinking its eyes at the sudden light. "Well," was all she said as she put it on the step. It sat up, raised its ears at her.

"It's quite socialized, thanks to the children," Annaliese said. "We released it, but it kept coming back. Not much of a watchdog, but good company, we hope."

"Well," Martha said again, but she finally stroked the soft, gleaming fur of its ears. While she did so, she looked over at the man with the horses.

Finally, he came around and stood off to the side. Martha stared at him with blatant interest.

"Oh, that's Floyd," Annaliese said as though she had forgotten he was there. Lucenia called him the mouthbreather. "He works at the mill, but we've asked him to help you with things at the school from time to time. Help with hauling, bringing you parcels, that sort of thing."

With three sets of ladies' eyes on him, Floyd went a little goofy in the shoulders for a minute, but he straightened and tried to look manly. He was slight in frame, fair-skinned and fair-haired, work-hardened in the arms. He took his hat off and grinned, which lit up his long, oval-shaped face.

"Hey," Floyd said. He raised a hand.

Lucenia smiled. He had been her idea.

Martha stood up, tried to smooth her hair and said, "Hey." She tilted her head to her shoulder, swayed the fleshy hips. "Where're you from?"

Floyd ran his hands along the brim of his hat. "Clayton County."

"So, everything's ready?" Lucenia said. "Books? Desks?"

Martha turned her attention back to her and nodded.

"Good," Annaliese said. "Well, Samuel and Darrison will be here first thing Monday morning. They certainly are excited."

Annaliese pointed to the sign. "I know Corinthia's excited, too, about her new academy."

Martha looked at the sign behind her. Corinthia was older by ten years.

"Sure would be a shame if anything happened that closed the school, wouldn't it?" Lucenia said. She swayed her own hips a little.

Martha's head nodded up and down slowly as the message sank in.

"Now, Lucenia," Annaliese said. "Don't be silly. What could happen?"

The wispy head turned back slowly, the eyes narrowed. "Thank ye for the presents," Martha said.

"See you Monday," Annaliese said. With a quick turn, she walked back to the wagon. Her skirt kicked up a little dust, as did Lucenia's. Floyd put his hat back on and, having had some time to look Martha over, turned without so much as a finger to his brim for her.

But Martha smiled as they drove away.

On the first day, Ben and John delivered their sons to the school-house. Martha made a show of waving the boys into the doorway heartily. After that, all the families could do was wait.

That afternoon when the boys returned, their mothers peppered them with questions. When nothing suspicious came forth, the women settled down and let them tell about classmates who rode mules to school and kept knives in their pockets. Bibles came to school, the boys said, for reading from every morning, and Sears and Roebuck catalogs, too. Everyone was barefoot. Some boys were way taller than Miss Meddling and had whiskers on their chins, not that that stopped her from cuffing their ears. Lucenia winced and shot a look over to Annaliese. Samuel said he was glad to be short.

The next morning, after Herschel had picked up the boys for their ride to school, Annaliese sat in her porch rocker, Venetian blind down. In her lap, a stack of stationery jostled as she bounced her foot. What would day two bring for Samuel? Would today be the day Martha showed her hand? She hoped not. So far, she did not have a backup plan.

Next door, Lucenia's Venetian blind clattered up. Against her better judgment, Annaliese peered around her blind. Lucenia returned her stare with insistent eyes. Annaliese acted as though she hadn't seen that and began writing a letter. Next door, the blind was zipping up and down.

Finally she threw down her pen, swept through the sea of hens at the foot of her steps and climbed Lucenia's steps.

"What," she sighed.

"Would you mind helping me with these butter beans?" Lucenia said sweetly. She scooped up bean pods from an apron spread across her lap. On the floor, shelled beans partially filled a blue-and-white enameled bowl.

Annaliese flopped down into a rocker beside her sister-in-law, scooped up a handful from a basket, and began slipping her thumbnail along the rim of a shell.

Lucenia put the bowl between them. "It's Darrison she'll go after, you know."

"What? And not Samuel?"

"Because of me."

Annaliese sighed and shook her head. "Let's wait and see."

"Nothing else we can do."

"Oh, I can't believe we are doing this on our front porches," Annaliese said.

"I can't believe we are doing this at all. My fingers are just ruined."

For a few moments, they silently mourned the loss of their smooth hands and smooth lives. They rocked slowly and worked their beans.

Lucenia suddenly dropped her hands into her apron. "I've been thinking about what you said about letting Darrison ride a horse."

Annaliese raised her eyebrows and looked over.

"But you have to bring the subject up with him because if I bring it up the idea will be dead on arrival. You'll ride with him?"

Annaliese smiled as she reached down to the basket for another handful. Running her thumbnail along the seam, she pressed until it yielded a trio of pale, shiny beans. They hit the side of the bowl and made the pinging sound she loved. "It would be a pleasure."

"All right, then." Lucenia's beans plopped into the bowl.

"And you'll be joining us?"

"Well, I've been thinking about that."

"Why are you afraid, Lucenia? My cousins and I never had one minute's trouble from a horse."

"You never fell off?"

"Well, yes, of course we fell off, but we just got back on. It wasn't the horse's doing."

"My father . . ." Lucenia's hands fell still. She leaned back and closed her eyes. "A horse killed my father."

"Oh, my God. Lucenia, I had no idea." She put her hand on her arm.

"Well, not directly."

Annaliese waited. Lucenia went back to her beans. Several minutes passed with only the sound of pinging into the bowl and the hens muttering in the yard. Annaliese even began to wish for Ruth The Inquisitor. Finally, she blurted, "What do you mean, not directly?"

"When I was ten years old, my father came home drunk one night. Well, he tried to come home. My mother wouldn't let him in the front door. He yelled that he was injured, not drunk, that he had fallen off his horse on the way home. All the boarders awoke, came down the stairs and gawked at my mother in her gown. I was mortified for her, but glad they were there, too, for if my father did get in, we would need their help. We darn well knew he was drunk again.

"Soon, he was at the back door, banging. I rushed back there just in time to see his arm breaking through the glass pane, his hand groping for the knob. He got the door open but he cut his arm badly in the process. He barreled inside, leaving a trail of blood. I saw an enormous gash that ran from his wrist to his elbow. He didn't get far before he collapsed."

Annaliese squeezed her arm again.

"One of the boarders cleaned up the gash and bandaged it. But it wouldn't stop bleeding. We didn't know what to do. It was the middle of the night, so late for fetching the doctor. The man wrapped a rag tightly around my father's arm, above the gash, and the bleeding stopped. We left him asleep on the floor."

Annaliese sucked in her breath. "Oh, no."

"In the morning, he was dead."

"The tourniquet."

"I know it doesn't make sense that I would be afraid of horses because of that." Lucenia finally looked over at Annaliese with eyes so full of pain that Annaliese was embarrassed. "In the morning, we saw bruises all over his right side. Looked like he *had* actually fallen off his horse. My ten-year-old mind linked that with his death, I suppose, though it was actually the whiskey."

Annaliese rubbed her hand up and down Lucenia's arm. "Perhaps it's time to face that fear. I can help you. There are some horses down at the mill yard. Not the riding kind, exactly, but we could see if they'd do."

"Won't Ben be surprised?" Lucenia's gentle laugh floated into the space between them. Her eyes were moist.

"Won't Darrison?"

Lucenia finished working her last pod and took off her apron. "I'll go get us some hand cream."

At the end of the day, the women again waited anxiously for the boys' return from school and again the boys reported nothing except that Miss Meddling had asked couldn't that Floyd fellow bring them to school next time. Herschel had brought the mail, too. Fingering through it, Annaliese found a letter with unfamiliar handwriting. The return address read, "Henry J. Chastain, Esq." She was surprised that he would write again so soon after his note for their hospitality. Perhaps an invitation? He wouldn't put an invitation on business stationery. In his own hand, Mr. Chastain had addressed the letter to Mr. and Mrs. John Stregal. She tucked the letter in her apron pocket and ran upstairs to her bedroom. She sat on the edge of the bed, her side. She studied the envelope again, lingering on the mark of his hand on the envelope: enormous, loopy letters in black ink. She imagined him finishing them with a flourish. Was he right-handed or left? She tore open the envelope.

Dear Mr. and Mrs. Stregal:

I have learned that Samuel and Darrison have acquired as a teacher a member of our community who is not known for letting bygones be bygones. Allow me to offer my condolences for this unfortunate turn of events, but most especially my professional services as necessary. This includes anything from legal advice to vile scheming, so long as my actions do not violate the Ten Commandments nor the Criminal Code of Georgia.

Most sincerely yours,

Henry Chastain (Colonel. Honorary.)

Annaliese fell backward with laughter. If they were going to need a hand, Henry's would be perfect. She returned the letter to the envelope and left it on John's side of the bed.

That night, John picked it up. "This is addressed to me," he said as he fingered its torn edges.

"And me," she replied as she flopped down on the bed. He was not going to dampen her mood tonight.

John looked at the envelope. With a weary grunt, he sat down on the bed.

"It's the cavalry coming over the hill," she said lightly.

As he unfolded the letter, she lay down and watched his face that bore the timber cruiser's two-tone—pale forehead and sunburned cheeks. Across his jaw, new flecks of silver flashed within the four-day beard he had allowed to grow, and she wondered about the toll the business was taking. Too proud to say, he bore everything silently and, she hoped, successfully. There had been no more demands from him of unwavering support.

A grin creased his tanned cheeks. He shook his head and chuckled. "This is silly. Martha was perfectly pleasant when we dropped the boys off the other day."

"Oh, surely you don't trust her! And that's not the point. Don't you think his letter is amusing?"

John rubbed his arms. "I suppose so, but I think you are making too much of her. We built the school. She knows who's in charge here."

Annaliese rolled onto her back.

John took his boots off and moved his hands toward his suspenders, but dropped them to his side instead. He turned to look at Annaliese. "Let me show you something." He walked around the bed and reached for her hand, leading her to the window that looked upon the bedroom of Ben and Lucenia only thirty yards away. Had Lucenia's curtains been open and several lamps going, the voyeurs would have been able to count the buttons on Ben's long underwear, but the room was dark. Annaliese didn't want to think about Ben in his underwear . . . or less. She squirmed a little, for she and John were backlit, visible to their neighbors who were not. John pulled her in front of him to look out the window and cupped his hands on her hips. He inhaled the night air, blew it against her ear and sucked in his next breath at the nape of her neck. For once, he did not smell like whiskey.

"Most nights, their lamps go out far earlier than ours. Ever notice that?"

She had, but she shook her head. "They're sleeping. I know I'm exhausted at this time of night."

"Doubt it. Ben is afraid of the dark, like Father was. Father went to sleep with the lamp on. The last thing he did each night was check to make sure it was full of kerosene. Anyway, Ben is not sleeping." His hands pressed harder on her hips.

Annaliese leaned back from the window. "They'll see us."

John was already shuffling backward, hands still on her hips and pulling her with him.

She pushed him lightly away. "Your imagination is filling in too many blanks." She lowered the blind.

John threw up his hands. "What, you don't think those two are capable of . . ."

"I don't want to think about them at all, thank you." Annaliese walked over to the bureau and pulled out a hairbrush. "I wanted to laugh with you about Mr. Chastain's letter." She began brushing her hair furiously. Moments later, she heard the bedsprings creak. In the mirror, she saw him sitting on the bed. Slowly, he pulled his suspenders off his shoulders, yanked off his pants, dropped them in a heap.

Through the window, the night sounds drifted in. Cricket songs rose and fell, *forte* and *piano*, in waves. Farther away, from a den hidden in a black mountain, came the thin, cat-like yips of foxes.

She washed her face and neck, undressed, and pulled on a gown. They climbed into bed in silence. As John dimmed the lamp, Annaliese asked, "Your father was afraid of the dark?"

She felt him settle back against her. "I should never have told you."

"Is there something you're afraid of John?"

Beside her, a deep sigh.

"Why do you run the mill so hard, work the men sunup to sundown?"

He rolled away. "Thought you were in a hurry to get this job done and get back to Louisville."

"Yes, but . . ."

John sat up. "We've just got to operate hell for leather, Anna, all right?" He stared off into the night. "In this business things change every day. Woodborers could eat away our future in a week's time. Blight could blow in. Fire." His words came faster and louder. "The feds are breathing down loggers' necks. They want to give us advice about selective cutting and what they call managing the forests." A puff of disgust exploded from his lips. "And if Teddy Roosevelt ever becomes president, he'll really clamp down on us." In the lamp's thin light, she could seem him shaking his head. "Gotta get in, get out with our take. That's all." He lay down again.

Shame washed over her. "I'm sorry," she said. Her hand reached over to his face to brush her fingers across his sunburned lips.

"Anna, I . . . " He leaned back down on one arm and looked over into her eyes for a long time. She strained to see them in the dark. "I love you," he whispered. "I do. More than the day I married you. I want you to know that."

His words fell on her face like a soft rain. It had been so long. In the early years, John had been open like this, but time it seemed had worn away the sweetest of words in his vocabulary. Now, into every pore, every parched cell of her body the honeyed words flooded again. It was a little strange that they came on the heels of Teddy Roosevelt, and in a back corner of her brain a tiny alarm was going off, but she pushed it aside. She went still, held her breath, the better to savor the words that still hung in the air and hope that he might say them again.

"I just want you to know that," he said. "And . . ."

She put her finger to his lips. "Ssh. Don't say anything else." She sat up to kiss him, felt his toughened lips push back. With one of her hands, she found one of his and brought it up to her hair to pull out the pins. One by one they fell on the bed until her hair was so wild he had to push it out of her face. John rolled on top of her.

"Wait, wait," she said. "Let me think."

"It's safe," John said as his hand swept over her breast. "Today's the seventeenth."

If she found it disconcerting that he had begun tracking her cycle along with board feet shipped out and receivables due, she pushed that aside, too. With her last focused thought, she counted and confirmed that it was the seventeenth and let John pull her gown over her shoulders.

☙

XV

July 22, 1901

Dear Mr. Chastain:

Thank you for your kind offer of assistance. A week of school has now passed without incident. Some actual learning seems to be taking place. In fact, Samuel and Darrison are even enjoying their Corinthia Meddling Academy experience. It appears, therefore, that we will not need to risk tarnishing your professional or religious reputation.

Mr. Stregal joins me in expressing our hope that you will be able to again join us for supper, perhaps following my return from my visit to Louisville, which I expect will occur in August at the end of the school term.

Very sincerely yours,

Mrs. John Stregal

The garden was at the height of its bounty in the middle of July, the hottest July any of the locals could remember. In the cool of the mornings, Ruth walked up one row and down the other, filling her basket with tomatoes and beans, pinching off dead leaves and suckers, fussing over the sickly. Emeline and James tripped along behind with itchy fingers, but they picked only what they were told.

One morning, the kitchen and the cooks were ready to process the first haul. Annaliese had four pots of water boiling on top of the stove.

At the sink, Lucenia rinsed the last of the mason jars and lined them up beside it. Colanders, baskets, and enameled bowls covered the center table. First stop was the iron tub of water on the back porch, where the children washed off the dirt. Then they carried the vegetables into the kitchen for a serious scouring. All morning long, the women fought the flies and the heat to put up as much as they could before noon. One by one the green glass jars were filled to the brim and sealed. Ruth smiled broadly as she wrote, for the first time in her life, the names of her vegetables on labels. One by one she tucked the jars of okra, tomatoes, and beans gently onto the pantry shelves, as though they were eggs on glass. A little after noon, the three women and two children, soggy with sweat, stood at the pantry door and smiled at their work.

Martha was beginning to deliver as well. Darrison reported that she had smacked a ruler over his knuckles. What his crime was, he had no idea. All he could see was that she was sweating a lot, he said. The next day, both boys came home sunburned and thirsty. She had put them outside on the steps for the afternoon because they could not recite from the Bible, which the other children knew backwards and forwards. Annaliese and Lucenia sent a note with Floyd reminding her that the curriculum called for the use of the textbooks. A few days later, the boys came home shaky with hunger. They wasted no time climbing out of Floyd's wagon and racing to Ruth and her kitchen. Floyd told the mothers the story.

Miss Meddling had accused Darrison of slipping crickets into her bedroom window. She hadn't gotten a lick of sleep, she had said as she glared at Darrison. While the other students hid smiles under their hands, she had scooped up Darrison's dinner pail and marched outside. The children heard the outhouse door open and close. They went wild with laughter. She came back in and handed him the pail. At the meal break, Samuel had shared his food with Darrison.

Floyd sat in the wagon seat and shook his head after he finished.

Lucenia crossed her arms and looked at her sister-in-law. "What did I tell you? Just Darrison."

Annaliese's fury fell on Floyd, who snapped to attention when he saw the finger she aimed at him. "Floyd, tomorrow morning, you tell her that if she so much as looks crossed-eyed at these boys, someone will slip something much worse than crickets in her bedroom window."

"Yes, ma'am," Floyd said, nodding frantically. "Sure will."

"She won't for a moment believe that," Lucenia said.

"Well, she might back off for a while and a while is all we need. The end of the term is just a few weeks away. Before we leave for our trip, we'll talk to Corinthia about finding another teacher."

Lucenia kicked some dirt at Floyd. "You were supposed to sweet talk her."

Floyd hooted. "Ain't a man in the next three counties that would take her on. Her nor none of them Meddling sisters."

"Well, it didn't take you long to learn that," Lucenia said.

"Gaw, they talk too dang much. Biggity, too. Turnin' off the lamp at night don't fix everything." He gave a lecherous grin without a hint of shame about the line he had just crossed.

Annaliese dared not look at Lucenia. "Well, we'll get her attention somehow," she said.

Cooling winds rolled down from North Carolina, Miss Meddling stopped fanning and sweating, and a week passed quietly, then another. The end of the brief summer term arrived.

For the last day of school, Herschel had asked to pick up the boys. He hurried through his chores and Annaliese tried not to notice. She was afraid that he wanted to leave early because he feared that Martha would save the best for last. Ruth, too, seemed tense. Her usual lilting gospel songs had today been songs of woe and pleas for divine protection. When it was time for Herschel to go, Annaliese watched Ruth murmur in his ear, pat his bony back. He nodded and turned the horses down the road.

The waiting seemed like days. The women kept busy washing clothes and packing. Finally, they heard Herschel's wagon coming. They rushed to their porches and saw right off that something was odd. The boys were sitting still, and they were up front in the seat with Herschel. Something wasn't right about the way they sat, bumping stiffly into Herschel as the wagon bounced along, heads down.

The wagon rolled to a stop. The boys' eyes were still on the ground and they were just too quiet—hands clasped between their knees, shoulders hunched, and eyes glazed. The women's eyes flew across the boys' bodies, but there wasn't a mark on them.

"Samuel?" Annaliese said. She hurried down the steps.

"I swear," Ruth said. "What are y'all so hang dog about?"

Herschel dropped the reins and looked over at Darrison. "Tell 'em."

Darrison stood up, then Samuel, as creaky as war veterans. Turning to climb down, Samuel cried out.

Annaliese and Lucenia rushed to the side of the wagon.

"What's wrong with y'all?" Annaliese cried.

For Samuel, the sight of his mother was too much. His eyes finally teared up and he reached for her. Though she did not trust her shaking arms, she pulled the whimpering boy down from the wagon.

"She switched 'em," Herschel said. "Took a hickory stick to their legs. That is the meanest, sorriest woman."

"Ow, ow, ow," Samuel wailed as his mother lowered him to the ground.

"Let me see," she said.

Samuel turned around and tugged his knee pants up a little. Red welts streaked the backs of his legs.

Lucenia ran to put her arms around Darrison. "You, too?"

"Yes, ma'am," Darrison said. He showed her the backs of his legs, scratched and swollen.

Lucenia pulled her son into her shelf of a bosom. "What on earth happened?"

"We didn't start it, Mother," Darrison said.

"Start what?" Ruth asked.

"The fight."

"Aw, Darrison, it weren't no fight," Samuel said.

"*Wasn't* a fight," Annaliese said. "What fight?"

"We just shoved Harley Wilkins back, that's all," Darrison said.

Ruth sucked her breath in between clenched teeth. "Not a Wilkins," she whispered.

"For what? Darrison, must you make this so hard?" Lucenia pleaded.

"Harley was saying things to rile me. About the logging..." Darrison paused to watch his mother's face, "... saying Papa was cutting down too many trees, running off the game, robbing them of their food."

"He said it was the devil's work," Samuel cried.

"Devil's work, nothin'," Ruth said. "Them Wilkinses never seen the inside of a Bible. They steal ever'thin' they eat. And more."

"And then he shoved me," Darrison said, with a wary eye on Lucenia.

"And you shoved back," she said. "Good for you!" She grabbed his shoulder and shook him.

Darrison's eyes went wide. "Yea, and then Sam showed up so he got shoved."

"But you were the only two she whipped, weren't you?" Annaliese asked.

"Yes, ma'am," Darrison said.

Annaliese gently rolled up Samuel's pant leg. "Ruth, look at this."

Ruth gasped at the boy's bleeding calves. "Let's get some pokeroot juice on that," she said. "Y'all come on with me." She led the boys, bow-legged and tentative, up the steps into Lucenia's home.

Lucenia kicked the wagon wheel. "That's it. Do what you want, Annaliese, but it's boarding school for Darrison Stregal." She picked up her skirts and ran up the stairs to follow Ruth.

Annaliese swung around to Herschel. "You go back and tell that woman she's got one hour to pack up and get out."

"Might want to think on that a while, Miss Annaliese," Herschel said.

"Why?"

"Might be best if you can figure a way to make her want to leave. Martha and her kin ain't never been known to let a good grudge go to waste."

She stared at him, certain that he was right and equally certain that Henry Chastain would be getting another letter from her.

The next day, six Stregals dressed for travel stood once again on Pinch's train depot platform, this time with the town at their backs. John and Ben walked out to their families from the depot office, having sent telegrams to those who would meet them. Samuel pulled John's watch out of his father's pocket and Annaliese snuck an anxious look over the boy's shoulder. Three minutes to go. Even the ache of her corset could not dilute her excitement. She looked over at Lucenia, who had found a bench in the shade and beckoned Emeline over to sit on her lap.

Finally, a whistle drifted in from the forests. Emeline jumped down from Lucenia's lap and ran for her mother's hand.

"Bye, Papa," James shouted as he reached up for his father's damp neck. Ben dabbed a handkerchief around his collar and went down to one knee to accept the thin arms.

John had his hand on Samuel's wiggling shoulder. "Now, Samuel, I don't like sending your mother off unescorted like this, so you take good care of her for me."

"Yes, sir." Samuel nodded, straightened his shoulders.

The rumble beneath their feet grew stronger. Again the whistle, closer now, blasted through the air.

Annaliese turned to John to press her cheek to his. He had had a rough night. Unable to sleep, he left their bed around 1:30 and had not returned. That made four fitful nights this week. As she looked at his weary face, something behind him caught her attention—the depot's waiting room door bursting open. Henry Chastain barreled through. Annaliese recognized that energy. For the first time, she realized that Henry reminded her of the John she had married, the John with strategy.

"I heard y'all were down here," he bellowed above the screeching wheels. "Did John get it in writing that you're comin' back?" He tipped his hat to Annaliese, then Lucenia.

"Henry!" John roared. "Good to see you."

"Why, Mr. Chastain," Annaliese said. "Of course, we'll come back. We have unfinished business to take care of." She gave him a long look. "Mr. Stregal will tell you."

Henry shot back a smile. "Oh? Very well. I'll be lookin' forward to that."

The train pulled alongside the platform, sending everyone backward to escape the billowing steam and grit. The final round of arms thrown around necks, cheeks patted, and good behavior promised swept through the family, ending with John pulling Emeline up into his arms. Finally, as the conductor leaned out to urge everyone aboard, he put her down. He held Annaliese in his embrace too long for the eyes watching, too long for propriety, too long for the woman in his arms eager to get on with the journey but afraid to leave him, too.

Henry Chastain stared at his shoes.

Lucenia climbed the car steps, followed by her sons and finally, Annaliese. A conductor in the doorway looked them over and directed them to their private car at the end. Soon, they were all in their seats waving to the men. Annaliese smiled down at them, noticing that John was the shortest of the three. He peered up at her, his face sunburned and leathery, from under a weathered hat coated with red powder. His tanned neck disappeared into a blue work shirt already ringed under the arms with sweat. Suddenly, he looked like the wood hick he was proud to be, while Henry stood a head taller and crisply professional in a suit and white shirt. Framed by the window, the men seemed to her to be subjects in a photograph shot as a study in contrasts. The train began pulling away. With increasing anxiety, she watched John grow smaller, darker, stranger. When he disappeared from view, she burst into tears.

Samuel leaned over to put his hand on her shoulder.

The other boys piled up at the window. They began naming the mountains, accurately and not, that rose into view. A hawk rose out of a treetop. "Red tail," James said. Brush-stroked clouds streaked a brilliantly blue sky. Annaliese stood to open the window and took a long, deep breath. Sitting down again, she looked over at Lucenia, bosom rocking, hat feathers bobbing.

"Has it truly been only five months?" Lucenia asked. She took off her hat to let her head fall back against the leather headrest. Emeline slid off the seat, stepped on Lucenia's boots, and began petting the feathers on the hat in her lap. Lucenia watched her quietly and smiled.

"How many times I've imagined going home," Annaliese said. How many times she had pictured her arrival at Louisville's station, seen her family and friends waiting for her there, tasted Aunt Gert's cooking, felt her smooth sheets. "I will indulge myself in every luxury I can find," she laughed.

"The first thing is . . ." Lucenia whispered in the tone of a starving man describing a roasted leg of lamb, "a professional shampoo. Hot water, oceans of it. Someone's fingers on my scalp." She closed her eyes.

That night, all four children were asleep an hour after sundown. Annaliese washed her stockings, took down her hair, and stepped into the sitting area to see if Lucenia was there. She was, in her gown and robe, looking out the window. Annaliese came out to sit on the facing seat and join her in vacant staring into the night. She didn't want to talk. She just didn't want to be alone. Despite the narcotic lull of the rocking train, she could not let go of the image of John at the train station, bleary-eyed, melancholy, shaky. Perhaps others did not see him as bleakly as she did. Perhaps she was worrying about nothing.

Lucenia tucked her feet under her. "We saw you two looking into our window."

She spoke in such a detached way, in a tone so flat, that Annaliese was too puzzled to respond.

Lucenia leaned forward and put her hand on Annaliese's knee. "Back in July . . . our bedroom window."

Blood shot up her neck and flooded her cheeks. "We didn't see a thing. I mean . . . not that we were looking." *What rot. John was looking.*

"Admiring the curtains then, were you?" Lucenia murmured with a smile. "It's all right. We knew you couldn't see us. We just hoped you wouldn't *hear* us."

Once again, Annaliese cooly regarded this woman so unlike any other she had ever known. Didn't she know that erotic pleasure was dangerous? Everyone knew that it distorted a woman's judgment. (Well, she *had* married Ben Stregal, so there was clear proof that this was so.) On the other hand, Lucenia's moral fiber could not be questioned. She was imperious, no argument, but not depraved. Even when painted, she did not actually *do* anything scandalous, at least not in public.

"All right, we won't speak of it if it disturbs you so." Lucenia picked up a hairbrush and pulled it through her brown hair.

But she did want to speak of it. If Lucenia was enjoying some form of entertainment in those hills with no theater, no debutante spectacles, no Belgian chocolates, and not even a thin newspaper, then Annaliese wanted to know more. Over the years with John, she had felt stirrings of pleasure now and then, just enough to hint at the hysteria she had heard about and might be hers if John would just slow down and match her rhythm, but she had never been able to ask him for what she needed, not that she really knew exactly. But Lucenia surely did.

"So . . ." Annaliese's voice was barely a whisper. "Tell me. It's pleasurable?"

"Well, given certain preliminaries." Lucenia's enormous breasts and hips shimmied under her nightgown. "Does that surprise you? My dear, do not think that one does not enjoy that of which one does not speak."

Annaliese smiled. Lucenia spoke of it every chance she got.

Lucenia took this as encouragement. "Even better, there is an undeniable utility to it."

A circus monkey could lead Ben around.

"With control over the bedroom and heirs, there is no question who's in power. I find that the most pleasurable part of all."

"Tell me." Annaliese was leaning so far forward she had to catch herself from slipping off the leather seat. She was fourteen years old again, listening to Irene and Dorothy in the night as they filled the dark with questions and fished for answers that none of them had. Now, finally, she had someone who did.

"The first thing is birth control, of course. You've heard of a womb veil?" Lucenia said.

Annaliese hadn't, didn't think the Pope would approve, but she wasn't going to stop Lucenia now.

❧

XVI

For the next two days on the train, she savored the image of her family meeting her at the station. Uncle Edward's oldest son, Ted, would bring his sister Kathryn and Dorothy for sure, and perhaps even Irene and her new baby. Once again she would be fretted over, indulged. Bags would be taken from her poor, cracked hands. Meals would be put in front of her. Pressed blouses would appear in her closet.

But on the last day, as she and the children finished supper in the dining car, she began to see Samuel and Emeline through Louisville eyes. Elbows on the table. Sticky fingers wiped on the tablecloth. The children were getting rough. Was she? Her face was freckled. Nothing to be done about that, and her hands looked like an old woman's. Kathryn for certain would notice and she would say something. Kathryn was like that. It was a miracle that she had survived for thirty-seven years without someone strangling her.

Five miles out from Louisville, Annaliese pulled on gloves.

At the sight of them on the platform—the large knot of Connelleys bustling about and craning their necks—she cried, ending her trip in the same soggy way she had begun it. As Lucenia spotted the Connelleys, she looked back from the window at Annaliese with soft, wet eyes. "Providence truly shines on you, my dear," she said.

A porter came to their door and gave a perfunctory salute. Lucenia stood up to tie Emeline's bonnet beneath her chin. Annaliese was up, too, handing Samuel a small leather valise. In the parlor, Darrison and

James hung back to watch quietly. The train rolled to its stop. The women faced each other, mirror images of awkwardness. They fell into a stiff embrace and pulled away quickly. At the door, Samuel whined to go. Finally, Annaliese managed, "Well, see you in two weeks." Lucenia nodded and patted her shoulder.

They flew down the steps and were immediately swallowed up by the family. Ted patted Samuel on the head until the boy had to duck away. Someone else had Emeline off her feet within seconds. As the train pulled away, Annaliese could only raise a gloved hand above feathered hats and her cousins' shoulders and hope that Lucenia had seen it.

By the time the two carriages pulled up to the Connelley home, the blue fingers of evening shadows were creeping across the manicured lawn, but the three-story home at the top of the hill blazed like a lighthouse. To the children, who had forgotten about electric lights, the warm glow streaming from every window seemed as startling as fire. But Annaliese brought her hands to her face in relief. Electricity meant ice boxes, ice cream, phonograph music, and finally tubs and tubs of hot water.

Ted pushed open the carriage door, got out and turned to help her down. Just before her feet touched the brick walk, she looked down for cow manure. When the children tumbled out and did the same, Ted threw his head back and laughed.

Inside, she found the merry bedlam she had hoped for. The house was throbbing with piano playing and a gang's singing in a far-off room. Her cousins Clark and Michael came running down the hallway, elbowing each other for Annaliese's first kisses. Eighteen and twenty years old, they were the last of the brood still living at home, but their bodies were men's. Annaliese began backing up. Clark got to her first. He threw gangly arms around her neck and gave her a jolting kiss. From the front door, Ted bellowed at them to help him with the trunks. Michael stole a kiss, too, then headed toward Ted.

Annaliese took off her gloves. "Mother?" she called out. "Aunt Gert?" From the dining room doorway, her mother rushed at her with open arms, squeezed her for a long, long moment, then pulled back to look her over.

"Anna, darling," Eleanor said. "I can't believe you're home."

Annaliese pulled her mother's hands into hers. "Nor can I."

"You look so well." Her eyes went up and down her daughter's body. "I told you."

Annaliese fanned at her face to stave off tears. A little croak escaped her throat.

Dorothy and Kathryn came up from behind, brushing off road dust. "Doesn't Annaliese look wonderful, Aunt Eleanor?" Kathryn said. "Look at her freckles."

Eleanor squeezed Annaliese's hands. "Yes, so I see. Thank God." Her eyes shifted to look beyond Annaliese. "Where are the children?"

"Right here," Kathryn said. She stepped away from the doorway and moved her skirt to reveal Samuel and Emeline.

They stood glued to the doorstep, blinking. Annaliese knew that they were overwhelmed by the noise and bodies and lights, though Samuel was timidly scanning the hall for his cousins. Four boys swarmed in with marbles to share. Emeline grabbed her brother's hand. As they all ran up the staircase, Annaliese saw her uncle beaming at her from the parlor doorway.

"Welcome home, Anna," he said. He took her face in his hands. "My little pioneer."

"A reluctant one," Annaliese laughed. Her cheek pressed against his.

Her aunt came out of a door at the back of the hallway, removing her apron as she came.

"Aunt Gert!" Annaliese shouted.

Gertrude wrapped her arms around Annaliese. "At last. Home!"

A wave of smells came off Gertrude: bread, onions, roasted meat. *Please, God*, Annaliese thought. *Let it be anything but ham.*

"Oh, my gracious, look at you." It was Irene coming downstairs. "So slender and brown."

Gertrude stepped back to let them grab each other. "Supper in an hour, darling. Silk sheets on your bed." She headed back down the hall.

They planted kisses on cheeks and hair, stood in the foyer swaying in joy. Dorothy joined them. Annaliese realized how dear the physicality of females was. The warmth, the comfort of unguarded embrace was so pure.

"How is it there, 'Liese?" Irene asked.

Annaliese looked at her sister and Irene and thought, *Where to start?*

"Oh, what am I thinking?" Irene asked. "Plenty of time to talk about that later. You must be exhausted. Let me help you upstairs." Irene pressed lightly on her back to urge her toward the stairs. "Come on before Clark brings out that awful banjo."

From the parlor, male voices erupted in laughter. Another Connelley bash was rolling.

Passing one of the bedrooms, Annaliese heard Samuel's voice. She stopped to listen.

"Sure we see snakes. I'm not afraid of 'em. Herschel says he's going to show me how to pick one up by the tail and snap its head off."

"Aw, go on," someone said. A round of grunts followed.

"Well, he will. Soon as I get back."

Another round of muttering.

"And I know how to find a bee that's going back to its hive. Ruth showed me that."

"So?"

"So that's how you find the honey. Ain't you never had honey?"

Annaliese winced at the grammar.

"No."

"Well, you go to the creek and wait to see a bee at the water. Then you follow him back to the hive. Bees always head straight back from water to the hive."

"Hey, Brian, give me back my cannon."

They were fifteen sitting down for supper. The table, with all extensions locked on, groaned under the silver and candelabra and china. Uncle Edward's prayer of grace included thanks for Annaliese's safe return. She settled back into her chair, savoring the sight and smells of a meal as only one who has not prepared it can. It was going to be standing rib roast.

As the servants lowered brimming platters to the diners, Edward turned toward his niece.

"How does the lumber business seem to be going, Anna?" he asked.

Annaliese looked up from tucking a napkin under Emeline's chin. "Quite well. The mill's operating six days a week and the railroad cars are bursting at the seams, hauling it all away."

Edward nodded with satisfaction. He smoothed a napkin onto his lap. "I knew the demand was out there. I just wasn't sure . . ."

"That John could operate a business?" Ted said barely under his breath. He waved at one of his brothers to pass the salt.

Edward frowned at Ted and turned back to Annaliese. "Of course, John is such a smart man."

"Well," Annaliese said, ". . . it has been a lot for him to take on, learning how to cruise timber, oversee a hundred men, sell our products." *Our* products. "You should see him in his mountain clothes. He's having a good time of it."

"And what about you?" her mother asked.

"Me?" Annaliese said. "Oh, I've learned how to kill chickens . . ."

"What?" Kathryn said.

". . . and plant by the signs."

"The what?" Irene asked.

"And I've learned so much about animals." Annaliese decided she wouldn't mention womb veils.

Samuel came to life. "Did you know that hogs love to eat snakes?"

A groan went around the table. Even the men looked disgusted. Annaliese winked at her son as she put a forkful of potatoes in her mouth.

Samuel started waving his hands. "And we had a mountain lion in our back yard."

Annaliese's throat clamped down.

"I knew it," Ted said.

"Dear God," Aunt Gert said.

"How exciting!" Eleanor said.

"He was trying to get Emmie in the chicken coop," Samuel said.

The table exploded.

"Sam," Annaliese said as soon as she got the potatoes down. "That's enough. I'll tell them."

Around the table, faces settled on her.

"A mountain lion was in the yard, it's true. No one was hurt. Got shot dead. That's all. We have put up a fence. Now . . . we're fine." She sent Samuel a shushing look.

"Mama shot him," Emeline said.

"Merciful heavens," Aunt Gert said.

For once, Annaliese's mother was speechless.

"Where was John?" Uncle Edward said.

Annaliese pushed peas around on her plate. "He was there, trying."

The table fell quiet, though the men looked at one another.

"Well, I told you she learned how to shoot," Eleanor said.

Forks and knives got busy again.

Annaliese put hers down. "You know what? I would like to receive more letters from y'all."

"Aw, Anna, nothing ever happens here," Clark said.

"I have some news," Dorothy said.

All heads turned to the end of the table, where Dorothy and her husband, Phillip, sat.

"We've heard the Atlantic and Pacific Tea Company is coming to town," Dorothy said.

"In the mercantile and produce business for ten years, but now we're going to lose customers for sure," Philip said.

"Could be," Patrick said. "They're known for buying huge amounts of food, right from producers."

"Hard to beat their prices," Dorothy said.

Annaliese dabbed her napkin to her mouth. "Well, what can you do?" *At last. Something that wasn't her problem.*

"We're organizing a hometown boosters association, that's what," Dorothy said.

"You are?" Eleanor turned to look at her oldest daughter with new regard.

Ted stood, picked up a bottle of wine from the sideboard, and began refilling wine glasses. "Going after that new rural free delivery law, too? That's got to cut into your mercantile sales."

"Can't get that repealed. They just passed it," Edward said.

"What are y'all talking about?" Irene asked.

"A new law says the postal service has to deliver parcels to all homes, even rural. People are ordering everything out of those infernal catalogs," Philip said.

"Oh, yes," Annaliese said. "We are . . ."

Dorothy threw up her hands. "It's not right. Every Bubba and Ida Bell in the sticks has access to anything now. Mail order is going to ruin merchants everywhere."

"Is that so?" Annaliese said with just enough ice to make Dorothy look startled.

"Please pass the peas," someone said, and the conversation moved on.

The next morning, Ted drove them to their home several blocks away. As he brought in their trunks, Samuel and Emeline ran upstairs to their old rooms. Annaliese roamed downstairs for a while, lifting sheets off the chairs and tables and throwing windows open. The house without the maids and their carpet sweepers, the cook's singing kettle, the butler at his pantry disturbed her, and it wasn't the quiet. She went to the dining room and pulled out of the breakfront a yellow tablecloth, spread it across the table despite the dust, and turned on all the lights for more cheer. But she still felt there was something wrong. She heard the children upstairs—barely—and she understood. They were too far away from her when they were beyond that wide staircase and down that vast hall. The house didn't fit them anymore.

Ted came upstairs from the basement to say that the hot water heater was on and she hugged him so hard he gave her a puzzled look.

They stocked the pantry with the provisions she had ordered and he left. Soon, the neighbors were over with covered dishes. She smiled through their questions about mountain life, questions she might have regarded as insulting had she not asked the same ones five months earlier.

One afternoon, Annaliese and Dorothy set out for the library. The humidity hung on Annaliese like a horse blanket, a suffocating part of Louisville's August she had forgotten. She wanted to roll up her sleeves and open her collar, which was out of the question here.

Their carriage let them out at the commercial district and immediately Dorothy began pulling her too fast past the window displays that she longed to see, but she knew there would be no peace until Dorothy showed her. As the women turned a corner, Dorothy stopped.

"There it is." She pointed at a red and gold sign on the largest store on the block.

The sign read, "The Great Atlantic and Pacific Tea Company." Smaller signs around the doors announced "Lower prices" "Free Delivery" and "Premiums for Lucky Customers." Green parrots swung from gilded swings in the windows.

"They sell fresh vegetables?" Annaliese asked.

Another sign announced "Band Music on Saturdays."

"And soap flakes and condensed milk and baking powder," Dorothy said. The women began moving toward the store.

"But y'all offer reliability and credit, Dottie. Do they?"

"People don't seem to care about credit so much anymore. The economy is strong now. They have money in their pockets. Look around." Dorothy swept a hand toward the street. Well-dressed men and women flowed in and out of the store's giant doors. "Look at those clothes. Made by machines now. It's getting hard to tell who belongs to our class and who doesn't. You certainly can't tell by the cut of their coat any more."

As they passed the store, Annaliese tried to look inside without too much eagerness. The place was packed with people trying to move through the aisles.

Dorothy grumbled all the way to the library.

Inside the hushed central corridor, the sisters separated. Annaliese walked to the card catalog files and pulled out one long drawer of cards. Minutes later, she was in the history section in the basement. The stone floors and walls radiated a chill that had attracted a dozen or so patrons who read quietly at a long table. She searched the shelves and pulled out what she was looking for.

"The History of Georgia, chapter one:

"Before the first white settlers came to the New World, Cherokee Indians claimed a nation that stretched over more than 124,000 square miles. Centered over northwest Georgia and northeast Alabama, it also covered parts of Tennessee and North Carolina. By 1721, the Europeans and the Cherokee had made the first of many cessions and treaties. After the American Revolutionary War, the Cherokee paid the price for allying with the British; they were forced to give up some of their most cherished land. By 1819, the Cherokee nation consisted of about 17,000 square miles, most of it in northwest Georgia. By then, the federal government had made a deal with the state of Georgia to remove the Indians in exchange for Georgia's ceding to the United States its huge tract of western land beyond the Mississippi.

"As the government pondered the Indian Removal issue, Georgia Cherokees began adopting the white man's lifestyle. They operated businesses and farms; some even owned Negro slaves. White missionaries helped them advance their education, made possible by the alphabet that their chief, Sequoyah, had developed for them. In 1828, they began publishing their own bilingual newspaper, the Cherokee Phoenix. *Firmly rooted in Georgia, the Cherokee were resistant to removal and drafted their own constitution in the hope of formalizing their independence. In the same year, the Georgia legislature ordered that this law be replaced with Georgia law.*

"The discovery of gold in the north Georgia mountains a year later triggered a rush of thousands of whites into the area. Anti-Indian sentiment had reached a fevered pitch. Finally, in 1830, the U. S. Congress

passed the Indian Removal Act, forcing the government to finally fulfill its promise. There were approximately 17,000 people of the Cherokee Nation at this time.

"In 1832, Georgia held a land lottery, which assigned Indian land to white settlers. Despite continued resistance by many Indians, the U. S. Army rounded up approximately 12,000 Cherokee in 1838. Over the next few months, thousands of them died on their trek to Oklahoma, commonly referred to as the Trail of Tears."

Annaliese stared off toward the milky trail of sunlight streaming in the one window. Only a few generations ago. Could be some of those who walked to Oklahoma were still alive, still grieving for those who died along the way, for their homes and property stolen. Perhaps some had returned somehow to Georgia. She had stared into the dark eyes of their kin, the men standing at the Pinch courthouse, and she lived in the pristine hills these people had cherished. How could she not have known about this sordid legacy of greed and cruelty?

She turned the page for more, but that was the end of the entry on the Cherokee.

But a chapter entitled "Vigilante Groups" caught her eye. She thumbed to it.

"Georgia history has long been marked by collective violence. Vigilantes assisted federal troops in driving the Indians out of north Georgia. During the War Between the States, squads of home guards were organized to keep order. After the war, a Ku Klux Klan formed to pay retribution on Union sympathizers.

"The group's method of disguising themselves in black or white hoods and capes and intimidating their victims at night earned them the nickname of 'night riders' or 'white caps.' Its purpose soon expanded into punishing general rural lawlessness or protecting a woman's virtue. When the federal government increased pressure in the late 1870s on brewers of homemade whisky to pay revenue taxes, nightriders soon rode again. Their goal was to punish informers.

"*As recently as the 1880s and 1890s, the night riders expanded their purpose to include the punishment of people whom they consider immoral.*"

Annaliese slumped against the shelf. The Klan she of course knew about and detested, but she did not know that it had thrown its net of hate and violence so wide, beyond race and religion to women's virtue and immorality, however they defined them. Ruth had never told her about such a threat, though Lucenia's paint had certainly kept tongues busy throughout the county. As recently as ten years ago nightriders were still riding, this book said, so was Herschel talking about that when he warned about Martha's grudges not going to waste? That she would unleash the wrath of her kin? Annaliese imagined uncles and cousins slipping on hoods and riding into the hills to punish an innocent neighbor.

Martha.

Punishment.

She slammed the book closed. *No, no. It's too hideous to even think about.*

Annaliese returned the book to the shelf. *But Mr. Chastain offered his help.*

She walked out to the stairwell and paused, hand on the rail. *It would be so wrong. Scaring Martha with nightriders, even pretend nightriders. Horrible. There has to be some other way to scare her enough to leave.*

But at the top of the stairs, she thought about the lashings on Samuel's legs, still healing. *Would Mr. Chastain even do such an illegal thing?*

Dorothy was waiting for her at the card catalog. "Find what you needed?" she asked.

"Yes," Annaliese said. "I'm afraid I did."

❧

XVII

"How many days until we go home, Mama?" Samuel spoke to his mother's reflection in the bedroom mirror as she stood behind him trying to brush his hair.

"Why, we are home, Sam," Annaliese said. She dipped the brush in the basin of water on the dresser and stabbed again at his moving head.

"I mean back at the mill, where Papa is," Samuel said. "Ouch."

"Well, hold still then," Annaliese said.

"It's noisy here," Emeline said from the bed.

Annaliese clamped her hand on her son's forehead and took aim again. "You mean your cousins?"

"No, outside," Emeline said, pointing at the window. "At night."

"Yea," Samuel said. "The horses on the street, the neighbors talking and slamming doors." He hooked his finger in his collar. "Papa wouldn't make me wear this."

"Of course he would if he were here." Annaliese cupped the boy's chin in her hand and finished smoothing his hair as best she could. She recalled the mountain noises that had scared him on the first night, that wall of creature sounds so massive it seemed to rise out of the black trees and fall on their house.

"I can't see the moon here," Emeline said.

"Well, only six days to go. This time next week, you'll be telling me how much you miss your grandmother." Annaliese held the brush above her son's head. "All done. Emmie, go find your shoes."

The girl slid off the bed and ran out the door.

Samuel was still looking at her in the mirror. "Papa's going to have a pony for me when I get back."

Annaliese shook her head.

"I'm nearly seven, Mama." He stood to hug her. "I've watched the men at the mill stables."

"We'll see."

"I could ride with you and Aunt Lucenia."

"Run downstairs and see if Uncle Edward is ready to go to church."

"Oh, all right." He dragged his feet on his way out.

Lucenia. She had not thought of her for days, but as the return to Georgia approached, the woman's raw wool on bare skin personality loomed. During their time apart, the accommodating attitude Annaliese had developed about Lucenia had melted away. Annaliese began thinking that perhaps Lucenia's was doing the same. Perhaps the ground Annaliese had won was already lost. Perhaps she would drive her crazy on the train ride again, this time pestering her about the Martha problem. Well, she was ready for that.

She rubbed balm into her hands. They were nearly healed—just in time to return to Pinch.

At the Cathedral of the Assumption, Annaliese and Samuel ambled behind the Connelley clump on its slow crawl down the main aisle. The front pew being their destination, it was a long walk. Assumption was enormous, the grande dame of the diocese, the oldest and wealthiest parish, and it attracted those whose aspirations matched its towering vaulted ceilings.

In the pews, black veils and hats turned slightly toward the Connelleys. Annaliese returned their gazes with a whisper of a smile. Heads dipped slowly in reply. Finally, as they reached their pew, she stood in the aisle and waited for her aunt and uncle to poke their way to their seats. One last time she glanced around and it was with this casual scan that she stumbled across the one dowager in the crowd who could make her heart race. Two rows away sat the mother of David Sullivan.

She returned Annaliese's shaken look with a sad smile. Annaliese gripped the wooden pew as she pushed Samuel too hard toward his seat. David. So many years ago.

The organ started up.

They were Sister Immaculata's piano students on Tuesday afternoons when they were fourteen. Waiting for their lessons in the hall outside her classroom, they whispered and laughed, reveling in their good luck to be left unsupervised. The opportunity to socialize with the opposite sex was rare. Even during recess the boys were segregated from the girls. In keeping their voices low and their heads just low enough under the glass window in Sister's door, Annaliese Lewis and David Sullivan, fueled by conspiratorial thrill and pulsing adolescent hormones, felt exactly the pull that they were not supposed to.

David wanted to be a professional baseball player. She wanted to be a dozen things she made up as they went, the more outrageous the better. Sometimes, if she was talking and he smiled at her, she had to look away so she could breathe. Together, they created a plan to sneak downtown to the Savoy, a music hall that ranked only a hair above a billiards hall in their parents' eyes. One Saturday afternoon, they slipped into the darkened balcony to watch a parade of jugglers, dancers, and leering singers. There in the dark, he reached over and stroked her long hair. A tingle went straight to her nipples, which suddenly seemed to feel every thread of her camisole. She squirmed in her seat, hot and itchy and intrigued. His hand swept behind her head and landed like a sack of rice on her shoulder. She felt the uneven pressure of each sweaty finger. They stared ahead at the stage and saw nothing.

But the rendezvous was soon reported.

Sister Immaculata called her to her office on Monday.

"Miss Lewis, you were with David Sullivan this weekend, unchaperoned at a music hall. Miss Lewis, this is immoral. You have sinned against God."

Annaliese was stunned to hear the Savoy dropped into the same category as lying and stealing. Sister hadn't even gotten to the sweating in the balcony part yet.

Sister said that Annaliese had placed her chastity at risk, that women were superior to men because they had a higher moral sense and therefore women had to make sure they were incapable of erotic feelings. Annaliese had never heard the word erotic, but she was beginning to make the connection between that word and the sensation between her legs that David had produced, and now that that wonderful feeling was linked with the tainting of her character, she felt sick.

Immaculata told Annaliese to close her eyes. Not what she expected to hear, but if they were going to pray she had just been given a reprieve, so she did. But she heard rummaging in a drawer, then "Don't move." She felt Sister's hand on her chin, pulled away and opened her eyes enough to see scissors coming at her. "Close them, I said," Sister said. She cupped her hand around Annaliese's chin again. In a few seconds, her destruction was complete. Annaliese's eyelashes were gone. When she opened her eyes, they felt sticky and naked.

"Pain makes us think, Miss Lewis. Now, go back to your classroom. But after school, go to the cathedral and think. Pray for forgiveness. Pray that God doesn't send his own punishment upon you."

By the time she got home that afternoon, her mother had heard, including the Savoy part. She looked at the damage, flew into a rant about twisted interpretations of morality and the chains of convention, but they both knew not even Eleanor would speak to the nun. As for the Savoy, she said it was more that part of town and being without a male chaperone—much as she hated to buckle to that—that was the problem, so that could not happen again.

David and Annaliese were never alone again. Every teacher and priest saw to that. The more the other students nagged for the scoop, the deeper the two retreated into silence.

But curiosity about the sensations that David had aroused sent her to her uncle's library, where she pulled down the dictionary. Soon, her fingers found "erotic" with its taint of abnormality echoing Sister's warnings. She stared at the facts before her on the page. Though the explicit cause and effect was still unclear, she had to accept that physical arousal eventually led to the degradation of society, which women were bound to prevent. But *David.* She thought of his broad, honest face, the way his eyes lit up when he saw her. She loved the way his hand whispered across her cheek when he swept her hair back. How could a lower force of nature be coursing through that sweet, pure body?

A week later, the first symptoms appeared. Annaliese writhed in her bed with headache, fever, and chills. A few days later, when the red pustules broke out on her face, the family doctor quarantined her in her room. It was smallpox—uncommon in Annaliese's part of town. As the rash spread to her arms, hands, and legs, her mother and aunt wracked their brains trying to figure out where Annaliese might have been exposed. But Annaliese knew. The Savoy. This was the divine punishment of which Sister had warned, and she would wear its mark the rest of her life.

For a long time, Annaliese tried to think of a way to ask her mother about those impure lower forces. She wanted her to refute the nun's statements, tell her that pleasure was part of God's human design, but could never bring herself to speak of it. Over time, she began to assume there was some truth to what Sister said. At night, with her cousins piled on Dorothy's bed, she would try to get more information, but they were all just guessing. Underneath the giggling, though, she heard fear.

Her lashes grew back, but they were stunted, pale little needles. Sometimes in class, she stared at the back of David's head or his hands. When he turned, she hid behind a book, certain he was staring at her fresh, pink smallpox scars.

Years later, she saw him across a Louisville street in a navy uniform. He raised his hand and crossed the street to tell her in long breathless sentences that he was going to see the world, make admiral. She allowed him a smile and a look that was probably too long for a woman about to marry someone else, but it closed their circle. He deserved that before he went away. Six years later, newspaper headlines screamed that the battleship U.S.S. Maine had exploded in the Havana harbor. Her eyes raced to the S's in that long list of the two hundred and sixty six lost sailors and there it was: David Sullivan, Lt., J.G. She went into her bedroom and cried into her pillows. For a long time afterward, she wore black in some little way, even if it was just a black ribbon tied on her camisole.

Annaliese was staring into space when she realized that her uncle was trying to get past her to go to the Communion rail. The priest and two altar boys were waiting for them, her included. Finally she stood and stepped into the aisle.

When Mass was over, she looked for Mrs. Sullivan, but she was exiting out a side door and there were too many people in between.

That night, as Annaliese brushed her hair, her mother came to her doorway.

"Wound up your clock for the night?"

"Yes, Mother, thanks."

Eleanor stepped into the room and watched Annaliese pull the brush through the long strands that were usually tucked.

"Your hair is still as lovely as ever, Anna."

"I wish I could say the same for my face and hands."

Her mother took over with the brush. "I think you've adjusted well to your situation."

Annaliese raised her eyebrows. "You do?"

"You seem to be making the best of it. Hogs in your yard, for heaven's sake."

"Yes, well, they eat snakes."

"See? You've become downright pragmatic." Eleanor worked Annaliese's hair into a braid and laid it across her shoulder. "Now." She squeezed her shoulders and looked at her in the mirror. "You want to tell me what's been bothering you?"

Annaliese stood up to take her mother's hands.

"It's not John, is it?" Eleanor asked.

"He's just not himself, Mother. He's angry so much, and sick and running that mill twelve hours a day, which can't be safe and . . ."

"Now, Anna, of course he would throw himself into it."

"No, no, there's more." Annaliese closed the door. "His nasty temper . . . cursing in front of the children . . . drinking too much . . ."

"Probably he's so worried about . . ."

"But he's spending so much money, Mother, on ridiculous things, like five bathtubs, which are four more than we can use, and barrels, barrels, Mother, of nails and hammers."

"Oh." The bed springs creaked as Eleanor sat down.

"From what I can gather from his conversations with Ben, the company is making a fortune." Annaliese sat down beside her. "So what could be wrong? He seems desperate."

"You've talked to him about this?"

"I've tried. He just keeps saying he needs my support." There was more, though.

Eleanor nodded. "Any insights from Lucenia?"

"Not really."

"Perhaps you need a male perspective on this."

"Uncle Edward?"

"Talk to him about the early years of his own business."

"I can't tell him all of this."

"No, no, of course not." Eleanor stood up. "Just ask him what it was like for him."

Annaliese reached for her mother's hand and kissed it. "Thank you."

Eleanor took her daughter's face in her hands. "It will be all right. You'll see."

After breakfast, Annaliese found him in his study, the least familiar room in the house. It had always been off-limits to the children, who knew that even a knock at his door carried risk. Nowadays, though, the door was open. He was pulling a book down from the wall of books behind his desk. On his right, two leather chairs hugged the fireplace. Above the mantel, awards from colleagues in the shipping business covered the wall. Her uncle's sovereignty would be forever thick here, no matter her age, though he waved her in immediately.

"Uncle Edward, did you ever have any business dealings with B. F. Avery and Sons?" she asked.

"Of course. For years we shipped their plows all over the world." He still held his finger on his place in the book.

"John's father worked there, you know."

"Yes, twenty-some odd years ago. John's mother mentioned it a *few* times." He rolled his eyes.

"Can you help me find someone who knew him? Someone he might have worked with there?"

"I suppose." He studied her face.

Annaliese put her hands behind her back. "I thought the children should know more about him. John was only ten when he died. He can't tell them much."

Edward closed his book. "Everything all right, sweetheart?"

She nodded.

He reshelved it. "Yes, quite right. A man's professional accomplishments should be recorded for posterity."

He told her he would see what he could do.

A few days later, Annaliese knocked on a door on Walnut Street, a tidy but morose neighborhood of brick row homes with struggling bushes in the front yards. A white-haired woman opened it already smiling. Annaliese handed her a calling card.

The woman barely scanned it. "Yes, Mrs. Stregal, come in. A pleasure. They called from the office about you." She stepped back to open the door. "I'm Jeremiah's wife, Sarah. Please excuse the way I look. I've been in the kitchen all morning." She peeled off an apron from her thick waist.

Annaliese stepped over the threshold into a dark hall thick with the odor of cooking sauerkraut.

Sarah led her to a room on the right. "Please, have a seat. I'll tell Jeremiah that you're here."

Annaliese lowered herself onto a velvet-covered chair and put her leather satchel on the floor. The room looked like the aftermath of a flea market explosion. On every wall tapestries hung alongside ancestral photographs, mirrors, shelves. On the shelves and tables sat plants and more photographs, vases, a zither, and a violin. Palms reached to the ceiling from wicker plant stands.

The sound of shuffling footsteps rose in the hall and an elderly man appeared with Sarah in the doorway. A cane wobbled helplessly beneath his hand.

"Mrs. Stregal, how do you do?" Jeremiah Bracken came in, smiling. Sarah followed him in and nodded.

"A pleasure to meet you. Thank you for seeing me," Annaliese said.

"May we offer you something? Water? Tea? So warm today."

"No, thank you. You're so kind."

Jeremiah sat down on one end of the over-pillowed sofa and his plump wife sat on the other, sending pillow feathers flying. Sarah folded her hands.

"Yes, well," Annaliese said. "I understand that you once worked with my father-in-law, Lawrence Stregal, at B. F. Avery."

"Yes. Fine man. Had two sons as I recall," Jeremiah said. "And so you are married to . . .?"

"John," Annaliese said quickly.

Jeremiah nodded with faint interest. "John, yes. I trust he's well?"

"Yes, thank you. He and Ben have started a lumber business in the Georgia mountains, so we are living there at the moment."

Sarah gasped. "The Georgia mountains. Pretty thing like you?"

"Well, it's just for a little while," Annaliese said. "Anyway, I am putting together a little family history as a surprise for John and our children."

"Lord! You took children into those mountains?" Sarah said.

Jeremiah batted at his wife.

Annaliese kept her eyes on Jeremiah. "And since he doesn't remember much about his father's professional life—he was just a boy when his father died—and his mother has passed on, I was hoping that you could tell me a little about him. What Lawrence was like." Bending down to the satchel, she pulled out a pencil and pad of paper.

"Well, when we started out together around 1867 . . ."

"1865," Sarah said.

"All right, all right," he said, waving her down again. "We were both about twenty, greenhorns anxious to make our mark. He kept impeccable financial records, which was his job, but he was also able to keep a dozen other things organized in his head. Smart as a whip."

"So he started out keeping the books?" Annaliese made notes.

"Right." Jeremiah's long explanation of subsequent jobs at the company followed. Annaliese got as much on paper as she could and didn't worry about what she couldn't. She looked up occasionally to smile. When she felt she had given this enough time, she asked, "And his demeanor?"

"Oh, easy-going, a regular kind of guy," Jeremiah said.

Sarah shot a look at Jeremiah and scooted to the edge of the sofa.

"He sure loved those boys," he continued.

"Did he?" Annaliese could see Sarah cock her head at Jeremiah.

"Heck, yes. I seem to recall something about a bicycle they were building together."

"So, you worked with Lawrence for about 15 years?"

"Yes." Jeremiah shook his head. "It was hard to watch him change so fast at the end."

Annaliese tried to control her face. "Yes, I know it must have been. How, well, that is, what was that like?"

"Now, you don't want to know about that," he said, sitting back into the sofa.

"Certainly she does," Sarah said, wetting her lips.

Annaliese held her pencil above the paper, eyes shifting between Sarah and Jeremiah.

"You want to know, honey," Sarah said. She inched forward again to pat at the air near Annaliese's knee.

Jeremiah looked over at his wife, then at the floor. "Well, he became so grouchy. We couldn't figure out why. And he started swearing like a longshoreman."

Annaliese put the pencil down. "And this came over him around what time?"

"When we began managing the machinists, so I suppose it was around 1880."

"So he would have been about thirty-five years old." *Five years older than John.*

"And then he began that running around," Sarah said.

"Sarah Bracken!" Jeremiah said. "Hold your tongue." He strangled her with his eyes.

Sarah moved back on the sofa, smoothed her hair.

"He did some things . . . let's just say out of character. We didn't know what was coming over him. He would stay up for days and nights, working like a maniac. This impressed the Averys, who promoted him, of course, because he could convince anyone that he could succeed at anything. Naturally, his health suffered. He caught every cold in the factory. Then he'd stay home for days. It's a miracle it never turned into pneumonia."

"But . . ." Annaliese said.

"What is it, dear?" Sarah said.

"I thought he died of pneumonia."

"Oh, honey, he died from jumping off a bridge into the Ohio River," Sarah said.

"Oh, my God!" Annaliese cried.

Jeremiah's head flipped around to his wife. She squeezed herself back into the corner of the sofa, nodding and patting her pillows into place. Annaliese put her hand on her chair seat to brace herself, trying to breathe. The pencil slipped to the floor.

"I'm sorry," Jeremiah said finally. "I thought you knew."

"Tell her about all that money he ran through," Sarah said.

Though she did not trust her legs, Annaliese rose from her chair, groped for her satchel, shoved the tablet of paper in. She turned toward the hallway, did not say a word that would give Sarah any satisfaction, though the woman had provided exactly what Annaliese had come for: the naked truth.

Behind her she heard the cane whistle through the air and land on something soft. Sarah yelped.

"I have to go," Annaliese said. The hallway reeked. She put her hand over her mouth.

"Mrs. Stregal." Shuffling footsteps and the tap of the cane were behind her. "Wait."

Get hold of the glass doorknob. Turn it quickly. Bright sunlight hurts but oh, fresh air. Stone steps. Hurry down. One step at a time, but hurry. She clutched the satchel to her chest, turned left, and never looked back at the raspy apologies from the old man.

The cathedral was dark, save the amber glow of votives flickering in an alcove. Low voices filtered in from some distant chamber. She went to a pew, genuflected, and sat down. Her thoughts were irrational, wild. To crowd them out, she forced Hail Marys out of her mouth, but they quickly trailed away.

She cursed herself for crossing that row house threshold, wished for the ignorance she had enjoyed just minutes ago. Why had she such done such a reckless thing? What did she think she could do with the information? Well, she had it now, this family specter gripping her lungs, and what was she going to do? What *could* she do? She was a woman, so not much of anything. Life swept over her with the force of the Ohio River. *The Ohio River.*

Something moved at the altar and she tried to focus on it, the very place she and John had said their vows. An altar boy was lighting the candles that sat on both ends of that marble slab. Their light spread up and across the mosaic tiles, igniting the flecks of gold in the Mary's robes, her baby's tunic. Annaliese looked at the windows atop the towering columns as the last of the day's light slipped away and relaxed enough to grant that she had at least chosen the right place to come, this building so vast and yet so soothing in its feeling of patriarchal embrace.

Annaliese squeezed her hands between her knees and tried to compare John with the father-in-law she had never known. While the evening outside deepened, so, too, did her conviction that John was nothing like his father, nor were his demons.

∽

XVIII

A crisp September wind clipped across the platform where Annaliese and her children and Ted stared down the tracks for the Cincinnati train, eight minutes late. Ted wrapped an arm around her and squeezed. She dabbed at her tears and looked away from his eyes that said he wanted her to get back in the carriage. She thought about how many different kinds of tears there were. If Ted had known what she was really crying about, they never would have even left the house.

The family lie was burning a hole in her brain. Lawrence Stregal killed himself. He jumped off a bridge. Did John know? Did Ben? Should she tell Lucenia? If she did, Lucenia would drive her mad with fretting. No, she couldn't tell her. But it was her problem, too, wasn't it? Of course she should tell her. She would tell her tonight.

Maybe.

Finally, they heard the whistle, felt the tremor in the soles of their shoes. Annaliese clamped her hands over Emeline's ears as wheels screeched on iron rails. People picked up valises and threw one-armed hugs around their companions. Ear hairs tickled. Babies cried.

Ted kissed her and split off to help the porter with baggage. Like the gentleman his father had asked him to be, Samuel helped his mother up the stairs to the private car. But inside he nearly knocked her down trying to get to his cousins. Emeline was right behind him.

Lucenia pulled Annaliese into an embrace so energetic she could only pat at the air until released. Lucenia wore a cocoa-colored wool suit, which she smoothed down as Annaliese pulled away. The cocoa eye shadow was subdued.

"I have the most wonderful surprise," Lucenia said, pulling her deeper into the car.

A slender woman rose from her seat to greet them. Rumpled and young—barely out of her teens, Annaliese guessed—she had the uncertain bearing of a new pastor's wife in an old congregation. Her eyes and mouth were delicate but pinched, as though if she would just relax they might bloom into something more luscious. Brown hair straggled from a bun tucked into a straw hat and did little to hide two white ears that sprung from her head at right angles.

Lucenia grabbed the woman by the arm. "Allow me to introduce our new governess."

Annaliese blinked. *Governess? We don't need a governess. And hired without a word to me?*

"Minerva Meally," Lucenia said to Annaliese's fixed smile, "this is Mrs. John Stregal."

Minerva lurched forward to take Annaliese's hand, saw that it hadn't been offered, touched her straw hat, stepped backward, tripped over her feet, and fell down. Annaliese started to help her, but Lucenia placed a firm hand on Annaliese's arm. The three boys came out of their seats, though, to clamp grubby hands on her wrists and elbows. They hoisted her up so energetically that she went sailing into one of the seats. The boys rushed over with apologies. Laughing, she reached out to rub as many heads as she could before they pulled away. Then she sailed her hat at them.

Annaliese leaned toward her sister-in-law and whispered, "She actually has references?"

Lucenia giggled. "She's perfect. This one knows her place."

The train shuddered with its first movement, so the women urged everyone back to their seats. Outside, Ted was pacing and peering up at the windows until he saw Annaliese. He raised his hand, more salute than farewell, it seemed to her—his way, she figured, of sending her off on as happy a note as he could muster. Samuel and Emeline rushed over to throw kisses. The cars picked up speed and in seconds Ted was out of sight.

After the train settled into a steady rhythm, the children moved to seats around a table in a far corner of the parlor. They crowded around Samuel's new prize, a stereoscope from his grandmother. Emeline held the pictures of the "Wonders of the World" that were to be viewed in the stereoscope and dished them out to her brother cheerfully despite his condemnations of her sticky fingers. Minerva stood over them, providing a running travelogue on the Wonders.

Lucenia leaned over to Annaliese. "Sorry about surprising you. There wasn't time. I found her at my door two days ago, abandoned by a family that owes her three months' wages."

"Well . . ." Annaliese took another look at her. "She seems to like the children."

"Imagine that. And, yes, she brought good references, all of whom I contacted."

"But where's she going to live?" Annaliese could already hear Herschel's hammer.

"With us. In the back bedroom for now."

Annaliese relaxed against the leather headrest. What was done was done.

"How was your visit?" Lucenia asked.

"Fine. Too short, of course."

"Darrison thought ours was too long. He missed the mountains. Can you believe it?"

Annaliese smiled. "I heard something like that, too." Behind Lucenia's shoulder, the last of Louisville's warehouses rolled by. "How's your sister?"

"She's married! Finally. She waited to tell me in person. An architect."

"What do you mean, 'finally'?"

"Well, Rose is thirty years old, for heaven's sake." Lucenia lowered her voice. "She hasn't had many prospects." She fluffed the lace at her collar. "She doesn't take the care with appearance the way I do. And she is . . . well, not a petite woman. But she finally followed my advice." She pointed to her eyelids.

Annaliese envisioned another Lucenia, painted with a different brush and palette but, above all, painted.

"She's done well, as I did," Lucenia said.

"Does she love him?"

"Oh," Lucenia shrugged. "I have no idea."

Annaliese watched the landscape for a while. Was she a fool to be thinking at this point in her life that love should glimmer at the outset of a marriage, or had she been right to yearn above all else for security? Perhaps it was better when love was born along the way, richer as it became the sum of many small things: charitable moments, other cheeks turned, trials survived. Was that what she had now with John? The man she had cleaved to years ago wasn't the man she was returning to. Tougher and less refined, yes, but also brighter, more alive than ever and only because she was working alongside him now could she see every brilliant quality. If John was struggling under the yoke of his father's legacy, she owed it to him to pull harder, too.

"Mother would be so happy to see what's become of us," Lucenia was saying. "And that's all that matters." She put her hat on the shelf. "Now, what about your family?"

Annaliese looked at Lucenia for a long while—too long, for Lucenia was now looking back with raised eyebrows.

"What?" Lucenia said.

"I found some helpful information in the library."

Lucenia threw her a puzzled look. "About?"

"It seems that the Georgia folks have a time-honored punishment already in place."

"We're talking about Martha."

Annaliese nodded.

"Well, what is it?"

"Night riders."

"Excuse me?"

"Bands of disguised men who arrive on their neighbors' doorsteps at night to terrorize them."

"The Klan?" Lucenia shrieked. Then, in a whisper, "We are *not* going to call up the Klan."

Annaliese fluttered her fingers at her. "No, no, of course not. But we are going to make Martha think that's who they are. And they are going to be incensed that men have been seen coming and going at night from her quarters behind the schoolhouse. Poor character for a school marm. Run her out of the county."

"You never told me men have been seen . . ."

"No, Lucenia. We're making this up."

"Oh. Well, who are 'they'?"

"Henry Chastain. And whoever he rounds up."

Lucenia eased back into the leather seat. "What makes you think that he would do such an outrageous thing? It's got to be illegal."

"He sent me and John a letter. He offered us help in dealing with her. Said that he wasn't above something vile."

A smile grew on Lucenia's lips. "Yes, he would do that, wouldn't he? For you."

"As I said, the letter was addressed to me and John."

Lucenia looked outside for a few minutes. Then she turned to eye her sister-in-law with new regard. "Anyone in the county would believe that about Martha."

"We just need Martha to believe that they believe it."

As the train rocked along, Lucenia bounced in her seat. "Such a horrible thing, though."

"Very well." Annaliese smoothed her skirt. "Just an idea."

For two and a half days they traveled through hills and fields where the last of summer was turning in. Cornstalks stood in withered rows. Rolls of hay spilled out of barn loft doors or dotted the fields, ready for the wagons. Inside the Stregals' car, another transition was going on, from two families back to one. They were at ease this time, familiar with one another, and unafraid of what lay ahead. The children fell into their sibling ways, picked up their games and books, while their mothers dropped in and out of conversations with Minerva. Many times, Annaliese looked at Lucenia and tried to push Lawrence's name out of her mouth. But as the miles slipped away, so, too, did her courage and her feeling of obligation to share. Pinch was on the horizon, and so she pushed the past into the shadows.

When they pulled in, Darrison was hanging out the window to be the first to spot the depot. The blast of mountain air through the window sent the women for coats and shawls.

"Look, it's Ruth," Darrison said. "I can see her waving down the train with a white rag. She's on the tracks."

Lucenia yanked him inside. "When will that girl get good sense?"

As the train slowed, Annaliese let out an enormous sigh.

Lucenia nodded. "Eighteen months to go," she said.

The train screeched to a halt.

James ran in from the berths. "Seen Papa and Uncle John yet?"

"Not yet," Lucenia said. "And I told you Uncle John won't be here today. He's tending the mill." She pulled on her gloves.

On the platform, Ruth and Herschel swept the children into their arms. By the time Lucenia and Annaliese joined them, Minerva was gaping at Ruth, a jolt of red from head to toe. Red bonnet, red dress trimmed in white eyelet at the neck and cuffs, and red stockings.

Ruth smiled and put Emeline down. "I got me a sewing machine," she said with a swish of her skirt. "Montgomery Ward delivered it right after y'all lef'."

"That's quite an ensemble," Lucenia said.

"I was trying to look like you in your red supper get-up. How'd I do?"

Lucenia's face went flat.

Annaliese held her handkerchief over her mouth. Finally, she managed to speak. "Ruth and Herschel, I would like to introduce you to Minerva. Minerva Meally. Our new governess."

Minerva dipped a little. "A pleasure."

"Ma'am," Herschel said with a finger tapped to his hat.

"Governess?" Ruth gave her a quick once-over.

"Mother's helper," Annaliese said.

Minerva straightened and sent a perplexed look to Lucenia, who had turned her back on the conversation.

Annaliese pointed at Ruth's feet. "New shoes, too, I see."

"Yes, ma'am. Herschel traced my feet on the paper like Miss Lucenia showed me and we sent it off to that Sears Roebuck fella." She stuck her tiny foot out to display brown boots with buttons as round and black as a squirrel's eyes. She dropped to her knee to speak to Emeline. "But wait till you see what I made for you, little darlin'."

"We gots a surprise for you, too, Rufe," Emeline said.

Samuel went rigid. "Wait," he said to his sister.

"Sure enough?" Ruth swept the girl up into her scrawny arms.

"It's a . . ."

"Emmie, wait," Samuel said. "It's supposed to be a surprise. We'll show her at home."

But Emeline grabbed Ruth's face with two chubby hands, pulled it into hers and said, "It's views."

Samuel stomped his foot. "Dang it, Emmie."

"Hang on, Sam, it's all right," Ruth said. "I ain't got no idea what views is."

Samuel pulled Darrison toward the depot. "We're going looking for Uncle Ben," he said over his shoulder.

As if on cue, Ben came out of the waiting room. For a man of his girth, he was covering ground quickly. His face was freshly shaved, his shirt immaculate white.

"At last," he said. "My family has returned to its bosom."

Annaliese heard Ruth say to Minerva, "That's Old Lizard Lids. Lord, he's bad to talk."

"Darling," Lucenia said, holding out her hand.

Ben took her hand as if she were the queen, bent down, bestowed his kiss, straightened just as tenderly. "And here is my little surprise. For your birthday." He pulled a tiny box out of his pocket.

"You remembered," she said, accepting it. As people streamed by, the Stregal family and entourage stood watching Lucenia fondle a box that was about the size of a man's gold watch. It was wrapped in shiny paper of tea roses of pink and plum, crowned with a wide, golden bow. After producing a shudder of anticipation worthy of the stage, Lucenia looked at her husband with genuine tenderness. Annaliese felt her heart seize with jealousy.

Ruth popped up at Annaliese's side to worm her way into their tight little circle. "Well, are you gone open it or not?" she asked.

Lucenia cut her eyes over at Ruth and for a moment Annaliese feared that she might stall to remind Ruth of her place. Annaliese was tired and ready to get back home, find out what John was up to. But Lucenia began to untie the ribbon, slowly, cooing as the ribbon slid away and the top of the box came off. With arched pinky, she brought out an enormous gold brooch. A garnet the size of a dime glistened in its center. It was encircled by a ring of gold leaves in which were embedded clusters of tiny pink pearls.

Annaliese thought it was the most vulgar piece of jewelry she had ever seen.

"Ain't that just the purtiest thing?" Ruth said.

Lucenia's face went still for a moment. Whether this was a reaction to the brooch or to Ruth's liking the brooch was hard for Annaliese to judge, but either way it was satisfying. Lucenia gave Ben a shaky smile. "It's beautiful, darling. I love it."

Herschel moved in to urge them all to the wagons. Eventually, everything was loaded. As Annaliese settled into her seat beside Herschel, he said, "Mr. John's got a right big surprise for you, too."

Annaliese studied his face. He kept his forward gaze, but underneath the red beard, a smile was forming. "You'll be tickled," he said finally, snapping the reins. "I reckon."

At the granite outcropping that meant home was about fifteen minutes away, the horses' ears pricked up. A horse was coming down the trail and coming fast. They all heard it: hooves pounding out a frantic rhythm. Herschel reached under his seat for his rifle. As he placed it across his knees, the rider came upon them so fast that the teams skittered sideways into the rush of red road dust.

"There you are," John shouted.

Herschel shook his head as he fought to control his team.

"John!" Annaliese said, coughing and rubbing her eyes.

"I couldn't wait any longer for y'all to get home," John said.

Annaliese made a final wipe. "We missed you, too."

Ben's wagon pulled up behind Herschel's. "Did you tell her?" Ben said.

"Wait till you see, Anna," John shouted. His movements were quick and careless, and the horse's jumpiness told her that he had been that way for too long. A ring of white foam bubbled from the bit in its mouth.

"Mr. John, that horse of yours is plum wore out," Herschel said softly. "Why don't you . . ."

"Nonsense," John shouted. "Come on." He pulled the horse around and took off.

They found him waiting in front of the homes, still jerking the jittery horse around. But as the wagon closed in, they saw something white behind the homes—an enormous stable. Nearby, there was a new corral and fences enclosing several horses.

"I knew it," Samuel shouted. "I knew he'd have a pony waiting for me."

"And me! There must be at least six horses in there," Darrison said.

"Oh, joy," Lucenia said. "Horses."

"Surprise!" Emeline shouted.

Annaliese closed her eyes.

The boys spilled out of Ben's wagon as it rolled to a stop. John guided his horse toward Emeline, and swept her up to lead the giddy parade to the corral.

Ben began unloading Lucenia's trunks and bags. She came over to Annaliese, still in the wagon seat and staring at the purple smears in the evening sky. She touched her knee. "We shall make the best of this."

Annaliese just shook her head.

"I know you'll have me riding by next spring."

Annaliese's face softened. "With Darrison."

"That's right. Good night, Anna."

"Night."

He came to her long after the children were asleep, after she had washed her stockings and slipped into bed. He reeked of sweat—his and the horse's. For a moment, he sat and tried to listen to her description of the visit. But while she talked, his eyes bounced around the room and soon he was up, looking into the water pitcher, lining up the shaving brushes on his dresser. Suddenly, he announced that he needed to clean his gun—he'd been practicing while she was gone, he said—and he bolted downstairs. During the night, he woke her off and on, trolling through the house. When the sun rose over Bunny Mountain, he was shooting tin cans out back.

Annaliese watched him at the window and thought, *I'll tell her tomorrow.*

After breakfast, Annaliese filled her arms with books and climbed the hill to Ruth's cabin. Annaliese had praise on her tongue, for she had opened her pantry that morning to discover rows of jars full of apples, okra, onions, and pumpkin. From floor to ceiling, green mason jars glistened back at her. Strings of dried peppers and pumpkin hung beside dangling burlap sacks of smoked hams. Sweet potatoes spilled out of sacks in the corner. Ready for winter, the room said, and Ruth had done it all.

Annaliese had never worried much about their food supply. The railroad into the sawmill made deliveries once a week. But the almanac warned of a hard winter coming. The unusually chilly September nights were already telling her that. Ruth was right to not rely too much on the train.

She glanced over at the corral, where two horses were circling back to watch her. Their fuzzy ears were up, backlit by the morning sun. Missouri Fox Trotters, at least. Strong and sure-footed. Her eyes shifted to the stable, which she now realized had two floors. Three windows dotted the upstairs wall of the brilliantly white building, yet another tap root going in.

She knocked gently on Ruth's door. Ruth waved her in as she untied her red apron.

The cabin was one room, lit only by windows at both ends and the robust fire Ruth had going. A kettle hung from an iron bar that ran across the fireplace opening. Coffee's rich aroma filled the air. Ruth pulled up two chairs with basket-weave seats.

"Ruth, you've been busy putting up food while I was gone," Annaliese said.

"Yes, ma'am. Herschel helped."

"I wanted to thank you."

Ruth shrugged. Her eyes were on the books Annaliese still clutched to her chest. "What you got thar?"

Annaliese released the books to her. "I brought you these from Louisville."

"Really and truly?" Ruth leaned forward to take them.

"They're elementary school books. Spelling, mathematics. We can study them together."

"Lord, Lord." The tiny head shook side to side. "They ain't enough words in my head can help me tell you how I feel right now."

"That's all right, Ruth. You don't need to say anything at all."

For once, she did not. Ruth thumbed through the pages of each book, mouthing a word here and there, smiling at pictures. The fire hissed in its cove, an invitation to Annaliese to hold her hands out to its golden glow. *Perhaps I could stay here all day. Perhaps no one will think to look for me here.*

Ruth put the books on the floor. "Lord, I can't wait no more. I got to show you what I sewed for Emeline." She ran to her sewing machine.

Annaliese strained to see what she was fetching. *It will be red*, she thought. *Red pinafores. Red frilly bonnets.* What was she going to say? Emeline would look like a big, fat strawberry.

Ruth sat down and held up a blue dress with a high, straight collar and long sleeves. Annaliese reached forward to feel it: a soft calico. It had been expertly gathered at the waistband and wrists into precise, little tucks. Yellow daisies dotted the field of rich blue.

"Oh, Ruth," Annaliese said. "This is exquisite."

"Don't look too close at them plackets."

"Nonsense. You do beautiful work."

"Look at this." Ruth held up a white pinafore bursting with ruffles. "It goes over the blue dress."

"Oh, it's adorable." The silky cotton ruffles at the shoulders flowed like cream. "Where did you get this beautiful material?"

"Ordered it, 'course."

"Well, you are amazing."

"Looky what else."

Ruth stood and beckoned Annaliese to the corner where a bed had been shoved against the wall. Beside it, a cradle hung from its wooden frame. Ruth reached inside and pulled up tiny caps and gowns, bibs, a blanket.

"Ruth! Are you . . . ?"

"Naw. Not yet." Ruth smoothed her apron over a stomach that was nearly concave. "But when it does happen, I'll be ready, won't I?" Sadness pulled at the edges of her eyes. "I want that more'n anythin'."

It was a yearning Annaliese easily understood, but childbirth was a risky matter. The older she got, the more she realized just how risky. Between the longing and the pushing, fate could take an ugly turn. Worse, it could wait for years to make its entire course plain. So many children died of typhoid, whooping cough, or just a simple cold or cut. Likely as not, a cold could turn into pneumonia, a cut could become septic. In the mountains, the dangers just piled on. And once the lumber company left, how would Ruth and Herschel come by cash?

Annaliese looked at the girl. Her hips were so narrow.

But Annaliese also saw a sewing machine that she had mastered and books she would surely would, too, and a face still bright with hope.

"Then I want that for you, too," she said.

༄

XIX

Court week was coming, they reminded their husbands. It was scheduled for the third week in October. Annaliese and Lucenia announced that they wanted to invite Mr. Chastain and Mr. Garland themselves this time. They had parcels to pick up in Pinch, things to buy, they explained, so they would extend the invitation in person and make the arrangements. To their amazement, the men said fine, they were too busy to leave the mill anyway.

As they waited on Lucenia's porch for Herschel, Annaliese stared at the garnet brooch perched on her shawl.

"Never, *never* issue the slightest disappointment over a gift of jewelry from a man," Lucenia said. "Or there won't be any more."

"I see." Annaliese pondered the merits of acquiring more ugly jewelry.

Lucenia pulled on gloves. "Are you feeling well, dear?"

"Yes. Fine." Annaliese put her hands on her hips and leaned back into a long stretch.

"You've been so quiet lately."

Annaliese shrugged.

"Is it John?"

"Just thinking about the conversation we hope to have with Mr. Chastain."

Lucenia flicked a chicken feather off her shawl. "Think he'll do it?"

"Shhh." Annaliese looked around at the front door. She pulled Lucenia down the steps into the yard. "We'll know soon enough."

"Oh, keeping this secret has been unbearable."

"Shhh!"

As Herschel drove the wagon through Pinch at a leisurely pace, the women glanced down the alleys, scanned the storefronts and doorways. In one window of Smith's Mercantile, a sign announced a new shipment of lightning rods. In the other, Mrs. Smith's attempt at a millinery display consisted of three poles sprouting from the naked display shelf, each one topped with a sad hat askew, each one creepy in its headlessness.

Looking down the boardwalk while the horses drank at a trough, they saw a new shingle swinging above a freshly painted blue door: "Calvin Chastain, M. D." They exchanged a look. A doctor in Pinch? Related to Mr. Chastain? Annaliese pulled her shawl across her chest. No doctor should have the good looks of Henry Chastain. She preferred her doctors old, gray, and slightly blind.

A few minutes later, they stood outside Henry's office. Annaliese drew in a deep breath. Back in that dark library, this had seemed like a good, if despicable, idea. On the train, telling Lucenia about it had been just sport. But now they were about to it spill it all to Mr. Chastain. He was a man. Men could make things happen.

"You knock," she said to Lucenia.

They heard a male voice call out and Henry opened the door. "Ladies! What a nice surprise." He took a quick scan of the road behind them. "By yourselves today?"

"Yes, Mr. Chastain, indeed we are," Lucenia said. She turned to look left and right, too. No one within earshot, but she said loudly anyway, "We've come with a dinner invitation."

"More than that, I'll wager. I heard what Martha did to the boys." He waved them into his one-room office.

He stood at the corner of his desk closing books and moving papers. They sat down in the cracked-leather chairs that faced it. Smiling, he settled into his chair and folded his hands on the desk.

Annaliese cleared her throat. "Mr. Chastain, as you are aware, we have had some trouble with a certain former employee who became disgruntled with us."

"Naw, she was born that way," Henry laughed.

"Well, in any case, she took a switch to our sons."

"And that was at the end of a long string of abuses," Lucenia said.

He leaned back in his chair. "Go on."

"So we'd like to accept your offer of help in . . ." Annaliese struggled to find acceptable words.

"Getting revenge," Lucenia said.

"At last," Henry said.

"We want her gone, out of the county, for good," Lucenia said.

Henry's eyes flew open.

"Well, she just keeps turning up," Annaliese said.

"You know I'll help you. But I'll have to think for a while on the how part."

"Oh, we have a plan," Lucenia said.

"Sure enough? Well, shoot, ladies. Let's hear it."

"It's vile," Annaliese said, wincing.

Henry, feigning impatience, waved to bring it on.

"Well, when school is in, Martha sleeps in the school's back room. So she is alone at night," Annaliese said. She brought out a handkerchief.

"You can be certain of that!" Henry said.

"We think some night riders should pay her a visit," Annaliese said slowly while she watched Henry's face.

Henry's eyebrows shot up. "Night riders? You expect me to find some night riders?"

Annaliese looked at him long and hard.

"Me?" he shouted.

"Think how much fun it would be," Lucenia said, leaning into the desk. "And you're too smart to get caught."

Henry sat up straight in his chair. "Me? It's illegal. I'm an officer of the court!"

Annaliese dabbed the hankie under her nose and sniffed. "You should see Samuel's legs."

He began drumming his fingers on the beat-up desk. "What's her alleged crime?"

"Consorting with several men, including a colored man," Annaliese said so tentatively it was nearly a question.

"There aren't any colored in the whole county," Henry said. He went silent when he saw on their faces that, yes, they already knew this. "But if anyone could find one and consort, it would be Martha."

"Precisely," Lucenia said. "Anyone would believe it. Even Martha will believe that the riders believe it."

The tempo of his fingertips picked up. Henry looked out his dirt-caked window. "I don't know. This is illegal, I tell you. And ... I haven't ridden a horse at night for years."

"Of course, if you feel your age would inhibit you," Lucenia said, nodding sympathetically.

"What! I didn't say that." Henry jerked his head back to look at the women. "Leave it to me."

"Wonderful," Lucenia said.

"Such a horrible thing," Annaliese said. "But we're desperate."

"Don't you worry about a thing, Mrs. Stregal."

His words washed over her like silk on bare skin. It was the mantra by which she had planned to spend her whole life. John had never said that back even when she had nothing to worry about. And now, well, if he said that now, she would worry.

"Worried? Us?" Lucenia said.

Oh, you have no idea, Annaliese thought.

"How soon do you think you can get to this, Mr. Chastain?" Lucenia said.

Henry sat back into his seat. "Not till court week's over. And it'll take me a while to make arrangements. Maybe I can get my brother ..."

"The new doctor in town?" Annaliese said.

"Had to drag him out of Savannah to dry out for a while."

"Oh, I see," Annaliese said quietly. Still, a recovering doctor in Pinch was better than a sober one five hours away in Atlanta. "One last thing."

"What's that?"

"When you tell our husbands, you know, when you come for supper, tell them this was your idea."

"You understand," Lucenia said.

"Indeed I do. When am I coming for supper?"

"How about Saturday, two weeks?" Annaliese said. "Do bring Dr. Chastain."

Henry and Calvin Chastain strode into Lucenia's dining room each presenting a bottle of apple brandy. Calvin turned out to be an anemic version of Henry in Annaliese's view. What little hair he had was banana peel limp and sparse at the top. Across this sad knob he had scraped a few wisps. The rest grew long down the back of his neck. Shorter and rounder, he literally stood in Henry's shadow. But his command of his body was sure, like Henry's, Annaliese noticed, and his tongue just as silver. Both were on their third glass of claret.

"Mrs. Stregal," Calvin said to Lucenia as he pulled out her chair at the table with a flourish. "I've never seen a finer home in these hills. Such remarkable craftsmanship. How appropriate that you have placed such handsome children in its embrace."

Lucenia smiled over her shoulder at Calvin as she sat down. Annaliese stifled a smile at the two and caught Henry doing the same, but when she passed through the warm light of the wall sconce she felt his eyes on her.

Spoons were soon lowered to soup.

Henry said, "I read in the *Atlanta Constitution* that a forestry school has just been endowed at Yale."

"Yes," John said, looking up. Dark circles swagged under his eyes. "The Pinchot family did it for 'the work ahead in American forests'."

"Gifford Pinchot is behind it, I can assure you," Ben said.

"Who's he?" Calvin asked.

"A fanatic," John said.

"A couple of years ago, he was George Vanderbilt's head forester for his estate in North Carolina," Ben said. "Pinchot made it his demonstration project for conservative land use and it boosted the hell out of his career."

John put his spoon on the table. "Damn, I've just lost my appetite." He waved at Ruth, who had entered the room with wine, to take away his soup. She threw a startled look at him and looked at the ground as she removed his bowl.

Ben waved his spoon. "Now he's the head of this new Division of Forestry in Washington. They've bought more than thirty million acres of forest to preserve."

"They aim to restrict logging," John said. He shook out a handkerchief and blew his nose.

"But surely not on private land such as yours," Calvin said.

"That will be next, mark my words," John said, dabbing.

"But the nation needs lumber," Henry said, lowering his spoon.

"Of course, it does!" John bellowed. "Americans are using 157 cubic feet of timber products per person per year."

Henry smiled at the statistic John could cite so easily, but he knew by now that that was John Stregal. "Well, I can understand your concern, gentlemen," Henry said. He waved Ruth over and leaned back in his chair. "The Progressives do seem to be gaining ground."

"They say our country faces a timber famine." John threw up his hands.

"Bah," Ben said.

"Well, perhaps we'll have a new president come March," Calvin said.

John shook his head. "McKinley or not, I aim to have my timbering done by then."

Annaliese looked over at Lucenia.

"Now about Vice President Roosevelt . . ." Ben said.

"Gentlemen," Lucenia said. "If we keep politics as our first course, I fear appetites will be quite dead by the time the stuffed quail arrives." She shot a meaningful look at Henry.

Henry's dark eyes responded. He pushed his chair back onto its two rear legs and swirled the claret in his glass while he waited for Ruth to leave. She finished clearing the table and left with a stack of too many bowls and plates. Lucenia winced as the door swung closed behind her.

"Calvin, reckon they might like to hear about our little adventure the other night?" Henry said.

"Henry, I reckon they would. It was more fun than St. Paddy's Day in Savannah," Calvin said.

"Adventure?" John smiled politely and leaned forward on his elbows.

Annaliese gripped her napkin in her lap.

"Well, Calvin and I thought we might could get rid of your Martha problem and have a little fun at the same time."

"Oh, no. Not the Martha problem," Ben said. "I have heard about the Martha problem *ad nauseum.*"

"Why, Mr. Chastain," Lucenia said. "What have you gone and done?"

"We rounded up a bunch of fellas and horses, threw feed sacks over our heads, and threatened her at her schoolhouse cabin coupla nights ago," Henry said.

"What!" John said.

"Ssh!" Henry warned sloppily, having lost all professional dignity in the wine long ago. He cast a wary eye toward the kitchen door and tossed back the rest of the claret.

"What exactly did you do to her?" John said.

"We lit our torches and hollered at her to come on out," Calvin said. "'Course she didn't. So we had to send one of the fellas in after her."

Lucenia grabbed Annaliese's hand so tightly that she let out a squeak.

"Who were these fellas?" Ben said.

"Coupla Cherokee buddies."

"What!" Annaliese blurted. "They'd be the last people I'd expect to . . ."

"I'm tellin' you, they had a big time ole with this," Henry laughed.

"So one of them—I don't know their names like Henry does—dragged her out of there kickin' and screamin'," Calvin said. "He forced her out into the yard there. She stood there all wild-eyed and cryin', but mean-lookin' too, you know? Like she was thinkin' she'd get us later for this."

Henry pounded the table. "She held her hand up against the torch light and said, 'I know that's you, Damascus, and I'll slap your fool head smack off next time I see you.' 'Ain't no Damascus here,' says one of the Cherokee men, serious as a judge. Says, 'We're honest-to-God night riders.' Martha took a step back, squinted at us some more and said, 'Go on. Ain't nobody done that around here for twelve, fifteen years.' 'But you've done something right serious, Martha,' says another Cherokee. 'And we aim to teach you a lesson.' "

John interrupted Henry. "You didn't say anything? She didn't recognize your voice?"

"Right," Henry said.

John began to smile, so Ben did, too.

Henry continued. "So she put her hands on her hips and said, 'What fer?' and we said, 'Consorting with a colored man.' She threw her hands in the air and said, 'Why, there ain't a colored man within a hunnert miles of here.' And we said, 'Well, if anybody could dig one up for funnin', it'd be you.' "

"Well, that took her aback, I must say," Calvin said. "She got real quiet. She looked at the ground for a while."

"Was she trembling?" Lucenia said, leaning forward.

"Can't say, Mrs. Stregal. It was real dark," Henry said. "But she seemed to be thinking over her reputation, sure enough. She looked up and said, 'Why I ain't been doin' nothing but havin' a little fun now and then, living my life jest like y'all out there.' And God so help me I blurted out, 'Do we take that as a plea of guilty, then?' "

John said, "Oh no. You sounded like a lawyer?"

"But I don't think she recognized my voice, she was so hopping mad. So she just called out, 'Aw, hell. What's my punishment?' and we said, 'Get out of town.' 'What?" she said. 'I got all these young-uns to teach. I love them so,'" Henry said in a falsetto voice.

Everyone broke into laughter. John leaned across the table to refill the brothers' wine glasses. No one noticed when Ruth swept in carrying a tray of roasted quail.

Calvin continued. "We said, 'You got some kin in Tennessee.' And she fell to her knees and said, 'Oh, no, not them holy rollers,' and we said, 'Be on the Thursday train.'

"Now at this point, one of the Indians began really getting into the swing of things because he began, um, departing from the script, shall we say," Henry said.

"Indians!" Ruth squealed. "It was y'all and some Indians what run Martha Meddling off?"

"Ssh," hissed Lucenia and Annaliese. They batted their hands at her and pointed to the kitchen. Ruth put the tray on the table and nodded at Henry for more.

"Then he accused her of being a moonshine informer, too," Henry said. "That's when I knew we had to leave. So I kicked my horse posse-leader style and we peeled out of there."

"We had a devil of a time getting back in the dark," Calvin said.

"Well, she sure enough did leave two days ago," Ruth said. "I heard she was powerful mad when she got on that train."

"Mr. Chastain, how can we ever thank you?" Annaliese said.

"Your wickedness is exceeded only by your wit," Lucenia said. "Such a raconteur."

"No need for thanks, dear friends, I assure you," Henry said.

"It is I who should thank you for introducing me to these unique mountain customs," Calvin said. "Quite amusing. Is there anyone else y'all are mad at?"

John was shaking with laughter. "Henry, I believe you left a few broken laws scattered along that dark road."

"Oooohh, and y'all have to wait until August for forgiveness," Ruth said, shaking her head.

Every head at the table turned toward the girl.

"Why, that's when the next revival will be." Ruth looked at the faces that had suddenly gone stern and took a step backward. "'Course, that's strictly between you and your Savior."

"And that's where it shall stay," Annaliese said, shooing her into the kitchen.

"Strictly," Ruth said.

X X

John Stregal stood on his back porch steps urinating into the morning fog still hanging in his yard. From the kitchen window, Annaliese and Ruth watched in stony silence, then turned and looked at each other, grim as fresh widows. They knew that he knew that they could see him.

The porch door squeaked. Annaliese turned to face him, hands on hips. Ruth kept at the dishes in the sink, dropping her head into her bony shoulders. He swept in and buttoned his pants as openly as if he were in a stand of oaks miles away. His cheeks were rosy from the brisk air, his hair so wild and long that Annaliese ached to take scissors to it, or a brush at least. With winter approaching, he had been pushing himself and the sawyers harder—up to 4,000 acres cleared now he had told her last night—until she prayed for snow and ice. Two colds and a sore throat in him had come and gone already and it was only early November. Now, he looked at her with bloodshot eyes that were about to announce something. She folded her arms across her chest and braced.

"Had our first hard freeze last night," he said.

Annaliese nodded. At dawn, she had found a thin crust of ice in the sink.

"Time to kill the hogs."

Annaliese raised an eyebrow. "Why?"

"That's what you do at first freeze."

"What does the weather have to do with it?"

"Any coffee left?" John said as he sailed over to the stove.

Annaliese stared at his back. Much as she hated the hogs, slaughtering them had to be a dangerous, messy job that the children would want to be in the middle of. And who was going to do it? Surely not Herschel, at least, not by himself. Surely not Joe. And why? Their pantry ceilings were thick with hanging hams. She turned to Ruth, but she wouldn't look up from the sink, though Annaliese saw her steal a sideways glance at John as she scrubbed the last plate for the third time.

"Why would we want to kill the hogs? We've got enough ham and bacon for an army," Annaliese said.

"But our hogs will taste better," John said, plucking a coffee cup from the shelf above the stove. "Isn't that right, Ruth?"

Ruth's shoulders clenched, but she finally turned around, eyes on the floor. "Yes, sir, but not all the hogs, Mr. John. Just one or two'll do. It's a mess of work."

John poured his coffee. "Guess you're right."

Ruth looked at Annaliese and relaxed a little. "They been eatin' acorns and chestnuts all year. Makes mighty sweet meat, Miss Anna. Plus you get all them parts, like the feet and head, so you can make headcheese."

Annaliese held up a flattened hand at Ruth, but the girl was just getting started. " 'Course you got to get the eyeballs out first 'fore you cook it. Got to soak all the blood out."

"Stop," Annaliese said. "I may never eat pork again."

John laughed as he waved his cup. "Don't worry so much, Anna. Herschel will do it. But he'll need some help."

Ruth nodded and turned back to the sink.

"I've sent word to our Cherokee friends," John said.

"Cherokee?" Annaliese said. "Our . . ." she lowered her voice, ". . . night riding friends?"

"They can use the cash and they'll get some smoked meat out of it, too."

She walked into the pantry and brought back a scoop of flour. Indians. In her back yard. Knives. Fire, scalding water, blood, curious children. "Where will these people do this?"

Ruth said, "Oh, they're all right."

"They'll work behind the stable, back at the woods' edge. We'll build a smokehouse," John said, striding back to the door.

Another building.

"Got to make sure hit's a full moon when we slaughter them hogs," Ruth said. "Else that meat'll be bad to shrink ever' time you cook it."

"I see," Annaliese sighed. She sprinkled the flour on the tabletop. "Well, how long does it all take?"

"Couple days. We'll bunk the men in the rooms above the stable." John shoved the back door open with his coffee cup and he was gone.

"Seems like a funny thing for him to be thinkin' about with the mill and all," Ruth said, standing on her toes to look out the window and watch him.

Annaliese bent down to open the stove's warming drawer, took out a bowl covered with a towel, and put it on the table. How she had hated being near that stove last summer, but now its halo of warmth and gently crackling fire was like Heaven blowing in. She removed the towel and rubbed flour into her hands before she plunged them into the soft mound of bread dough. As she kneaded it on the table, it released its yeasty fragrance, and she savored the familiar nutty smell. *Bread dough is such a sure thing,* she thought. How little it needed to become what she intended—just enough kneading to activate the yeast, a warm window in which to rise, a seasoned hand to test the oven temperature. How pleasant to work her hands into something that became more elastic the more she pushed.

The almanac predicted November's full moon would arrive on the 25th, and on the morning of the 25th they came. Four dark-haired strangers and Joe climbed the gentle slope that led from the commissary to the homes. At his parlor window, Darrison looked around Minerva and her lessons and saw them coming. He fled to Samuel's home with James and Minerva hurrying behind, and within seconds everyone was on Samuel's porch. The geese boiled out from their hiding places to hiss and charge.

Joe wore a thick black canvas coat over his apron, the last six inches of which fluttered like a flag. Behind him, the shivering men took their hats off as Joe introduced them. The children leaned over the porch railing, frozen still for once.

"Ma'am, this here is Walter Ferguson and Gideon Allen," Joe said of the two closest to him. The men nodded as jointly as they had been introduced, then raised lanky arms to return hats to heads. From underneath the lumpy brims, coal dark eyes sent back cautious stares. Their long faces were as tanned and creased as weathered shoe leather.

"And this 'un is Wade McClain." Joe pointed to a rounded-off man who had tucked his hands in the sleeves of his coat. "And this is Tote McClain. Brothers."

The McClains raised broader, smoother faces to the women and nodded.

"Pleased to meet y'all," said one of them.

Annaliese and Lucenia nodded back.

"Are y'all real Indians?" James asked.

One of the McClains nodded before he kicked at a nagging goose.

"Thank you for coming," Annaliese said.

Lucenia called out, "We are grateful to you for other previous assistance as well."

The Indians exchanged amused glances. Joe sent a puzzled look up to Annaliese, which surprised her. Ruth must have kept her mouth shut after all.

"How do you kill a hog?" Samuel asked as he jumped down the steps. Darrison and James came after him.

"Well," Tote said, "you shoot 'em between the eyes." He drew up an imaginary rifle, squeezed one eye shut against it, and pulled the trigger.

"My word," Minerva said.

"'Course that's how," Darrison said, swaggering past Samuel. One of the geese lowered its head at him and stuck out a black tongue. James stayed on his brother's heels. "Then you slit their throat so you can bleed 'em dry."

"Darrison," his mother said.

"No, ma'am, the boy's right," Tote said.

Lucenia put her hand to her neck. "Well, how about shooting a goose or two?"

A tremor of gentle laughter rippled through the group and the men fell into a more relaxed clump.

From the porch, Ruth's screech rang out. "Y'all be sure to save the bladder for the young 'uns."

"Whatever for?" Annaliese said, craning around at Ruth.

"Why you blow it up, tie it off. Young 'uns can toss it around like a ball," Ruth said.

"Yay!" Emeline yelled.

"No, Emmie," Annaliese said. "Nasty. Ruth, honestly."

"Well, at least she's not suggesting that we eat it," Lucenia said.

"Y'all want to come help?" Wade said. "We should be gutting 'em in 'bout an hour."

"Yes," shouted the two older boys. James backed up the steps toward his mother. She put her hands on his shoulders.

"No, no. We have plans for the day," Annaliese said. She turned to put one foot on the steps. "Come on, let's go." Her arm swept out to collect the boys.

"Quick! Just tell us what you're going to do," Darrison said.

Wade kicked at the dirt for a minute and looked up at the mothers, whose collecting arms were paused.

"Well, once the blood done all run out, you scald the hog in hot water."

Annaliese crossed her arms tightly under her breasts.

"Then you string the carcass up—we got to set up a rig to heft the hog up with ropes and a pulley first thing—and commence to scraping off the hair."

Tote stepped forward. "You take your knife and slice him open to get out the melt and the lights."

"The what?" Annaliese looked down at Joe.

"The organs, ma'am. And the lights are the lungs," Joe said.

"Don't ferget the chitlins," Ruth said.

"Right," Wade said. "You stuff the sausage meat into them at the end of the day."

"The intestines?" Lucenia said.

"Right," Joe said.

Wade continued. "We'll set up a cuttin' board on planks set across two sawhorses and cut him up. First the head comes off . . ."

James clutched his mother's skirts. Annaliese looked over at Emeline, who was captivated, leading her mother to wonder what that said about the child.

" . . . then the hams, picnics, belly, and sides. You trim all this and them trimmings is what gets you your sausage and lard. Slice off the streak o'lean . . ."

"From the sides," Joe said to the women.

" . . . into slabs and they get salted for the curing."

"In the smokehouse," Samuel said.

"Right, son," Wade said. His face creased into brown furrows as he smiled at the boy.

"Must you build a smokehouse?" Annaliese said.

"Now, Miss Anna, it'll be just a little ole thing," Ruth said, who had figured out how Annaliese felt about the buildings going up.

Tote said, "Then you set up your grinder and grind the trimmings, and maybe a little of the shoulder, into sausage. Shove it into the intestines."

"Eww," said one of the boys finally.

"By then it's nigh dark so you hump it to get them hams rubbed with salt, hang 'em in the smokehouse, along with the bacon and sausage, and clean up."

"Golly," Samuel said.

"Yup. It'll take all of us all day," Wade said.

"Just one hog," Annaliese said.

"Yes, ma'am."

"Lord, it's a mess a work," Ruth said. "Sorry I ain't goin' to be here to help y'all."

"Me, too," Samuel muttered.

James let go of his mother's skirt and she looked down at the two men behind Wade and Tote. They were rubbing their arms against the cold, looking around, ready to get on with it.

Lucenia said, "Joe, why don't you take them over to Herschel? In the woods beyond the stables. He's already got a hog penned up back there."

"Yes, ma'am," Joe said. "I'll be back directly. But first, a word with you, Mrs. Stregal?" Joe climbed the steps toward Annaliese.

Annaliese motioned to her children to wait. "All right."

Joe joined her on the porch, where they walked over to a corner.

"What is it, Joe?"

"It's that Slivey. He's hoppin' mad again."

"Oh, well, talk to Mr. Stregal," Annaliese said.

"I have, but he ain't hearin' me. Mr. Stregal has just announced that the mill is goin' to operate twenty hours a day until the snow shuts us down."

"What! At night?"

"Yes, ma'am. Slivey says it's dangerous to wear the men out like that. More'n that, though, he's like to spit fire that Mr. Ben is doin' his job, won't let him make decisions."

Annaliese rubbed her eyes. "He's not saying he'll quit, is he?" As much as she disliked Slivey, they needed him. She needed him. So she could leave a year from next spring.

"Well, that ain't what I'm worried about. That Slivey's got one nasty temper. Seems like he's always lookin' for a black eye."

By now, everyone in the yards and on the porches was staring at them.

"Mama?" Samuel called.

Annaliese started to pull away. "Talk to both Mr. Stregals again, Joe. I can't . . ."

"There's more."

"What."

"Mr. John, well, he's ordering things, too many things, and some things we got no call for."

"Joe, that doesn't sound so . . ."

"Four crates of water dippers? A hogshead of barb wedges when the warehouse is full of 'em? Ten crates of tobacco, the smoking kind, not the chewing kind. That's a dangerous choice for a mill owner."

Annaliese lowered her voice. "All right, all right. Let me think about this."

Joe gave a stiff nod and returned to the yard. The men shuffled on to their work, geese nipping at their heels.

"Let's go," Samuel shouted. He bolted for the back.

"Y'all just hold on a minute," Ruth said from the porch, hands on hips. "Y'all can't go rippin' and runnin' up to the stable on your own. Wait till Joe gets back to help us."

"Aw, Ruth," Sam said. He crossed his arms across his chest.

Lucenia walked over to the boys. "I think I saw a bowl of apples on Aunt Annaliese's back porch."

"Horses like apples," shouted Emeline as she slipped away from her mother to beat the boys into the house.

Ruth turned to Annaliese and Lucenia. "I got a surprise for y'all. Made somethin' for your ridin'."

Since their return, the women had been at the stable every day. For Lucenia's lessons, Annaliese had chosen Belle, a matronly mare as calm as she was wide. Annaliese showed Lucenia how to coax her over to the fence by shaking oats in a bucket. The scratchy sound triggered sweet memories for Annaliese—Saturday mornings at the riding club, laughing cousins in hay fights, wind-burned cheeks. Belle had dropped her graying nose into the bucket that Lucenia held out with a stiff arm while Annaliese guided Lucenia's other hand to the mare's velvet ears. In time, Lucenia learned to brush Belle's knotty mane, then the withers, the back, the rump, talking to herself to ease her fear as she worked her way down the glistening body. The women moved on to tack lessons. With the patience of a seasoned schoolmarm, Belle withstood the fumbling hands trying to put a bit in her mouth and many times Annaliese saw her stand still, untethered and free to run, while Lucenia fiddled with the bridle going over her ears. Finally, Lucenia had collected the courage to mount. The women had already agreed they would cast propriety aside and ride astride rather than sidesaddle for safety. Gathering her skirt up, checking to make sure the men were out of sight, Lucenia hoisted her left foot up into the stirrup, threw the right one over the rump and, with a mighty shove from Annaliese, landed on top of a horse for the first time. Annaliese led them around the corral, murmuring gently in Belle's ear, more for the benefit of rider than beast. Eventually, Lucenia's confidence in her hands at the reins grew, and one day Annaliese let her wave her away. At this point, Annaliese mounted, too, to ride alongside. So it was with stiff new saddles squeaking and uncertain knees clutching that the two mistresses of the manor rode around the corral. Eventually they ventured out into the sloping meadow off Bunny Mountain, where they successfully threaded their way around sheds and fences.

Today was to be their first ride into the hills behind the homes— probably the last ride before serious winter and certainly the best way to keep the children away from the butchering.

"A surprise?" Lucenia said, raising her eyebrows. "Something you sewed for us?"

"Wait right thar," Ruth said and she ran into Lucenia's house. Moments later, she returned with two small rolls of cloth. Holding them out, one in each hand, she let them unfurl.

Trousers. The women gasped and looked at each other.

"Oh, come on now. Y'all ain't gone be the only ones with britches," Ruth cackled. She yanked up her skirt to reveal her own pair. "I know it's a might irregular, but don't it make sense?"

Annaliese looked at Lucenia. "You know, it does."

Lucenia winced. "Oh, I don't know . . ."

"Well, jest take 'em," Ruth said as she shoved the bundles into their hands.

Lucenia held hers up against her broad hips. The pants were made of coffee-colored flannel, plain and blousey, with a button fly. "Mercy," she said.

"Oooh, they'll be so warm," Annaliese said as she smoothed her hand across hers.

"Now, lookit this," Ruth said, bringing a third roll out of her apron pocket. She snapped open a tiny but identical pair of flannel pants.

A gunshot rang out in the crisp, winter air. A riot of hog squeals followed.

"Gracious, let's put them on and go," Annaliese said.

"I don't suppose you could add a bit of lace or ribbon to these, Ruth?" Lucenia said.

"Might could," Ruth laughed.

Joe was hurrying through the last of the saddling, for the gunshots from the woods were making the horses jittery. While Ruth and Annaliese helped the boys mount, he began his final check on Belle's saddle. Just as he started to tighten the girth strap that ran under her belly, Emeline came alongside and flipped up her dress to display her new trousers. Lucenia arrived seconds later to find the man blushing and moving on to the next horse. She scooped the child up and headed outside. They found Annaliese in the corral, mounted on her horse and making irritated motions at Lucenia to lift Emeline to her.

Finally, Joe led the long string of riders out of the corral and toward the mountains. Annaliese was behind him, then Lucenia, followed by the boys. Ruth brought up the rear. Annaliese had laid down the rules: walking only—no cantering—and they would move single file to keep the horses from breaking into a run. The butchering was underway at the edge of the woods. Distance spared the riders the details, but they saw the men, backs bent, dragging the hog's body toward a steaming cauldron. Smoke billowed from a furious fire beneath. One man was chopping down a tree. No one waved at them.

"You know those men pretty well, Joe?" Annaliese called out.

"All my life," Joe said.

They plodded up a slope, picking their way through the gray trees and kicking up the blanket of decaying leaves, the detritus of summer's canopies. The papery sound floated through the naked limbs, scared up a hawk.

Joe took them around the base of the hill they knew until homes and stable disappeared. They walked beside a rushing stream, crossed it, and found an open field edged with blackened trees. The fire had swept through long ago, for young pine trees were already knee-high in the scruff. As the riders ambled through the field, the horses tried to drop their heads to munch around the sumac and vines. Annaliese turned around to check on Lucenia, who knew not to let a horse feed, but was pulling the reins too hard as Belle's head went down. Soon, the horse would be obeying this order to back up.

"Loosen up on the reins, Lucenia," Annaliese said.

Lucenia gave them some slack. Belle gave up and waddled on.

"That's good, Mother," called Darrison from behind her. "Good. Now just talk to her, tell her no."

"Yes, thank you, everyone," Lucenia said, not sounding thankful.

"Mama, look," Samuel said. "Up in the sky."

Annaliese and Joe pulled to a stop, as did the others behind them, and peered skyward. The leading edge of a swarm of black birds had just come over the mountain and now swept toward them, inky and slow and as thick as molasses. "Bullbats, heading south," shouted Joe just before the sound of hundreds of working wings drowned him out. Emeline pressed her body into her mother's. The horses skittered sideways and looked up, too. Now the swarm was overhead, the sky black and churning. The birds dipped into the tree tops to try to feed, even down into the field where the riders stood as still as their horses would allow. Hands flew to hold on to hats in the wash of air trailing off so many wings. Finally, the frontline disappeared over the next mountain, so the sky slowly returned to white as the swarm thinned out to a hundred, then a dozen, then nothing but the retreating dark line of creatures responding to their timeless call.

Annaliese watched them in awe of nature's forces that sent the flock on its way, this same way for hundreds of years. All around her other ancient cycles of life slept, waiting for signals that no eye could see.

Joe raised his hand. "Everybody ready?"

They kicked their mounts.

At the sight of the next stream, Emeline felt her own call from nature, which she announced more loudly than her mother would have preferred. Joe nodded and said he had already planned to stop in the next meadow. Once there, some headed for a stream or tree. Ruth joined Annaliese and Emeline in disappearing into a grove.

Afterward, the three huddled against the wind for a moment, listening to the creaking branches above their heads. Against the ashen sky, the chapped limbs looked so dead Annaliese feared they would snap. She turned to leave, but Ruth was lingering, talking to herself, the latest in recent odd behavior that Annaliese was tiring of trying to get her to explain.

Ruth kicked at the carpet of leaves. "Looks dead under here, don't it?" she said.

Annaliese looked at what Ruth had turned up—a soggy brown mat, a little ash-colored mold, and the black, bare earth underneath.

"Come March, the sun will stream though them bare branches, warm up this forest floor," Ruth said. "In a few days, little green shoots'll come pokin' up through these here leaves."

The wind was picking up, sending the branches into broader sweeps. Emeline started to whimper and pull at her mother. Annaliese said, "We need to be going."

Ruth swept a bony arm above the leaf mat, like the Creator at His seas. "Then, in June this here will be covered with big green umbrellas and under those umbrellas—guess what?"

"What," Annaliese said as she picked up Emeline.

"The mayapple blossom—the purtiest white flower you ever seen. Looks like a cup—one of them creamy-colored cups y'all save for company? Now isn't that the fiestiest plant you ever heard of?"

"Fiesty? A plant? Really, Ruth, let's go."

"It puts all it's got into producin' one blossom, one fruit." Ruth turned her pale face up to the sky. "Couple of weeks to rise up while the sun can still come through the trees. After that, the leaves fill in, darkness returns. Weeks later, the plant's done what it came to do—make one mayapple—and then it's done, gone, for good."

Ruth turned solemn eyes to Annaliese.

Annaliese froze. This was not about flowers.

"Sometimes, darkness comes in on people, too," she said.

A chill went up Annaliese's spine. She wrapped her arms tighter around Emeline.

"If they feel it coming, they might hurry through their business, too."

Annaliese stared at the mat of leaves and absorbed Ruth's words like the cold she felt seeping into her boots. The girl was talking about John and his urgency, the urgency they all couldn't understand. Working the men too hard, ruining his health. His race against tomorrow's darkness.

Ruth kicked leaves back over the bare spot.

If Ruth was right, then that meant that John did know the truth about his father's death. He knew that Lawrence Stregal had waited too long, let too many lucid days slip by before they were gone for good. John saw that in families, things get passed down along with the furniture. Good looks and brains, yes, but also demons and misery. Something had happened back in Louisville, who knew when, that told John his time of playing his odds were over. He had faced his choices. He could wait and find out what his later years held for him or he could act boldly while he was still able.

Annaliese looked at the ground as she finally understood. The lumber company was not the reason she and the children were here. They were the reason the lumber company was here.

She stormed over to Ruth and slapped her. "Stop it," she screamed as her eyes tore into Ruth's horrified face. "It's not true."

Emeline clapped her hands over her ears. Annaliese dropped her to the ground.

"Why, Miss Anna, I didn't . . ." Ruth stuttered.

"He's not what you think he is. I've seen the way you shy away from him, like he's some sort of diseased vagrant."

Ruth's face went white.

Annaliese raised a shaking finger. "See! See there! I was right. You think he's disgusting." She yanked Emeline away. They tore across the forest toward the riding party. Ruth scrambled to follow her, shouting pitiful denials as she went.

"You will respect him, no matter what." Annaliese was shouting as she burst out of the underbrush. By now, Emeline was wailing at the top of her lungs. Together, they scared a flock of birds out of the trees overhead.

Lucenia had just remounted Belle, who was sidling toward the forest and trying to drop her head to nibble, so both were absorbed in a battle for control when Annaliese and Emeline arrived. Belle bolted forward, Lucenia fell backward, bounced left, then right, but stayed in the saddle somehow while Belle raced off across the meadow.

"Pull her in," Darrison shouted. "The reins!"

Joe jumped on his horse and tore after them.

Belle circled back toward the party. Everyone could see that Lucenia was, in fact, getting control of the reins and she was leaning forward, clamping her knees into the saddle as she should. But the saddle was slipping to the left and as Belle continued to lope around the field, it slid farther and farther down. Joe had reached them by now, but his grabbing at the reins was pointless. Seeing that Lucenia was about to fall between his horse and hers, he had to pull away. Again the saddle shifted. Lucenia saw the ground coming at her and let go. She fell off the horse and slammed into the ground at full gallop.

Everyone raced over. As Annaliese fell to her knees beside Lucenia, she scanned the ground for stumps or rocks. Nothing but matted brush and leaves. With some relief, she put her hands on Lucenia's shoulders, patting for broken bones.

"Mother," James gasped as he dropped down beside her.

Darrison wormed his way past the others to see. "Are you all right?" he asked.

With a moan, Lucenia opened her eyes. She twisted her shoulders and arched her back, prompting cries from the crowd.

"Don't move yet," Annaliese said. "Let me check." Annaliese threw Lucenia's skirt up and ran her hands over the trousered legs. Seeing nothing wrong and not hearing otherwise, she bent Lucenia's legs, testing her knees.

Lucenia swatted her away. "Put my skirt down," she groaned.

"Thank God for this soft meadow," Darrison said.

"What about your arms?" Annaliese said as her hands began creeping up her sister-in-law's sleeves.

Lucenia raised her arms, bent them, wiggled her hands. "Battered but operating, it appears."

Joe arrived leading Belle and his horse by the reins. "She all right?" he asked.

Lucenia rolled from side to side and sat up. "I have a headache. Let's go home. I'm walking."

Annaliese and Joe looked at each other. Joe took the plunge. "Well, ma'am, you know the best thang is fer you to get right back on."

Darrison was helping his mother to her feet. As she straightened her back, he threw himself against her in an awkward embrace. "Joe's right, Mother. You'll never ride again if you don't," he said.

Her face softened as her son leaned backward to look her over again. "Well, then," Lucenia said. "All right, Joe. Fix that saddle cinch, would you?"

Joe grabbed the cinch that ran under the horse's belly and gave a yank until it seemed as tight as possible. Then he jabbed his knee into her ribs. With a grunt, Belle exhaled the last of her resistance, and the cinch got its final tug.

Annaliese shook her head. "I thought I knew that horse."

"Still got a few tricks up her old sleeves, I reckon," Joe said.

Lucenia mounted Belle with Joe's help. Ruth crept toward Annaliese. "Mrs. Stregal," she said. "I'm . . ."

Annaliese looked at the ground. "Not now, Ruth."

Joe waved everyone to their horses and the group began its return home. Ruth was uncharacteristically quiet in the rear.

At dusk, Annaliese took supper to the McClain brothers and their friends. Ruth had raised her eyebrows when she was asked to hand over the basket she had packed for them. She didn't say a word but she held onto the basket too long when Annaliese reached for it. Annaliese would not look at her.

The sound of her footsteps on the stairs to the second floor of the stable announced her arrival. The door opened just as she raised her knuckles to knock. Wade McClain smiled and lifted his hand to a hat that wasn't there. He laughed at himself.

"Evening, ma'am," he said. The smell of soggy flannel and smoke came off him. Another man came to stand behind him.

She put the basket in Wade's hands.

"Hope you like chicken," she said. Wade was not an old man, she could now see. His face was smooth as a brown egg and framed in the blackest hair she had ever seen. "You do like . . . chicken?" She fumbled for what she really wanted to say.

There was an awkward silence. Then, "Yes, ma'am. I grew up in these mountains. Cain't not like chicken." Wade looked beyond her at the sun slipping behind the hills. "Over by Two Knees."

"What do you do when you're not slaughtering hogs?" she tried again. *Really, this was too nosy.*

"Sometimes, me and Tote . . ." He turned to look at the man behind him, who nodded at Annaliese, "we work in the blacksmith's shop in Pinch."

"The smith is our father," Tote said. His cheekbones were higher, the skin a deeper brown.

"Please tell me your name again. Sorry that I don't remember it," she said.

"Wade, ma'am."

"Oh, yes, that's right. I do recall that Joe said that," she said, fiddling with her collar. "Well, I hope you enjoy the supper."

"Yes, ma'am. Much obliged."

They closed the door.

By ten o'clock, the house was quiet enough. After checking on the children, Annaliese led John downstairs to the kitchen where embers still throbbed in the wood stove. Steam curled out of the three buckets of water she had placed atop. She and John wrapped rags around the handles. Together they carried them into a small room beside the kitchen and poured the water into a tub. John staggered to a chair and fell into it, shoulders slumped, head down. She stood behind him and brought scissors out of a pocket. While the bath water cooled, her hands went to work, sending soft brown clumps to the pine floor. The scissor's whisper was the only sound in the room. Slowly, she pulled a brush through his hair, patted it, checked her work. When she was satisfied, she brushed it once more, then ran her fingers through it in wild destruction. John spun around on the stool to stare at her, stunned. She flipped open his shirt, then hers. He stood, helped her out of her skirt and underclothes. They slipped into the warm water. With her eyes closed, she found his mouth and guided his fingers down her body to the swollen folds that he had hurried by for too long. If peace was not to be John Stregal's by nature, perhaps she would make it his by design. Neither of them gave a thought to her cycle.

When the snow finally came, it came serious, as the locals said. For three weeks, it fell and blew and piled, so that by the middle of December their lifeline to the outside world—the railroad—had been severed. Neither food nor mail arrived for weeks. Every morning, Annaliese stood in her pantry eyeing the shelves. On the bottom shelf sat a ten-pound cheese wheel and a few cans of salmon and tomatoes, the last of the store-bought goods. But above them rose the wall of jars brimming with Ruth's garden. In the smokehouse, dozens of salt-caked hams hung from the ceiling, curing. It seemed enough, but for how long? There were ten people to feed.

Every man and machine in the compound was still. At six inches of snow, John had finally suspended the logging and sent the workers home, save a trusted few who would repair and re-tool the mill machines under Slivey's supervision. But John walked down to the office every day.

From her porch, Annaliese would squint against the snow's glare and watch him go. She prayed that he would leave Slivey be.

John seemed to accept Mother Nature's forcing his hand. With relief, Annaliese watched him uncoil more each day, though sometimes, when he rubbed his temples, she suspected headaches. He spent only the mornings at the office, walking back at mid-day to remove soggy clothes, eat dinner, and read. On good days, he read to the children.

Annaliese watched their small faces react to his gravelly, daddy bear voice or pleading orphan eyes and other histrionics and she thought of the juries who must have followed his performances just as avidly, as they would again one day, she told herself.

As for Ruth, she said nothing again about John but blatantly avoided him. When he entered a room, Ruth left it. When he spoke, she looked away. It made Annaliese tense the way the girl reacted to him, but she understood it and forgave her, as she had months ago forgiven her the conversation about the mayapple. One especially frosty day, Annaliese found her sitting at the piano trying out the keys. Bits of a song that Ruth sometimes sang began to emerge. Annaliese stood beside the piano and listened, impressed with the musical ear Ruth clearly had. She sat down, and together, with one woman humming the gospel song and the other showing her the right keys for the melody, they found some of their way back to their easy way with each other.

Lucenia, on the other hand, was a wreck. By December twenty-second, she was frantic about her missing catalog orders.

"Christmas is just days away," she said for the third time one afternoon.

They sat in Lucenia's parlor cutting paper dolls and clothes out of magazines. The aroma of Ruth's dessert—pumpkin pie from the smell of it—wafted through the house. "These paper dolls will jolly Emeline for a while, but what about the boys? All of the presents I ordered for them are sitting on a trestle somewhere."

"Uh huh," Annaliese said, having run out of meaningful responses the day before. She finished cutting out a fur coat and laid it on the table. Lucenia picked it up, worked her scissors delicately around to refine the trimming, and returned it to the table. "Can't John do something?" she asked.

Annaliese sighed again. "I think he's telegraphed the man at the Pinch depot."

"Maybe they'll send a gang to dig out the tracks."

"I don't suppose they have a gang on hand, Lucenia. Besides, everyone down there knows we're all right, that we have plenty of food."

Lucenia put the scissors in her lap. "Don't you want to see what I've ordered for you?"

"Rouge and black lingerie, no doubt."

Lucenia straightened in her seat, looking startled. Without a word, she began flipping through the magazine again, scissors held agape in her right hand, but she smiled.

Outside, the muffled sounds of dogs barking drifted across the snow. The women went to the parlor window and moved the drapes aside. The sawmill dogs had not barked since the last six inches had arrived.

"Who on earth?" Lucenia asked.

"Surely there are no strangers down there."

"When it'll be dark soon."

Two bundled figures came out of the commissary and walked toward the mill. The dogs sent up a chorus of frenetic yelps. Annaliese and Lucenia scooped up blankets and ran for the porch where they heard the rumble of a locomotive and the screech of a dozen iron wheels grabbing the rails. The women shot off the porch and tumbled through the snow, hands raised against the sun that was setting. They arrived at the commissary panting, dragging their blankets, and raced toward the last building that stood between them and the railroad yard. Annaliese got there first, turned the corner, and ran into a wall of black wool.

"Whoa!" said the black coat as Annaliese fell into the snow.

Lucenia slid to a stop in time to teeter above Annaliese.

Henry Chastain reached down and put one hand in Annaliese's and the other at her elbow. "Can you stand?"

"Oh, yes, of course," Annaliese said, though she did not want to stand. She wanted to crawl away to the nearest door, so she concentrated on brushing snow off of her skirt.

"Mr. Chastain, how nice to see you," Lucenia blurted. "But how did you . . . ?"

Calvin Chastain, pink in the face and puffing, came up behind Henry. Beside him, Wade and Tote McClain waved bundled hands.

"We heard y'all were in trouble up here," Henry said.

"I should say. Desperate conditions," Lucenia said.

"Snow was blockin' the tracks at Big Cut, we heard. Train's been sitting on the tracks for a long time. The engineer couldn't back it out, so he jumped on the hand-car and came back to town," Calvin said.

"This morning we went out lookin' for volunteers to dig out, and see who stepped right up?" Henry said, gesturing at the McClains.

"We shoveled out the tracks from Big Cut to here," Calvin said. "I swear, this manual labor business is hard on a man of medicine."

"You brought up the whole train?" Lucenia asked.

"Wade knew how to run it," Henry said.

"Our heroes," Lucenia sang.

"Oh, my, I can't believe it," Annaliese said. "You just don't know what's on that train. Chocolates and books from my family and . . ."

Lucenia shot her an expectant look.

"And my Christmas gift from Lucenia," Annaliese laughed.

"Six cars behind that engine," Calvin said.

Annaliese realized that Henry was staring at her. She was a chapped-cheeked, runny-nosed mountain woman in a hairy blanket and she didn't care. She started giggling.

"Anna?" Lucenia said. "What is the matter with you?"

"Oh, I'm just so happy, of course."

"Come on." Lucenia turned toward the men. "You all must be starving."

"I've already promised 'em supper," called John from the rail car. He strode forward to stand beside Henry. "Sure do appreciate this."

"And Christmas supper, too," Lucenia said. "Mercy, stay for as long as you like."

"Well, just the night," Henry said. "Got to get back to town tomorrow."

Ruth fried extra chickens and opened more jars and the informal meal that unfolded was the most relaxing entertaining that Annaliese could remember. At the table, the children sat alert and excited, for Henry had announced Christmas gifts and his stories geared toward them were mesmerizing. Laughter spilled out of the kitchen, where the McClains were happily settling in with Ruth and Herschel and

Minerva. Afterward, though Christmas was still three days away, the mothers nodded yes at the gift opening. Everyone moved by the fire in Lucenia's parlor to watch.

The boys tore into their packages and were soon dumping toy cannons, horses, and soldiers on the rug. War was declared. Emeline edged around the conflict to go to her father, who was seated in a chair. While the battle raged, she wedged herself between his knees and opened her gift. It was a tiny wooden wagon and horse.

"Papa, look. A wagon." She shoved it under his nose.

John turned it slowly in his hands. On the side of the wagon, painted in red: "Stregal Brothers Lumber Company." His haggard face broke into a smile.

"Thank you, Mr. Chastain," Emeline said. "My dolly can go for a ride."

From her chair, Lucenia waved at the boys sprawled on the floor. "Boys?" she prompted.

"Thank you, Mr. Chastain and Dr. Chastain," they sang.

Leaning against the fireplace mantel, Henry and Calvin nodded.

Lucenia was beaming. "Thank you, Henry. And may I say, since we're being so informal these days—here we are, in the wilderness, abandoning so many of the conventions we used to hold dear—may I call you Henry?" She turned to Calvin. "Calvin?"

Ben's eyes strained at their sockets.

Henry and Calvin, however, reacted as though she had just offered them apple brandy.

"Why, yes," Calvin said, waving the question away.

"Of course," Henry said. "Y'all feel like family."

Annaliese was beginning to feel that she could say the same.

XXI

A cross the glens and meadows of north Georgia, spring moved in as slowly and silently as fog. Frozen slabs of black leaves thawed into puddles that became trickles, icy but moving. The trickles meandered through the forest, carving trails in the snow until they merged into streams and the streams into rivers. To the banks of these rushing waters the mountain creatures came, heads bent down in quick lapping, ears cocked to listen for hunger on four feet. Birds called to one another, their songs of seduction drifting away to other branches where potential mates listened and judged. Wildflowers unfurled the shiny new leaves that were mere backdrops for the coming glory: the Trout Lily, with its butter-colored blossoms that would bob gently above its leaves, the pinkish Pussytoes, the purple-striped Jack-in-the-Pulpit.

Into these rustling hills John Stregal fled. While the last of the snow still clung to the highest hollows, he and Hoyt saddled their horses to cruise the farthest reaches of the Stregal timber rights. The sawmill's whistle sent out its urgent call and the workers came back to their mules and saws and cash. Soon, the screams of the mill's massive machinery again drifted up to the side-by-side homes on the hill. The schedule was back to six days a week.

The Stregal children shot out of their houses, too. They ventured farther and farther from home each day. With Herschel or Ruth or even the tottering Minerva along, the children explored the surrounding canyons and brackens. Herschel started them on building a raft. The boys could not put Emeline off by denying her saw or nail and she was the first one aboard and the last one off on the day they launched on the strongest stream that Herschel would allow.

On a damp March morning, Annaliese walked out her back door and saw Ruth walking the borders of the old garden. Herschel stood nearby, arms crossed, head down in careful listening. Annaliese headed in their direction, straining to hear the details about what would be going in.

"This year, this here garden's goin' to be put in right," Ruth said. "Don't let's forget some castor oil plants. And calamus and hoarhound."

Herschel's scruffy red beard wagged side to side.

"If you was to plow way out to here . . ." she walked eight feet beyond last year's edge ". . . we'd be able to plant enough white potatoes to keep Mr. Ben happy." She kicked at the ground. "Lord, he loves them things."

Herschel nodded, but Annaliese knew that he hated plowing.

Ruth turned at the garden's future corner and walked off another five feet, with her back to Annaliese.

"Reckon you could stop right there, Ruth?" Herschel said, following his wife.

"Hmmm. Maybe some turnips."

Herschel squinted into the bright sun and sighed.

Ruth smiled. "And what shall we plant to make you happy?"

He pulled her into his arms and wiggled her playfully. "I reckon I like what we already been plantin'."

Annaliese, only a few yards away now, stopped in her tracks. At the sound of her boots, Herschel and Ruth dropped their embrace, shuffled apart awkwardly. Annaliese made a U turn and said over her shoulder, "Don't forget the okra."

Later that day, Annaliese walked out on her front porch, lowered her Venetian blind, and sat down with a crisp new copy of *Walden*, a Christmas gift from her cousin Kathryn. Only now, with spring's deliverance of everyone into the outdoors, had she found peace enough to open it. "Comfort against the solitude," Kathryn had written on the card. *Solitude*? Well, now, she finally had some. She dutifully opened the book, but several paragraphs later, she couldn't remember a word of what she had just read.

John's January had been bad, February even worse. He had battled constant chills and fevers, ranted at the weather, paced the floors wanting to get the mill up and running again. Other times, he slept too much. The dark moods could last for days no matter what Annaliese did or said, then just when she despaired of ever sharing a flash of happiness with him again, he rose out of it. But the upswings unnerved her as well, for then he did not sleep at all and he boasted so convincingly she couldn't sort out the truth in what he said. She discovered that if the truth was to be found in John any more, it was in his eyes when they were inches above her face, lit only by moonlight. To savor it, she slowed his hands as they moved across her skin. She guided his fingers with an encouragement that he had learned to follow now that he was realizing the intricacies of the landscape and the benefits of knowing it. If once she had thought that that kind of pleasure was never to stir within her again after David and that it was depraved, she now knew otherwise. Finally, together, unbridled and astonished, they finished what David had started. On the mornings after, she did not think that it was just her imagination that John was calmer. Sometimes the calm lasted an hour, sometimes a day. It was all she knew to do. But now he was exhausted at night from his days in the hills. The bond was gone. He was short-tempered and edgy. She hated his being out in the cold where he could get sick again. Today, at least he was going to be inside going over contracts and invoices with Ben.

She slammed the book closed and stood up. "Ruth, I'm going to the office," she called into the front door and started down the hill.

At the commissary, Joe was cleaning windows. He turned at the sound of her boots on the road. She waved back and pointed at the office. Joe nodded.

Ben and John looked up from the desk and raised their eyebrows at her.

"Just thought I'd stop by," she said, wishing now that she had brought something—food at least—as her reason. Last time, she had brought Ben a hat he didn't need. Now they were on to her, especially John whose lips were pressed firmly together. They just nodded and turned back to their papers, leaving Annaliese to wander around. Even now, the grimy office conditions still surprised her. Along the walls, yellowing calendars and schedules hung cock-eyed from nails. A coat of fine sawdust covered the dark oak floor and shelves. The miasma of forgotten coffee and acidic kerosene burned her nostrils.

She noticed a stack of papers spilling across the top of a wooden filing cabinet: folders, letters, ledgers, bank statements. Without a word, Annaliese began organizing them.

"I was about to get to that, Anna," Ben said gently.

"Is there something you want?" John asked, less so.

"Oh, well, I suppose I am just anxious to get out of that house. Perhaps I could file these for you?"

The doorknob rattled and Hoyt stuck his head in. "Ready, Mr. Stregal?"

John nodded. "Be right there."

"See you 'round back."

John began scraping his papers together.

"You're going out?" Annaliese knew it was a ridiculous question, but she couldn't stop herself.

"Yup."

"Where are you going?"

The men looked up at her with hooded eyes. "Not sure yet," John said in a way that made her doubt that.

"May I come with you?"

"What?" John's voice rose. "This isn't pleasure ridin', Annaliese." He pushed the papers back to Ben and straightened up in his chair. "I can't have you wearing pants and riding astride a horse around Hoyt."

A jolt of embarrassment shot through her. He had no call to bring this argument of theirs up in front of Ben. She had tried to tell John how much safer it was with her legs wrapped around the horse. Nor did she care for the curl in his lip as he said "astride." He shouldn't have used that word in front of Ben, either. Her face turned crimson.

"*Cross saddle*, John," she said in a steely whisper.

He shook his head. "I don't care what you call it. Answer's no. Do what you want when you're riding with Ruth or Lucenia, but . . ."

"I will," she said. "In fact, we'll go today."

They heard Ben inhale sharply.

John slapped his hat on and moved toward her. "Fine. But don't go into the mountains, especially not near Black Face."

She crossed her arms. "Why?"

"The trails are too wet and slick. Your horse slips, breaks a leg, it's too far for you to walk back." John stalked to the door, opened it, and looked outside as he spoke. "Shit, Anna. What's gotten into you?" He stormed out the door.

"Me? What's gotten into me?" she shouted at the door.

At the desk, Ben held his head in his hands. "Annaliese, leave him be."

She stared at the door, wishing all of her words back into her mouth.

Ben turned his broad face up to her and folded his hands on the paperwork. "You can't watch him all the time."

She turned around to look at him. "Is it that obvious?"

He laced his fingers together over his belly.

"Ben, help me." She walked over to his desk.

"What do you want me to do?"

Annaliese weighed her next words carefully. The secret she had stifled all winter had finally gnawed through her resolve. She felt she was going to spill it all to Lucenia any day but first she had to find out how much Ben knew. She crossed her arms as she looked down at him. "I know about your father."

Ben's eyelids slid down over his eyes and back up slowly. "What are you talking about?"

"You know what I'm talking about. The cause of his death."

Ben shifted in his seat. "How?"

"I spoke with someone who worked with him."

"All right. So?"

"Why didn't you tell me?" She stopped at the edge of the desk and rested her fingertips on it.

"Has nothing to do with us, Anna." Ben crossed his arms across his barrel chest.

A burst of air exploded from her lungs. "What?"

"My father's end has nothing to do with us."

"How can you say that?"

"Well, what are *you* saying? That John will choose the same course?"

"I've lived long enough to see that certain family histories repeat themselves. And your father's behavior. . . what I heard . . . sounds like some of the things John's doing."

"Bah. He doesn't even know what Father was like at work. He was ten when Father died. Mother and I told him it was pneumonia."

"And Lucenia? Does she know?"

Ben pointed one plump index finger at her. "No." Annaliese took a step backward. "I don't want her worrying about me the way you're worrying over John."

"Worrying about *you!*"

"What, you assume a bad end for one son, but not the other?"

She hadn't thought of that. "Oh, Ben, I'm . . ."

"Relax, Anna. John's got a lot on his mind is all."

Annaliese grabbed the ledge of the desk. "But is it the same, Ben? The way John's acting? You were eighteen. You remember."

He slowly shook his head. "No, no, not the same." He shrugged. "Look, I know John's been cranky and extravagant and that he's started highballing the operation around here, but so what? He's a good businessman. We're making a fortune."

At this, she pulled away. "So that's all you care about? Making money?"

Ben rose from his chair, came around the desk, and put an arm around her shoulder. She stiffened at his touch.

"That didn't sound right," he said. "I just meant that he's unlike Father in that way. Near the end of his life, Father *lost* a fortune. Look, John's a genius, a smarter man drunk than four of my law partners sober and together in church. Not to mention more honest. I've joined him in this because I think he'll succeed and . . ." His voice went watery. " . . . he would've done this without me, Anna. I am here to see him through this."

Annaliese stared at his florid face, so close to hers that she could see the red veins crisscrossing his swollen nose. She hadn't thought of that: Ben as protector.

"I'm watching out for him, too, you know," he finished. He squeezed her again.

She leaned into his grasp as a way of relenting, but she was not relieved. Ben was not a man who inspired confidence. But clearly he was a man who loved his only brother. If he had agreed to this venture out of concern for John, a statement that she had no reason to disbelieve, then she had to appreciate that. And if Lucenia had come along to watch the watcher, well, that was understandable. Fate was not theirs to control anyway. They were all tied together, like tails on John's kite.

As Ben released her, she said, "All right."

❧

XXII

The road under the horses' hooves was indeed too muddy and slick, but Annaliese and Lucenia weren't turning back for anything. They had made it past Herschel. Like schoolgirls slipping the headmistress, they had pulled on their trousers and stolen away without him. Lucenia rode Belle, whom she had forgiven and groomed and fed with Darrison during the winter, which had bolstered her confidence, as had Annaliese's tightening the cinch belt twice before they left. They headed toward the sawmill.

"Where shall we go today?" Lucenia asked.

"The schoolhouse," Annaliese said.

"That's kind of far, isn't it?"

"Aren't you curious about it?" Annaliese's eyes were on the office door.

Lucenia shot her a perplexed look but nodded.

They passed the mill yard and the commissary undetected and turned onto the road to Pinch.

"Herschel's going to worry about us the whole time," Lucenia said.

"We'll be fine," Annaliese said. Finally, her face relaxed.

Lucenia shifted in the saddle, sending Belle into a burst of grunts and snorts. "I know, Belle. We'll both be sore tomorrow, won't we, girl?"

They rode along in silence for a while. When the road became steep, they got off and walked, as much for the feel of exercising their softened calves and the brisk air pumping into their lungs as for the safety of the horses. When the path became rocky, they climbed back on. A gunmetal-cold pall hung overhead in the gray trees, but underfoot tiny green shoots nudged their way out of the soil along the edges of what would become the lush forest. The wildflowers were rushing for their sun just as Ruth had said.

"It's breathtaking," Lucenia said. "Life's sprouting from every crevice." She pointed to a granite ledge furry with ferns. "Even the rocks are green."

Annaliese looked at the columns of trees lining the road, gazed up at their limbs overhead that arched toward one another, bare now but soon to leaf out and form the vaults that would nurture all life below. Even without green canopies, the embrace of the towering trees brought her a sense of peace.

"It'll be April soon, Anna. One year in Pinch," Lucenia said.

Annaliese smiled. "Seems much longer than that."

Lucenia cocked her head. "You've been unusually quiet lately."

"Just a lot on my mind."

"John."

Annaliese nodded.

"But he seems to be all right lately."

"Not really."

The horses rounded a bend in the road and the women pulled their reins to slow down to admire the view ahead—a breathtaking view of pristine meadows and forested slopes leading up to Black Face Mountain. But as the bend straightened, the view was an ugly surprise.

Waves of naked land, scraped down to nothing but red mud and limb trash, rose on slope after slope. The majestic trees that for centuries had stood as sovereigns of the valley were now jagged stumps. Ashen branches lay scattered along the gouged-out trails to the river, where the logs had been sent on their way.

"Oh, my God," Lucenia said.

Annaliese gasped. "Everything. Gone. Even the saplings."

The few young trees that still stood were nicked and bent into a black fate. Already, some of them were yellowing into death, taking the future of this hillside with them. Last spring, there had been a wall of trees and brush, a forest so thick that a man could not have ridden a horse through it. Now, only the muddy tracks of mules and men climbed the hill to meet the riders. The wind picked up and blew down the hill, unchecked by the pines that last spring had rustled softly. The quiet was so deep even the horses turned their heads toward the valley.

"He's always said he'd cut only the mature trees." Annaliese turned to look at Lucenia. "Oh, my God. It's this he didn't want me to see."

"What do you mean?"

"This morning he told me not to come up here."

"But that's ludicrous. You'd find out as soon as we reopened the school. What's the man thinking?"

Annaliese's head fell backward as she moaned, "Oh, Ben is so wrong."

"About what?" Lucenia guided Belle over to Annaliese.

"He's just like their father."

"What are you talking about? What's their father got to do with this?"

"He was wild, they said. Shocking everyone with his behavior."

"Who's 'they'? What was shocking? Annaliese!"

"He was destructive, uncontrollable, Lucenia. And to end his misery, he jumped off a bridge into the Ohio River."

Lucenia brought a gloved hand to her mouth. "Lawrence Stregal?"

"They were right." Annaliese slapped tears away.

"Who?"

"An old man who worked with him. I spoke to him when I was home." Annaliese was sobbing now, rocking in her saddle. Belle began sidling away.

"But . . ." Lucenia looked down at the valley as this sank in. "Ben never told me any of this."

"John swore he'd never do anything like this. He lied to us." Annaliese dropped the reins and buried her face in her hands.

"I thought . . ." muttered Lucenia, still shaking her head, " . . . but Ben tells me everything."

"It's happening. Despite all I've done."

Lucenia guided Belle back over. She picked up the reins Annaliese had dropped and tried to place them in her hands. "Anna. Dear? Are you listening to me?"

Annaliese shook her head.

"This devastation might be haste, it might be workers out of control. Maybe even just plain greed. But not John's unraveling on us."

"You don't know everything . . ."

Lucenia shook her sister-in-law's shoulder. "We'll figure something out. This is a family matter. And I'm family."

Annaliese looped an arm around Lucenia's neck, but she could not raise her head for the sobs that robbed her of breath. "I wasn't supposed to tell you. Ben asked me not to."

"Really?" Lucenia's face went still.

"I'm sorry."

"It's all right."

"Lucenia, what am I going to do about him?"

"Anna, let's just go home."

As they turned the horses around, they looked away from the valley. The ruin, literal and figurative, present and future, was too overwhelming.

Later, as they approached the split in the road where the road from Pinch came in, their horses' ears stiffened. Through the trees came the sound of a wagon and voices. Men laughing. The women pulled their horses to a stop and waited in the shadows.

When the wagon pulled into view, they saw four familiar dark-skinned faces in the back of Joe's wagon. The Cherokees. Then they remembered—it was spring. They had come for their share of the smoked meat.

That night, John was asleep when she came to bed, so she was left awake with the conversation she was going to have with him in the morning. As she lay staring at the full moon, the sound of the horses whinnying in the stables floated up to her window, then an odd snapping and popping. Annaliese got up on her elbows. She felt him stir.

"It's the wind," John said, still on his side. "Makes them nervous."

But the horses got louder. She heard them bumping into stall walls. John sat up, too. They heard men's cries of alarm, shouting, doors slamming. John threw off his blanket and ran to the window, cursing by the time she got there.

The hill behind the stables was a wall of fire. A white-hot inferno was racing down the hill, treetop to treetop. Flames stretched a hundred yards across the slope and twice that back up to the hilltop. Only a thin green ribbon of chestnut trees stood between the blaze and the scruffy grass that carpeted the grounds from the stable to Herschel and Ruth's cabin and on down to the Stregal homes.

Samuel and Emeline ran in wailing. John jerked on some pants and pushed past them. Annaliese found her riding trousers and pulled them on, barely registering that the children were behind her on the way down the stairs and on to the back porch. They saw John running to the stable, where Ruth was already throwing open the door. The two ran inside the stable and within seconds, horses bolted out and raced downhill, right past the homes. John came back out with a mattock and disappeared behind the stable.

He found Walter and Gideon frantically digging a trough in the grass. The leading edge of the fire was still about fifty yards uphill, but the wind was holding steady, pushing the blaze toward them. Flames leaped out to the top of a chestnut tree—sixty feet high—and within minutes the massive tree was aflame. It sent out an ominous crack, like a shot across a battlefield. Herschel rushed in just in time to see it pitch toward Walter and Gideon. Finally, they heard Herschel's screams. They ran as the chestnut thudded across the ditch they had just dug. Its red-hot corpse instantly set the grass afire. They raced back and began shoveling and covering it with dirt.

At the corner of the stable Wade and Tote McClain were slamming axes into a pine tree, the first in a string of pines that dotted the yard from the woods to the houses—a horribly perfect wick to their doors.

Ben stumbled up, axe in hand, heaving for breath and pointing at the fist-sized embers landing throughout the yard. John threw his mattock at Ben's feet and yanked the axe out of his hand. He ran downhill to the second pine in the string and began hacking.

On Annaliese's back porch everyone else in the family watched the amber sky, flinching with each red bloom that meant another tree had gone up in flames. Across the back yard, Ruth and Minerva were ferrying chickens from the henhouse to Annaliese's porch, dodging the falling embers and their little fires.

"We can stamp those out," Darrison shouted. "Let's go." He and Samuel started down the porch steps.

"No!" Lucenia shouted, yanking Samuel back up the steps. "You two stay right here."

"Sam!" Annaliese cried. "Go get Joe and Slivey. Find a horse if you can and ride down there."

Darrison snapped around to look at his mother.

Lucenia waved him on. "Oh, all right. You, too."

"Take this," Annaliese shouted as she picked up a lantern from the porch steps.

The boys disappeared around the corner of the house.

"This wind," Lucenia cried. "There's no fighting it."

In the yard, Minerva's and Ruth's skirts were brushing through the grass fires as they ran after chickens.

Back at the pine tree near the stable, Wade stepped away from the undercut he had finished to let Tote make the final back cut that would drop the tree uphill into the fire. As Tote swung, Wade ran back to Herschel and the others to warn them. Without even looking up, they fled their frantic digging. The branches of Tote's tree, no less the widow-maker than the trunk, came down in their footsteps.

Annaliese and Lucenia held onto each other and their youngest children in agony, coughing and peering into the hell. John was well lit by the flaming tree he worked under. Burning branches rained down around him. Finally Wade ran over to help him finish chopping it down.

Ruth and Minerva were trying to drag furniture out of Ruth's cabin, but they had to stop to beat out flames on Minerva's skirt.

"We can't just stand here," Annaliese said. She turned to Emeline. "Stay here with Aunt Lucenia."

Emeline shook her head, clutched at her mother.

"I'm coming, too," Lucenia said.

"No! I've got on pants," Annaliese shouted as she ran down the steps, tying an apron over her head. She headed for John, stomping grass fires as she went.

The tree that John and Wade were working on was disintegrating from the top down into red-hot chunks. Annaliese screamed at them to get away. John threw his axe down and grabbed Wade by the arm, but he waved him off. Wade's final back cut sent the tree down across the corral into nothing but dirt.

Out of the corner of her eye, Annaliese saw movement near the house—horses and dark figures sliding off. As Slivey and Joe ran up the hill, Slivey peeled off toward the other men.

"Damn, Mrs. Stregal," Joe said as he reached her. "You all right?"

"Yes, yes, we're all right here, but go help the others. Over there." She waved at the stable, where the other men were still digging and chopping. Behind it, the conflagration still raged, but it seemed to have stopped moving and the tallest trees that could have kept it advancing were down.

John rushed over. "Wind's dying, thank God," he shouted.

"Mr. Stregal," Joe said. "I got to tell you somethin'."

"Later." He started for the stable.

"Sir, these fires were set all along there. They weren't no accident."

John jerked to a stop and turned. "That's obvious, man. You know something?"

"I heard the men talkin' . . ."

"You knew this was going to happen?" John shouted in Joe's face.

"No! No, I just heard 'em sayin' that Slivey had been runnin' his mouth . . ."

"Damn it, man! Spit it out!" John grabbed Joe's shirt.

"John! He's trying to," Annaliese said.

"Slivey started a rumor in the mill that you all were the ones who sent the nightriders to scare Martha. He knew it would get around in the hills. Martha's got kin in every hollow out there."

"Oh, no," Annaliese said.

"I tried to tell everyone Slivey was lyin' but they was already suspectin' y'all of reportin' that hidden still you stumbled over a while back."

"But why would Slivey do such a thing?" Annaliese cried.

"To run y'all outta here."

"Damn!" John said.

"Yes, sir. And leave the mill in his hands. I never dreamed it would come to this," Joe said. "But I've been tryin' to tell you he was trouble." He looked at Annaliese.

"I'll kill him," John screamed, turning back to the fire.

"Joe, stop him!" Annaliese said. "Slivey's too big."

But John was already halfway to the stable. Behind it, the six men stood simply watching the fire, which had stopped at the ditches. Just as Slivey turned toward John's thunder, John hurled his five feet nine inches into Slivey's six feet two.

Samuel and Darrison raced in from the shadows.

John landed squarely on top of Slivey and had gotten a hell-bent round of punches in to his face before Slivey grabbed his wrists. John jabbed a knee into his crotch. With a howl, Slivey crumpled and John wrenched free.

The other men jumped away from the two and shot questioning looks at Joe.

"His fault. All of this," Joe shouted.

Some of the men stepped backward again. Others, not so interested in fairness for Slivey, leaned forward with clenched fists.

Annaliese couldn't believe her eyes. John's arms were pounding as relentlessly as the pumping arms of a locomotive, keeping the larger man too busy to return harm. John grunted like an ape as he threw each punch. He was filthy and he was ruthless—throwing dirt in Slivey's eyes, kicking him, anything to rain pain. It was horrible, this savage rage spilling out of him, she felt. Never could she have imagined such violence from a man who used to mete out revenge with court orders and indictments. But it thrilled her, too, seeing John's raw power. For the first time in Georgia, she felt on firmer ground.

"John!" Ben shouted. "Stop."

"Get him, Papa," Samuel said.

"Yes!" Annaliese said.

Slivey got his hands on John's neck, threw him over to the side, and climbed on top. Holding John's upper arms down with a knee and a hand, Slivey sent his other hand to pummeling John's face. Herschel and Tote moved to grab Slivey, but Samuel got to him first with a fistful of dirt. Slivey, blinking the grit away, lost his grip on John, which freed him to launch into Slivey's stomach.

Finally, the men pulled Slivey off. He rolled around for a few seconds, then staggered to his feet, coughing and spitting blood and sneering at everyone as he wiped his eyes. Annaliese and Samuel helped John to his feet. He straightened up right off, but a gash on his forehead gushed.

Slivey took a step in John's direction.

"Enough!" Ben said. He held up an arm.

Slivey spit over Ben's shoulder, looked at John, then back to Ben. "I'll fix you yet, you moron." He scanned the rest of the men. "And you, Rosetta!" he snarled, pointing a crooked finger at him.

"This time," John said, "I'm gonna let that North Carolina sheriff lock you up."

Slivey started to run.

From the shadows came the sound of a rifle being cocked. "Stop right there," someone shouted. Wade stepped into the firelight and raised the barrel. "Or I'll shoot your head smack off. Tie him up, Tote."

As Annaliese watched Tote tie Slivey, it hit her that he was binding the hands that were supposed to have set her free.

ᕲᕲ

XXIII

John rolled over to check the clock.

Annaliese said, "Almost five?"

"Right."

"We might as well give up."

The children were sleeping on a quilt on the floor.

Rubbing his temples out of habit, John gasped when he hit the lump at the edge of one eyebrow.

"John, I have to tell you something."

He turned to look at her. She lowered her shoulder to allow a slice of moonlight to hit his face so she could see his expression, and then she regretted it. The shadows added to the bruises, making him seem even more battered than he was.

"I'm sorry about Martha."

"What?"

"Running her off. That was our . . . my idea. Not Lucenia's. Not Mr. Chastain's."

Silence.

She raised up her shoulder to cast him in darkness again. "I didn't want you to blame the Chastains for this."

"You telling me you came up with the night riders idea and the Chastains did it?"

"Yes."

"Of all the fool . . ."

Annaliese slid back into her pillow. Outside, the wind combed through the blackened carcasses on the hill. "It was for Samuel," she whispered. "And Darrison. I just wanted to protect them from her." Tears rolled down into her ears. Such a brilliant schemer she thought she was. Such a big shot showing Lucenia who was in charge.

John wiped her cheeks with his bandaged hand. "Anna, I'm the only one to blame. I shouldn't have brought Slivey here. He was trouble and I knew it."

"Not your fault."

"So that's what's gotten into you," he said gently.

She threw her arms around him and buried her face in his chest, began rocking both of them with her sobs. John said nothing, stroked her hair. After a while, she came up for air.

"There's something else," she cried. "I have to get it out."

"Now what."

"I know why you brought us here," she ventured, lowering her voice again.

"I've told you all along..."

"The creation of the lumber company. The move into these hills. These huge financial investments. I know what you're doing."

"Anna, come on..."

"You are afraid you don't have much time, aren't you?" she whispered. "Like your father." She held her breath.

John pressed his lips together. She felt the sheets go cold. He turned onto his back and blinked at the ceiling. Finally, he said, "How'd you find out?"

"At home. Someone who worked with your father."

"You had no call to go poking around like that."

"This venture, it's supposed to set us up, isn't it? So that no matter what..." She groped for the least bleak words. "... no matter what the future holds, we're financially secure."

John faced the ceiling. "And people will speak my name in the halls of power, not in the darkened corners of pubs."

"But John, the destruction on the mountains."

His head flipped toward her. "What are you talking about?"

"Black Face Mountain."

"You went there?"

"How could you allow that?"

He threw the bed covers off and stepped over Samuel to pluck his pants off a chair. "It's called 'cut out and get out,' Anna. Lots of reasons to hurry now. People are turning more to metals and masonry for buildings. Lumber prices will be dropping soon. Gotta hump it while we can." Pulling his pants on, he said, "You shouldn't have gone over there." He picked up a lamp and went out the door.

It was the silence that woke everyone else that morning. Outside their windows, a leaden quiet arrived with the dawn. They lay in their beds, listening for anything that they had heard the morning before—the horses bumping around in the stable, chicken conversations, the wind in the leaves—anything that would prove that last night had not happened. Finally, into the emptiness a displaced but dutiful rooster crowed. They threw off their dread and got up, went out, and gaped at the night's destruction.

From the top of Bunny Mountain to the corral where the Cherokee men had finally stopped the fire's push, scorch covered the hill like black mange. A few charred snags still stood in ugly contrast to the rosy, hopeful sky. Ruth kicked at the edges of her garden, now a muddy mash of boot prints and ash. The backside of the stable was scorched and buckled. The corral fences lay in splintered heaps under the tree that had landed across it.

Samuel stared at the stable. "Good you got the horses out, Papa."

John turned his head and shoulders in one stiff movement to look down at his son. He winced as he nodded.

"Ruth said they're all right," Darrison said.

Annaliese walked over to pat Darrison's shoulder. "They ended up at the mule barns down by the mill."

Samuel nudged his head under her other arm and raised his face to hers. "She said people out there . . ." He pointed to the hills. ". . . set this fire?"

"Our neighbors?" Darrison asked.

"Well, we just don't know much right now, boys," Lucenia said.

"But why would Mr. Lowman lie and try to make people mad at us?" Samuel said.

Darrison spun around. "So that's what happened?"

Annaliese looked over at John. He shook his head and walked back to the house. She dropped her gaze down on her son, whose round eyes were still swollen from sleep. Samuel pressed his warm body against hers as he searched her face. "Papa's going to fix him, right?"

"With the sheriff?" Darrison said.

She pulled both boys in for a hug. "Right."

"But what about those other people, Aunt Anna?" Darrison said. His anxious eyes flew to the hills beyond their mountain.

Annaliese and Lucenia shared a look.

Lucenia said, "Aunt Annaliese and I will fix them."

By mid-morning, everyone was waiting for John outside the mill office. Ben sat on the seat of the first wagon, reins in hand, elbows on knees, nodding at the whispers of his wife beside him. Behind them, Slivey, bound hands and feet, scowled in a corner as he eyed the McClain brothers and their rifles in the opposite corner. In the second wagon, Annaliese sat on the seat beside Herschel, who tapped his boot to his rifle under the seat one more time.

John stiff-armed the office door and came through yelling. "I've telegraphed the sheriff in North Carolina. Told him I've got the man who fathered his grandson."

Annaliese and Lucenia narrowed their eyes at Slivey.

"Ain't mine," Slivey said.

"Thought I could let that go, you were said to be such a good foreman," John said. "Should've known." He walked over to the wagon rail and peered in at Slivey's hands and feet. Nodding, he looked at the McClains. "Don't take your eyes off him till you hand him over in Pinch. Sheriff there knows you're coming."

"Yes, sir," Wade said.

He called over to Ben, "You all right takin' care of this?"

"Of course, he is," Lucenia said.

Ben turned and gave an energetic nod, which sent the seat squeaking.

"I'd like nothing better than to personally hand this scum over to the law," John said, "but I'm worried about leaving the grounds."

Slivey snorted. Wade kicked him in the knee.

"And I'm going to give those damn mill workers a good piece of my mind," John said.

"What's left of it," Slivey said. Wade kicked him again.

Ben raised the reins. "We should go."

"Wait a minute," John said. He walked over to Annaliese. "Get your business taken care of quickly, ya hear? I want y'all to get back as soon as possible."

"We will," Annaliese said. "And you'll check on the children? I know Ruth and Minerva will be with them, but still . . ."

"I'll check on them." John pushed away and raised both arms. "Better get going."

The schoolyard was alive with children when Annaliese and Lucenia arrived. In clumps of twos and threes they dotted the grassy hill, digging through lard buckets and dinner sacks.

Corinthia Meddling looked up from her desk at the silhouettes in the doorway. She stood and planted her fingertips lightly on the desk, squinted into the light. "Mrs. Stregal?"

"Yes, it's me, Miss Meddling," Annaliese said in a tone that said there was more to say. "And my sister-in-law, Mrs. Benjamin Stregal."

Corinthia came from around the desk. "What's wrong? Y'all look a fright."

"We've come to ask you to help us call a truce," Annaliese said.

Corinthia held her hands up. "Is there a war?"

"Martha," Lucenia said.

"Martha?" Corinthia frowned. "But she's gone."

"No, it's *about* Martha. We think some people believe that we had something to do with her being asked to leave town," Lucenia said.

Corinthia opened her mouth, but Annaliese jumped in. "We want them to know that as of last night the score is settled. We want this to end. Can you help us let them know?"

Corinthia still shook her head. "Somethin' happen last night?"

Annaliese and Lucenia watched her face as carefully as a suspicious wife on a wayward husband's. The blue eyes staring back revealed nothing but frustration.

"I cain't help y'all if y'all don't tell me what happened." She threw up her meaty arms. "As for Martha, I don't have no bone to pick with y'all about her. I'm glad she's gone."

"You are?" Annaliese said.

"Shoot, she's 'bout driven me crazy since the day she was born. Half-sister, you know. But from what I hear, she's glad she's gone, too."

"What do you mean?" Lucenia said.

"I heard she's done found herself a lightning rod salesman in Tennessee."

"Well, someone seems to still be holding a grudge against us," Lucenia said.

Corinthia put her hand on her hips. "Y'all gonna tell me what happened or not?"

Lucenia lowered her voice. "A fire, Miss Meddling. Someone, several people set fires to burn us out last night. It nearly reached our homes."

Corinthia gasped. "Land sakes. Anyone get hurt?"

They shook their heads.

"Ruth? Herschel? They're all right?"

"Yes."

"Your children?"

Yes," Annaliese whispered. She blinked back tears.

Finally, Corinthia waved the women toward the chairs near her desk. "Lord, Lord." She shook her head as she sat down behind the desk.

"Will you help us put a stop to this?" Lucenia said, sitting down.

"You sayin' I know who did this?" Corinthia's shoulders went square.

Annaliese leaned over the desk. "Heavens, no. Just that we thought you would know who to talk to. Get the word out."

Corinthia's eyes drifted over to the window, leaving her visitors to wonder about the web of familial conflict festering in the hills.

"Tell them we'll make sure the school near Black Face re-opens."

The teacher's head swung back. "My academy?"

"We will provide the teacher," Lucenia said to Annaliese as though she had just thought of it.

"That Minerva?" Corinthia asked.

They nodded.

Corinthia's mouth puckered like the blossom end of a rotten squash. "I got to tell you, them families in the hills don't care about schoolin' for young 'uns. They need 'em around to help with the crops."

"Tell them we'll order shoes for every child," Lucenia said.

"Hmmm." The blue eyes fluttered faster now that a purse had come out. "You know I could use some new shoes, too."

Lucenia looked startled but Annaliese patted the desk. "Of course, you could. And how about a new hat? I heard the milliner is in town taking orders for Easter."

"Why, I believe I heard that, too." Corinthia's head was as still as a hunter's on a raised rifle as she watched Annaliese.

Out of the corner of her eye, Annaliese saw Lucenia's straw hat turn in her direction. She was way, way off course from what they had planned to say.

"Order you one. Tell her to send us the bill," Annaliese said.

Corinthia wiggled in the chair. "Why that sounds right nice," she said, patting her tangle of hair. "Something with them new parrot feathers." She looked at Lucenia for approval.

"Oh, that would be so smart." Lucenia waved her hands above her head in imaginary fluffing of feathers.

"Then you'll tell the families school's on again? And shoes for the children?" Annaliese said.

"Sure enough."

"We can have the school building ready in a week," Lucenia said, standing up.

Annaliese stretched her hand out to Corinthia's. "We just want to live here in peace, Miss Meddling."

" 'Course you do." Corinthia's hand slid over to pat the fingertips. "We'll be gone in a year."

"Tell them that, too, would you?" Lucenia said as she pulled Annaliese's arm. They moved slowly toward the door, where light streamed in to gild every nail and gouge in the pine floor. Annaliese felt Corinthia's eyes on her back.

"I'm real sorry, Mrs. Stregal, 'bout your scare," the teacher said.

In the doorway, they held up their hands in thanks and farewell.

Thessalonia, on the other hand, had already heard. They found her bustling among the dinner crowd in her boardinghouse, a news organ faster and less restrained than any newspaper, which was precisely why Annaliese and Lucenia were there.

It was the top of the dinner hour. Chair legs scraped the floors as diners came and went. Thessalonia glided from table to table, checking on her customers, mostly men. Annaliese searched their faces, sensing that the truth she sought was just under someone's greasy lips. Her gaze ended at the window-framed nook that faced on the street. Lawyers' corner. Henry wasn't there, thank goodness. She didn't have the energy to accept his condolences, so it was with relief that she noted that the sunny spot was full of train depot workers—a boisterous knot of fellows who were filling the room with laughter and smoke. Into their haze Thessalonia sailed with a platter of biscuits. One of the men shouted something to her as she lowered it to the table, something that made his leering tablemates watch for her response. She laughed and looked away, finding Annaliese and Lucenia in the doorway. Her face fell, and she came at them with two plump outstretched arms. "Lord ham mercy, you poor things," she screeched, sending heads turning. "Y'all all right?"

Lucenia took a step forward to accept the clutching hands. She said loudly, "Yes, we are. We are all fine, thank you." Her eyes made a circuit around the room. Several heads flipped back to their plates.

"Your children? Darrison and James? Please tell me none of them young 'uns ain't hurt."

Hot tears pooled in Annaliese's eyes, but she managed to shake her head.

"Praise the Almighty! And your homes? The fire didn't get them?"

"No, just the stable," Lucenia said. "We stopped it in time."

Thessalonia gave Lucenia's hands a firm squeeze and dropped them. "They say that y'all's mill manager rode into town this morning hog tied in the back of your wagon."

"He told a lot of lies about us," Lucenia said loudly.

Thessalonia's white lips parted, revealing a collision of yellowing teeth. "Sheriff's arresting him for *that*?"

Annaliese lowered her voice. "A fugitive from North Carolina justice, we've learned."

"Go on," Thessalonia said.

The men who were sitting at the tables nearest the door pushed their food slowly around on their plates, as if tending tiny animals.

"Of course, we are devastated," Lucenia said, pulling a handkerchief from her pocket, "and baffled."

"As to who did it," Thessalonia said. "I'll bet it was them Wilkenses."

Lucenia shrugged. "We've done nothing to warrant such treachery."

"If our neighbors are making corn whisky, our husbands don't care a thing about it," Annaliese said.

"Sure enough?"

"People here have been making it for generations," Lucenia said.

A couple of the animal tenders exchanged glances.

"We just want to be good neighbors," Annaliese said.

"But, you are!" Thessalonia patted Annaliese's hand.

"We are?" Annaliese said shakily.

"Look in there." Thessalonia pointed at the crowded dining room.

"Half of them is drummers comin' through town to sell to Miller's Mercantile or Billy's General Store, both of which are doin' a right good business. And the other half is people who used to eat their dinner out of a poke. Yes, ma'am, y'all and your cash money are downright perfect neighbors." Thessalonia smiled and winked a white-lashed eye.

It was not exactly sentimental, but it was the first positive comment Annaliese had heard from the community. As her composure dissolved, she reached over to borrow Lucenia's handkerchief.

Thessalonia's smile disappeared. She stepped forward and wiped her hands down her apron anxiously. "Oooooh, look at what I done, makin' you cry. What I meant was an old maid like me's got to survive, you know. I'm ever so grateful to y'all." She lowered her voice. "I know I ain't behaved like a Christian woman toward y'all."

Annaliese dabbed at her eyes until Lucenia took the handkerchief back for her own dabbing. They pulled each other away from the doorway and into the hall.

Thessalonia followed them. Her hands flew to her face. "Here am I runnin' my mouth, upsettin' y'all. Why don't we get y'all some dinner?" She turned to wave at a server. "Pinky! A table for two."

"No, no, we can't stay. We have to get back to the children," Annaliese said. "Thank you." She slapped at her moist cheeks and pulled in a deep breath. "But we would like to take some food for the ride back. There are six of us."

Thessalonia was already heading for the dining room. "I'll have someone bring some fixin's right out."

As they waited, Annaliese and Lucenia lingered in the dining room doorway scanning the faces, nodding at those that looked back, and noticing that all around the room, conversations were starting up again.

ℰℐ

XXIV

As night fell, Annaliese lowered the bedroom blinds so that her children would stop looking at it. They bent down to catch the last sight of Bunny Mountain, as though the scene would right itself if they just blinked. Afterward, they clung to her, as they had all afternoon. Samuel's hair was still full of the fire smell. She had never gotten him to clean up from the night before. Every time she had stooped down to wash Samuel, Emeline had slipped between them, grabbed her mother's face with grubby little hands and pulled it to hers. Samuel's fingers then dug into his sister's shoulders, howling ensued, and the cleaning was put aside again.

She led them over to the pallet on the floor beside her bed. Together—one child still on each side of her—they crawled onto the quilts and flopped, eyes on the ceiling. Outside, the voices of the Cherokee men came and went as they brought up a few of the dogs.

"They'll be out there all night," Annaliese said, and she felt the children nodding beside her. "Don't worry about the bad people any more. And Aunt Lucenia and I have settled the matter."

Aunt Lucenia and I have settled the matter. Just hushing words for anxious children, but how she hoped they would prove to be true. So often in these months of wrestling with various miseries, Annaliese felt that she and Lucenia had simply taken turns leading each other into disaster. Today, they had agreed on their course, and now they could only hope that the Meddling sisters would live up to their names.

A soft gust rattled the blinds, flinging the lamplight's gauzy shadows across the walls. Annaliese felt the warm, still bodies of her children against her and she realized that their breathing was becoming heavier. She pressed her lips on Samuel's forehead to feel the baby fat. Too little of it pushed back, as she had always feared. Next, the same for Emeline, but she could only reach the top of her head. The tension in Annaliese's neck melted. Slivey and Martha were gone for good. Four more men were on the grounds, their presence as comforting as an extra blanket at night. She and Lucenia were united—united in misery, but united at least—and the Meddlings' softening had been a pleasant surprise.

But still there was John.

The Corinthia Meddling Academy re-opened on April 2, 1902, running counter to the Coosawattee County school calendar that ran January through March. Minerva stood on the schoolhouse steps with clipboard and class roster firmly in hand. She had taken the news of her new responsibilities well and had adopted a fresh air of authority. Now she watched the forest's edges with the zeal of a missionary, waiting for the first sign of a mountain child she could save. Behind her, a fidgety Ruth held a basket of dried apples and biscuits.

Across the dirt yard, the four Stregal children raced around their mothers and the wagons and horses. Corinthia told them to expect the children who had attended before. Fifteen more or less, ages six to fourteen. Samuel and Darrison settled in front of the women to tell them who that would be.

"Well, there will be those Wilkins boys," Darrison said, clenching his fists.

From the steps came Ruth's snort. "Them no 'counts," she said.

"The two who picked on you last fall?" Lucenia said.

"Yea," Darrison said.

"They're awful big," Samuel said.

"How big?" Minerva asked, shifting her gaze from the woods to Samuel.

"We're bigger now, Sam," Darrison said. "We can take 'em on."

"Now, none of that," Lucenia said. "You leave the discipline to Miss Meally."

Minerva turned an anxious face back to the woods.

"I guess we'll have some of them girls back, too," Samuel said, rolling his eyes.

"Those girls," Lucenia said. "And you boys will be perfect gentlemen."

The first to arrive were in fact three girls, uniform in wiry build and caramel-colored skin but stair steps in height. They were slow to leave the stand of pines behind them, being the focus of everyone's attention, but finally the tallest one took the smallest one's hand and the three crept toward the schoolhouse. They mashed tattered Bibles to their chests and took solemn steps until they saw Samuel and Darrison. The boys, hands shoved in pockets, shuffled around in a goofy dance that Annaliese wanted to watch, but Lucenia was acting even weirder.

"Lucenia, what is it?" Annaliese whispered.

Lucenia held her hand over her mouth and shook her head, eyes softening as they followed the three sisters all the way to the boys.

A fourth girl arrived and stared for a while from behind one of the wagons. Then a couple of boys, whom Darrison nodded to with false indifference, ambled in from the dirt road. Ruth hurried down the steps and into the yard to give out the food. Minerva called out a welcome and invited them all inside. As they came toward her, she asked their names and checked them off.

Inside, the women spread sheets of white paper on the floor. Annaliese picked up a pencil and began tracing a boy's bare foot on the paper that was going to go to Sears Roebuck and come back as his new shoes.

Lucenia scooped up Emeline and walked over to the smallest of the three sisters. The child wore a yellow sleeveless dress—so thin that Lucenia could read the flour sack that was her undergarment—and a shy smile. Her pale green eyes were a surprise against her brown skin, like candlelight in a mossy cove. A yellow strip of the dress fabric hung in a limp bow from a hank of black hair over one eye. Lucenia dropped to one knee, positioning Emeline between herself and the girl. Emeline pointed to the girl's sisters, whose feet were being traced by Minerva, and began a windy explanation of shoes and hookworms and Sears Roebuck. When the child warmed to them, Lucenia moved Emeline aside to be able to hold a pencil and paper up to the child, who nodded and put one mud-stained foot forward. While Lucenia traced, she felt the little feather of a hand on her hair.

"Purty," the child said.

Lucenia's pencil wobbled around the tiny heel. "And you have pretty feet," Lucenia said.

The child peered down at her feet and blinked in surprise.

"Look at my feet," Emeline said as she climbed into Lucenia's lap. "Aren't my feet pretty, too, Aunt Lucenia?"

"Yes," Lucenia said. "Yours are pretty, too." Lucenia slipped her hands under Emeline's bottom and boosted the child up and out. "Have you asked this little girl her name yet?"

A storm began gathering on Emeline's face. "I want to take my shoes off, too," she said.

"You'll have to ask your mother about that."

Twice wounded, Emeline returned to her mother and crossed her arms, glaring at the girl.

"So, what is your name?" Lucenia said, tracing the other foot.

"Sarah Frances."

"Pretty name, too. I'll bet you are about five, six years old, Sarah Frances?"

The child shrugged and looked around the room.

Turning to look with her, Lucenia said, "And those are your older sisters."

At the sight of them moving toward a desk, Sarah Frances began inching away. "Got two brothers, too. They won't come."

"Well, welcome to school, Sarah Frances," Lucenia said to the back of the yellow dress. She lifted the tracing paper and ran her hands over the image.

༄

XXV

With John as the foreman, the sawmill operated twelve hours a day, seven days a week and even then it seemed to the family that he would have pushed for longer hours but for Ben's warnings about the danger of exhausted workers. When the wind was right, the women could hear the saws at their brutal work, and they would move from room to room in search of relief. Their back porches were the quietest place, but there it was their eyes that could not rest, for they constantly picked at the scarred, black mountain. The children would not leave it alone either. They threw rocks at the limbs that hung precariously, yanked weeds and anything else green they could find, and tried to plant them into the ash.

One day, Annaliese and Lucenia came outside with the mending and saw Wade with the children at the lip of the hill where the black mange had stopped. He was digging a hole. James and Darrison held wispy little pines. Emeline and Samuel stood by in unusual stillness—Samuel held another shovel—heads bent down in an absorption that was almost prayerful. Lucenia's boys lowered the pines into the scorched earth. Even Samuel's shoveling was slow and reverent. After each tree went in, Emeline knelt and finished the job with gentle patting. An hour later, there were enough seedlings in the ground to form a bright green froth along the edge of that miserable black sea.

It was a green so young and innocent, a sea so vast and sterile, it made a mother's heart ache.

"Look at this," Annaliese said as she came into Lucenia's kitchen a few days later. She waved a thin booklet at her.

Ruth and Lucenia stood at a table, slicing potatoes and swatting at the flies that had arrived with the first days of May. Lucenia wiped her hands on her apron and took the booklet. Ruth leaned over to try to read it, shook her head, and returned to her potatoes.

Lucenia said, "Circular 21: Practical Assistance to Farmers, Lumbermen, and Others in Handling Forest Lands." Her eyes went to the bottom of the page. "Published by the Division of Forestry, U. S. Department of Agriculture." She looked up at Annaliese. "The enemy," she gasped. "Does John know this is in the house?"

Annaliese waved her hand. "Oh, it's all right. I found this in his office. It came with the quarterly forestry magazine he and Ben read."

"Oh." Lucenia's eyes relaxed for moment before a question creased her brow. "Well, why are you reading it?"

"The children's seedlings got me to thinking." Annaliese took the booklet and flipped to an inside page.

Ruth looked up to join Lucenia in staring at Annaliese.

"Look. Here." With an index finger jab, she gave the booklet back to Lucenia. "It says the Division of Forestry offers a consulting service on replanting forests."

Lucenia slowly shook her head. "You can't be serious."

"Which part?"

"All of it. Replanting forests? Consultant? John would shoot a consultant right off the train."

"No. It's all by mail."

"Annaliese."

"But Lucenia, it's Bunny Mountain, our mountain, and we need to take it back."

Ruth moved away from the potatoes to look out the window. Her gaze moved left to right across the acres. "Ooooh, Lord."

Lucenia swept her hair off her forehead with the back of her hand. "Anna, we won't be here to enjoy the shade."

Annaliese shook her head. "Someone will enjoy it one day. Call it a gift. Oh, call it folly, I don't care."

Lucenia smiled gently. "Sounds rather progressive."

"Now don't turn this into activism on me."

Ruth came back to the table and sighed as she picked up the knife again. "Pines will volunteer out there soon enough."

"Yes, yes, I know. It says that in here." Annaliese jabbed at the open page again. "And that as the pines grow they provide the shade and protection that enable the hardwood seeds to take off. I just want our beautiful oaks and poplars back," Annaliese said. "I don't want to wait on the volunteers."

"Yes," Lucenia said. "I agree."

"And we do have four Cherokee men with time on their hands." Annaliese gestured toward the stable.

"Yes."

"And you know the children will be wild about it." She took Lucenia's hands and pumped them up and down. The booklet fell to the floor.

"Anna, I'm saying yes," Lucenia laughed. "I'm with you. I'll talk Ben into paying whatever expenses we'll have. You just take care of John's knowing."

Annaliese threw her arms around Lucenia's wide shoulders and pressed her cheek to hers. Lucenia hugged back, startled and stiff. Ruth ran over to nudge under their arms and began crying.

"Ruth, what's the matter?" Annaliese said, wiping the girl's freckled face.

Ruth's hands flew to her face. "Oh, I'm just so tired of all these flies in here," she said before running out the door.

They heard the porch door slam.

"What on earth is wrong with her?" Annaliese said.

Lucenia picked up the knife to finish the potatoes. "Haven't you noticed how moody she's been lately?"

Annaliese looked out the window. "Perhaps we shouldn't talk so openly about our leaving."

"Probably." Lucenia threw a towel over the potatoes and picked up the booklet from the floor. "So, how will we get these baby pines?"

"Why, they'll ship them to us."

Lucenia slapped the booklet against her chest and giggled. "So it's come to this: ordering trees by mail along with our Tula Water for the Complexion."

A month later, at dawn on a mild, windless June day that was going to be perfect, Annaliese sent Wade and Tote to the Pinch train station. Hours later, they were back, waving their hats the minute they emerged from the forest. The children sprang up from their steps with shouts that brought their mothers and Ruth and Minerva out. Slowly the horses labored up the hill to them, too slowly for the boys, who swarmed down to meet them. As the exhausted horses made the final pull toward the homes, Wade called out to the women, "Had to stop in town and get some water on the roots, like you said."

"Here we go," Lucenia called to Annaliese from her porch. "Get your knickers."

The men drove the wagon around the houses and began struggling to unload wet burlap bags of seedlings. Herschel arrived and helped the children untie the bags. They untangled the seedlings one by one, the first one going into Emeline's outstretched hands. She and her brother and James fanned out across the hillside, where they had to stop and wait for Darrison and his hoe and Herschel with his mattock. Soon, rounded backs large and small dotted the hillside. Lucenia and Annaliese arrived, pulling on their gloves.

"Now, Darrison, be sure to spread out those little roots in the hole," Lucenia said.

"We've got it, Mother," Darrison said, pointing to his brother kneeling near him, tree in hand.

Darrison swung his hoe into the blackened earth, gave it a yank to widen the gap, and waved his brother over. With one hand James deepened the hole, and with the other he gently lowered the seedling, shaking roots out as he went. He finished with three firm tamps of his boot.

The boys looked up at their mother, who was having trouble ignoring the crooked seedling, but she nodded. Her bonnet glided up and down and left to right, son to son, to ensure they could see her smiling face under the brim. "Off to the next one, then," she said as she headed back to the wagon.

Walter and Gideon brought up a wagon full of pine straw. The women fell in line behind the workers, sprinkling the straw on the turned earth. Wade came upon them on his way back to the first wagon, grinning at their earnest faces and their trousers. The women did not find it offensive. Instead, his amusement was a sign of a comfort between them, an ease born in the weeks of walking the charred fields together, reading the forestry circulars, talking about slope and soil. Wade and Tote, blacksmiths, knew only a hair more about forestry than the women did. As their knowledge grew, a bond of trust and excitement did as well. There were still boundaries of propriety, of course, but neither of the men had crossed them. In fact, the women felt the men's respect, especially Wade's, was growing as their project unfolded. They had come to know him as an honest, intelligent man whose flash of a raised eyebrow at their trousers felt perfectly acceptable.

Wade stopped beside them to wipe the sweat from his brow. "Ain't no call for y'all to get your hands dirty out here with us."

Lucenia pulled her gloves tighter on her hands. "Don't you worry about us."

"Worry ain't never crossed my mind for you two."

"This is a big day," Annaliese said.

"Yes, ma'am."

They feathered pine straw over seedlings until their bag was empty and climbed to a granite ledge above the workers. Across the sky, a string of white clouds slid by.

Lucenia removed her gloves and rubbed her eyes. "This is one huge, preposterous undertaking," she whispered as she sat down.

Annaliese looked left, right, and eased onto the rock. "I know."

Lucenia patted her hand. "And I'm in full support."

"I know." Annaliese squeezed back and grinned.

"We could use a breeze," Lucenia pulled off her top layer—a man's work shirt—and dropped it on the ground. "This reminds me of another huge job we took on."

"What was that?" Annaliese said. She dragged the shirt behind her and leaned back on it on her elbows.

"Remember the day we took all your furniture apart looking for bedbugs?" Lucenia said.

Annaliese laughed into Lucenia's shoulder, nearly knocking her off her perch. "Look at us now. We wouldn't care if we had bedbugs in our knickers."

"Speak for yourself," Lucenia said.

Downhill, Wade held his hand above his eyes, turning and looking around the hills. Spotting the two women above, he began climbing the hill.

"Such a gentle soul," Lucenia whispered.

Wade's arms swung as he came, pushing his square body higher with each step. His stringy, black hair swung side to side. Perspiration stains seeped from the seams of his blue shirt, open at the neck. Coming closer, he took his leather hat off and waved it at his face.

"Now I'm wishin' for a little wind," he said as he stopped near them. He dragged a forearm across his leathery face.

"A little rain, too," Annaliese said. "But not until tonight."

Wade looked at the clouds hurrying by. "Might could get some." He put his hat on and crossed his arms as he watched the work below. "In a coupla years, them pine trees we planted down at the edge will be big enough for yore boys to go pine ridin' on."

Lucenia turned to him. "Pine riding?"

"Yes, ma'am. Used to do it all the time when I was a young 'un. We'd find us a patch of young pines and climb one to where it started to bend under our weight. Then we'd swing to the next one and do it again."

"Sounds dangerous," Lucenia said.

"Oh, yes, ma'am. It was right fun." Wade's chin fell to his chest as he chuckled silently.

"Wade, well, you know we won't be here by then," Lucenia said. Putting her hand up to shade her forehead, she looked at him.

"Oh, yes, ma'am. I forgot," he said quietly. He adjusted his hat unnecessarily.

Annaliese felt his disappointment settle on her shoulders. She plucked a blade of grass and curled it around her finger. It was getting so that the subject of leaving just could not be aired—not around the children, not around Ruth, and now Wade.

"You know, I been wonderin' . . ." Wade began.

They watched him kick at the grass.

". . . thinkin' on what will happen to the land when y'all go back."

Lucenia searched for something distant to look at. "The timber cutting will wind down, our husbands will return now and then to check on things, and later they'll shut down the mill," she said.

"And sell the land?"

"Well, yes," Lucenia said, though this was more assumption than established fact. She snuck an uneasy look at Annaliese and saw that she did not like the direction the conversation was taking either.

"Who do you reckon will buy it?"

Annaliese thought of the butchered hillsides, the muddied rivers, the lifeless slopes so still and barren and airless. She squirmed on her granite seat.

"It ain't good for farming neither," Wade said, reading her mind, "unless you get you some bottom land in the deal."

Lucenia laughed. "My goodness, Wade. It sounds as though you're already negotiating for a rock bottom price."

Wade's snort said what he thought of his ability to buy any land. He shook his head. "No, ma'am. Was jest thinkin'."

Annaliese rose to stand beside him. "I don't think I can even begin to imagine the kinds of ties your family has to this place."

"Yes, ma'am."

Lucenia stood, too. "How is it that your family was able to stay when thousands of others . . ."

"Was run off by soldiers?"

Annaliese and Lucenia nodded.

"They hid." Wade crossed his arms and fixed his gaze on the valley. "My grandfather told me that on the day the soldiers came, he was playin' on a hillside with his little sisters. He was just a boy, 'course, 'bout ten. Their mama was collectin' plants near the branch. The soldiers come out of the woods, yelling at them. Grandfather and his sisters ran for the bushes. The soldiers pointed their guns at their mother, made her walk away even though she was screamin' to be allowed to get the children. But they couldn't understand her tongue, 'course."

"Dear Lord," Annaliese whispered. Her eyes raced downhill to count the children.

"They hid in the forest that day and night and the next day. Heard gunshots, saw the smoke of a fire on a distant hill, so they stayed where they were, scared and hungry. At the end of that second day, their mama came back. She whistled a little sign they knew and they came runnin' out to her."

"How did she get away from the soldiers?" Lucenia said.

"One of the soldiers took pity on her, she was so tore up. He went and got somebody who could understand her, and when they realized what she wailin' about, he snuck her out of the fort."

"Where was the children's father?" Lucenia said.

"In the fort. They wouldn't let him go with her."

"Then what happened?" Lucenia said.

"Well, they couldn't go back to their house. Whites had moved in, taken their livestock. So they lived in the hills with a few other Cherokee who had escaped. After a while, when ever'thing all settled down, they came into the towns and lived among the whites. Started over."

"What happened to his father?"

Wade shook his head in answer. "Don't know. We reckon he died walkin' to Oklahoma with the others. Thousands of our people died on the way." He shoved his hands in his pocket.

Annaliese and Lucenia stared at their children digging in the earth.

"Ain't but a handful of us around here now. My father took up smithin' so he wouldn't end up like my grandfather, yearnin' to live in the forests for good but not really knowin' how. Nothin' would do him but to visit Trackrock every coupla weeks 'cept in the winter. He'd go up 'ere and just touch that rock and touch it. Then my father would go up 'ere and get him."

"Trackrock," Annaliese said. "I've read about that. People think the scratches on it are Indian drawings."

"Yes, ma'am. So, anyway, we've been raised white, get along good with folks in Pinch. Tote and me help our father in smithin'." He turned to smile at the women. "And help y'all."

"Yes," was all Annaliese could say.

"Well, I reckon I better get back to work."

Lucenia was nodding. "We'll be along shortly."

He started down the hill, but turned back and said, "I just got somethin' to say."

They stared at him.

"I'm much obliged to y'all." He raised his arm to sweep it over the slopes below where the children and the others worked. "For this. I ain't never worked the earth like this. There's somethin' to it, I'm findin'. The smell of the warm dirt, maybe, or the mountains standin' watch over me. Seems like there's a presence of some kind, and it ain't grandfather's spirit or any of that bull." He peered back at the ladies to judge the word's offensiveness. Their faces were on the distant summits, their expressions as calm as a baby's at the breast. Wade turned back to the view. "More like the mountains themselves, I reckon. Like they're pretty good company all by themselves."

Without waiting for a response, he finished walking back down.

That evening, a light rain began just as everyone had come in to wash up. It was the best kind of rain for fragile life, a steady but gentle shower that filled air pockets and settled the soil where the roots were already taking hold.

⁕

XXVI

Henry Chastain scanned the sawmill grounds, hoping to catch sight of a child or a worker who might tell him where she was and soon, but the July heat had run everyone inside. A couple of dogs inched out from under the planing mill, coughed up a few thin barks, stretched their scruffy forelegs, and slipped back to the shadows. But at the office building, his eye caught something else moving—a flash of blue skirt disappearing around the corner. He came off his horse and pulled it along in a hurry, veering away from the office windows. At the corner, he stopped, and peered around. Annaliese was pressed against the wall, head cocked at the window. He dropped the reins and walked toward her.

"Have you taken up lip reading?" he whispered over her shoulder.

"Mercy!" Annaliese spun around, bringing her face within inches of his. "I thought you weren't coming until . . ."

"I need to talk to you." He crossed in front of her, brushing his hips softly against her skirt, and peeked in the window long enough to see John and Hoyt talking at John's desk. "Some place private."

She was already sidling away from the window, back the way he had come. They came to his horse, looked around it both ways, and adopted an air of nonchalance as they strolled toward the planing mill. Finding a spot among the stacks of wood slabs and warped strips that rose eight feet on each side, they stopped.

Annaliese pointed toward the office. "Just so you know, what you saw back there, well, that wasn't snooping."

Henry took off his hat and fanned her with it. "I reckon you have your reasons."

She twisted her apron. "I don't want you to think ill of me."

"I could never do that." His fingers rose to smooth away the strands of hair that curled at her damp neck, but went back to his pocket, the pocket that held the reason he had come. He had wanted to get to her alone like this long before supper when John would undoubtedly make his announcement, but now he realized he was going to have to look at her up close as she absorbed his news, steel himself against her pain, fight the urge to tell her it would be all right because it wouldn't.

She leaned against the building. "It's just that John . . ."

Henry moved closer so that his shadow would shield her eyes. "I know."

"Oh, Mr. Chastain, you don't."

"Henry. It should be Henry by now. Remember?"

She rubbed her neck but did not turn away from his steady gaze.

"You have to watch him, don't you?" he asked.

She felt the air leave her lungs.

"He's not his old self," he said.

"You see it, too?"

Henry nodded.

"Yes, I suppose you do. You've seen enough of him in the last few months. I know he's been to town calling on you."

"We've had several meetings about the business." He rubbed his brow. "Anna. . . ."

It was the first time he had called her by her nickname. She twisted her apron tighter.

"I know something's not right with him," he said. "I . . ."

Inside the planing mill, men's voices rose before a saw screamed again. He lowered his mouth to her ear as he said, "We can't stay here long, so listen carefully."

Alarm swept through her eyes. "All right."

"I've brought some contracts that John and Ben asked me to prepare for their signature."

"What kind of contracts?" she said, grabbing his arms.

Her touch jarred the words right out of him, but his silence made her tighten her grip. He said, "I have always had the impression that you expected to be going home after a couple of years."

"Yes?" She dug her fingers in.

"Anna, this isn't good news."

"Just say it."

"John and Ben are buying five thousand acres of timber land on the other side of Skipjack Mountain and the timber rights to eight thousand more."

Annaliese released him as if she had been scalded. She brought her hands down on top of her head. Her mouth formed an anguished "no", a long, drawn-out silent howl.

Henry ran his hands around the edges of his hat, looked at his boots. There was more.

Suddenly, the saw fell silent. Henry whispered. "He said his father told him to buy these acres."

Annaliese's mouth fell open. "But . . ."

"I know, I know. He's dead." Henry leaned against the building and closed his eyes.

"What about Ben? He's going along with this?"

"Hard for them to turn away such demand, Anna. They can't fill the orders fast enough. And from what I can see, Ben doesn't like to turn John away."

"Please don't tell anyone about John," she whispered. Her fingers went back to his arm. "I've got to keep things together here until I can get him home, get him some help."

Henry pulled a handkerchief out of his pocket for her. "Couple of months ago, I knew something was wrong when he wanted to talk about naval stores."

"What's that?" She put the handkerchief to her nose.

"Tar, turpentine, sealants for ships, all made from long leaf pine. Everyone knows that kind of pine doesn't grow here in these mountains."

"He wanted to set up another business?"

"But I stopped him."

"That's not the point."

"One thing at a time." He ran his fingers through his matted hair. "Listen, I'm guessing that John will announce these contracts at supper tonight. I came early today to warn you, so you could be ready."

Annaliese shoved his handkerchief into her sleeve and put her hands on her hips. "Oh, I'm ready."

His head fell back. "Whoa."

"Any more surprises?"

"Well, no. You sure you're all right?" Henry fanned her with his hat.

"I am now, now that I know that you know." Annaliese's hands flopped to her side. "I'm glad you know."

Henry dropped his hat to the ground and finally allowed his fingers to move toward hers. As he lifted her hand, she took a step back. Inside the planing mill, voices grew louder, people were moving toward the door. Henry and Annaliese jumped apart and strode into the mill yard.

"Sure was a long, hot ride up here, Mrs. Stregal," Henry said as he picked up a wooden bucket from the ground. "My horse could use some water."

"Well, you know where the trough is, Mr. Chastain. And we look forward to seeing you at the house later." Annaliese turned for home.

The sisters-in-law were still exchanging acidic whispers as they lit the sconces in Lucenia's dining room. Annaliese's news had cranked up the temperature in the stifling kitchen where Ruth and Lucenia were working on the meal. Lucenia had slapped a dishtowel against the sink, saying Ben had some explaining to do. Ruth said she was sorry, that she wanted whatever the women wanted, but looked at the floor as she spoke. Lucenia scooped up Ben's beloved salt mackerel and stormed off toward the hog pen to give it to them.

John was having one of his loud nights. He led the men into the dining room, hands waving, spit flying as he finished a rambling tale.

He pulled out a chair for Annaliese and then one for himself between her and Ben, who sat at the head of the table. To Ben's right sat Lucenia, then Henry.

John threw a challenging look at him. "Henry, you need another drink. You're too quiet tonight."

Henry gave a flat smile and raised his hands in defense. "No, thanks, John. I've had enough."

John pushed his chair away from the table to grab a decanter from the sideboard. "But we've got some celebrating to do." He brought the decanter toward Henry's glass, but Henry waved it away.

Ruth came in and lowered a platter of pan-fried trout and parsley potatoes onto the table.

Annaliese leaned her head toward John. "Moderation is next to God, they say, dear."

"Moderation is overrated," John said.

"Hear, hear," Ben said as he reached for the platter.

"Hold on, Ben." John watched Ruth as she was leaving. "Ruth!" She spun around. "Champagne glasses for everyone."

Ruth nodded as though she had heard of champagne and disappeared into the kitchen.

"John, we don't have any champagne," Annaliese said.

"Well, bourbon then." John banged a spoon on the table, though every face was already turned toward him. "I think you all know— you, Henry more than anyone else—that the Stregal Brothers Lumber Company has been doing very well. Succeeding beyond our wildest dreams, isn't that so, Ben?"

Ben pressed his chins into his neck and smiled. "Yes. Railroad ties are keeping us in business, and roof shingles, and furniture . . ."

"And so it's time for us to take the next step," John said.

Henry folded his hands on the table and looked at the saltshaker.

"Ben and I have decided to make a new investment in the Stregal Brothers Lumber Company. And this is something that we expect will make our dear ladies' lives easier as well."

The dear ladies' spines stiffened.

"We are going to install an electric generator at the mill." John leaned back in his chair and grinned at the women. "That means we might as well put one in here, too."

"That's it?" Lucenia asked. "That's your news?"

"What about . . .?" Annaliese fought to keep from looking at Henry, directly across the table.

Henry, however, stole a glance at her.

"No," John said, catching it. "Isn't that enough?"

"How could you do this?" Annaliese rose from her seat.

"But . . ." John said as he rose to meet her fury, " . . . you can have an electric icebox now. Electric lights . . ." His hands spun in circles, implying the rest of whatever Sears Roebuck could ship on a train.

Ben pushed away from the table and said, "A proper stove."

"You wouldn't make such an investment unless . . ." Annaliese, grasping for words that wouldn't betray Henry, finally looked at Lucenia for help.

Lucenia shot up from her seat and cocked her body across the table at Ben. "It sounds like we aren't leaving any time soon."

"What is wrong with you two?" Ben asked, struggling to stand.

"In April, as agreed," Lucenia said.

Ben shot a look at John. "April?"

"Who ever said we were leaving in April?" John asked.

"You did! And we're counting on it," Annaliese said.

"Leave?" John shouted. "When we're making a fortune?"

Henry leaned back into his chair, tucked his head to study the table-cloth's lace.

"You're committing too much," Annaliese cried. "Sawmill, commissary, houses, stables, cabins, fencing. And now this—this huge investment."

"And don't you try to tell us you did it for us," Lucenia said.

"John Stregal, when are we leaving?" Annaliese shouted.

"When I'm goddamn finished!" John flopped back down into his chair. "Uppity women. Been reading all of that suffragette shit," he said to Henry as he reached for the decanter again, but his wife yanked it away.

"Come on, Lucenia." Annaliese pressed the decanter to her chest. "Get the glasses."

Lucenia plucked two wine glasses from the table while delivering her last blistering look.

"That's right. Y'all go on. I've got more," John bellowed. "Henry, take that drink now?"

Henry closed his eyes slowly. "Oh, yes."

"We're leaving in the morning," Annaliese said.

Henry's eyes flew open.

The women stormed through the kitchen, ignoring Ruth's stares, and were heading out the back door when Annaliese stopped so quickly that Lucenia ran into her.

"Wait a minute," she said, staring at the wash hanging on the porch.

A few minutes later, when the men had just put forks to potatoes, Annaliese and Lucenia marched back into the dining room and made one circuit around the table, one slow, saucy pass, with their fannies packed quite clearly into trousers.

"Feel anything yet?" Lucenia looked into the bottom of her empty glass.

"B'lieve so," Annaliese said. She licked lips that felt like cotton.

They sat in solidarity on their granite shelf on Bunny Mountain, where they had watched the McClains and the children plant the trees three short weeks ago. The sun was slipping behind a summit's silhouette. They could see their houses and the houses could see them, which was as far as they were willing to go without a lantern, which pretty much summed up the boundaries of their civil disobedience.

"An electric generator," Lucenia said.

"Not a word about the thirteen thousand acres," Annaliese said. "Suffragette shit, he said."

Lucenia poured herself more bourbon, then more for Annaliese. "Trying to sweeten us up before telling us."

They grimaced into their glasses, as if facing cod liver oil, and drank it down just as hopefully.

"I have to get him out of here, Luce," Annaliese said.

"A hospital."

Annaliese stared at the darkening sky. "No. I can't turn him over to *them*. Do you know what they do to people in those asylums? I've been reading about it. Some places, they wrap them in wet sheets for hours." She shook her head. "That's their treatment."

"No, I don't mean an asylum," Lucenia said gently. "Just, well, someone to make him see that this can't go on. All this spending."

"But he'll have no peace until he finishes this, proves to himself that he can do it." Annaliese's voice became quieter. "Provides for us."

In the deepening chill, Lucenia moved closer to Annaliese on the slab. "But, Anna, we just can't stay here putting up butterbeans, waiting for the next surprise."

Annaliese pulled her knees under her chin. "If I could just get him home."

They watched the lamp lights move room to room in Annaliese's upstairs, which meant Ruth was getting the children ready for bed. Over at Lucenia's, a light appeared in the guest bedroom.

"Henry." Annaliese was having trouble focusing. Her tongue felt like it was wearing a coat.

Lucenia's head wobbled. "He's a good frien'."

"John and Ben will listen to him."

All around them cricket song was rising. The women fell silent for a while, letting the roar sweep over them in waves of loud and louder.

"I say we stay out here until they're all asleep," Annaliese said.

"Yup."

Finally, the last of the day's light had seeped away. They watched the stars crystalize in the gunmetal sky. Down the hill, at the back of Lucenia's house, a door opened and someone lit a lantern. Its dim light began moving toward them, swinging back and forth at the end of someone's arm, and the effort was so labored they knew it was Ben. When he got within earshot, they screeched at him.

"Go away," Annaliese said.

"Go back in the house," Lucenia bellowed.

And he did.

Annaliese's eyes swept over the grounds below, where the buildings that made up her entire world were shrouded in darkness. "Look at all that we've built here. It's a compound. And I made it worse, buildin' that schoolhouse," she muttered. She rested her chin on her knees.

"Oh, I don't know 'bout that."

"Another stake in the ground."

"Our children and the mountain children have benefited, though."

Since the day they had reopened the school, Annaliese had wondered about Lucenia's reaction to the three sisters. Now, in the intimacy of the dark, with an untethered tongue, she managed to push out the subject she had held since then. "Especially the mountain children."

At this, Lucenia stared off into the sky, where there was little to see but the blackened backbones of the mountains rolling away.

"Those three stair-step sisters," Annaliese said, straining to see her face.

"Little Sarah Frances." Lucenia plucked at a cushion of moss between them.

Annaliese took a sloppy swipe across her mouth. "I saw you crying that day. You told me it was nothing."

"She reminded me of my little sister."

"Rose."

"No." She left the moss alone. "My littlest sister."

"Littlest?" Annaliese said. "I thought there were just the two of you."

"One more. There was Alice, the baby."

Annaliese felt her heartbeat in her throat. She hated women's stories about babies dying on their mothers, whole sets of children wiped out by one diseased visitor.

Lucenia shook her head as she brought the edge of the glass to her lips. She pulled the last of her drink in noisy slurps. "My father took her."

"But you told me he died on the kitchen floor."

"Oh, I wish he had. I've wished it so hard I've come to believe it, I suppose. I wish the tourniquet had killed him like I told you it did before he could . . ." Lucenia let out a raspy cry and began shaking her head. "It is true that my mother wouldn't let him in that night, when we thought he was just drunk again, and we did wrap him with the tourniquet, but when he came to in the morning and remembered everything, he ripped it off his arm and left. To spite my mother, he came back a few weeks later and stole my baby sister. Three years old. From her warm place in the bed right beside me. I never heard him. How could I not have heard him? I was the oldest. I should have protected her." Lucenia's voice broke.

The glass slipped from Annaliese's hand as she threw an arm around Lucenia's shoulder.

"For days, my mother and I scoured Cincinnati, asking after the two of them. We even went to the river docks, though it made no sense since they had taken off on that horse."

"You had no means to get any help?"

"No. No family to help us look, no money to grease palms or to pay for travel . . ." Lucenia struggled with her words, squeezing them out in a slow, jagged stream, ". . . not that we knew where else to look." She shrugged. "After a few weeks, we stopped searching."

Annaliese held her breath high in her chest.

"Months later, a man came to our door. He said he was from the railroad company, said there had been a terrible accident near Akron. A man and a little girl had been on a horse, waiting at a railroad crossing. So stupid. Just as the train was on them, the horse spooked, ran right onto the tracks. The man found Mother through the saddle maker. She never blamed me outright, but sometimes, when she sat on the edge of my bed to say good-night, I could see that question in her eyes, the same one I asked myself so many nights. How? How could I not have heard him, stopped him?" A wail rose from her now, in barely controlled waves.

Annaliese was crying, too. "You couldn't have known he was capable of such a thing."

Lucenia shook her head. "It's true. We never dreamed . . ." Her words trailed into whispers. She hugged her knees and rocked for a while, nose buried in her trousers. "Rose clung to me for years, we were that scared that somehow he was still alive, that perhaps he'd paid that man to lie to us. Maybe he'd come back for Rose. How many times I promised her that I'd see after her, that we wouldn't be poor and help-less when we were grown." She turned her head and pressed a wet cheek against Annaliese's.

Annaliese swept her hand over Lucenia's back in slow circles. "You kept your promise, Luce."

Lucenia brushed her tears with fierce little swipes. "Yep. Rose is happily settled and well taken care of."

Annaliese finally dropped her hand. "And you have two sturdy sons."

"Yep." Lucenia smiled. "Listen to me saying yep. Sloppy mouth."

Downhill, gauzy figures moved in the dim light of the children's bedrooms.

Lucenia leaned back on her elbows. "Don't be sorry for the school-house. I like to think about Sarah Frances learning about the world beyond these hollows."

Annaliese patted the dark ground, groping for the decanter. "Our children will soon need more, though."

Lucenia lifted the decanter from her other side and handed it over. "Uh huh. And we'll be in Cincinnati and Louisville, giving it to them."

"Yes. We're leaving in the morning."

They were silent for a while.

"They do grow here in other ways, though," Annaliese said.

"Look at all those trees they planted." Lucenia waved her hand over the hill in an arc.

Annaliese nodded. "I believe they would've planted trees for as long as Wade pulled bags off the wagon."

"We have to keep goin'."

"What? But we finished Bunny Mountain."

"There's Black Face."

"That's hundreds of acres."

"Moderation is overrated." Lucenia waved her glass around sloppily.

"But we're leaving in the morning, remember?"

Half a laugh. "You know we're not."

"You're drunk."

"You started it."

"But . . ." Annaliese paused, remembering the children working so hard, their eager little hands as they planted the seedlings, their faces set with thoughtful and earnest attention as they listened to Wade's gentle directions, their eyes rich with satisfaction. Each night, they said prayers at their bedsides for cool days and enough rain, a ritual they had begun, not she, and the perfect weather had in fact come, hadn't it? The coolest June that Ruth and Joe could remember and gentle showers, too, all of which had nudged the seedlings along into the tiny forest that now thrived on Bunny Mountain. *We took it back from you*, she said to whomever was out there in the brooding mountains who needed to hear it. She looked over at Lucenia. "But we had to show them."

"So let's really show them. John and Ben, too." Lucenia swung an arm around Annaliese. "We'll call it our suffragette project."

Annaliese smiled. "No. Our suffragette shit project."

They fell into each other's shoulders helpless with laughter.

Ben was coming back. His timid calls came floating up to them, little impotent bleatings that brought their scowls raining down again on his head. But they were getting cold. They stood up, wobbling into each other at first before steadying themselves. Behind Ben's shuffling frame, Annaliese saw Henry—taller and thicker than John—standing in the kitchen doorway.

"The children would like it," Annaliese said.

Lucenia brushed off her pants. "Wade, too."

"Gotta put up the peaches first, though."

"Yup."

July 15, 1902

Dear Mother and Aunt Gert;

We are all well and of good cheer, though John continues to battle mysterious fevers and nighttime chills. The mountain air is quite cool after sunset, even though our July days have been sweltering. The heat and cold seem to bother him more than the rest of us.

We have put up butterbeans and corn and tomatoes until I thought I would scream. But I know that next winter we shall be glad that our garden was so bounteous

Our little mountain school will begin a new term tomorrow. Over the last few weeks, Samuel has read two more Zane Gray books and he is hoping that the local boys will sit still for a few chapters being read to them. You should see him now, Mother. He is as tall as my shoulder, as brown and agile as a deer. His face is not so round anymore. It's longer and firmer, like John's, though sometimes I think I see Clark's square chin in there as well. With his horse, his confidence grows every day, and it is well-placed, for he guides that animal with a sure hand. I do so regret that we were unable to be home for his birthday last month, but John's illnesses require my full attention. Nothing for you to worry about, really.

Emeline might as well be a boy, she is so assertive. You should see her recruiting Samuel and her cousins to pick violets with her – and they agree to it! She shows no fear of bees. In fact, Ruth has taught her how to follow them from the streams to their hives. Be assured, however, that she is learning her stitches and her Baltimore catechism.

Lucenia and I are planning to plant a few trees around the schoolhouse.

The only sad news other than John's illnesses is the puzzling melancholy that has befallen our cook, Ruth. I am at a loss to understand it. This is a drastic change in her boisterous personality. Her manner is still kind and helpful, but there seems to be no bounce in her any more and she will barely allow her eyes to meet mine. Herschel seems just as baffled as I.

You will be surprised at my last piece of news. John has decided to install an electric generator at the sawmill and another near our homes. We will have the only electricity within five counties, which I pray won't cause too much resentment.

As you can tell, the company is doing well, growing beyond John's expectations, and he does not appear ready to leave soon. It is difficult to say just how much longer we will be here. And so, I am extending an invitation to you and Dorothy and anyone else in the family to come and visit me. I cannot abandon the school while it is in session (which continues to the middle of September), nor can I leave John to his illnesses, so I hope that you will come here. The cool evenings are quite restful.

Please keep me in your prayers. You are always in mine.
Lovingly,
Annaliese

∾

XXVII

"Oooh, won't these taste good come January?" Ruth wiped the last glass jar down with a damp towel. She stepped back from the kitchen table to join Annaliese and Lucenia at the sink, where they were mopping July off their necks. The women looked over their day's work—twenty-four glistening jars packed with warm peaches. Even the green Mason jar tinge could not ruin the golden glow of the fruit, flecked with red at the pit pockets, drowning in its sweet glaze.

"Twenty-four quarts," Lucenia said. "Whew."

"Would've been twenty-six if you hadn't eaten so many peaches," Annaliese said with an elbow to Lucenia's ribs.

"Ouch." Lucenia clamped her arms to her sides.

"Ain't you one to talk," Ruth said. "I couldn't cut a slice into the bowl afore you was eatin' it."

"I had the worst job, cooking the sugar water," Annaliese said. "Look at me." She held up two hands for inspection, tried to wiggle her fingers. "My fingers are fused. My arms are sticky."

"Worst job, nothin'," Ruth said. "I had to boil all of them rubbers and lids and jars."

"Well, I peeled those infernal peaches," Lucenia said. "And neither of you warned me about the afflictions of peach fuzz." She clawed at her neck and arms.

Ruth walked over to the wood stove, choosing her steps slowly around the spills on the floor. She kneeled down before the open door and spread out the last of the hot coals with a stick. "Lord, it's some kinda hot in here. But we'll have electric stoves next summer, won't we?" She clamped her hand over her mouth. Two sore spots in one sentence: electricity and next summer.

Annaliese pulled her damp blouse away from her chest and blew into the gap. "Whose idea was it to put up all these peaches on a day this hot anyway?"

"Yours." Lucenia shoved her gently and the women fell against each other. Jumping up from the stove to join them, Ruth slipped on a peach peel and started falling, heading straight for the legs of the table that held the day's work. Annaliese rushed for the girl's arms, Lucenia for the table legs, and soon all three slid into a heap under the table, helpless when John appeared in the doorway. A coffee cup dangled from a finger. Barefoot and shirtless, he scratched at the fly of the pants he had slept in. Two o'clock in the afternoon and John had just gotten out of bed.

Silence swept through the room like a gust before a rainstorm. Three sets of cool eyes stared back at his bloodshot ones. He took a step backward and raised his cup. No one moved, not even Ruth—still on her hands and knees—save the narrowing of her eyes. Flies darted through John's open door and circled the room. Their excited droning sliced through the tension while everyone stared. John took a step backward, then another, and he was gone.

Annaliese and Lucenia helped Ruth up.

"Well, time to clean up, I reckon," she said.

A tower of peach baskets slumped against a corner near the pantry. In the sink, a sugar-crusted iron pot soaked. Flies were drowning happily in its sweet scum. Peach pits and peels filled several tin buckets that sat under the table and when Annaliese walked over to pick them up, her shoes made loud sucking noises.

"Let's get out of here." She pulled the towel off her shoulder and threw it on the floor.

Ruth snapped her dishrag at a knot of flies on one of the peach jars. "Oh, y'all go on. I'll straighten up."

"Where are you going?" Lucenia said, scratching at her neck again.

Annaliese grabbed Ruth by the arm and pulled her to the doorway. "Come on. Before the children get home."

They followed Annaliese down the road that led to the sawmill, kicking up red dust as they ran, feeling hot and dangerous. One hundred yards down, at the stream that paralleled the path worn well by now, Annaliese stopped to untie her apron and dropped it, then her boots. Ruth and Lucenia, looking left and right, joined her.

The stream was shallow at this point in its meandering course, bubbling just barely over its wide cobbled bed of smooth, dark stones. Born a few miles away in a mossy cove on Skipjack Mountain, it ran cool even in the scorching days of summer. Just sitting beside it, the women could feel the air temperature drop. Annaliese looked over at Ruth, whose old mirth seemed to have returned for the moment, and smiled. Leaving the aprons in a heap beside the road, the women ran into the creek with skirts hiked high. They walked up the middle of the streambed until they were in the forest's shadows. A curtain of leaves fell behind them as they pressed on. Deeper into the woods they ventured, kicking up a spray, following Annaliese without a word. Finally, she pointed to a wide sandy shelf and Lucenia hurried over to plop down on it.

"Take off your skirt, for heaven's sake," Annaliese shouted, unfastening hers. She tossed it to the bank and began unbuttoning her shirtwaist.

"And get sand in my knickers?" Lucenia asked.

"Well, your blouse at least." Annaliese pulled hers off, tossed it beside the skirt, and now stood in the middle of the creek in pantaloons and camisole, splashing water on her arms and legs. "You're the lusty one after all."

"I beg your pardon," Lucenia said from the bank.

"Oh, take yore shirt off, Miss Lucenia," Ruth said. "You know it's full of peach fuzz."

"Oh, all right." Lucenia's fingers began working on the buttons of her blouse. Soon the billowing skirt was in a heap on the sandy bank, too.

"Me? I am shuckin' it all." Ruth threw her skirt over her head.

When the girl's camisole came off, Annaliese and Lucenia peeked while they doused their arms, though she didn't seem to care. Soon, there was more peeking than dousing. Ruth stripped down to nothing but papery-thin, white bloomers, which would soon be transparent. She sat down and splashed herself with glee. From the girl's thin chest two breasts rose swollen and full, fuller than one would expect on such a small frame. Fuller than Annaliese and Lucenia could ever remember them being, or, rather, ever judged them being. They looked at each other wide-eyed and then back to be sure. Two erect nipples stared back, intensely pink against the creamy skin. Unnaturally pink. Purplish pink.

The sisters-in-law exchanged raised eyebrows and turned their eyes one more time to their suspicions. Sunlight was falling through an opening in the forest canopy directly on those glistening mounds, making them translucent and shining, and underneath that skin a blue network of veins stood out, as vivid and stark as fresh scars, doing what God intended: carrying blood for two.

"Ruth! You're pregnant?" Annaliese shouted. She took two steps toward the girl and reached down for her hands. "Look at you."

Lucenia struggled to get up. "Wait! Wait for me."

Ruth shot up and looked down at her chest. "What? Look at what?"

"Why your breasts."

Ruth clamped her hands over as much of them as she could.

"You've embarrassed her," Lucenia said, finally arriving at the middle of the stream. "You weren't ready to tell us, were you?"

"But how do y'all know?" Ruth whispered. Confusion raced through her eyes, but Annaliese thought she saw fear as well. Why wasn't pure happiness glowing there? Blood was rising on the girl's neck, spreading across her face. Ruth's chin fell again to the chest that spilled over her crisscrossed arms. "Y'all see somethin' I don't?"

"Your veins," Lucenia said. "Your . . . voluptuousness."

As Annaliese nodded, Ruth's anxious eyes slid from Lucenia to Annaliese and back again. She did not relax her shoulders, held as rigid now as her thin, pursed lips. It wasn't from embarrassment.

"But it's wonderful, isn't it, Ruth?" Annaliese asked. "The baby you've pined for?"

The girl nodded stiffly.

"Perhaps you'd like to put your blouse on." Annaliese turned toward the bank to pick it up. As she bent down for it, she heard Ruth say, "Well, I had my 'spicions. These thangs sure enough hurt."

Annaliese waded back, offering the blouse. As Ruth reached for it, Annaliese held it back slightly to force Ruth's eyes to meet hers. What was wrong, for heaven's sake? Annaliese wanted to read her eyes again, the eyes that usually gave away whatever her mouth did not. Perhaps Herschel was the problem. Perhaps he only liked the planting, as she had heard him say, and not necessarily the fruit. Annaliese released the blouse. "Herschel will be pleased."

"Oh, yea. He will be." She took the blouse, blinking her pale eyes at her briefly, but long enough to give Annaliese the impression that Ruth was eyeing *her*.

The wet blouse was proving difficult to pull on. Lucenia stepped forward to help.

"Well, he'll be thrilled," Annaliese said, though she imagined how difficult it might be to gauge thrill in Herschel.

"Yes, ma'am." Ruth concentrated on the buttons.

"Well, now, there's something I need to warn you about," Lucenia said as she delivered pats on the girl's back. "Your hair will fall out in handfuls after the delivery."

"Lucenia," Annaliese said, still trying to worm her way into Ruth's eyes, "you don't need to get into that right now."

"But I have a salve for it," Lucenia said, wounded.

Ruth allowed a weak smile upon her lips. "I reckon there will be right many thangs to learn 'bout this. But y'all are sure?"

"We'll send you to Dr. Chastain soon to confirm it," Lucenia said.

Ruth's head turned downstream. She held her hand up for silence, staring at the bend in the stream thirty yards down. "Your clothes," she hissed, pointing to the bank. Annaliese and Lucenia hurried over. Just as Annaliese fastened her skirt, she heard it.

"Yoo hoo," called a female voice.

Splashing echoed up the creek.

Lucenia fumbled with her blouse buttons. Annaliese jerked her wet arm into a dry sleeve that would not slide.

"Mizz Stregal?" the woman called.

"Who on earth . . .?" Lucenia asked.

The sleeve seam in Annaliese's shirtwaist ripped at her tugging.

The woman emerged from the stream's bend, skirt gathered up in one hand, boots in the other.

"Well, I'll be," Ruth said.

Thessalonia Meddling grinned back at the bathers.

"Slow her down, Ruth," Annaliese whispered, fumbling with buttons.

"I knowed y'all was in here," Thessalonia shouted as she waded toward them. "Them boots and aprons out yonder on the road. Somethin' came in on the train for y'all. I know y'all been looking fer it. Boxes said Sears Roebuck."

"The shoes," Lucenia said. "For the students."

"We'd just about given up on that," Annaliese said.

Thessalonia finally arrived at their circle. "Came in on the one o'clock from Atlanta. Big ole heap of boxes. Loaded them in my wagon and came on up."

"All by yourself?" Annaliese said.

"Sure."

"Why, thank you," Lucenia said. She pulled up a wad of skirt and wrung it.

Thessalonia turned to Ruth. "Ruth, how you doin'?" She eyed her transparent clothes with a cocked eyebrow. "You're looking right roundish for once."

"Doin' fine, Thessalonia," Ruth said, folding her arms across herself. Somehow, she found herself shivering. "We was puttin' up peaches all day," she shrugged.

"Well, no wonder," Thessalonia said of the scene, but her eyes took note of whose skirts were wet and whose had stayed dry on the bank.

"Well, come on to the house. Have something cool to drink," Annaliese said, moving to leave.

"Don't care if I do, thanky."

"So kind of you to go to this trouble," Lucenia said as she waded downstream to her.

"Wanted them young 'uns to have their shoes," Thessalonia said. Blinking with a new thought, she touched Lucenia's arm. "Reckon I shoulda been the schoolmarm instead of Corinthia? She don't care a lick for young 'uns."

"Why, we hadn't noticed," Lucenia said as she looped her arm through Thessalonia's.

That night, by the light of the lamp that Darrison held over her shoulder, Lucenia opened each parcel. Three boxes later, she found them—the smallest pair of boots. She turned them over to read the name and be sure. She stuffed a small porcelain doll deep down inside. On top of the doll, she tucked a coil of glossy yellow ribbon. Then, mother and son rewrapped and labeled the fifteen pairs. As Darrison turned to go— the kerosene was getting low—his mother called him back. In the final moments of the lamp's soupy glow, they organized the boots by gender, then size. By the time she was delivering her lecture on the importance of order, the lamp was dead, which gave Darrison the dark that allowed his adolescent eyes freedom of expression in all of its forms.

"Wade says if we're going to plant trees over by the school that we need to do it soon," said Lucenia one September afternoon when she and Annaliese were pulling wash off the line. "Before the cold sets in."

Annaliese squeezed a shirt to judge its dampness and sighed. They had not spoken of Lucenia's drunken proposal since their night of anarchy, the memory of which still gave Annaliese a headache. She had hoped that Lucenia had forgotten. Planting trees on Bunny Mountain was one thing, mostly a way to bury the memory of that terrible night, something hopeful to rest their eyes against as they washed the dishes. But planting those acres was crazy. They couldn't just go behind John and right his wrongs. Worse, they couldn't recreate the primeval forest. Annaliese repinned the shirt to the line and looked off into the rolling hills. Forests were cathedrals of life, built over time, from the towering oaks and chestnuts whose canopies protected the smaller dogwoods and redbuds, to the understory of shrubs and vines and mosses. Forests were fungi and moles, birds, mites and slugs unearthed by grubby little Stregal hands, all of it linked. Trees were but one aspect of the teeming, throbbing organism.

Still, without columns, one could not create a cathedral, and she had agreed to it.

"Well, I suppose a ride up that way to take a look wouldn't hurt," Annaliese said. "Perhaps tomorrow? Take Wade with us?"

"Tomorrow?" Lucenia put the laundry basket down and leaned back into a long stretch. "But Belle has been ailing. We should wait a couple of days until she's healed."

"You could ride any horse in that stable now." Annaliese folded a pinafore and put it in the basket. Lucenia had worked hard with Belle in the corral for many months. As she forgave her for the fall of last November, Lucenia's fear faded enough that she could now mount the horse unaided, turn her, and stop her. Darrison often appeared at the fence to watch. Recently, Lucenia had asked him to come in, help her dismount. Annaliese made up a reason to leave them alone. When she returned, they were leading the mare around the ring, deep in discussion about the differences between quarter horses and thoroughbreds.

"Oh, I don't know about that." Lucenia's frown creased her brow.

Annaliese recalled how on that train ride to Georgia eighteen months ago, she had admired her sister-in-law's smooth, flawless skin. Now there were freckles and the beginnings of a leathery look. She pulled her bonnet on. "Well, I do. Your riding is coming along nicely," she said.

"Truly?"

"Truly."

Lucenia turned to eye the rest of the clothing on the line. "Who should I ride, then?"

"How about Brownie?"

"The bay? You think she's all right?" Lucenia squeezed the next shirt.

"Of course."

"But tomorrow's Sunday."

"So?"

"Wade's going to tell us we shouldn't be out on the Lord's day."

Annaliese snapped the wrinkles out of an apron a little too hard. "Who brought this up and said we should get started soon?"

"You're right. We'll go tomorrow." She raised her eyebrows at Annaliese. "There I go again."

"Again what?"

"Letting you talk me into something," Lucenia laughed. "Look at what you've done to me."

The next morning, Lucenia, Annaliese, and Wade rode past the sawmill at half past ten, its doors closed, the machines all locked down. Beside the dry kiln building rested a new electric boiler. Crates full of generator parts littered the yard. A raceway from pond to mill was already finished. The women would not look at any of it.

A steady night rain had cooled the air and slicked the road to Pinch. Brown puddles still shimmered in the ruts Herschel's wagon had made on its way to and from the schoolhouse. The riders guided their horses around the mire and watched for the fork, where the left branch that led to Pinch would be muck and the right branch leading to the school-house would be strewn with bark and other lumber offal. To this firmer ground the horses headed and, once all hooves steadied, the women and Wade relaxed in their saddles.

Overhead, the leaf canopy sagged with moisture and dusky scents. Every surface was cleansed, fresh and spring-green, though the tips of some leaves were beginning to turn. To the horses' right, the damp mountain rose up to meet a mist so thick that the slope disappeared into the gray sky. To their left, the hillside fell away toward the river.

The forest closed in on them, heavy and sheltering, lulling them into drowsiness. Annaliese let the reins go slack in her fingers. Even Wade, who should have known better, allowed his grip and spine to relax.

The wild hog darted in front of them so quickly they were aware of it only as a brown blur. All three horses bolted to the left, as if tethered together. Annaliese's horse started a sideways fall, but she had time to kick her feet out of the stirrups. As the road rose to meet her face, she panicked for Lucenia, out of sight. Annaliese's thud into the muck knocked the breath out of her, but immediately she began trying to wriggle away from the horse, which had landed on one of her legs. Somehow she twisted away from him. She pushed herself up with one arm, struggling to refill her lungs and find Lucenia.

Brownie and Lucenia were disappearing over the lip of the cliff.

Wade pulled Annaliese the rest of the way up. She cursed her throbbing foot into working to get her to the road's edge. She had never seen a horse go so fast down a hill. Lucenia's elbows were flapping at her sides and she was leaning way too far back in the saddle. When Annaliese saw the ravine beyond them—a chasm about eight feet across and too deep to judge—she knew what the horse was going to do.

"Get off!" Annaliese screamed.

"She's gonna jump!" Wade yelled.

They started running downhill, shouting commands they knew she could not hear. Brownie bore down on the ravine, lifted her front legs as they knew she would, and sprang across the gap in one frantic, flailing, ugly thrust. But she could not overcome her rider's misplaced weight and the mud. Only the front legs made it across. Her rear feet caught just under the lip and she began clawing at the slippery slope, filling the air with desperate, angry grunts.

"Kick away," Annaliese shouted as she weaved through the trees, impossibly hopeful that Lucenia could slide off before the horse went down any farther.

But Lucenia pulled on the reins, dooming the struggling horse to fall backward. With outraged whinnying, Brownie fell into the ravine just as Wade and Annaliese arrived at its edge. Wade put his hand on Annaliese's shoulder as they peered over.

Ten feet below, Brownie was on her back, finally still. Sickeningly still. All four legs in the air. One boot stuck out on the right side of the horse. The quiet was nauseating. Annaliese and Wade scrambled down, trying to speak calmly to the horse that was heaving for air. Brownie's eyes ripped around the ravine, but she kept still, as though she realized the danger her rider faced. Annaliese's stomach lurched as she saw that the ravine was lined with boulders. Where was Lucenia's head? Her arms? She moved around the other side of the horse, patting it, trying to force Lucenia's name out of her throat.

A groan came from under the horse. Lucenia's head and torso were nearly buried in mud.

"Uhfff," she coughed.

"Oh, thank God," Annaliese cried. She took Lucenia's mud-caked face in her hands.

Wade, on the other side of Brownie's heaving belly, was already whispering into the horse's quivering ear. "You're all right, girl. You're all right. You got to calm down and do what I say, girl."

Slowly, he coaxed the horse to roll over toward him.

Annaliese sucked air through her teeth as she watched the saddle horn pull away from Lucenia's upper abdomen.

"Didn't know what to do," Lucenia moaned.

"Ssh, darling," Annaliese said. "Don't move."

"All right so far?" Wade called to Annaliese.

No, her mind screamed. *Nothing is all right.*

Lucenia's eyes were closed and her chest was laboring hard in short, shallow bursts as if she could not fill her lungs. *Please, God. Not her lungs.* Annaliese stared at the crushed blouse. *Not her heart. Not her liver.* Annaliese's eyes moved down to Lucenia's waist. Everything below it was still under the horse.

"Miss Annaliese!" Wade pleaded for an answer.

Annaliese whispered into Lucenia's ear. "We've got to finish getting Brownie up, darling. Are you ready?"

Lucenia grimaced and squeezed her eyes even tighter, but she managed a nod.

"Go ahead, Wade. Slowly," Annaliese said.

Brownie's slow rise quickly turned into a flailing of hooves as the horse tried to plant them on something solid. Lucenia began screaming about her leg, sending Annaliese into pushing the horse and Wade pulling until Brownie finally scrambled up.

Wade dropped to his knees at Lucenia's side and scanned her body. Every part of her had landed on rocks. One of her feet twisted away from the leg at an impossible angle, but the leg itself was worse. Just below the knee, a ragged bone protruded through her trousers. A crimson stain was fanning out across the fabric. Wade tore his shirt off and wrapped it around the leg. Meanwhile, Annaliese was gaping at Lucenia's concave belly.

But it was Lucenia's silence that was the most terrifying of all. Annaliese clawed at Wade's arm.

"We have to get her out of here," Annaliese cried.

"There's a wagon at the schoolhouse." Wade grabbed Brownie's reins and began pulling her up the hill.

"But the children are at the schoolhouse," Annaliese cried. "Don't let them . . ."

"No, ma'am. It's Sunday."

"Of course . . ." Annaliese closed her eyes and heard what he was thinking. *Shouldn't have been out here on a Sunday.*

"Be back fast as I can."

And he was off, somehow dragging a panicked horse back up a slippery hillside, leaving her looking at a woman who should not be moved by anyone but Atlanta's finest doctors. She picked up Lucenia's hands and brought them to her lips, where she did the only thing she could think to do. She kissed them.

"Our Father which art in heaven," she began, and her mind hit a wall. She could not remember the next words, could not think of anything but Lucenia's words from the day before: "There I go again, letting you talk me into something."

Lucenia's shook her head. "Go," came the weak sound. She opened her eyes and said, "Don't stop praying, Anna."

Annaliese pressed Lucenia's limp hand to her cheek. Between sobs, she managed, "Wade's gone for help."

"Uh-huh."

Annaliese's heart was thudding against her ribs. "Hallowed be thy name . . ."

"My leg," Lucenia groaned.

"We've wrapped it, darling." Annaliese could not force herself to check on it.

Lucenia's lips began to move. "Pray."

But Annaliese found that she could not pray at all, so absorbed she was by the gnawing sense of something else. Prayer assumed hope, but she felt hope slipping away like Lucenia's dim pulse. Annaliese's skin grew cold as she felt something dark coiling around her soul—the specter of waste. She was wasting precious minutes. Lucenia's life was ebbing away. *Wade will never be back in time.* All of their tomorrows were telescoped down into the next few minutes. If she denied this, their final moments together would be just panic talk, words to distract Lucenia from her leg, mere vapors by next week. If she embraced it, she would have a few gems to give and a few to receive—pearls on a string to finger for the rest of her days.

Annaliese spat on the tail of her shirt and wiped away some of the mud from Lucenia's eyes. Lucenia looked back, tears welling up at the corners and over to track down her cheeks.

"In the name of God, Lucenia, forgive me," Annaliese cried. "I never should have put you on a horse. You were afraid. I should have left you alone about it." Her eyes bore into Lucenia's.

Lucenia lifted her arm toward Annaliese's neck, but the motion caused her to cry out. She touched her stomach. "No. No. It's been a gift. Darrison . . . He's unfolded to me. I've seen the flickerings of the fine man he'll be. And he'll be nothing like my father." A weak squeeze of her hand.

"No, of course, he won't," Annaliese said, squeezing back.

"Now . . . you'll . . . finish him."

And there it was. Her mind struggled to shove it back, but she knew she must not.

"And James." Lucenia picked up her head to stare at Annaliese with a strength that surprised her. "He's too young. Don't know yet."

"Why, he's like Ben, Luce," Annaliese said, hoping that that was all right.

"Yes," came the weak whisper as Lucenia lay back and closed her eyes.

Annaliese straightened to look for Wade. Her ears, full of her pounding heart, were not to be relied upon. *Come on. Come on.*

Lucenia began pulling on Annaliese's arm. "Promise me . . . "

Don't she wanted to scream. But they had to.

"Promise me you'll help Ben raise them."

"Yes."

"And Ben."

"Yes."

"Take care of Ben for me." A weak smile appeared at her lips. "He needs . . ." A groan rose in Lucenia's throat. Again, Annaliese turned to look up the hillside. Her ankle burned with pain.

When she turned back, she saw Lucenia's eyes on the hill, too.

Annaliese dabbed at her muddy face again. "Oh, darling, we never asked for this, did we?" she whispered.

Lucenia's head began rolling side to side. "Perhaps I did."

"What . . ."

She forced herself up on one elbow to meet Annaliese's bewildered stare. "Can you forgive *me?*"

"Ssh," Annaliese whispered. "You've done nothing." She pushed Lucenia's shoulder toward the ground but Lucenia resisted. Words began pouring out of her mouth, strong and fast and as surprising as the strength with which she pushed back.

"I nagged him. To start a business."

Annaliese squeezed her eyes. "Lucenia, stop."

"Carpe diem, I told him." She coughed. "But I never meant this!" Lucenia's eyes pleaded for understanding. "No, I never meant Georgia."

"Dear, this was all John's idea."

"This place . . . not of our choosing."

"But it brought us together, didn't it?"

"Forgive me?"

"Lucenia."

"We don't have much time."

"All right. I forgive you." She leaned down to press her lips on Lucenia's forehead. Her skin was clammy and her hands were growing limper. What was taking Wade so long? She remembered his shirt girdling Lucenia's leg and forced her eyes toward the road so she could not look at it. Such a steep slope. They would have to strap her to something flat—maybe they could pull off one of the wagon's side railings somehow—to haul her out of there. And then the wagon ride. It would be torture for her and would only bring them to the sawmill. Then what? On to Pinch or send for Dr. Chastain? But that would take hours. All this blood. Lucenia's leg. All my fault. Dear God, there just isn't enough time.

Annaliese turned back to kiss Lucenia again and saw that her head had fallen to the side. Her eyes were closed, and the anxious forehead of seconds ago was now smooth and relaxed. Her lips had parted slightly.

Across her bottom lip, a fly walked, unchallenged.

"No!" Annaliese shook Lucenia's limp arm. The fly shot away. She dropped down to press her ear to Lucenia's chest. The silence tore through her brain like a bullet.

"No, no, no," she screamed. "Don't leave me!"

Wade found her slumped over Lucenia, smoothing her hair.

"I'll see you home," she sobbed. "Please, God, tell her. I'll take her home."

Wade crouched next to Lucenia, took her hand, turned it over and pressed his fingers into her wrist. He stood up and took off his hat. Annaliese rose and attacked him.

"Put it back on!" she cried.

He did, but it didn't stop her blows. Finally, her hands slowed into childish slaps, landed on his shoulder for the last time, hung there while Annaliese struggled for breath between sobs, and began sliding down his taut arm in a long, slow, clutching slide that made his blood run cold. At the bottom, where her fingers wrapped around his, Annaliese fell against his knees.

"I didn't get to tell her," she cried.

"What?"

"That I would be sure she got home. That she taught me so much. That I loved her."

"Oh, Miss Annaliese," Wade moaned. "She sure enough knew."

❧

XXVIII

The sight of Rose, every inch Lucenia in build and bearing, sent Annaliese to the porch railing to steady herself while Herschel's wagon brought her closer. Rose perched on the seat with the same haughty posture, the same squaring of broad shoulders. Even the lay of the woman's hands in her lap, one hand cupped inside the other, was Lucenia.

Ben pulled out a handkerchief and wiped his nose. Herschel stopped the wagon in front of them. They knew they should be moving toward her, but the sight of her was too much. When she turned her face up to them as she approached the steps, Annaliese beheld the same wide forehead and narrow chin, the same smooth complexion. Her head, like Lucenia's, was too small for her heavy body. But the eyes were rounder and darker, thought Annaliese, and very swollen.

Finally, Rose raised both arms to Ben and waited for him to come down the steps. He shuffled down and she lifted shaky arms to embrace him. Ben buried his face in her neck. Her black hat tumbled down into the dust. Annaliese stared at it listlessly, as did Herschel, who, on another day, would have hurried to pluck it up.

Behind Annaliese, the screen door squeaked. She turned around to find James and Darrison shuffling toward her. Everyone in the families had become more attuned to sounds in these last few days since John had suspended the sawmill. Mute as wooden soldiers, the children wandered between the houses, avoiding not so much the casket in their parlor as the callers coming through at all hours. Thessalonia and Corinthia had arrived days ago with a clump of women from their church to direct visitors and their rag-covered plates of chicken, ham biscuits, and apple bettys. Yesterday, Henry and Calvin brought Dorothy and Annaliese's cousins Michael, Ted, Patrick, and Irene from the train. For the children, all these new voices, the hands that tried to land on their shoulders, even just the gritty shuffle of too many feet on the floors was so jarring that they fled outdoors most of the time. They stayed there until the deathly quiet of the stilled saws drove them even crazier and sent them, especially Lucenia's boys, looking for Annaliese. Now, as she turned to her nephews, she heard Ruth's distant crying—as the boys must have, too—and she waved them to come to her.

The boys scurried across the porch and grasped Annaliese's hands. They watched their father and aunt sobbing, patting. When Rose saw the boys, her face broke into a tender smile. James buried his face in Annaliese's skirt.

" 'Lo, Aunt Rose," Darrison said.

Rose rushed up the steps and pressed a body so much like his mother's into Darrison that Annaliese ached for the boy. His head landed in her hearty bosom, where he began sobbing. Annaliese nudged James over to join them.

Watching them cling to one another, she felt her chest lighten. She would never call the boys a burden, but it had been a long three days waiting for this woman to arrive. Annaliese had planned that it would be the other way around, that they would take Lucenia to Rose in Cincinnati. But Ben wouldn't hear of it.

"What do you mean, send Lucenia back to Cincinnati?" he cried when she brought it up the morning after the night no one had slept. He held his head in his hands, elbows on his kitchen table. In his parlor, Ruth was draping the boards on which Lucenia's body would be laid out.

"But I promised her I would see her home," Annaliese said.

"This is her home." Dark skin bagged under his eyes.

Annaliese lowered her voice, having no stomach for arguing with the poor man, but guilt pushed her on. "But by next spring it won't be." Her fingers crept toward his hand like a beaten dog stealing back to the master.

"Will you stop saying that!" Ben slammed his hand on the table. "I'm here now. Her sons are here. We need her near us." He ground his palms into his eyes.

Of course, you do. She could feel that yearning herself.

Annaliese laid her throbbing head on the table. The cool tin surface felt good on her hot cheeks. She couldn't think straight. Was she just crazy with pain and guilt? *Is this home enough? What would Lucenia say?*

"I just can't send her away," Ben was whispering. "Think of the boys, Anna." He fought his quivering lips, finally clamping a handkerchief over them.

Annaliese sat up and looked out the window at the summits of the mountains behind the home, still shrouded in morning's blue shadows. She thought of the day Ruth stood at this table and spoke of her mother's words about place shaping one's destiny.

I ain't this dirt.

And yet, Ruth had done nothing that would enable her to flee. Just the opposite. She took on a husband, a cabin, and now a child that would grow up strong and self-reliant to a fault, like all the Scots-Irish before him. Ruth's soul had sunk in this earth, stubborn as kudzu.

Had Lucenia's?

They had been so smug at the outset, she and Lucenia, and so different in every way. Annaliese wiped a tear from her cheek and as her finger lifted it from her skin, she felt a speck of red dirt, that dirt that had blown into their eyes, slid between their sheets, and rubbed raw their upended city lives. It was though it had abraded away their differences. At times, each woman had risen in strength and each had sunk to low deeds, and in the end both had settled into a smooth understanding in the middle.

Annaliese reached over to squeeze Ben's hand. "Find her a nice spot out there, Ben." Her hand swept toward the hills behind the house. "Somewhere near us."

John placed his hand at the small of his wife's back as they followed Ben, Rose, and the boys up the rocky hill. Samuel and Emeline walked, heads down, alongside their parents. Ahead, the wagon bearing Lucenia's casket swayed and creaked into the quiet mountain air. The preacher stood at the crest, a soft mound of earth on the backside of Bunny Hill. Ben had chosen it for being far enough way to not run into every day but close enough to get to when he needed. It was a lofty ledge, perched above the wide, calm valley that spread toward Skipjack Mountain, a place where Lucenia would see every dawn and catch every crisp breeze.

A towering red cedar tree flourished there. Annaliese caught its scent as she followed the small sad party that was trying not to look at the fresh hole in the ground. She smiled that Ben had found the perfect spot for a woman who had been so enamored with pleasant odors and—like the red cedar—thrived independently in the sunlight, not in the shadow of the overstory of others.

The dreary sky churned indecisively, sent columns of cold air down on their heads. The preacher looked up and scowled, then scanned the valley to check the western sky. Black clouds were coiling. He turned back to the crowd trudging up the hill and patted his limp leather Bible impatiently.

It took several minutes for the mourners to gather. Ben and his sons and Rose walked over to stand beside the preacher. John and Annaliese and their children settled in beside them. John's fingers laced into his wife's as they watched the others come: Ruth and Minerva, Henry and Calvin Chastain, the Connelleys. The Chastains still lingered close to these visitors in quiet hospitality. Extending his hand in Annaliese's direction, Henry sent the Connelleys to stand near her while he and his brother went to help Herschel at the wagon. Irene stood behind Annaliese, where she lifted Annaliese's shawl up and over her shoulders.

Dorothy patted her back. Next came Thessalonia and Corinthia leading the First Methodist crowd. They shot shy looks at the Stregals. Joe and Hoyt, the foreman, came along in crisp white shirts. Behind them, Wade, Tote, Gideon, and Walter took off their hats and raised their eyes from the ground to see where they should stand. They followed Joe to the other side of the preacher, raising Connelley eyebrows. Out of the corner of her eye, Annaliese saw John make a slow nod at the men.

Still more people came. Mill workers and their families poured out of the forest and trudged up the hill. Rail-thin women pulled shy children along as they followed the gang of men that strode before them. Shirts had been washed, hair combed and plastered down. Heads dipped whenever a Stregal eye landed on them. Annaliese heard Darrison murmuring names to Rose, whose enormous black hat bobbed as she listened.

The wagon sent up deeper creaks and groans as Henry, Calvin and Herschel began working the casket out. John joined them to help carry it toward the grave. Ruth began to sing, creating a sound so thin and pained at first that Annaliese did not recognize the voice as Ruth's. Into the air her lament wafted, went around them and through them like the gusts of the September wind that buffeted them on this high ledge. She sang,

"Comin' home, comin' home. Never more to roam.
Open wide Thine arms of love. Lord, I'm comin' home."

Annaliese twisted around to grab Irene's arm. Other mountain voices rose shakily to join Ruth's.

"My soul is sick, my heart is sore.
"Now I'm comin' home. My strength renew, my hope restore.
Lord, I'm comin' home."

Ben began dabbing a handkerchief frantically into his eyes, prompting James to bury his face in Rose's skirts. The big black hat swung side to side with the song. Darrison stepped aside to let the casket bearers through and it was soon laid at the family's feet.

The casket, hewn from flawless oak, had been polished into a gleaming gem. Men who usually worked saws and drove mules had created this casket when Ben asked for volunteers. Caramel-colored rings swirled against the amber background like ripples in a pond, a testament to the wealth of skills within dirt-poor hands. Its main adornment was a molding that ran along the bottom, but on the lid, a pair of crude roses had been carved into the otherwise unbroken surface. Here was the result of the day that the men had called James and Darrison to join them at their work and had guided the boys' unsteady hands. Rose leaned to run her fingers over their rough edges and smiled at the unselfishness that had allowed the children to mar such beautiful work.

The preacher was the Reverend Damascus Cobb, second cousin of Thessalonia and Corinthia. He eyed the darkening sky again and the crowd that was still growing. Opening his Bible, he stepped forward to stand beside the casket. He cleared his throat. But Ruth and her shaky choir continued into the refrain. People who were still coming out of the woods picked up the song as well.

"Comin' home, comin' home.
Never more to roam.
Open wide thine arms of love.
Lord, I'm comin' home."

Through her tears, Annaliese looked up. The sound, growing surer, came from the formerly faceless—the sawyers and mule drivers, the millpond pole pigs, and the dry kiln operators. *There must be fifty, sixty of them*, she thought. *But, of course there are.* The company had a workforce of more than eighty. Every day of the last year and a half she had heard them at their work. Whistling and calling. Cursing. Grunting. These were the voices that had filtered up to her porch along with the sawdust, scorched her ears with vulgarities as she walked beside the sawmill. She had hated them off and on. Now, for the first time she looked at the faces, creased with yesterday's rough road and today's honest pain.

Samuel and Emeline, who knew the song from Ruth's piano practices, were humming softly. Irene's hand patted in time on Annaliese's back.

John returned to Annaliese's side, trembling from his task. He beckoned the crowd to hurry on. The last stragglers found their spots and Reverend Cobb cleared his throat again.

"We gather today to say farewell to our sister in faith, Lucenia Hopewell Stregal, whom Jesus has called home," he said.

"Amen," came a voice from the crowd.

"She leaves behind a devoted husband and two sons, a sister, a brother-in-law and sister-in-law, a niece and nephew."

Emeline stepped forward and touched the casket. Darrison came behind her and wrapped his arms around her.

The preacher raised his hand and swept it toward the crowd. "And us."

A murmur of agreement rose.

"May the Lord help us with his abounding grace to bear our loss."

"Amen," Annaliese whispered. Irene squeezed her arm again.

"Mrs. Stregal was well known in our community for her devotion to our children's education and their welfare. She was even known to provide them with clothing and food."

"Yes, Lord!" came another voice, stronger this time.

"She embodied the ideals of fine Christian womanhood and we will miss her sorely. She will live on in each of us." Reverend Cobb turned to Ben. "And now, Mr. Stregal would like to say a few words."

James pulled his face out of Rose's skirt to watch.

Ben tucked away his handkerchief and stepped forward. "Thank y'all for coming," he began. "I know Mrs. Stregal would be touched by your outpouring." He paused to fight for control of his lips. "Some of y'all know that she wasn't crazy about coming here. No, this place wasn't a place of her choosing. She'd look at me and say, 'I never meant this!' Or, rather, she said that when we first arrived."

Darrison now left Emeline to back up and stand beside his father.

"Lot of hard work for her here. But every challenge, well, she rose to meet it and as she did so, she came to love this place, I think. Every day, my admiration and love for her grew as I saw more of her and more in her than I ever had before." He looked up to a spot above the cedar trees. "She was strong when I faltered, perceptive when I was blind. Her curiosity and fearlessness empowered me so many times that I shudder to think what might have become of me if I had not known her. My sons . . ." Ben placed one hand on Darrison's shoulder. " . . . will be strong, principled men because of her. I see the evidence of it already. And I am so . . ." Ben brought his eyes back down to her casket. ". . . thankful."

People hugged their Bibles, nodded in sympathy.

"What sweet joy," Ben began breaking down. "She brought us all," he finally sputtered. "From the moment people met her, they loved her."

Ruth stole a look at Annaliese, whose face bore a trace of a bitter-sweet smile.

Ben dissolved into tears. Darrison fished in his father's pocket for his handkerchief and gave it to him. Ben stepped back from the grave.

People shifted foot to foot.

Rose stepped forward to speak with a confidence and volume that reminded all of the woman they had come to bury. She raised her head, enabling everyone to see the pale face under the hat brim. Fixing her eyes just above everyone's heads, she took a deep breath and began.

"My sister was exhausting," she said.

Throughout the crowd, eyes blinked and froze upon the speaker. Some of the children looked up at their parents' sudden stiffness.

Rose put her hands out as if to calm the sea. "It's true. Now, we all know she had the qualities Mr. Stregal just mentioned, but it was also true that with her it was 'My kingdom come, my will be done'."

With this blasphemy in the air, eyes flew to Reverend Cobb. He turned his entire body toward Rose, who clearly needed watching.

"Because I was younger, this could actually be comforting sometimes," continued Rose. "As I matured, though, I wanted to make my own way. But as she pressed me to care about this cause or that injustice or even just my own self-betterment, I also could see that she was often trying to convince herself of her conviction. I saw that if she was afraid, she faced her fears straight on." Rose shook her head slightly. "No one ever talked my sister into doing anything she did not want to do. If she did something she feared, she had her reasons." She looked straight at Annaliese.

At this, John squeezed Annaliese's hand. Rose had already tried to deliver this message to her that first night, when the two of them were alone on Annaliese's front porch, weeping and talking about that awful day. But Annaliese would have none of it. She countered with all of the reasons why she was to blame, agonized over what a tragedy it was for a woman to have survived childhood diseases, childbirth, consumption, and all forms of contagion only to die in an accident caused by a hog. This time, Rose's message was for everyone else who might have heard of Annaliese's role in the accident. Annaliese squeezed back and looked at John, whose eyes urged the same message on her.

"In her letters, I sensed an uncoiling, however. As she described this beautiful place and how the children loved it so . . ." Rose patted James's shoulder. The boy's face crumpled, but he did not cry. ". . . I felt she was learning that there are many paths that can take us where we want to go."

"The divine hand guides us on those paths," inserted the Reverend Cobb, nodding solemnly.

"God's will," came a voice from the crowd that had not experienced the luxury of more than one path.

Rose nodded gently and pulled James into her. "It's true that this place was not of her choosing, but I believe it became the place where her eyes were opened."

"Praise His holy name," Reverend Cobb said in a conclusive tone.

A blast of cold air swept over the crowd and kicked up grit into wet eyes.

"Let us pray," Cobb said.

All heads bowed.

"Heavenly Father, we place our beloved sister Lucenia Stregal in your eternal care, to sit beside your golden throne and beside your Son, Jesus Christ, at your right hand, and join you in watching us down here every day. Let us continue to feel her loving presence, Lord. And yours. In your holy name we pray."

"Amen," everyone said.

"May God keep you, Lucenia dear," Annaliese whispered. "I'll love your boys as my own." She crossed herself.

Reverend Cobb made a quick nod at Henry and Calvin, who stepped out of the circle. John and Herschel did the same. The men picked up the four ends of two leather straps that were under the casket. They struggled to lift it, then began moving it over the hole. Slowly they lowered it. Down it went in jerks and slips until it finally arrived at the bottom. They threw the leather straps in.

As the last sight of Lucenia slipped below ground, Annaliese felt her knees give way. Even a presence as large as Lucenia was nothing against this vast earth now swallowing the last trace of her. Soon, there would be nothing left to see except a gleaming marble headstone. She would be truly gone forever, buried in the cold, red earth.

Annaliese felt an arm loop around her waist. A handkerchief appeared. She took it and tossed a small sliver of the Venetian blind from Annaliese's front porch into the grave.

With a moan that made stomachs turn, Ben fell to his knees. James and Darrison looked down at him, gaping and clearly on the brink of joining him. Annaliese started to go to them, but Dorothy's arms held her. In the time it took her to realize that her legs were not to be depended upon, John and Rose had coaxed Ben up and pulled the boys into a tight circle.

Ruth stepped forward and began singing.

> *On Jordan's stormy banks I stand*
> *And cast a wishful eye*
> *To Canaan's fair and happy land*
> *Where my possessions lie.*

As the melody hit Annaliese's ears, she realized that she knew it. This simple, plodding song had filled her home many times as Ruth had poked it out on the piano.

All along the hill, the song's words rose sure and strong from the crowd.

We will rest in the fair and happy land by and by
Just across on the evergreen shore
Sing the song of Moses and the Lamb by and by
And dwell with Jesus ever more.

This refrain, repeated after several verses, was picked up by all with increasing confidence, so that by the end, even Ben and John had added their voices. The brothers leaned into each other, pale and weakened by different forces, but each struggling for the other while their wide-eyed sons watched. And there on either end of the men stood Rose and Ruth, mismatched book-ends, swaying side to side as the song ended.

In the silence, everyone heard distant thunder rumbling across the valley. The gray gauze of the sky had turned into a roiling mass of sure trouble. Herschel motioned to Wade and Tote, who followed him to the wagon and pulled out shovels.

The crowd turned to go, grateful for having a reason to not watch.

Annaliese stood on her front porch holding the plate of food that Thessalonia had forced into her hands. Through the parlor window behind her, cracked open about three inches, she could hear forks on plates and soft conversations. Rain poured off the roof in a shimmering curtain in front of her. Occasional gusts showered her shoulders and legs, but she did not move nor did she reach for the Venetian blind to lower it against the spray. Instead, she looked over at Lucenia's porch where the blind remained up, too.

The screen door squeaked as Ted Connelley pushed through. Annaliese straightened to face the conversation. She had seen her cousins' eyes on this house, the hogs and chickens. She caught the glances they exchanged, and she had seen them watching John, too. Sure enough, Patrick and Michael were right behind Ted.

"Annaliese," Ted said as he pulled her gently out of the spray. "We need to talk."

Annaliese's swollen eyes bounced from Ted to Patrick without expression.

"Maybe now's not the time to talk about this, but . . ." Michael began.

"We want you to go back home with us tomorrow," Ted said.

She took a step backward and bumped into the porch railing. Michael reached for her arms to pull her away from the rain again. She shied away from his grasp, shoving the plate of food into his hands and sitting down in one of the soaked rockers. Michael stared at her for a moment and put the plate on the floor.

"I can't do that," Annaliese said.

"What?" Ted said. "You don't want to leave this hole?"

"Anna, we had no idea how bad it is here," Michael said.

"This is no place for you. Or the children," Ted said, leaning over her.

"The children are thriving," Annaliese said.

"What! They are becoming little . . ."

Michael grabbed Ted's arm and he stopped. Ted straightened and crossed his arms. "It's you we're worried about."

"Well, I'm not ready to go yet. I can't leave Darrison and James right now. Y'all can understand that, can't you?"

Michael sat down in a rocker beside her. "Anna, all of you need to get out of this place."

Patrick finally stepped in. "Especially John."

Annaliese winced and looked at the open window behind her. "Ssh!"

"Why didn't you write to tell us?" Patrick said.

"He's dangerous for God's sake," Ted said.

Annaliese spun around at Ted.

"He looks awful," Patrick added. "That sunken face, the long, dirty hair."

"What's happened to him?" Michael said.

Annaliese opened her mouth to speak, but Ted cut in. "He's gone mad, that's what," he said.

Michael twisted around in his seat to glare at Ted.

Annaliese cried, "Don't say that."

"I tried to talk to him yesterday," Ted whispered. "Couldn't get a word in. He's hardly in mourning. He went on and on about his accomplishments, the money he's making, the future of this business, how he can't wait to get the mill up and running again. Began a rant about the Department of Forestry. When I tried to respond, he left. Went into the dining room and began counting the flatware."

"He wanders the house at night," Patrick said.

"All right," Annaliese sighed.

"Enough," Michael said. He put his arm around Annaliese. "We'll talk about this later."

Ted's broad shoulders rose and fell. "We're leaving tomorrow. You and the children are coming with us. We'll have your things shipped back. That's it."

Annaliese shook her head. "I told you. I can't leave."

"Why not?" Ted shouted.

Annaliese waved at him to quiet down. "Because . . ." she said slowly ". . . there's something I have to finish."

"Of all the . . ."

Someone tapped on the window. "There you are," Dorothy said. Moments later, she was on the porch with them.

"Good!" Ted said as he waved her over. "Dottie, will you please talk some sense into her?"

"She has plenty of sense," Dorothy said. Her eyes fell on Michael's arm clamped around Annaliese. "What's going on?"

"Tell her she needs to come on home with us," Ted said.

"Not yet," Annaliese pleaded.

"Oh," Dorothy said, shaking her head side to side. "Yes. Those two poor motherless boys."

"I promised her I'd look after them."

Patrick touched her hand. "For how long?"

Annaliese looked at the four pairs of eyes facing her and said, "We'll be fine."

"Not in John's care you won't," Ted said.

Again the screen door screeched and everyone turned to find Henry Chastain coming through, elbows out, grasping two plates of food. He stopped short at the tense faces before him, which sent his biscuits sliding onto the wet floor. The Connelley brothers shifted apart. Henry extended a plate to Annaliese with careful control of his eyes as they fell on her puffy face.

Taking the plate, she said softly, "John needs to be here, too, to finish. Just a few more months."

Ted stuck out an arm and leaned against a post, head down, lips pursed for a moment before he whispered, "He's full-blown mad."

"Father will be frantic when he finds out," Patrick said.

"Oh, Patrick, you're not going to tell him," Annaliese said. She jabbed the plate at Dorothy as she came out of her chair.

Patrick threw his hands up and backed away.

Ted's eyes flew open in surprise. "Why, of course we are."

Henry put his hand on Ted's shoulder. "Gentlemen."

Everyone looked at Henry.

"I'm the company's attorney and, as you know, a family friend. I can assure you I've got my eye on John."

"What about Ben?" Michael said. "With this death . . . two sons to raise . . . John to deal with. Is Ben going to be able to carry on?"

"We've been doing all right," Henry said.

The brothers, suddenly silent, seemed to be absorbing the "we."

Henry caught that. "I've been watching out for this family for some time now. I'll keep you informed. You have my word."

"Well, I don't know," Patrick said. Ted, shaking his head, looked out at the sea of red muck that was the front yard.

"Mrs. Stregal and I have discussed this," Henry said.

Now it was Annaliese's turn to control her face. They had done no such thing.

"We'll have him and everyone else out of here by next spring," Henry said.

"But that's six months from now," Ted said.

"I'll stay," Dorothy said. "Here. With Anna." She patted Annaliese's arm. "Now then, that settles it."

"What?" Ted threw up his hands.

"No, no," Michael said.

"Oh, Dottie, are you sure?" Annaliese said. "The almanac says we'll have a hard winter. The snow might block the tracks. You may not be able to leave for weeks."

"Yes," Dorothy declared, though her nod was stiff. "I'm sure."

"What about your husband?" Michael asked.

Dorothy shrugged.

Patrick patted his older brother's back. "They're ganging up on us again, buddy," he said. "Let's let this go for now."

Ted turned back to Annaliese. "Anna?"

"I know he's not right," she said. "Just give me some more time to figure out how to get him out of here."

Ted walked over to Annaliese and wrapped his lanky arms around her. "What's gotten into you, Anna? You used to be so reasonable." He kissed her forehead. Looking up, he noticed movement at the open window behind Annaliese. John Stregal held two plates of food behind the misted glass. He stared back at Ted with murky eyes veiled by a tangle of hair. Annaliese turned away from Ted's embrace and saw her husband's twisted expression, the grim set of his mouth. He threw her a black look and disappeared into the crowd behind him.

At nine, the house was finally quiet, the dishes having been washed and put away by long before sundown, good-byes said and condolences accepted, the kin waved away to bed, the children's prayers heard. Annaliese sat on the edge of her bed barely able to drag the brush through the hair that spilled over her shoulders. Her hands were as heavy as marble but she kept at it while she waited for John. The bedroom door was wide open. Across the hall, the other door was cracked enough that she could hear the calm rhythm of pillow talk between Irene and Dorothy.

Downstairs, the back door slammed. John had been next door for hours, consoling Ben she hoped, but more likely polishing off his bourbon. She heard his tread on the first step. She worked on a knot. The next footsteps came slow and sloppy. With eyes fixed on the doorway, she waited to read his face. How much had he heard?

Irene and Dorothy fell silent.

John came in and closed the door. As he walked to her, her eyes searched the wounded face and she found her answer. Her hand pulled the brush through a final sweep of her hair and lowered it to the bed.

"Out of here by next spring, huh?" The stench of liquor floated down to her nostrils.

Annaliese tucked her hands against her stomach. "There are people who can help you, John."

"Never." He turned away and walked to the window. "Years after my father died, I found out what they'd done to him to help him."

"But there are kinder treatments now. The Quakers in Pennsylvania have . . ."

"No." He flipped around to face her. "You think I can tell anyone about the voices I hear? The despair coursing through my veins one day, the feeling I could swim against the strongest rivers out there the next?" He pointed at her. "You should see your face as I lay bare these awful truths."

Annaliese threw up her hands. "I buried my best friend today."

From the other side of the door, Dorothy's cough had the intended effect. Annaliese pulled the quilt down and crawled in.

John sat down on his side of the bed and yanked off a boot. "Go on home. You and the children. Just go, like Ted said. Tomorrow."

She could barely shake her head. "Can't."

"I've got things to finish here." John wiped his nose on the back of his sleeve before he began unbuttoning. "Far as I'm concerned, you've kept your end of the bargain." One boot still on and fully clothed, he fell against his pillow, where he threw one arm across his eyes.

She turned down the lamp. The door across the hall closed. Finally, she was allowed to grant her bones rest, but the blanket of her grief and fear was suffocating. As John snored, she went to the window and opened it.

∞

XXIX

"Want to turn back?" Wade pulled at the horses to slow them and held up his hand to stop Tote's wagon and the four others behind him.

Annaliese shook her head. "Let's get it over with." Her fingers urged him to keep going before all the other wagons stopped, too. "I'll be all right once we're past it."

He looked over at her. Under the brim of her bonnet, her face was as colorless as white marble. "All right, then," he said before clicking his tongue at the horses.

In truth, she couldn't remember exactly where it was. She knew it would be just a narrow place in the road with an ordinary canopy above and the usual dense forest to the right, not the kind of spot where the trees or rocks were so distinctive that anyone would recognize it and point to the left and say there, precisely there is where Lucenia Stregal's horse took her over the edge. Nothing there to make one wary, either, Annaliese thought, except that the woods were so thick that anything could hide there, anything shaking in its feral fear that made it so irrational it would jump into the humans' path just as they arrived. She should've known that could happen. At the least, she and Wade should have made more noise as they rode along that day, that Sunday when they shouldn't have been riding at all.

She had to look down at the floorboards. After a while, when Wade stopped slapping the reins on the horses' flanks, she figured they were past it. She lifted her face to let the bracing September wind kick-start her breathing again.

Finally, the road widened and the forest fell away into the stark, bright light that shone on the sins committed upon Black Face Mountain. The wagons emptied of the dozen men recruited by Wade and Tote. Annaliese started to climb out, but Wade fussed at her to wait for him to come around and help her.

"You all right?" he asked.

With a shrug, she took a few unsteady steps toward the edge of the road. For what seemed like the hundredth time that morning, she sucked in a deep breath to make the nausea go away.

"Just nervous indigestion," Dorothy had said after breakfast. "Not surprising, considering."

With her eyes locked on the earth, she made her way to the ledge. The slash and debris spanned for miles. Where there should have been slopes thick with autumn's crimsons and golds, there was only death. The few branches that had been clinging to life when she had last been here now rattled dry and copper-colored in the wind.

Wade arrived beside her. "Hit's goin' to look better come next spring, Miss Annaliese."

She shook her head. "You don't really believe that, do you, Wade? You think these seedlings won't survive the winter."

"Well, ma'am, we been over that. The booklet says we should plant these bare root trees when it's colder, December even, so they won't start growing until next spring. But I reckon you just got to do this right now." He turned his whiskerless face, brown as an acorn, toward the valley. "Maybe I do, too. We'll just pray for a long cold fall." He went back to the wagon and picked up the *Forestry Quarterly* she had left on the seat. He waved it at her. "Says the northern side has the best soil. This here's the north side so I reckon we got that goin' for us. Now let's go. We got a hunnert acres to plant."

The men brought out axes and shovels and headed over the lip of the ledge then down the hill toward the river to begin the cleanup. Runoff had laid naked huge patches of earth. Across the hill fissures fanned out, tiny rivulets choked with rocks and the last of the precious topsoil.

Annaliese went to her wagon for her gloves but they were not there.

"Here," Wade said. "Take mine." He pulled off a mismatched pair—one as brown and wrinkled as dried tobacco, the other bright blue denim with a band at the wrist of yellow and red plaid.

She was slipping them on when she heard the rumble of a wagon coming from the direction of the schoolhouse. Herschel and Minerva had taken the children to school an hour ago. They weren't due to come back this way until the afternoon.

Not again, she thought.

As the wagon rounded a bend, Annaliese saw that it was Herschel. Beside him sat James and Darrison, arms crossed, faces dark with the latest storm. Whatever they had done this time must have been pretty bad for the tender-hearted Minerva to send them home. She had already reported that James spat at a little girl and Darrison recited a poem aloud substituting bawdy words. Both had picked fights with the other children. Ben's response had been half-hearted lectures on his best days, whippings on his worst. Always, Annaliese and Ruth followed behind to console or hug or just feed. The boys seemed calmest when they were helping Wade with his chores or, as Annaliese found them one afternoon, nestled with him in the stable hay, carving whistles out of maple boughs under his soft instructions.

Summoning a patience she did not possess, Annaliese waved them to her. Darrison's shoulders slumped, and he twisted around in his seat. But James jumped off and ran to her.

"Hey, there, buddy." Annaliese's arms wrapped around him as he plowed into her trousers. "Want to help us with this?"

"Yes, ma'am," James said. He looked up at her and for an agonizing instant she saw his mother's soft curve of the brow.

A wad grew in her throat. She forced herself to cough a little and only then could she nod back at him. "Let's find you a shovel," she said as she waved him away to Wade's wagon.

Darrison finally slid off Herschel's seat. Herschel never stopped, just slowed down, then turned his horses in a circle and went back up the road as though this was a regular delivery on his route.

Down by the river, the men were swarming across the hills. The air was filled with their axe blows and the soft scraping of the tree limbs they dragged into gullies that had split the earth. When those were full, they threw the extra scags and limbs into heaps and set them aflame. Others followed behind bringing bags of pine straw and hay.

Annaliese and the boys brought down the first boxes of burlap-wrapped seedlings in a pallet. Cupping a loblolly pine in her hands, Annaliese waited while Darrison shoved a dibble into the ground, wiggled it back and forth, and held the ground open for her to drop in the seedling. James tamped the ground around it back down. Wade and Tote dragged down more bags and pallets to ready hands. Jackets came off as the morning chill lifted. By noon, nearly seven acres were planted with loblolly, white pines, and yellow pines.

Just before the dinner break, they stood at the top of the hill and looked over their work. A new landscape was emerging—a scalped hillside still airless and sunbaked, but hopeful with its little wisps of green planted in the orderly way the human eye craves.

After eating, the men returned with new energy to finish the upper half of the hill. They called out to one another in cheerful challenges and jabs. After the debris fires burned down, they dragged out the last bags on the wagon, which were the wood slabs and bark strips from the sawmill that would be the final protective layer. They scattered them around the tender trees and stomped the mulch carefully. The last trees were planted—ten acres in all—with plenty of time to get home and wash up before everyone else got home from school.

"How'd it go?" Joe asked as he came out of the commissary.

Annaliese and the boys were washing their hands under the pump spout.

"Fine," Annaliese said. "Planted everything we had." She wiped her freezing hands on her skirt.

"Come in and get you some of these warm ginger cakes Ruth just brought down."

"Don't mind if I do," Darrison said as he and James ran in the door.

"Joe, I'm going on to the house." Annaliese said. "See that they leave some for Sam and Emmie. They'll be along soon."

Joe held up a finger for her to wait and he disappeared inside. He came back with a small bundle of mail tied with string. "Just a few pieces for you today," he said.

Now, every mail bundle was just a few pieces. No more catalogues from Montgomery Ward or California Perfume, for Annaliese had cancelled everything but the *Journal of Public Vocation*.

She was filthy and cold, her shoulders ached, but it was a good ache, and so for the first time since the funeral, she walked up the hill to her home with a light step. Ruth and Dorothy would be in the kitchen, which would be heavenly warm and full of the smell of gingercakes or perhaps Ruth's applesauce. They would hand her something hot to drink and wave her into a chair to listen to all she had to report. She walked even faster, sending her breath into the brisk air in short, quick puffs.

The geese raised their usual alarm. Out from under the porch they came, black beaks aimed up at the sky while they tried to look at her slaunchways, as Ruth would say. She strode right past them toward the back of her home.

Annaliese leaned against the porch handrail to kick the mud off her boots. Hearing the chickens squawk and scatter, she looked across the back yard and found John standing beside the chicken house, head down as if listening. As she started to call out to him, he crossed his arms and leaned against the coop, leisurely, but still listening for something, so she hesitated. The sound of Ruth's cabin door slamming shut drifted downhill. The girl was heading toward the house, past the coop.

John dipped into a crouch.

Annaliese let go of the stair rail and slipped back into the shadow of the house to watch.

As Ruth rounded the chicken coop corner, John jumped out to force her to slam right into him. She reared back, but he grabbed her arms, spewed some message into her face, from which she twisted side to side to avoid. Finally, he stroked one of her cheeks and she stopped.

Annaliese knew that stroke, the way he turned his hand to offer only the soft backside of his fingers, not the calloused side. She could not breathe.

Ruth was scowling at him. His hand on her cheek slid down to her neck. Finally, she said something that made him let her go, but he laughed at her. Ruth ran back to her cabin. John headed uphill toward the stables.

Annaliese pinned herself against the house and groped for something to hang onto. There was no question about what she had just seen—a quarrel between intimates. With her pulse pounding at her temples, she shot out of the shadow and raced up the hill. She pushed open Ruth's cabin door. Ruth, poring over her Bible at the kitchen table, yelped.

Annaliese shook with rage. "You!"

Ruth pushed herself away from the table.

"How could you?" Annaliese picked up a broom and slammed it on the table. "I saw the whole thing."

Ruth sucked in her breath. Her eyes froze on Annaliese's twisted face. Her hand flew to her belly.

Annaliese's eyes followed. *Was it possible? John's baby?* She picked up the Bible and threw it into the fireplace.

Ruth raked her hands through her hair. "Wait, Miss Anna . . ."

"Don't you ever call me that again." Annaliese pounded on the table. "What a fool I've been."

"Oh, no, no. Think again about what you seen out yonder. Didn't you see how scared I was?"

"I saw two lovers arguing, that's what I saw," Annaliese screamed as she leaned over the table between them.

"No, ma'am, that ain't . . ." Ruth's whole body shook.

"How long's this been going on?"

"Ain't nothin' *goin' on!*" The words flew from Ruth's tiny mouth as fast as steam from a kettle. " 'Cept my runnin' away from him ever chance I get." She ran her hands down her apron while she looked at Annaliese sideways. Annaliese ran around the table and slapped Ruth's face, but her head merely flipped right back to spit out the rest of her story. "I have asked the Lord ever day to help me figure out a way to tell you what he done to me."

"Shut up!" She grabbed Ruth's shoulders and began shaking her.

Ruth shoved her away and staggered to a rocking chair that faced the fireplace, tucked her hands between her knees, and began a furious rocking.

Annaliese grabbed her own throat. The black air of the dark cabin suddenly seemed unbreatheable. She turned toward the open door. The move made her head ache and her gut began churning in a familiar way that meant her misery would soon be boiling up into her throat, onto the floor. Instinct drove her toward the door, but her legs would not take her. Seconds later, she was vomiting all over the stove wood stacked in a bin beside the table.

Ruth rushed over and wrung her hands above Annaliese's heaving back. Spying a rag on the table, she shoved it under Annaliese's nose and waved it until it was taken, and then Annaliese was staggering toward the door, somehow willing her body out toward the light and the air. With a stone-faced Ruth watching, Annaliese stormed toward the stables.

Only a couple of the mill's mule drivers were in the stable, mucking out a stall. As she steamed by them, one of them stuck his head out. "Ma'am?" he said.

She found him in her kitchen. He was leaning against the sink talking to Dorothy as she sliced an apple into slender crescents, Emeline at her elbow. As Annaliese stood in the doorway, heaving for breath, John stood up straight. "Anna. You're home early," he said, stealing a quick look over the sink at the yard.

The blood in Annaliese's eyes blurred her sight and she did not even hear herself say, "Dorothy, take Emeline out."

Dorothy's hand froze above the apple.

"But Mama . . ." Emeline said.

"What's wrong?" Dorothy blurted.

"Get out!" Annaliese shot a rigid arm toward the dining room door.

Emeline burst into a wail, sending Dorothy scurrying to pull her through the door.

John's eyes darted around the kitchen, out the window again.

Annaliese stepped toward him while her hands groped for loose objects. They landed on a coffee cup. She threw it at him. "Damn you!"

He ducked as the cup sailed into the pantry.

"What a fool I am." Her hands found a ladle.

"What's wrong with you?" John yelled. He sidled toward the dining room door.

The ladle hit his chest. "Damn you, John Stregal! Ruth!"

"What about her?"

"How could you? I saw y'all just now."

"Saw what?" He raised one shoulder up and down. "I jumped out and scared her is all."

"Stop it!" She slammed her hand on the table between them. Two knives bounced into each other. She picked one up, gripped its cool, hard handle, felt the sudden shift in power as her husband's eyes landed on it. John's hand moved toward the other knife, but Annaliese swept it off the table onto the floor.

"How long have you been fooling me, John? Since the beginning of this fiasco? Here I've been working harder than any Louisville servant I ever knew. Working my hands raw. Growing gray before my time." Her fingers clenched the handle hard enough to strangle a dog and she found herself raising the blade tip to the level of his chest. She started around the table.

"Anna . . ." Hands splayed, John inched closer to the dining room door but kept his eyes on the knife.

"Tell me, John. Are you really crazy? Or is that a performance, too?" Annaliese's mouth curled around the last of her words.

John put his shoulder to the door, found it would not budge, pushed harder.

"But it takes a keen mind to pull off deception, doesn't it? Oh, damn you, John." She took another step on shaky legs. Again John tried the door and he finally gave up. He squared his shoulders.

Annaliese began crying. The blade wobbled now two feet from John's chest. "I thought I could help you. I thought loving you, making love with you, would heal you. I'm the one who's crazy."

Suddenly, John snatched the knife from her hands and with one long, nauseating pull along his shirt sleeve, sliced into his arm. A crimson stain welled up.

The back porch door squeaked. "Mama?" came the call. "We're home." Samuel bounced in.

Annaliese lunged for the knife. It went sailing across the floor, but she kept at him, clawing at his face, his chest, even the bloody arm he held up in defense. She landed a few good slaps before he pushed her away and ran past Samuel. The boy dropped back, then turned to look at his mother, whose bloodied hands sent him running to her.

On the other side of the dining room door, a chair was being pulled across the pine floor, away from the door. Dorothy and Emeline rushed in.

"Mama!" Emeline cried. She tried to pull out of her aunt's grip, but Dorothy was holding fast as she scanned the room. She spotted the bloody knife on the floor.

"Dear God," Dorothy said. Her eyes flew to her sister. She saw the blood on her hands. "He attacked you? What on earth . . ."

Emeline wriggled free and ran to her mother.

"You're bleeding!" Samuel cried.

"No, no . . . it's not me," Annaliese said, shaking so much that none of them believed her. The children pinned themselves against her, tried to keep their eyes off of her hands, which she held away from them while she could.

Dorothy rushed to her and pried Annaliese's hands away while the children squirmed underneath. She swiped her apron across one hand, then the other, eyes frantically scanning until she looked back up with relief. "Then it's John who's injured? You mean you . . ."

"No, no, I didn't. He was the one who took the knife and . . ." Annaliese looked into the frantic eyes below her and stopped. "It was an accident. A small cut."

"And you're not hurt, Mama?" Samuel's eyes raced over her body.

Annaliese shook her throbbing head.

"But Papa?" Emeline asked.

"Just a small cut I said." Annaliese smoothed her daughter's hair, felt Dorothy's eyes burning into her. "He'll be all right."

Outside, excited voices were at the porch steps. Footsteps fell quick and light on the stairs to the door. Darrison and James rushed in.

"Uncle John's down at the commissary . . ." Darrison began. He looked at the knot of people in front of him. His aunt's face was red and swollen. Blood on the floor.

"Arm's all tore up," finished James, still oblivious.

"Someone tending to it?" Dorothy asked.

"Yes, ma'am, but Papa's on his way up here," Darrison said.

Annaliese peeled the children off of her. "Everyone stay right here."

Outside, she looked toward Ruth's cabin. She was there, standing in her doorway, still and straight as a sentinel. Annaliese shot off the steps, past her muddy boots, to run as best she could in bare feet toward the sawmill.

The laboring form of Ben appeared at the bottom of the hill. He looked up at her. By the time they met up, he was heaving for breath. "What in hell . . ." was all he could manage.

"Is it bad?"

"Not too deep. Joe's got it bandaged." He took out a handkerchief and dabbed at his forehead. "Did you see it happen?"

"We were having an argument. He took the knife from my hand." Instantly, she regretted her words, for they gave shape to the most violent thing she had ever considered. Worse, it was clear from Ben's face that John hadn't told him that yet.

His eyes widened into a stare that made her sick. "From your hand?"

"I tried to keep it away from him. But he was so quick. He did it to himself, Ben."

"You held a knife on him?"

"But you don't understand. I saw . . ." Annaliese stopped. What *had* she seen? Intimacy. Pain. A clear history between a man and a woman. John's nervous look over the sink window. Nothing as concrete as a lawyer would want, but in her mind every bit the conviction. Ben waited, gape-mouthed, eyes bulging at her. She wanted to slap them right out of those runny sockets. "I know what I saw."

From the homes on the hill, the sound of children made them both turn. The four were pouring out of Annaliese's house.

"What are you going to tell them?" he said.

She lay with them on Samuel's bed for a long time, one ear on their prayers, one on the stairs. No one had seen John for hours, but now it was close to midnight. The children grew still, their questions fell away into murmurs of nonsense, and their baby snores began. Annaliese peeled one arm off her waist, another off her shoulder to tiptoe to her bedroom. Two warped floorboards creaked under her footsteps. She winced and stole a look down the steps for the flickering light of an approaching lamp. Nothing but pitch black.

Dorothy cracked open her door. "Now?" she whispered.

Annaliese nodded.

His shirts, still laundered every week in town and delivered crisp and folded, lined the first drawer. The day before, Annaliese had laid them there in neat stacks, smoothed out the last of the wrinkles as though he was still the John who put them on carefully each morning. Now she grabbed a handful and headed for the open window to snap them open one by one and fling them out into the night. She leaned over the sill to watch them float down in ghostly waves, her only regret being that the moonless night robbed her of seeing the shirts hit the goose droppings. Back to the bureau she went to accept Dorothy's handfuls and back to the window. She did not rush. She savored each step of this fetch and fling, which she had plotted throughout the evening, while she prepared supper without Ruth, while she pretended to listen to the children's prayers. In slow, thoughtful pitches she sent his pants, suspenders, collar stays, underwear, socks, garters, brushes, and shaving cup out the window.

She threw his shaving razor under the bed.

Downstairs, the back door slammed. The women looked at each other, startled in spite of this certain result. Wordlessly, they ran to the bed and sat down—rigid and hot and twelve noon awake.

John stormed up the stairs and into the doorway, gripping his kerosene lamp as though it were a weapon he was about to fling into the nearest soft tissue. He still wore the blood-stained shirt of the afternoon, one sleeve rolled high on the arm wrapped in white muslin strips. His other hand held a bottle of whisky. Bloodshot eyes went straight to Annaliese, over to Dorothy, then back to his wife.

"What the hell you think you're doin?"

"That's all you have to say?" Annaliese jumped up.

"Oh, no." He took a couple of unsteady steps toward her. "I got lots more to say." He pointed the bottle at Dorothy. "And you don't need to be here."

Dorothy took Annaliese's hand.

"All right, then. You two can both just go out there right now and pick up all that shit."

They did not move.

With a grunt, John staggered over to the chest of drawers that held Annaliese's clothes. He pulled on a drawer, grabbed a fistful of something filmy and white, and threw it out the window. "There!"

"Get out of my room," Annaliese shouted.

"Your room? I'll show you whose room it is." John dropped the bottle and the lamp and lunged at Dorothy. With surprising accuracy, he caught her wrist and began pulling her toward the door. The lamp burst into flames, sending a streak of fire across the pine floor toward the bed. Annaliese yanked the quilt off and threw it and herself on top of the flames. Dorothy's clawing and slapping had no effect on her brother-in-law's intoxicated might. He quickly had her in the hall. While Annaliese watched from the floor, he gave Dorothy a shove that sent her flying and he slammed the door. Her outraged cries were muffled behind the door. He turned the key.

"For cryin' out loud, Dottie, shut up!" John put the key in his pocket.

Dorothy fell silent, but worked the doorknob in vain. Annaliese sat up on her knees, coughing in the smoke.

John stood over her. "Now you listen to me. You and the children are going home on the next train."

Annaliese shot up from the floor. "I'm finished listening to you." She charged toward him. "And I'm finished taking your orders." Eye to eye, she could see the depth of his raw anger, feel the simmering violence. Like a woman who had tripped over a snake, she knew that she had just made a very bad move.

John read her revulsion on her face, another mistake. "Think I'm mad, don't you?"

She looked at the doorknob.

"I'll die before I let you lock me up." His watery eyes were just inches away from hers now. He grabbed her arm and twisted it just enough to make her cry, but he let out a gasp, too. He looked down at the bandage on his arm. In the middle of the white muslin, a circle of bright red was seeping anew. Annaliese writhed against his grasp.

Dorothy pounded on the door.

"Shut up!" John shouted over his shoulder. He flipped back around to face her. "Or was it Henry's idea?"

Between coughs, Annaliese shook her head.

"Let's say I believe that. That's more trust than you offered me this afternoon. After I transferred $400,000 into our bank account in Louisville. For you and the children. How 'bout that, huh? That's what this has always been about Anna. You and the children."

She nodded weakly.

"And then . . ." John looked down at his arm again. The spot had spread into a long, fresh stain running the length of his arm. "You went and made me do this."

Rage flooded her brain again. "What?"

He pushed her toward the bed. "After all I've done for you."

In the hallway, Dorothy was hysterical. The doorknob rattled impotently.

Annaliese stumbled backward for a moment, found her feet, planted them firmly against his intentions. "Done for *me*?" The rational core of her brain told her to shut up, that this was an angry, dangerous man, but the irrational part won out and she slapped him.

In a flash, his hand was over her mouth and he was pushing her down on the bed. As she struggled to breathe, he began yanking up her skirt. She bit one of his fingers. His hand slid down to her neck, where he pressed his message into her windpipe. "Bitch," he said.

Dorothy called from the hallway. "Annaliese! I'm going for Ben."

Annaliese tried to wriggle away, but his fingers closed tighter with each move, so she stopped. Hope slipped away with the sound of Dorothy's footsteps on the stairs.

"Let her go for him," he hissed. "This won't take long." With his other hand, he worked his belt free until his pants hit the floor.

With one arm jammed under Annaliese's chin, John tore away her underpants. He slid on top of her, a sudden crush of weight that pressed the last resistance out of her, and he was immediately in, burning her dry insides with each revengeful thrust. She turned her face away and focused on the black void outside the window, the moonless night that robbed her of sight. Her eyes stung with the fumes and her outrage, so much so that she truly was blind. But now she saw what had been in front of her all along and she knew what she had to do.

XXX

By dawn, the black and blue covered her arms and neck like algae. She rose from the bed she had shared with Dorothy for a few fitful hours and went to the water basin to splash her face. Taking care not to look in the mirror, Annaliese dried off and pulled on one of Dorothy's housedresses. She crept down the stairs and walked out her front door into September air so cold it bit her breath away. She thought about her shawl, but she was not going back.

He was there, as he had been every morning since Lucenia had died, rocking in her chair on the porch, staring at the vast sky. A new sun was warming the valley below. At the sound of her front door closing, Ben looked over. Last night, he had come to her aid, had knocked timidly despite Dorothy's hysteria, but in the end had bought John's muffled assurances that everything was all right. Just a little argument was all. Couldn't a man argue with his own wife? So Ben left.

Annaliese climbed his steps like a woman twice her age. Her thighs and back ached, her stomach throbbed with nausea again. Ben got up and reached down for her hand. He had not slept since he left her house disturbed and embarrassed, but she did not know that so she wouldn't take it. Standing in the middle of the steps, they stared at each other.

Ben looked her over. "Anna, are you all right?"

"No." She rubbed her arms.

Ben took off his coat and laid it across her shoulders. "What happened last night? John was saying through the door that everything was all right . . ."

"Do I look all right to you?"

"God, I'm sorry. I . . ."

She gripped the stair rail. "We've waited too long."

"I just don't know what to do." Ben backed up and flopped down into the rocking chair.

Anna struggled to climb the last step. "Ben, John's done something terrible. You have to help me get him home, get him some help. We have to leave this place."

Ben blinked, but he could not staunch the tears that began to pool at the bottom of the red rims. "How can I leave her behind, Anna?"

Annaliese's back softened. Why did he have to bring her up? She needed Lucenia more than ever. But of course he would. Every morning, he climbed Bunny Mountain to visit her. Every night, his bedroom stayed lit. To anyone who would listen, he fretted over the fading of her scent embedded in the bedding and the dresses that still hung in their armoire, but surely slipping away day by day.

"And what about all the trees you've planted?" Ben was saying. "Don't you want to be here to see if they survive the winter?"

She sucked in a long, deep breath of the frigid air. The nausea faded for a moment. The sun was rising quickly now, blanketing the valley with rosy light and warming the hollows. A strand of wispy clouds hung above the hills that eventually rolled on to Tennessee. Down at the mill, a saw started up. Men's voices rose out of the mill yard and mule stalls. Another day of scraping money off the north Georgia hillsides was beginning. John would be downstairs soon.

She would get help from someone else.

If once she had seen herself as saving Black Face Mountain, she soon saw it as the other way around. Day after day, she plunged into the reforestation like a laborer desperate for every nickel. Pushing her body harder than the day before worked the various poisons out of her veins—nausea, images, rage, guilt, Ruth. The quiet hillsides gave her a place to think about all that Ruth had said. Pieces of things she had noticed about the girl's behavior, especially around John, over recent months began to fit together. Wade and the other men worked nearby, but when they tried to help her with shovel or burlap bag, she sent them away. One afternoon, a soft rain came at the best possible time—just as she and the men were finishing the last acre. By then the bruises were gone, innocence was acknowledged, and her plan was formed.

Annaliese peered at Ruth's cabin from her back porch steps still moist from the rain, the weather-beaten, gray little cube perched at the foot of the mountain's swell. The new pine trees fanned out behind it, soggy and muted under the gray sky. But a cheerful ribbon of smoke was rising from the chimney, and a splash of Ruth's red curtains framed the windows.

Annaliese crossed her arms against the cold and started up the hill.

At the door, she paused to listen for Herschel, whose presence would change what she had come to say. She heard only the click, click of the sewing machine pedal beneath Ruth's foot. Annaliese rapped quickly on the door so she couldn't turn back.

When Ruth saw her visitor, she simply dropped her hands to her sides and waited.

"Ruth . . ." Annaliese was still catching her breath. "I need to say something to you."

The little squirrel eyes did not move.

"Um . . . may I come in?"

Ruth shrugged and stepped aside.

Annaliese's eyes fell on a cradle beside the fireplace. Across the cradle's bonnet a pink quilt lay, as tiny and new as the baby it waited for, and on its sides hung cotton gowns and shirts, infant caps trimmed in eyelet, calico sun bonnets, and a pair of tiny overalls. From underneath the pink quilt, the edges of a red one peeked out—just as detailed and tightly stitched as the pastel one. Annaliese ran her hands across it and

smiled at the intricate squares of red plaids, red flowers, red stripes—
her smile an act of acceptance and intimacy that signaled her intentions, she hoped.

"In case hit's a boy," Ruth murmured. She came over to stand next
to Annaliese, wary, waiting.

Stacks of tiny garments sat folded on top of a trunk at the foot of the
bed, while beside the trunk, the legs and seat of a high chair awaited the
arms and back that lay on the floor. A pocketknife rested among curled
bits of wood on the floor.

"Looks like Herschel is excited, too."

"Oh, yes, he's worse than I am."

The two women lingered beside the cradle. Annaliese fingered the
overalls to have something to do with her eyes while she absorbed the
news that Herschel did not know.

"He's been whittlin' on that chair and singin' ever night. 'Bout driving me crazy callin' out names we might use."

Annaliese looked up at Ruth's shining eyes, but she was sharply
aware of the round belly Ruth was rubbing and the thin shoulders that
would bear an enormous weight for the rest of her days.

Suddenly, Ruth threw her arms around Annaliese's neck. "Don't
look at me like that."

She hugged back fiercely. "Ruth, I'm so sorry."

Ruth pulled back to grab her shoulders. "This baby's a gift, don't
you see? The Lord's work." She dropped her voice to a whisper. "I
thought I was all dried up inside, like Abraham's Sarah. Or an empty,
seedless gourd. I felt so puny about lettin' Herschel down, with him
wantin' a son so bad. You know we tried and tried to plant those
seeds . . ."

Annaliese's eyes widened.

". . . but now I know it wasn't me, wasn't my insides at all. Herschel
and I might have gone on the rest of our days without a child. I know
it's hard on you to hear this, Miss Anna, but I've come to see this as a
blessin' sure enough. And if only the Lord ever knows who is the father,
then I accept that."

"A blessing," Annaliese whispered.

Ruth pulled a handkerchief from her apron pocket and gave it to her. "Now what we goin' to do about you? You're lookin' might puny lately."

Annaliese dabbed at her nose. "I've missed your bald observations, Ruth."

"Well, somebody's got to tell you. I'm worried about you."

"Someone's going to help me, Ruth."

Ruth's face hardened. "Help you with Mr. John."

"Yes."

"What you goin' to do?"

"Let's sit down." She moved toward the chairs at the kitchen table. "I'll get us some coffee."

The front door traffic at Thessalonia's boarding house was unusual—well-attired, well-fed, and self-assured. Annaliese explained court week to Dorothy while their wagon rolled by the men in suits huddled in the dining room's front window.

"Court week?" Dorothy said. "Court is held only for a week?"

"'Course not," Herschel said. "There's another week in May."

"What if he's in court?"

Henry's office was coming up on the right, on the corner. Annaliese noticed that the front door was ajar.

"I just wish you would've called," Dorothy said.

"Couldn't very well use the office telephone, Dottie," Annaliese said in a tone that discouraged further fretting.

From the back of the wagon, James squealed, "Herschel, stop. We want to get out."

Herschel shook his head. "Just hold on." Horses were hitched to every rail, tucked into every pocket of space. "Maybe down one of these here sides." He peered left and right at the narrower streets.

Though the wagon was still moving, the three boys had flung four legs over the railings.

"I done told y'all to hold on," Herschel said. He pulled the horses to a stop and turned around but two more legs went over. Samuel was perched on the rail about to jump and Emeline was right behind him.

"It's all right," Annaliese said. "Let them go." She twisted around in her seat. "Sam, don't let Mr. Miller give you any free candy."

"Oh, all right." Samuel helped his sister out and the children ran down the street.

"Good luck, Anna." Dorothy squeezed her hand, then slid off the seat to follow the children. "Y'all wait," she called. "Wait for me."

Henry and a young woman emerged from his office. She was in her late twenties, Annaliese judged, and graceful as she moved ahead of him. She wore a royal blue wool suit and matching hat, a hat so large and flowing with ribbons and blue poms that it might've a been challenge for such a thin neck, but she was managing nicely. Her swaying movements were so sensual and deliberate that she and Henry seemed to be finishing a dance. They now stood just inches apart, smiling and talking, while Annaliese and Herschel looked on.

Annaliese's ear tips were on fire. "Who's that?"

"New hat lady. She's just set up shop down yonder at Miller's," Herschel said.

Annaliese pulled her wrap off her neck, which was suddenly too warm. The woman was beautiful, light-hearted. Clearly, the conversation was not about a matter of law.

Annaliese's feet hit the ground. She tried to adopt a loose-armed, friendly gait, but felt mechanical and creepy and fourteen. "Why, good morning, Mr. Chastain," she called out.

Henry finally looked in her direction. "Anna . . . Mrs. Stregal!" he blurted. "What a surprise. A pleasure." He took a step toward her and smiled, though he searched her face for clues to the answer to his question. "What brings you into town?"

The woman looked at Henry to introduce her.

Annaliese stepped up onto the wooden boards. "I'm so glad I caught you."

Herschel slapped the reins and moved on.

Annaliese saw that the young woman in blue was no longer smiling. She had stopped her skirt swishing, too, as she eyed Annaliese carefully with serious little green eyes. "I don't believe I've had the pleasure of making your acquaintance," she said.

"Oh, excuse me," Henry said. "Miss Campbell, I would like to introduce you to Mrs. Annaliese Stregal, a dear family friend." He stood between the two, looking first at one, then the other while his dancing air evaporated. "Miss Campbell is new to town as of last month."

"A pleasure," Annaliese said.

Miss Campbell offered a terse nod. The blue poms and ribbons bobbed. "Mrs. Stregal."

"Everything all right?" Henry said. "Is this something that can wait until this afternoon? Miss Campbell and I were just on our way to . . ."

"No, I'm afraid not. It's a pressing legal matter."

The green eyes shot to Henry, whose worried look at Annaliese was sufficient response. "Perhaps we'll have our dinner some other time, Mr. Chastain," she said. She nodded again at Annaliese. "I hope to see you again, Mrs. Stregal. Do stop by my millinery shop inside Miller's Mercantile some time. Or send Mr. Stregal to get a little something for you."

Anna's lips thinned. "A kind invitation."

Miss Campbell flipped her skirt and walked away.

"Please, Mrs. Stregal," Henry said. "Come inside."

Henry closed the door and came around her to study her face. In front of Miss Campbell, he had worked hard to keep the corners of his mouth turned up, but now he frowned. "You are so pale, Anna." He put his hand to her cheek. "In this cold weather, your cheeks should be rosy. And your eyes . . . What's he done now?"

His gentle fingers on her face stunned her into being aware only of the three square feet their bodies occupied in the corner behind Henry's door. She looked up at his broad, honest face, those concerned brown eyes and allowed herself to look at them for a long time. Too long. They lit up with surprise. He cupped her face in his hands and she let him. In this tiny, dark corner, his body was a wall of warmth and relief closing in, his male breath above her mouth blinding. His hips pushed into hers. His brown eyes pressed, too. She was so tired. With all self-control sliding into her boots, she tilted her lips up. Henry's mouth fell on them hard, so hard it hurt, but she kissed him back just as hard. His hands slipped down to her waist, hers went to his neck to complete the lock, and their lips pumped and slid in frantic snatches.

When they pulled apart, they gaped at each other.

"Oh, my God," Annaliese said.

Henry tried to run his fingers through the golden hair he had ached to touch for a year and a half, but she pulled away. He held up his palms in acknowledgement.

Her eyes fell on the window where people scurried by and she stiffened. Those people were in a hurry and the window was filthy, but still.

Henry pulled her deeper into the corner. "Tell me," he said.

"You have to help me. Ben won't. Can't."

"Why haven't you written me? What's he done?"

"Four nights ago . . ." Her voice failed.

"What?"

"He . . ." She shook her head and tugged her wrap around her shoulders. "I can't say it . . ." She rolled up her sleeve to the place where the bruises had been. All that was left were a few spots of yellowing skin, but Henry understood, or at least understood enough.

"God in heaven!" He pulled her closer.

"But it's worse than that."

"Not the children. He's not hurt the children."

"No, no. Ruth's baby." She couldn't say that either.

His eyes went cold. "John's?"

"Ruth said so. He hasn't denied it."

"But Ruth wouldn't . . ."

"She says he got her alone one day."

Henry released her. "Why didn't you let me know?"

"For the last week I've just been out there with Wade . . ."

"Out where?"

"Planting trees. Lucenia and I wanted to repair the damage he's done."

"You've been planting trees?" He grabbed her hands and turned them over and saw the red stains no amount of scrubbing had discouraged. "Good Lord."

"No, no, it's saved me, Henry."

"No, darling, it's just distracted you. But I'm to blame for all this. I should've acted sooner."

"Help me now. Get John to Pennsylvania. There's a humane place there."

"Yes, yes, of course. As soon as we can."

Finally. She closed her eyes and dropped her head to his chest again.

"I'll come Sunday. I'll bring Arthur Garland. He's here again for court. We'll hog tie John if we have to. You tell him we're coming for dinner."

"Yes, yes, that'll sound good to him." Annaliese grabbed his shirt and pulled. "He's been wanting to show you the new generator."

"All right, then. Call the place in Pennsylvania. Here, use my telephone."

She looked at the telephone. "They'll want to talk to a doctor, too."

"I'll get Calvin to call later."

She wrote the number on a piece of paper, but still did not move toward the phone.

"Anna, we'll come in three days."

"Sunday." She gripped her face. "God help me."

Footsteps on the wooden planks stopped outside the door. Someone knocked too gently, as though on a bedroom door. Henry, whose back was mashed against the door, jumped.

"It's probably Dorothy." Annaliese took a step backward to give him room to open the door.

Henry put his hands in the pockets of his pants, shuffled everything inside around for a minute. Suspenders stretched up and down. He put his hand on the doorknob. "Sunday, then."

They stared at each other for a while. Annaliese nodded at his hand on the knob. "Let her in. I'll make the call."

On Saturday morning, the mill was screaming with efficiency as it roared toward the end of the workweek. John Stregal and his son walked beside the railroad track that snaked through his lumberyard until they came to the final car on the line. He handed Samuel the Brownie camera and pointed out the spot ten yards away where the boy was to go to shoot. John centered himself against the "Stregal Brothers Lumber Company" painted on the car and waited. He smoothed his wild hair into place with a shaky hand. Samuel took the photo.

They moved through the massive yard of finished lumber, craning their necks to look up at the stacks of oak, walnut, poplar, and chestnut. John told the boy again how black walnut was strong and good for gunstocks and cabinets, that white oak was used for flooring and furniture. They moved on to the acre of crates that held hundreds of golden, raw-wood shingles. Samuel took another picture.

But inside the mill, Samuel handed the camera to his father and put his hands over his ears. Shafts of light sliced through the air, spotlighting the sawdust that hung there, milky and moving. Four band saws were working. As logs were fed into them, their screams rose up to the tin roof and fell back twice as hard on the ears. Slabs of bark and boards thudded to the floor. Men yelled to one another to pick them up together or carry the boards to the kiln. But the most terrifying noise came from the far corner opposite John and Samuel. It was the sovereign headsaw with its ten feet of quivering steel teeth and the man-carrying headrig that Samuel still could not watch. As John walked toward it, he held the camera out to the boy and soon realized that he was way behind him. He waved him over and Samuel—eight years old now and almost five foot four—took a deep breath and obeyed. John went to stand so close to the headsaw that the water splashed onto his coat. The head rig was approaching the saw with its iron-gut rider in place, his hands firmly holding the gears that held the log. The man's eyes shifted from the saw to John. The boss was too close. The rig would knock him down if he didn't move soon, but he did. John leaned forward to give Samuel the camera. Just as steel teeth met heart pine, Samuel shot his picture. Wood bits flew into John's hair. The boy backed up and shot again. When his father released him with a wave home, Samuel ran out like a gust of wind. John stayed to walk the floor, hands clasped behind his bony back, and watch the sawyers at their work. They nodded in respect as he passed, this odd man with wood bits in his long hair who had just doubled everyone's pay.

That evening, at six o'clock, the men quieted the saws, wiped things down, cleared the floor of the day's offal, and left the machines ready for operation on Monday morning.

⤲

XXXI

Emeline's squeals rang down the hall. "Mama, come see what Mr. Chastain's brought!"

In the kitchen, Dorothy and Ruth looked up from cutting onions. Annaliese was at the sink, rinsing blood off the shaky finger she had just sliced. The women threw down their knives and ran to the porch.

The goat was objecting with lusty bleating to being lifted out of the wagon. It kicked and twisted in Henry's arms until he finally dropped it on the ground, where it shook its wiry-haired head. Emeline raced out the front door, down the steps, and grabbed the end of the rope that was looped around the goat's neck. The women arrived on the porch in time to see the goat jump away and jerk her off her feet. Everyone began shouting instructions, heeded by neither animal nor child. The goat headed to the right of a small tree, so Emeline veered left. She dug in her heels, which finally strangled the goat into obedience for the moment.

Henry acknowledged the women and Minerva who had appeared on Lucenia's porch. From his seat on the wagon, Arthur Garland tipped his hat. The women did not move.

Finally, Arthur said, "Good morning."

Annaliese walked down a few steps. "Welcome, Mr. Garland, Mr. Chastain." She looked over at Emeline. "A goat?"

Henry opened the wagon gate and pulled out a glistening red cart.

"Wasn't my idea," Arthur said. "I'd as soon dumped that stupid animal on the side of the road a couple of times this morning on the way up here."

As Henry put the cart on the ground, the boys ran in from behind the house. They slid to a stop at the sight of the cart, but within seconds were trying to climb into it. Ruth's scalding words stopped their flying elbows.

"Boys, boys! I didn't raise y'all to act like this," she said. "Ain't heard a word of thanks to Mr. Chastain." She flapped her apron at them. "Now get on outta that cart."

The boys withdrew legs and arms as though they were made of lead. "Thank you, sir," someone mumbled in a tone as limp as the boys' posture. Each kept a hand on the cart.

"Look at me," Emeline shouted from her tree. With the goat being merely reflective for the moment, she took one hand off the rope and waved.

"Emmie, you let that thing go before you get hurt," Dorothy shouted.

Annaliese untied her apron and draped it across the porch railing. "Mr. Chastain, what's this?"

"Why, I couldn't come without a gift for the children." His look told her he had his reasons.

"Ya hear that, Emmie?" Samuel shouted. "It's for all of us."

Henry turned back to the wagon and withdrew a small riding crop. "But the driver is to be Miss Emeline."

The boys stiffened. "But . . ." Darrison said.

"But nothing!" Annaliese said. "Would you all just hush for once."

Arthur dragged the goat back to the cart. Its wild eyes fell upon the boys and it began bleating again.

Henry handed Emeline the crop. "Now be gentle, Emmie. A light tap's all that's called for."

Ruth snorted.

Henry pointed a finger at the boys. "One passenger at a time, not including the driver."

James jumped in. The other boys stepped back to sulk.

"What do you say, Emmie?" Annaliese called from the porch.

"Thank you, Mr. Chastain." Emeline dipped into a clumsy curtsey.

As James got a good grip on the cart rails, Arthur tethered the animal to the harness. Emeline climbed in beside James on the narrow wooden seat.

"Shouldn't someone tell her how to stop it?" Dorothy said.

Arthur bent down to speak into Emeline's ear, his hands making pulling motions on the leather straps.

"Goats ain't got a lick a sense," Ruth muttered.

"Mr. Garland," Annaliese said. "Lead the goat and cart to the back yard, where there's a fence at least."

He gave a quick wave and began pulling the goat to get the wheels rolling.

"You're just going to let her go off like that?" Dorothy said, pulling on her sister's sleeve.

"Miss Dorothy's right," Ruth said. "You cain't trust a goat. It's them eyes. Lucifer eyes. I'm going out back to see how things go." She waddled down the steps. Minerva came down her steps and followed her.

Henry ran up the steps. "Where is he?"

"Down at the office," Annaliese said.

"And Ben?"

"Not sure."

The thwack of Emeline's crop on the goat's hide sent the cart forward, James fell backward, and off they went, nearly running Arthur and Ruth down but heading, at least, toward the fenced yard.

"Have you packed your things?" Henry asked.

"Yes."

"Must she go with you?" Dorothy looped her hand through her sister's arm.

Arthur joined them on the steps. "She has to sign papers at the . . ." He looked at Henry, who turned away " . . . place in Pennsylvania."

"How're you going to do this? How're you going to get him to go with us to the train station?" Annaliese whispered.

Henry's head flipped left and right. "Joe. Where's Joe?"

"Why?"

"We might need him to help us tie him up," Arthur said. "Get him in this wagon."

Annaliese winced as she realized that was why they had brought the goat and cart.

"Joe's at home. It's Sunday," Dorothy said.

"All right. Never mind him, then. How soon is dinner?"

"In about an hour," Annaliese said. "What about Ben? He'll try to stop us."

"We thought of that. Has Ruth made the pies?" Henry said.

"Not yet. We should go inside," Dorothy hissed.

In the quiet of the kitchen, where footsteps could be heard on the back porch or in the front hallway, Henry unfurled the plan. The four stood at the sink, heads bowed to catch his whispers. Henry and Arthur would tell John that to finish up some legal paperwork, they would have to leave before dessert. When the pies came out, John would walk the men to the door for their good-byes, with Ben likely staying in the dining room for pie, a particular pie that Ruth was going to lace with dried wormgrass root, which would send him to the privvy within minutes, by which time they would have thrown a bag over John's head and wrestled him into the wagon.

"Oh, God, tell me this is the right thing to do," Annaliese said.

The front door slammed. Henry and Arthur straightened, smoothed their shirts, and turned toward the hall.

None of them at the dinner table could look at him for long. His greasy hair hung in ropes long past his ears. Specks of chicken and potatoes clung to his ragged beard, though he had eaten little. Every ten seconds it seemed, he sniffed to stem the dripping of his nose rubbed raw. His conversation was nonsense one minute, fascinating the next, but, toward the end of the meal, morose. For several uncomfortable seconds, John stroked Samuel's hair over and over to the point of annoying the boy. What little food Annaliese had forced down churned in her stomach.

Ben was quiet and had barely eaten, too. Arthur tried to cajole him into conversation, even opening up the subject of military history, usually a sure bet to get him going. Ben's rheumy eyes brightened, as though a good story was bubbling up, but he turned his attention back down to his plate. Lucenia's absence at his right hand was deeply felt by all at this social gathering, the first since her death. The small presence of Emeline sitting there now seemed to reinforce the gaping hole the death had brought to the circle of friends. Still, Arthur persevered. He told several entertaining stories from the court week trials, which with the children's reports on the goat and cart kept the conversation moving.

Annaliese watched Ben push his food around his plate. She shot a worried look across the table at Dorothy.

About the time everyone had placed forks and knives across the rims of their plates, something in the kitchen burst into fragments that tinkled across the floor.

"What's the matter with Ruth?" Darrison said. "She's been dropping things all day."

"Hope that wasn't the apple pie," Samuel laughed. "I've been looking forward to that."

"Oh, but Ruth's made her wonderful gingerbread for you children," Annaliese said. She patted her hand on the table at Samuel, too hard.

Henry pulled his watch out of his pocket. "Hate to say this again, but we have to be getting back to town," he said.

"Oh, yeah," John said.

"Sorry to miss the pie," Arthur said, pushing his chair away.

"Been wanting to show you my new generator," John said. "Got a few minutes for that?"

Henry stared at the napkin he had just placed on the table. The generator was John's justifiable point of pride, the only one within seven counties. Resignation and guilt washed over Henry's face. He stood, nodded at Arthur as if to say they would give the man his due, and said, "Sure."

John smiled and stood, too. "Let's go, then. Ben, no need for you to come."

Ben opened his mouth, but Arthur cut in. "We'll come back and say goodbye to you before we leave."

Again Ben started to speak and again he did not get his response out, this time because of Ruth's noisy entrance from the kitchen with two pies in hand.

"I made your favorite, Mr. Ben. Apple." She put the dishes on the sideboard and began slicing into the one at which too many people were looking. "And I'll wrap up some for Mr. Chastain and Mr. Garland for them to carry back."

"Well then, let's go," John said again. He turned toward his wife who peered up at him from her chair, took her face in his hands, and turned his right hand over to stroke her cheek with its less rough side, a stroke that at one time had quickened her pulse but now ignited a bitter memory. His eyes bore into hers with more clarity and love than she thought he was capable of mustering any more, and that jolted her, too. She began to rise, but he pressed her shoulder down, then rubbed it as if to sooth a sorrow. Her hand grabbed his for so many reasons that she could only hope he could not read in her eyes, and as everyone in the room watched, he kissed her forehead, straightened quickly, and said, "No need for to you to get out in this cold either, Anna."

Ruth plunked the apple pie down in front of Ben, who pushed it away. "Not today, Ruth. I'm going to see Lucenia. I'll be saying my goodbyes now." He leaned over the table to shake Henry's hand, then Arthur's. "I hope you understand."

They nodded at him. "A pleasure, as always, to be with y'all," Arthur said.

"Indeed, indeed," Henry said. "Wonderful hospitality."

Annaliese, murmuring good wishes for safe travels as they all moved toward the front door, tried to read John's face, but he was too far ahead. He opened the door, slapped Henry on the back, and they were off. She watched them from the door as long as a good hostess would, then went inside to pull the curtain aside and watch them some more, hopeful that Henry would make his move right now, though the guilt she saw on his face told her that wasn't likely. John walked between the brothers, head turning side to side in easy conversation, and they were giving him space. She let the curtain go angrily and began pacing, trying to calm down about this delay, weighing the meaning of John's look. The John she had known had left her long ago—she had almost accepted that—but just now she saw a whisper of him in those eyes. But why now? Had he sensed something between her and Henry and he was making his claim on her in public—vulgar but clear? That did not fit with the rub on her shoulder, which sent a completely different message, almost apologetic.

She went back to the window. The men were tiny figures in the distance but their same relaxed gait was clear enough and she wanted to scream at Henry to pick up the pace, hurry John through his business, get on with their ugly scheme. She grabbed her coat to resume her pacing on the porch, where she could think for a moment before Ruth found her. John's hand on her shoulder had felt apologetic, yes, and something else. It felt final, like the kind of pat that accompanies a farewell, and if John was telling her good-bye, she knew that meant he was as clever as he had ever been and he was leaving Pinch, Georgia on his own terms.

The sawmill was as quiet and dark as a bunker when she flew in. Water buckets hung from hooks in long straight lines down the walls, at the ready in case of a sawmill owner's worst nightmare. Whorls of sawdust coiled slowly in the meager sunlight streaming down from the overhead bank of windows. The ports and doors that were ordinarily open were shut, except for the one door the men had just come through. Annaliese picked her way through the machinery to the lightless spot where the generator was being set up but they weren't there. On the tin roof, something skittered across in a panic. She heard feet shuffling across the gritty floor, voices to her left. A metal chain dropped onto the wooden floor. A click, then the cough of an engine, and the head saw roared to life in the corner opposite the generator. Above the stacks of fresh-cut planks, she could see the top of its enormous steel band of jagged teeth beginning its circuit. She ran, tripped over a pile of chains, got up, and groped her way through the tables of saws following the smell of smoke. She came to an opening between the machines and found Arthur stomping out a fire on the floor. Henry writhed on the floor holding his head. An axe lay beside him.

Annaliese dropped to her knees beside Henry, but he was already struggling to his feet.

Arthur yelled at her for her coat. She ripped it off and threw it on the fire. Henry took off, waving Annaliese away.

In the distance, she saw John walking alongside the moving head rig carriage, loaded with a log for Monday. He jumped atop, swung his leg over the log. The saw's spinning teeth loomed ahead, fifteen feet away.

"No!" she screamed.

Fighting for air, she made her way through the smoke to the carriage. Henry got there first, and began feeling his way down the long, shuddering log toward John, who faced the saw with a resolute calm. But suddenly, John began flailing his arms. A few feet ahead of him, just out of his arm's range, a head appeared. A ham of a hand clawed for a solid grip on the log. The man hoisted himself up and threw a leg over.

Ben.

In an instant, John was on him, punching his back and shoulders, yanking his hair to try to pull him off, but John's wasted body was no match for Ben's heft and his meaty legs that clenched the log. Finally, with inches to go, John threw his arms around his brother's shoulders and buried his face in the back of his neck. Henry pushed Annaliese's face into his chest. They heard the saw's pitch drop as the steel teeth bit into hard oak. Then a man's scream.

Annaliese vomited all over Henry's shirt. He pushed her backward until his legs wouldn't work any more. The saw droned on as it ripped through the rest of the log, and then the jagged scream became a smooth whirr, the saw set free, its work finished.

Arthur found them behind a stack and fell to the floor. They sat there, gulping for breath in the foul air, lungs, hearts and brains afire, unable to move. And the whirr continued like a taunt until someone from the outside came and turned it off.

ᴄᵔᴐ

XXXII

Annaliese lay on the floor of an upstairs bedroom in Meddling's Boarding House. Her children pressed their bodies into her, one on each side, eyeing each other across her bosom or staring at the ceiling as she was. Dawn's soft fingers of light crept along its plaster cracks. Outside, beyond Thessalonia's limp curtains of yellowing lawn, the town was waking. They could hear the scrape of barrels being pulled out of the Mercantile onto the boardwalk and a wagon rattling by, as though it was going to be just another ordinary Monday. Annaliese twisted her shoulders left, right, arched her back, and settled back. The children dug their fingers in and hung on.

Bed springs squeaked as Dorothy rolled over and reached for Annaliese. At the feel of the empty spot next to her, she threw off the quilt and bolted upright. Only when she found them on the floor did she breathe.

"Oh, Anna," Dorothy murmured, shivering in her thin gown.

Annaliese's gaze moved across the ceiling to the place where it met the wall. The light was just beginning its crawl down the dingy paper of faded peonies and lavender sprigs. She knew there must be things she should do today, but she could not isolate one.

Dorothy ran her hands up and down her thighs. "Come back to bed," she said.

The children's eyes flew to their mother's face.

"I lost him anyway," Annaliese said.

Dorothy moved closer to them. They still wore yesterday's dust from the frantic ride to get to town before sundown, but she had at least gotten them into bedclothes. Their clothes lay piled in a corner next to a suitcase that she hoped held enough for a couple of days while Henry steered them through the fallout.

The metal doorknob scraped softly. Darrison stuck his head in to stare at his aunt for a moment before creeping in. His arms hung at his sides like he didn't know where to put them. James followed, then finally Ruth, wild-haired and puffy-eyed. She tugged her shawl around her nightdress and tiptoed in to stand at Emeline's elbow, then near Annaliese's head, then beside James. Finally, she settled into a chair beside the suitcase and began rocking.

Through the open door, the smell of bacon and coffee wafted in.

Annaliese came up on her elbows. "Shut that door," she said. "That's making me sick."

Ruth shot out of the chair to close it.

In the street, the wagon traffic was picking up. Somewhere, a hammering began.

"Hope Mr. Chastain can reach them this time," Ruth said.

"Who?" Samuel asked. He sat up and tucked his legs under him, one hand on his mother.

"Uncle Edward and Mother," Dorothy said. "He's trying to call them again this morning."

"What's going to happen to us, Mama?" Samuel said.

Annaliese lay back down and threw her arm over her eyes.

"Darling, please come get in this bed," Dorothy said.

Annaliese shook her head.

"What about us?" James said. He leaned forward to look past his brother at Dorothy.

A moan boiled out of Annaliese's throat. Samuel scrambled back down to her side. Emeline's mouth curled down and quivered as she clung to her mother.

"We're goin' to pray on that." Ruth stepped forward to pat the Bible that lay on the bedside table.

"But . . ." Samuel began.

Ruth shot him an anxious glance. "Tell you what. Let's get y'all some breakfast."

"Not hungry," Darrison said, sliding off the bed. He dropped to the floor and crawled over to his aunt to clutch at her hand.

"Now y'all come on." Dorothy stood and made collecting motions at the children. "Let's get dressed and go downstairs."

"I can bring you some food, Aunt Anna," Darrison said, rising from floor. He clenched a wadded handkerchief monogrammed with a B.

Annaliese shrugged and nodded. "Some coffee maybe," though she didn't drink coffee. With labored thrusting of knees and arms, she got to her feet. "You go on down, too, Dorothy."

"What? And leave you here alone?"

"I've got to get dressed. Henry will be here soon. I'll be all right."

"I don't want to go," Samuel said.

"Samuel, please." Annaliese pressed her fingers to her temples.

Ruth stroked his hair. "Come on, baby. Miss Meddling will have you some biscuits time we get down there." She swept up the children's suitcase in her push toward the door and got everyone moving into the hall. Dorothy went to one of the valises and snatched out a dress, some stockings, and shut the door behind Ruth. Minutes later, with one long look back at her sister, she went downstairs.

Annaliese closed the door and pressed her forehead on the smooth doorframe for a blessed, quiet minute before running to the bed to snatch a pillow and stuff it with hot screams. They came in waves, her lungs filling and purging until her knees buckled. She collapsed back down on the floor, where she stayed face down in the pillow, fighting the images and sounds that she knew were going to live in the core of her brain for the rest of her life like tumors, malignant and inoperable— John straddling the log on his way into that hideous saw, the sound of the steel talons ripping into the massive trunk. Ben's scream.

She rolled over and threw her arm across her forehead, furious and shamed. John knew about her and Henry. Sometime in the night she had realized it, worked it all out in the quiet, and now her punishment was these tumors, just as smallpox had scarred her face as the price of immorality so long ago.

A gentle knock came at the door.

"Just leave the coffee out there," she called.

"Anna." It was Henry.

She threw someone's coat over her nightdress and hurried to the door. Henry rushed in, scanning the room briskly before planting both hands on her shoulders. He hooked the door with his foot and kicked it closed. "I finally got your uncle. They're coming as soon as they can."

She let her head fall back. "Thank God. Oh, Henry, what have we done?"

"Anna, you had no choice. You were trying to help him, remember?" He cupped her face in his hands and turned it toward his.

"No, you don't understand." She slapped the tears off her cheeks. "He knew, Henry. He knew about us."

Henry's head turned slowly side to side. "No, no, I don't think so."

She stepped back, shook off his grasp.

Henry held up his hands. "All right, all right."

She ran her sleeve under her nose. "What was I thinking? John always meant what he said, and he'd said that he would never go to a hospital, no matter what we called it. What was I thinking, that he'd just let you tie him up, throw him in a wagon, take him away?"

Henry raked his fingers through his hair. "Did you get any sleep at all?"

One shoulder rose and fell. "I've been tired for so long."

"Annaliese, of course you're tired. Look at what you've shouldered."

"Stop. I've done nothing. I'm a weakling."

"Anna, I won't hear this. You're the strongest woman I know." He closed the gap between them. "Strong enough to lose your best friend and love her two boys like your own without a lick of support from Ben. Plant trees with your bare hands when you're pale as death and nauseated and in a delicate condition." Annaliese's cheeks turned pink. He nodded gently. "Ruth told me. And you're strong enough to bear Ruth's secret and not run her off out of spite. All this time you've tried to help John despite what he put you through. No, you're no weakling."

But his words fell on her like raindrops on a stream. She looked down at the floor. "All my fault. We shouldn't have..." Henry's hands reached for her again but she twisted away to leave them hanging in the air. "Mother," she whispered. "I just want Mother to come and take me home."

Henry nodded. "They'll be here by Wednesday. Day after tomorrow."

Annaliese pulled apart the curtains. Below, the Mercantile clerk swept the storefront walk sending pinkish bursts of Georgia dirt into the water trough below. A cow ambled over and dropped her head in. "I don't belong here."

"Try to eat something. I'll leave you so you can get dressed."

She did not leave the window.

Henry's hand paused on the doorknob. "I'm going to try to reach Rose now."

They stood on the train station platform, all of them dressed in black dresses or knee pants that had appeared one evening in neat stacks outside their bedrooms. Henry and Arthur paced behind the family, hands in and out of watch pockets. Annaliese gave weak nods to several strangers who tipped their hats timidly to her. Tiring of that, she fixed her eyes on the tracks.

Even before the train had completely stopped, Eleanor rushed off the last step. With arms raised, she swept through the steam to grab her daughter. Edward Connelley was not far behind, slowed by arthritis but bent forward with urgency, stabbing his cane before his shuffling feet until he reached her. They wrapped their arms around her, hands landing on her head and shoulders and then Dorothy's. Samuel and Emeline clamped on. Next, Dorothy's husband, Phillip, came down the steps and rushed for her. A squeak of surprise flew out of her mouth as he pressed her to him. Ruth stayed back to pat the shoulders of Lucenia's boys. Finally, Annaliese waved them into their circle.

The train emptied of more Connelleys—Michael and Ted helped Irene and Kathryn down the steps. A porter held them up for a minute with questions, pointing at the trunks coming off. Finally, a string of uniformed Connelley servants filed down the steps—two women and a man—who headed off with porters to collect the empty trunks and crates they had brought.

As soon as Ruth saw the servants, she broke down, pierced to the core with the loss of hope.

As the afternoon began its slide into the mountain canyons, four wagons stopped at the granite landmark.

Henry, sitting next to Annaliese, leaned over to look at her as long as he dared and said, "You ready?"

Annaliese nodded. Her mother beside her squeezed her hand.

"Don't look at it." He slapped the reins.

But she had to.

In the long shadows that spilled across the mill yard, dozens of men ambled about. A few stood atop a tower of lumber to catch the planks their fellow sawyers hoisted up to them. Others were working over the mules with brushes and hoof picks. The doors to the mill were closed, the saws quiet, yet the yard overflowed with stacks of finished lumber row after row. The hounds sent up their barking and the men stopped as the wagons emerged from the woods. Slowly, the sawyers came off the stacks and out of the railcars and away from the mill's doors to head toward Annaliese. As they came, they picked up hats from posts and ledges and banged them against their overalls to knock the dust off.

"Mercy," Eleanor said.

They lined up shoulder to shoulder along the road. The mules were led out, too, every last one of the twelve, from the corrals. Joe Rosetta ran out of his commissary, ripping off his apron on his way.

Annaliese shot a look back at Samuel and Emeline in the wagon bed. Through the blur of her tears, she managed to see that Emeline was in her brother's lap, waving. In the wagons beyond, she could see the Connelleys staring at the workers. The men—forty, fifty of them—were in front of her wagon now, forming a long, dusty column of log pushers, saw operators, lumber finishers, and mule drivers holding their hats over their chests. Joe was the first one in line, hands at his side, watching her come. Her head dipped to him as she went past, then to a man with a blue shirt, then a short one with black, curly hair, a man with no teeth and on and on—one respectful face after another. Her acknowledgements ended with a tired smile at the scruffy mules, ears up and alert at the hubbub.

Up the hill, smoke streamed from the two chimneys in Annaliese's home. She pictured Herschel there, and likely Wade, too, feeding oak splits into the fireplaces. Annaliese pointed to her home. "That one, Mother. The one on the right," she said.

Minerva came through the front door.

"That's Minerva," Samuel said, standing now at his grandmother's back. "Our teacher."

Two little girls ran into the front yard holding their hands above their eyes to look down at them.

"Who are they?" Eleanor asked.

Annaliese shook her head. "I don't know," she said.

The girls took off to the back.

"Where are the geese?" Samuel said.

"Henry, hurry," Annaliese whispered.

Henry urged the horses on and stayed on them until they got to the house. Minerva came down the steps, elbows out as she lifted her black skirt out of her way, solemn eyes pinned on her mistress and the children. "Thank goodness," she murmured to everyone piling out of seats. "We've been lookin' for you." She patted Annaliese's hands. To the questions from her and her mother, Minerva simply said, "Come see."

Behind the homes, all they saw of the two girls were their backs as they left with a group of women. Only when they completely disappeared into the woods did Annaliese scan the yard. She found the geese inside a pen of split chestnut rails beside the chicken coop. On the empty wash line, dozens of wooden pins bounced in the breeze.

"That's our mountain, Uncle Edward," Emeline said. The child pulled at the old man's hand and pointed at the swell of land behind Ruth and Herschel's cabin.

Edward leaned on his cane as he heaved for air.

"Come on," Minerva said to Annaliese with another pat on her arm. Eleanor took her other arm and they led her up her own steps. Her eyes fell on two laundry baskets sitting on the back porch—aprons, folded with crisp corners, topped off a stack of tablecloths and towels.

In the kitchen, platters of covered food lined the tables. The aroma of cinnamon and baked apples and fresh bread washed over the travelers as they trickled in. Emeline and Samuel shot over to a basket of muffins and shoved their hands into the golden stack, but Annaliese's stomach turned at the sight. The men stretched out their hands to the woodstove, where a coffee pot muttered. Henry poured the first two cups and handed them to Eleanor and Annaliese, who wrapped their hands around them. Irene and Kathryn walked in, rubbing hands together and looking around the kitchen with thinly veiled shock. The children moved on to peeling back the edges of every cloth on every platter. Everyone waited for Annaliese to tell them to stop, but she did not. Eleanor looked around for a way to another room, somewhere to take off her hat, sit and drink the coffee, but Annaliese kept looking at the dining room door. Beyond the dining room lay the parlor. She pulled Minerva into a corner beside the door.

"Where is he?" she managed to say, eyes squeezed shut.

"Next door," Minerva said with a stiff nod toward Lucenia's house. "Two caskets in the parlor. Is that all right? Me and Wade weren't sure but..."

Annaliese exhaled in relief. She turned to look toward Lucenia's house. There was another question on her lips.

Minerva brushed her arm. "What?"

She opened her mouth but she could not assemble the right string of words, much less release them.

"Was it possible to . . .?" Annaliese pressed her lips together and stared at Minerva's eyes, just inches away from her own. ". . . dress him? He would've wanted to be dressed nicely."

Finally the girl's eyes widened in comprehension. "Oh, oh. Wade and Tote took care of that, Miss Annaliese. They didn't want the women who came today to have to do it." Annaliese winced. Instantly Minerva mashed her lips in regret. "You'd be proud of how he looks, is what Wade said." Minerva patted her hand again.

Would be proud. The caskets were nailed shut then. Wade was lying about how peaceful John looked. Against reason she had hoped otherwise.

Emeline pushed between them, knocking her mother's elbow and cup. Annaliese's hands flew apart to prevent the spill from landing on the child.

"Come on, pumpkin," Minerva said, picking her up. "Would you like to show your grandma your room upstairs?"

The child shook her head. "Mama," she said, leaning out of Minerva's arms toward her mother.

Annaliese pushed through the dining room door, ran her hand along the table, and put the cup down. She collapsed into one of the chairs beside the parlor fireplace. Behind the kitchen door, Emeline's wails were swallowed by a chorus of female fretting. Herschel's fire throbbed behind the metal screen. She pulled the chair closer to its pocket of warmth and leaned in, closed her swollen eyelids against it. For the first time since the accident—two days was it?—she felt moorings beneath her feet. What had she done in those two days? She had no idea. In this familiar glow, the first rays of feeling began to come back and with them snatches of memories of the aftermath. Being pulled up from the sawmill floor. Staggering out of the dark mill into the white light. Ruth and Herschel running downhill to her. Samuel's fawn eyes. Someone pushing her into a wagon. People in town mumbling things to her. The yellow telegrams thrust under the door. But who had sent them?

Edward Connelley's cane tapped in the hall. When it stopped, she felt his eyes on her freezing back. "I'm all right," she said.

"Ruth's taking some food next door to feed the help."

"Of course." She peered around and caught his gaze traveling around the humble fireplace that framed her, the curtainless windows, the bare oak floors scuffed under a thousand treads of a working man's boots.

"You've been so strong, Annaliese," he said. "We'll have you out of here as quickly as possible, sweetheart."

Annaliese pulled her chair closer to the fire. "I know."

The cane took him back down the hallway.

She focused on the fireplace mantel, where a string of Lucenia's photographs from her brown box camera sat atop a lace cloth. Emeline, the largest photograph, holding a baby chick in her outstretched hands. Darrison and Samuel showing off a string of fish.

John and Ben—John's hands on Ben's shoulders—beside the millpond. Annaliese tried to remember the last time John had put his hands lovingly on her. She yearned for such a memory, so that she could lay it over the one of his arm pinning her down on their bed, his knees shoving her thighs apart. As her memory continued to thaw, she did recall his last pat on her shoulder, and other images opened. His kiss on the back of her neck came to her, his hand at the small of her back as they walked home from the sawmill one warm afternoon. Was that August? July perhaps or even before. So many months he had been leaving her.

Other snatches of summer came to her: golden peaches in shining jars of green tinted glass. The scrape of her fingernails on her skin as she scratched at peach fuzz on her arms. The scent of the red cedars that overlooked Lucenia's grave.

The dining room door cracked open. She saw Irene and Kathryn peering at her in the darkness, then glancing at each other. Without waiting for her to beckon, they pushed on through the door. After them, the rest of the family tide rolled in.

As Annaliese watched from the doorway of Lucenia's room, Ruth spread the red evening dress across Lucenia's and Ben's bed, stripped an hour earlier of linen and pillows by the servants. They had packed up the curtains, washbasins and lamps and everything else that would fit in their crates, but Ruth had run them off when they came at the wardrobe, she told Annaliese. She would do it, she told them. They weren't family like she was. She ran her fingers over the bodice's black lace overlay.

"She would've wanted you to have it, Ruth," Annaliese said.

Ruth shook her head. "What would I do with a dress like this in these parts?"

Annaliese stepped in. "But you'll be back in Pinch, have your baby in a few more months. Maybe you can use the fabric in some way."

The girl slumped onto the bed. "Oh, no, ma'am. We're stayin' right here. This is home. Our baby's gonna be born in that cabin out yonder."

The "our" snagged in Annaliese's brain, but she pushed it aside. Her eyes went straight to Ruth's hips. *So narrow.* "What if you need help?" *Due in January.* "What if the snow is too deep and you can't get to the doctor?"

Ruth shrugged as she stood. "I got somethin' to say. There ain't been time a good time fer it and now you're leaving so I reckon it's now or never." Her hand swept across her swollen belly as introduction to what she had to say. She blinked her pale eyelashes nervously, giving Annaliese the impression that for once, the girl was having trouble saying what was on her mind. "I'll have my baby in Pinch if you'll have yours there, too."

They threw their arms around each other and rocked back and forth, locked in sorrow and fate and the certainty that the four hearts between them would be forever bound to the man who had left them.

While the others ate dinner, Annaliese climbed Bunny Mountain and easily found the trail Ben had worn through the weeds and brambles to Lucenia's resting place. Underneath one of her boots, a chinquapin acorn made its sweet crunch, then another, then she sought the acorns out for this small, silly pleasure. Her family would never understand the truth, that she owed it to Lucenia to apologize for abandoning her. Worse, giving up. Soon, Ted or Michael would be climbing the hill to come after her, which was all right. She wouldn't be long in saying such a painful good-bye.

The crisp scent of the red cedars tumbled downhill to meet her. As she lifted her face to savor it, she could see the crown of the new marble tombstone against the gray sky, and then after a few more steps its inscription: *Lucenia Hopewell Stregal, loving wife and mother, October 1, 1868 – September 8, 1902.* Finally, as she heaved for breath with the last steps of her climb, she saw the mound of disturbed earth, now hardened. But beside it—a fresh grave and beside that another. A mound of moist red clay was off to the side of each and someone had covered them with broadcloths. A shovel leaned against one of the cedars. A snatch of blue near the base of the tree caught her eye. She crept closer and saw that it was a man's glove—bright denim blue with a band at the wrist of yellow and red. Wade. He had made an assumption, as all the others who called this place home had, that the mountains had taken hold of her, enfolded her into their mystery and peace, and that she would settle against them now for comfort. He thought she would stay and wait to see if their loblollies made it, and after that to see the glorious spring dawns and bursts of wildflowers along the meadows, and hear the thrumming of the pheasant hidden in her tall grass. These images came easily to her as she stared off into the valley beyond the lip of this ledge. A peace came over her, like the last of a morning fog lifting from a valley, making the way clear.

A twig snapped. Ted Connelley crested the hill. She leaned over to pick up the blue glove and smoothed it out, watched him come.

"I have something to tell you," she said.

XXXIII

The search party crested one of Skipjack Mountain's milder slopes, a hillock thick with white pines and hickorys and sugar maples. Sunlight streamed through their bare branches to warm rosy cheeks and the hands of those who had forgotten gloves. The four children slowed the group's progress with their discoveries, but no one hurried them along. James turned over every other rock hopefully, Mason jar in hand. For Samuel, the pleasure was in poking a stick into flaps of the orange fungi—big as apple pies—that perched along the tree trunks. Every now and then, someone's boot kicked up the last of the frost that was sandwiched between soggy leaves dark as coffee grinds. The spring wildflower outing had turned into more meander than mission and that was all right with Annaliese. She caught a familiar, musky smell and reached out for Dorothy's arm to stop her. The scent came off the soft ground like a mist, soaking their clothes. "Fresh leaf mold," Annaliese said. They turned their faces to the sun without a thought given to freckles. Winter was over.

"Yonder's some, y'all," Ruth said, shifting the baby from one hip to the other. "See them little white flowers?" She looked back at Dorothy and Annaliese and pointed to a patch of pale green leaves. Phillip walked over to get a better look.

"What is it?" Emeline said, looking over from her watch on a woodpecker.

"Bloodroot," Annaliese said. She leaned backward into a long stretch and let the others move on. Straightening up, she scratched the taut, dry skin of the underside of her bulbous belly. Inside, an elbow or heel slid by.

"Bloodroot, ewww," James said.

"Well, come on," Emeline said, reaching for her mother's hand.

Annaliese shook her head and waved her on. "You go on, Emmie. I'm going to sit for a minute."

Emeline leaned forward to go, but hesitated at the sight of her swollen mother wobbling her way down to the ground. Darrison appeared at her elbow, box camera in hand. He held her elbow uselessly as she went down.

"Thank you, sweetheart," she sputtered, landing with as much dignity as a fat woman in tight pants could command. The mat of leaves was sodden and now her backside was, too, but she didn't care, it was so good to be outdoors, especially in her eighth month.

Ruth and Phillip stood over the pool of pale green leaves that sprouted through the forest duff. The leaves, with deep lobes separating the shiny skin into stubby fingers, looked like the palms of hands. They were in various stages of releasing into the March air their prizes: delicate clusters of white petals with yellow centers. Dorothy bunched up her skirt and bent down with Emeline for a closer look. As each flower grew taller on its round, red stem, the leaf relaxed toward the ground. But some flowers were still enfolded in their leaves, tightly coiled and waiting for the sun to coax them open.

"What's this used for, Ruth?" Phillip asked. He pulled two spades out of his coat pocket.

"Fever. Aches and pains." Ruth looked around for a rock, sat down, and pulled the baby's red hat down over the tiny ears. A ray of sun hit the baby square in the face, sending her to sneezing and blinking in baby confusion. Ruth moved to a shadier spot and turned her around to watch. "Ulcers, ringworm, warts. Got to be careful with it. Too much of it can turn yore stomach inside out."

Phillip dropped to his knees and began digging. Dorothy took the other spade and joined him. Soon, they had gouged out several plants dripping with thin, red roots. Phillip shook off the dirt and held them up to the sky. A red stain spread across his fingertips. He dropped the plants into a burlap bag at his side. "Dried plants and roots by mail order," he said as he shoved the spade under another stem. "From grocers to mail order business owners." Phillip looked over at his wife. "Well, it's worth a try."

Dorothy dropped a handful of plants and roots into his bag and turned back to tuck a few dislocated plants back into the earth. "But the rest stay. For next year."

Ruth bounced the infant. "Ya hear that, Lucy? Next year. They'll be here next year."

"What's the other one you said we'd look for?" Phillip asked. "The mayapple?"

Ruth looked back at Annaliese to see if she had heard that, the name of the plant whose costly life cycle Ruth had dared to explain on that windy November day more than a year ago. Annaliese's eyes were half-closed, still as death and her face was, too, and Ruth started to worry that the memory of John's death would do her in again. It had been a long winter. In December, just as Ruth had gotten her and Dorothy and Phillip and the children into Pinch, packed for Louisville, a blizzard dumped two feet of snow. Henry hurried everyone to his home where Ruth noticed that he had fresh linens on the beds and a tree decorated more carefully than one would expect of a bachelor. A week later, Lucy was born at Thessalonia's during another snowstorm, but the doctor was sober and the birth was over in four hours. Ruth didn't push Annaliese to hold her. It was enough to see her smile, the first smile since the tragedy that Annaliese had produced without someone's coaxing. Ruth watched her face when Herschel said, "We're naming her Lucenia." They saw a flash of pain, but then honest joy. They had figured the Lord would understand why they had chosen that name and forgive them for not taking one from Scripture.

The second time Annaliese's smile came on its own was on that freezing last day of January when she mastered blasting tin cans off a stump with a shotgun. To help her get her shooting eye back, Henry and Wade had started her out with the last dried pumpkin in the pantry.

The cracks of her blasts sank into the snow on Bunny Mountain and brought the children running from all corners of the house. Eventually, an orange chunk of pumpkin went flying and everyone cheered. Then the men moved her down to flour sacks filled with pinecones. Day after day, she went outside into the bitter air to load, aim, fire. Ruth and Dorothy watched her from the kitchen, one of them worrying about her catching her death of cold, the other worrying about her mental state. Dorothy said that clearly there was some element of anger at work, but they left her alone. The men moved her on to tin cans. Even after she finally nailed that first can, she kept on shooting every day—one can, two cans on top of each other, three in a pyramid. By February, her stomach and breasts were getting in her way and she had to stop. But her face was softer by then, Ruth noted, her eyes held more light, and she stared off into space less and less.

Another smile rose on the day Annaliese found baby chicks, born at the wrong time of year to a young hen, in the warming drawer.

Now, Ruth watched Annaliese set her face and figured she must have heard the conversation about the mayapple, but she appeared to be merely pensive. Her eyes were on the ground, her mouth at rest.

"What's the mayapple used for?" Samuel said to no one in particular. He stood next to Darrison and James, stick in hand.

"Warts. Throwing up if you need to." Ruth hooked an arm around Lucy and wiggled up. "But I ain't seen any sign of it yet."

"What about liverleaf then?" Phillip helped Ruth finish getting up. The baby had spit up all over her shoulder during the wiggling. He gave her a handkerchief. "I read about that, too. It goes into liver tonic."

"Right." Ruth cocked her wispy head at the man. "You're a bright feller, ain't ya? Let's go find us some liverleaf."

Emeline ran back to her mother. "Mama, come on."

Annaliese rolled onto her knees, then onto her hands and was halfway up when Dorothy arrived to help her the rest of the way. "Today's wagon ride is the last one for you, Anna," she said. "You shouldn't be out here."

"You know I have to see them, Dottie." Annaliese took Emeline's hand.

"But Wade's already told you . . ."

Annaliese started toward the others following Ruth along the edge of the woods. "He said he wants to see my face when I look down the slopes of Black Face." She tightened the wool scarf around her neck and pressed on.

Ruth pointed toward the forest floor. "Look for leaves that are droopy and brownish at the edges and cut into three round parts, like a mitten of three parts 'stead of two. Looks like a liver, book-learned people say."

Darrison ran toward a colony of bright green plants with broad leaves. "Is this it?"

Everyone arrived to peer down at about a dozen plants that perched a foot off the ground on thin stalks.

"Those look more like umbrellas than livers," Phillip said.

Annaliese smiled at the comparison—so true—and at the hearty green of these plants in the midst of crisp-dead leaves and naked trees. Many were still making their way up through the leaf litter. Annaliese bent down to one tubular head that wore a broad-brimmed hat of Red Maple leaf. Several feet away from the colony, a solitary one had just arrived, its seven leaves still pinched into a pinwheel shape as it grew out and up. So much effort from such a small plant, she thought. She turned to ask Ruth what this brave little umbrella struggling toward the sun was, but just as she turned, she knew. The adjectives all lined up.

"It's mayapple, isn't it?" Annaliese said.

Ruth nodded and squeezed her baby into her neck. The women stood looking down at the plants that were linked by an eternal root system just as surely as they were by their babies.

Phillip brought out his spades again. "What part do we want, Ruth? Roots? Leaves?"

Ruth knelt down to turn over a few leaves. "Leave 'em be. Come July, we'll come back, see if the deer have left us any of the fruit."

"I'm guessing it's one mayapple per plant?" Phillip asked. "Is it going to be worth the effort?"

Annaliese looked up at the latticework of branches overhead. No leaf buds yet. But soon. "It is for the mayapple," she said, linking her arm in Ruth's.

The last clump of roots was tucked into Dorothy's bag. "All right, let's go," she said. She took her sister's elbow in hand.

They were waiting for her on the side of the trail that opened to Black Face. "Wait till you see, Miss Annaliese," Tote said as he and Wade helped her out of the wagon and through the slush to the ledge. Everyone else emptied out of the wagon and followed quietly.

Annaliese's head turned slowly, left to right, as she scanned the hillsides. "They made it," she whispered.

Little bright green pines studded the mountain's flank from the ledge all the way down to the river. Most of the twigs and bark that the planters had scattered to protect the seedlings had held on somehow during the snowmelts, and now they would trap the spring rains for the tender roots. The stumps of the old sovereigns that had reigned here still remained, black sores scattered across the acres. But they had their own surprise for Annaliese and the men: stump sprouts. In time, this generation of hardwoods would once again lift sturdy limbs to the sky. In time, their shade would starve the pines of the sunshine and send them withering back down into the soil—their job done—to close that timeless cycle of the forest.

Wade slapped his arms for warmth. "One day, Miss Annaliese, I'll show my young 'uns and Tote's a better way to harvest them oaks and poplars and chestnuts."

Annaliese smiled to herself. They didn't have children, not even wives—not that they weren't both working on it with Minerva—but they did have these trees and the right to make decisions about their fate. She had seen to that.

All winter, Wade had pored over each *Forest Quarterly* when it arrived in the commissary and later he would come to her to work out some of the language or concepts. Far as he could tell, he would say, the government was itching to share its recommendations on this new thing it called forestry. The journal told you not to cut along the waterways, which made sense to him, for anyone could see that it caused mudslides and clogged up the rivers. He agreed that a young forest with trees of different heights and kind was best left alone so it could provide cover and food for the woodcock, the ruffled grouse, and many small critters, for he had observed that for years. But he didn't much hold with the government's call to go into a mature forest and cut out the largest, most economically valuable trees. It seemed to him that taking the best stock out of the hills would leave behind only the sorriest kind of tree to reproduce, like taking the preachers and teachers and Stregals out of the county. Annaliese had watched him at his reading, many times by the light of her own fireplace, and one morning she pulled him and Tote aside and said she wanted them to have it: Black Face Mountain's three hundred acres and two thousand acres beyond it as well. They stared at her, mute as rocks. She said she would arrange it with Colonel Chastain next time he visited. It was rightfully theirs and their community's she said, and she expected they would do right by it. The only condition she laid down was that Wade and Tote would build her a house in town where she and the children would live until the baby came. Plenty of lumber for it, she had murmured, and added that they could have all that was in the lumberyard, too. They built her house with the help of the other nightriders and when it was finished they had learned enough carpentry to pick up other customers in town.

Wade looked out across his mountain. "Shoot, maybe we won't cut a stick of it. Ever."

Samuel came over to stand next to Wade. "Golly," he said. "Look at that."

"Coupla years, they'll be taller than you, Sam," Wade said. He wrapped his arm around the boy. "I'll show you how to go pine riding."

"Aw, Wade, I'll be taller then, too, you know."

"Well, 'course," Wade said. He looked back at the other children coming. "Look how much y'all have changed in just two years."

Annaliese did not lift her eyes from her gaze on the hills as she heard this, but the phrase took her back to the day John had promised the limit. *Just two years.* And now those years had passed and there was a baby to be born, a homemade Georgia native, in the very month that would mark the anniversary. Probably all along John had meant to take longer than two years, but he had his reasons, and now that she knew them, a timetable bent hardly mattered.

Why did you agree to come, Lucenia? Because you did, Annaliese. What had Lucenia's intentions been at the outset? To become a wealthy woman, no question, and win female agitators and converts for social injustice, again no question. But also perhaps to meet the bar Annaliese had unknowingly raised. *Me, Annaliese Lewis Stregal, raising a bar.* She laughed to herself. But she had come to realize that that was what she had actually done. Both of them had climbed over it so unhappily. How bitterly she and Lucenia had railed against the loss of their comforts. The irony was that in their new world, they were much more free to create and build and wield power than women elsewhere might have won in years of marches on city hall. Annaliese smiled, stealing a glance backward at Ruth who now could read and sew on a machine and would soon share in the profits of the new medicinal plants by mail order business. She had organized her own women's sewing and prayer group at her church in town and the first thing they decided was to hold meetings without the preacher, who immediately objected. When they asked him why, he declared that he was afraid of what they might pray for. Ruth and the women had gone limp as possums laughing over that. There was the schoolhouse that would reopen soon with new textbooks, copies of the history of the Cherokee nation, and newspapers from Atlanta and Louisville. And now some of the Cherokees had at least some of their land back, where they could build new homes and a new way of life. And next summer, when the baby was sleeping through the night and Annaliese could put two thoughts together, she would begin the Pinch Library Society. Her subscriptions to *The Journal of Public Vocation* and *Renewable Resources of the Forest* would be her first donations. In Lucenia's honor, the catalog from the California Perfume Company would be on the shelves, too.

The winter had indeed been the long, bitter one the almanac had promised, but Annaliese was grateful for the solitude and the time to for prayer and reflection. She emerged from her own personal winter to see that John would never have emerged from his. The John she had followed to Georgia had been unraveling even before they had left Louisville. Only through his powerful intelligence and will had he been able to hide it as he first sensed it. The John who ended his life in front of her was just a shell that masked the tempest. Still, she knew that he had done what he could while he could and she would embrace that for the rest of her life. Some memories she would put away for good and others she would take out now and then to linger over, like the photographs John had left behind for her to find in his dresser drawer. With her heart in her throat, she had unfolded the brown wrapper and walked over to the window to hold them up. There was a photograph of him and Samuel in front of the towering bandsaw. She tore it up with trembling hands. Next came a shot of him and the children in front of the dry kiln. They wore matching brown felt hats. John's hand gripped Samuel's shoulder. He held Emeline up at his chest with the other. Another one had father and son in front of the enormous "Stregal Brothers' Lumber Company" sign by the mill. She ran her fingers over the shot. In it, Samuel's hand was clasped without embarrassment in John's. John's face was proud, relaxed, his body turned slightly toward the mill so the photographer would capture the entire name, bigger than John's own body.

There was a photograph of Henry and Calvin, too, in front of the courthouse during what must have been an October court week. Henry's brown eyes, looking away to something other than the photographer, were full of the devil and his lips were slightly parted. She knew that set of his lips. He was about to tell one of his stories—no doubt a wild yarn to a lawyer he had not lied to since the last court week. Over the course of the winter, she had looked back into those eyes longer than she should have, but each time she did so longer than before. And when she spoke, telling her own funny story from her childhood or ranting after reading the Louisville newspaper accounts of local politics, he still looked at her, wanting nothing more than to laugh with her or wag his head in sympathetic outrage. She found him to be a patient man. He would wait for her to unfold on her own timetable.

Dorothy came up from behind her and wrapped an arm around her shoulder. As she joined Annaliese in staring at the slopes, she said, "There now, see? They're doing fine, just as Wade said." Her fingers squeezed her sister's arm. "Let's get you home. You've done enough for one day."

Annaliese threw her shoulders back and lifted her chin to the breeze whispering across her cheeks. Her fingers fiddled with the strings of her bonnet until they fell away and she was able to pluck it off her head. Closing her eyes, she turned her face toward the sun, the face that had sought shadows for so long, and said, "I'm just getting started."

⁓

Lindy Keane Carter is a journalist whose work has appeared in a variety of national magazines, trade publications, and academic medical magazines. She is the author of award-winning short stories, including two that placed in the South Carolina Arts Commission's Fiction Project contest. *ANNALIESE FROM OFF* is her debut novel. Lindy has two daughters and a son and lives in South Carolina.

35224856R00223

Made in the USA
Charleston, SC
02 November 2014